MW00573096

TURNING THE STORM

LEE JACKSON

Severn River
PUBLISHING

TURNING THE STORM

Severn River Publishing
www.SevernRiverPublishing.com

ISBN: 978-1-64875-152-3 (Paperback)
ISBN: 979-8-54474-369-9 (Hardback)

ALSO BY LEE JACKSON

The After Dunkirk Series

After Dunkirk

Eagles Over Britain

Turning the Storm

The Giant Awakens

The Reluctant Assassin Series

The Reluctant Assassin

Rasputin's Legacy

Vortex: Berlin

Fahrenheit Kuwait

Target: New York

Never miss a new release! Sign up to receive exclusive updates from author Lee Jackson.

AuthorLeeJackson.com/Newsletter

To the men and women who knew that their lives would likely end within weeks,
But they went anyway,
To fight our wars in dark places and shadows,
That we might live in freedom.
To them we owe a debt that can never be repaid,
And we honor them and our progeny best,
By never resting in the eternal fight for Liberty.

PROLOGUE

September 22, 1940
Sark Island, English Channel Isles

"Must we meet yet another Nazi *kommandant*?" Marian Little-field, the Dame of Sark, grumbled. "I wonder if the new one will let me keep my anti-Fascist books. Major Lanz did, and aside from that, he did a perfectly good job of making our lives wretched. I suppose in the German high command's view, he could have been more rigorous about imposing martial law for nothing more than the propaganda value of occupying British territory. These islands are insignificant to Hitler's war effort."

She sat with her husband, Stephen, in the drawing room of the *Seigneurie*, the medieval mansion that served as both her home and the seat of government in the middle of the tiny island in the Guernsey Bailiwick. Stephen, born American but having taken British citizenship after serving with the Royal Air Force as a fighter pilot during the Great War, had found himself, upon marrying Marian, in the odd position of being the senior co-ruler by "right of wife" in this last vestige of a western feudal system. However, in matters of state and governance, he deferred to Marian.

He sat near her on a divan while she occupied an overstuffed chair. In front of them, a low fire that barely took the chill out of the air burned in the hearth and two white poodles snuggled together for warmth. The couple wore layers of clothing and sat with blankets over their shoulders and across their legs to hold back the cold.

"The Germans see our islands as a heavy gun platform to help stave off an amphibious invasion through France," Stephen said. "Besides, we chose to stay, dear. That was your choice and your advice to our people. On the strength of your guidance and example, our entire population remained rather than evacuate to the mainland. For what it's worth, I think you were correct."

"I know, I know, but we had no choice. We would have lost our Sark culture and way of life if we hadn't stayed. But these Nazis make things tedious, and that's being kind. I hope I haven't set our friends and neighbors on a slow plod to death." She stood and surveyed her figure in a mirror across from the fireplace. "I'm already looking skeletal, and I don't know how much more of that blackberry ersatz tea I can stomach. And it would be nice to know how our children are doing. The Red Cross messages don't tell us much, and the letters are limited and censored."

She fussed as she turned back and forth, opening her coat and observing her dress hanging on thin shoulders. "I'm glad to know that Jeremy escaped that awful evacuation in Dunkirk, but what is Claire doing in London? Do you think she's still playing at the Royal Academy while the war is on? And where is Paul?" She sniffed as she fought back a sob. "And Lance is in that awful POW camp in God only knows where."

Stephen rose from his seat, crossed the room to stand behind her, and embraced her. "It's near Leipzig."

"What?"

"Colditz, the town where the prisoner of war camp is located. I looked it up in the atlas and read about it in the encyclopedia. The last Red Cross message instructed us to send mail to Lance there. A very imposing feudal castle overlooks Colditz from a steep hill. If I had to guess, I'd say he's in that fortress."

"Show me."

Stephen went to the fireplace, removed a book from the mantel, and opened it to a place saved with a bookmarker. The article included a small black-and-white photo of the castle in winter, with snow blanketing its roof and the ground below.

Marian peered at it. "Oh dear, it looks gloomy; centuries old." She sighed. "And invincible. Maybe we can hope that he won't get himself killed doing something foolish like trying to escape."

Stephen chuckled. "He's got far too much of you in him for us to nurse that faint hope." He swept a finger across the photograph. "And one element might further dash that optimism."

"What's that?" Marian took the volume from Stephen's hands and examined the image closely.

"The castle is nearly a thousand years old and mammoth in size. Look at it compared to the buildings that surround it and then at all of its steepled roofs and dormers. It rises to six stories above the hill it's built on, and that's not including the attics. The article says it has an extensive cellar too—probably used as a dungeon in times past and maybe the present too—and all by itself, the castle occupies nearly five acres. That doesn't include all the property and outbuildings around it."

Marian stared at the photograph. "I'm not getting your point."

Stephen closed the book and replaced it on the mantel. "The Germans will hold hundreds of prisoners there," he said while rubbing his forehead. "They'll keep large numbers of guards, put weapons at key points, and string miles of barbed wire." He cast Marian a doleful glance. "But Colditz Castle was built to keep people out, not in. If Lance decides to escape, he'll find a way out." He started for the door. "Come on. The new *kommandant* will be here shortly. We want to be ready."

"We're getting good at this pretense, Stephen," Marian said.

They sat at two desks placed side by side in their grand ballroom. Low stacks of folders rested on the wooden surfaces, and when they heard a knock on the door, they each picked up a document and began studiously reading.

"Come in," Stephen called without looking up.

The door opened, and a servant girl appeared, followed by a German officer in full dress uniform. "Major Bandelor is here to see you," she announced.

Neither Marian nor Stephen glanced up, both continuing to peruse their documents and annotating them with pens. "Madame," the girl called.

"Excuse me?" Marian said distantly. Glancing up, she focused on the servant, and then her gaze shifted to the major. "Ah, yes," she said, rising. "I apologize. I had forgotten our appointment." She turned to Stephen and leaned over to nudge him. "Dear, the new *kommandant* is here to greet us."

"Oh, yes," Stephen said, taking to his feet. "Please excuse us," he called across the room. "We've both been quite busy.

Nothing like trying to manage scarce resources during a war, you know." He bestowed a gratuitous smile.

The servant gestured for the major to advance, and as he did, Marian held her hand out. Bandelor hesitated, and then took it in his own and kissed it. "My pleasure, Madame Little-field. My predecessor, Major Lanz, told me many good things about you."

"We're as sorry as is possible under the circumstances to see him go, understanding that the occupation continues."

The major smiled wryly. "I hope we can work together to keep everyone as comfortable as possible."

"Which is going to be increasingly difficult as your army builds gunnery sites on Sark and neighboring islands, and food becomes increasingly scarce. Our island is not completely self-sustaining. You take a good portion of the vegetables we grow, and now we're headed into autumn. Your bureaucrats try to regulate fishing hours as though sea creatures understand the concept of punching a clock; and our poultry, cows, and pigs won't last forever, particularly when much of it goes to feed your soldiers. We need more basic supplies."

Major Bandelor's eyes glinted, and he turned to Stephen. "I have not yet greeted you." He held out his hand. "Your wife certainly shows no fear of us."

"Why would she?" Stephen said, shaking the major's hand. "We understand our rights, and Major Lanz made plain that Germany intends to honor them."

The major coughed again. "True, for as long as that is possible. Our *führer* commands our army in these islands to be good ambassadors to the British people; to convey that we neither intend nor wish them harm. He sees our two peoples as natural friends, believing that we should be allies. But the continued fighting on your mainland—how shall I say this—muddies the water."

"I see," Marian cut in. "You know we British get our backs up when we're bombed every night; and that practice tends to —as you say—muddy the waters."

The major peered into Marian's eyes as if taking her measure. "We Germans don't like our own cities being bombed either. The same goes for our military installations." He gave an ingratiating smile. "But I came to make your acquaintance, not debate politics. Major Lanz complimented your leadership with the people of Sark, particularly in this war footing. I want to continue the goodwill. What needs of your people are not being met? Perhaps we can help."

"Do you mean beyond mere food?"

The *kommandant* smiled sardonically and nodded.

Marian harrumphed. "There is something I hope you can alleviate. We lost our doctor. She had been visiting once or twice a week from Guernsey but chose to evacuate before your army arrived. We have pregnant women needing checkups, children with injuries to treat, elderly with ailments..."

"I see your point. Would it help if I sent our physician to spend a day here weekly? Your population isn't large, but if that's not enough time, we can see about doing more."

The surprise in Marian's gaze showed that she had considered her request futile. "Thank you," she said with a gracious nod. "That's most kind. The German medical profession is well known for the quality of its care."

"Then consider it done," Bandelor said, obviously pleased. "I have other news too. Your son will soon be at a permanent prison camp at Colditz."

"We'd heard about that through the Red Cross," Stephen cut in anxiously, "but the message said that he's already there. Is he all right? Is he safe?"

Bandelor chuckled softly. "About as safe as anyone can be as a POW. For bureaucratic reasons that I don't understand, his transfer was delayed. Somehow, he ended up in a transit facility for RAF prisoners. That's why Major Lanz had difficulty finding him. A British army noncom among RAF pilots is rare.

"As for Colditz, that prison is a special one. It's where they send escape artists. Your son tried to break out at least once and probably several times. At Colditz, we've brought such prisoners into one place under the most intense security. The intent is to keep them busy and as well treated as possible so that they have no incentive to escape." He shrugged. "The situation is not ideal, but if he makes no more escape attempts, he should be safe."

"I sent letters to him there. Will he receive them?"

"In due time, I'm sure. They would have been delivered to the senior British officer for safekeeping. Part of the difficulty in tracing him is that the camp was not yet set up to take in British prisoners at the time he was slotted to go to Colditz. That won't happen until early November, at least six weeks away. And if he tries to escape again—" The major shrugged. "If he's caught and confined in solitary, he could be looking at more time before he's sent to Colditz. I have no doubt that's where he's permanently assigned, and whenever he arrives, your letters will be delivered to him."

He watched as Stephen and Marian exchanged neutral glances. "There's another aspect to discuss which Major Lanz brought to my attention, the fact of your son's being a *prominente*. That status and his propensity to escape all but assures that Colditz will be your son's new home for the duration of the war. Let's hope it's short."

Marian scoffed. "This is a tiny island that England didn't care enough about to defend. I hardly think that anyone would consider my husband or me or any of our offspring to be particularly prominent."

Bandelor smiled unctuously. "You say that, yet you had your servant guide me through the finery of your home and bring me to your office, which you've set up in your grand ballroom; and then you held me at bay on entry and compelled me to kiss your hand." He glanced around with an amused expression. "Very Mussolini-esque."

Marian chuckled and patted her hair. "A lady must keep her airs," she murmured. "I read that Benito used the technique quite effectively with your officers. Then again, you transferred into these islands a month ago, and we're just seeing you."

Bandelor laughed gently. "I respect that Sark's fighting spirit is not vanquished. The fact is, your king knows you by name, milady, as does Adolf Hitler. These islands are strategic for propaganda and for shore-based big guns. You and the citizens of Sark chose to remain. You could set an example for people in other countries when the war is over, and Germany has won. We wish to live in harmony, not be tyrants."

Marian stared at the major, hoping her hostility and rising anger did not show. *Can he possibly believe what he is saying?*

"The issue," he went on, "is that your son is already assigned to Colditz permanently, and when he arrives, he'll be moved in with the other *prominentes* there."

After the major had departed, Marian took Stephen's hand and led him into the drawing room. Closing the door, she wrapped her arms around him and held him close.

"Are you all right?" he asked, returning her embrace. "You're shaking."

"I'm scared," she cried hoarsely, staving off sniffles. "There's only one reason why they would put all the so-called *prominentes* together. They're bargaining chips. If things go badly for Germany, and if haggling doesn't work, Hitler will take out his revenge on them. Even before then, if the thought occurs to the Germans, they might try to use Lance as leverage against our family. They have access to the public records of everyone on Sark, and we would have been checked out almost immediately. How else would they learn about Lance? I'm sure they've also informed their highers of the existence of Paul, Claire, and Jeremy, and whatever they can learn of their activities."

Saint-Louis, France

So loud was the wailing of horror and anguish at dawn on a backroad near the French border with Germany that neighbors appeared on the narrow blacktop, looking curiously at each other and then toward the frantic cries. A middle-aged man with graying, disheveled hair emerged from the house, the front of his shirt smeared with blood.

"She's dead," he shrieked repeatedly, pointing back at the house. "She's dead."

Two men, leaders in the community, gestured to two women to comfort and care for him, and then proceeded cautiously up the front path and entered the house.

They gagged at the stench that greeted them. The sight was one they had never imagined. Blood splattered the walls and ceiling and pooled on the floor around the legs of a wooden chair. Tied to the seat was the grieving Frenchman's wife, also middle-aged, heavyset, graying, and still bleeding over her blouse. Her throat had been slit wide, her head pulled back, and around her chest, daubed in finger markings with her own blood, was a one-word sign that read: *COLLAB-ORATEUR.*

1

October 19, 1940
RAF Middle Wallop, Wales, UK

Flight Lieutenant Jeremy Littlefield entered the dispersal hut of RAF 609 Squadron with a disconsolate air. This was his first time at the airfield since being wounded in a frantic dogfight during which he had been downed with a bullet fragment in his shoulder.

Two Spitfires were parked near an adjacent maintenance and repair hangar. On looking at the bulletin board inside the hut, Jeremy saw what he had expected: a list of pilots assigned to the unit. Absent from it was Eugene "Red" Tobin, Andrew Mamedoff, and Vernon "Shorty" Keough, three American pilots he had befriended during his initial flight training. He had since flown combat missions with them from here, this very airfield, this squadron. While he convalesced, they had transferred to a new Royal Air Force all-American unit, the Eagle Squadron.

A shadow crossed the bulletin board. He turned to find one of the mechanics standing in the door of the hut. The man wiped his grimy right hand on an oily cloth and extended it toward Jeremy. "So good to see you, sir, all mended and in one piece. Right glad to have you back, we are."

"And glad I am to be back," Jeremy said, glancing down at the dirty hand and then grasping it firmly. "The only reason I'm alive is because you chaps do such a wonderful job of keeping our kites flight-ready."

"Ah, sir, you honor us, but it's you pilots that give so much in the air..." His voice trailed off, and Jeremy noted the strain and sadness that ringed his eyes. The mechanic sniffed. "It's not easy seein' you all fly off and some don't come back. It's wonderful when we thought we'd lost one and he shows up, like you just did."

He gestured toward the door. "The squadron's out training now. Most of the chaps are new because of losses and the transfer of the Americans to that new squadron. The commander told us you might arrive today. He left a message. He said you was to go to the officers' mess at lunchtime and meet Commanding Officer Anderson of 604 Squadron and Squadron Leader Cunningham."

Jeremy squinted and wrinkled his brow. "Did he say why?"

"No, sir. That's the full message."

Jeremy glanced at his watch. "I'd best get over there. It's almost that time now."

He had no difficulty finding the two officers. They had been watching for him and called to him as he entered the mess. Anderson cut straight to business after greetings and taking their seats at one of the tables. "We're night fighters, Lieutenant. We want you to join us."

Jeremy stared at him, speechless. The two officers sat across from him, both appearing affable but deadly serious.

"You're fighting in the dark," Jeremy managed at last. "The odds haven't favored you, and the results have been dismal."

He took in a deep breath. "I'm ready to die for my country, but I'm not suicidal."

"None of us are," Cunningham interjected evenly. "But England will cease to exist if we can't defend her from these nightly raids. You know how close Hitler came to defeating the RAF. We must beat him at night as well. We have the means to do that." He paused, and then reached across the table to grasp Jeremy's shoulder. When Jeremy glanced down at it, Cunningham removed his hand and continued. "I won't glamorize what we're doing. Night fighting is a highly special- ized game. We have to set a standard of inner strength and determination for everyone around us. You've demonstrated that. Our system has to be made to work, and we have to be the ones to master it."

Jeremy leaned back to take the measure of both men. Neither was much older than he, if at all. Their air was one of having been battle-tested.

"I'm listening, but even if I agree, my transfer will have to be approved—"

"We spoke to both your squadron leader and wing commander," Anderson broke in. "They would not like to lose you, but since your unit is still reconstituting almost from scratch, they said they'd release you if that is what *you* want. We're hoping it is.

"We know your story," he continued. "The odds have been against you since you went to build roads and airfields in France ahead of the battle there, but you've beaten them every time. Your tenacity did that.

"You told your former boss at MI-9, Major Crockatt, that the reason you wanted to fly with the RAF was that you needed to be where you could be most effective during Britain's fight for existence. That place now is flying with us.

What they're doing to our cities between dusk and dawn is proof enough of that."

The three pilots sat quietly, eyeing each other. "You talked to Major Crockatt?" Jeremy said at last. "You went to some trouble."

"We're actively recruiting, and we need the best," Anderson said. "You'll need steel nerves, but if you do as you're trained, you'll come home to fight again and again, and we'll blow a wide hole in the *Luftwaffe*. We will defeat them." He added wryly, "It won't be immediate. As of now, there are only the two of us."

Jeremy studied Anderson. He perceived no bluff or bravado. "How will you do that?"

"We have new technology that will change everything. It's a project developed and supervised by Air Marshal Sholto Douglas under a group he formed, the Night Fighting Committee at RAF headquarters."

Jeremy arched his brow. "At Bentley Priory? That must be under Air Chief Marshal Dowding. I'd say that's high-level enough."

Anderson agreed with a nod. "Germany won't be free to bomb our cities at will night after night." He leaned in. "We've put direction-finding on our fighters. We can see in the dark."

Jeremy stared at him. "Air-to-air radar?"

Anderson gestured toward Cunningham. "This man played a big part in re-designing the device to fit our aircraft, and then he flew the trials. It works." He took in Jeremy's skeptical expression. "Don't think this was easy. Our scientists and engineers were tasked with making a miniature version of what we have at stations of the Chain Home system, each of which has six massive towers, receiving stations, operators, and phone lines. To put that capability into an aircraft and making it useful was unthinkable. But they did it."

"The first successful air-to-air interception against a German was back in May. Another pilot, Flight Officer Ashfield, flew a Blenheim fitted with a prototype of our system and intercepted a German bomber.

"That flight proved the system's worth, but the aircraft and the configuration of the apparatus were ungainly. In the months since then, Cunningham worked with the engineers to reconfigure the system and modified a new aircraft to receive it."

Observing a vestige of remaining doubt, Anderson added, "A lot of fliers risked their lives flying blind at night and getting us to this point. It's time to take the system operational." He hesitated. "You should know that we don't fly together in formation. We go out singly."

Jeremy sat back and stared. "That sounds a bit scary. Are you hunting, then?"

Anderson shook his head. "No, and it doesn't mean that we have only one aircraft in the sky at a time. The controllers can see us. Chain Home has been fitted with radar to look inward across Great Britain now, as opposed to only looking out to sea and beyond. They keep us separated and vector us individually toward the enemy. Then, as we get nearer to our targets, our 'magic box' operators in the turrets pick them up on their cathode screens and guide us in. Final target acquisition is done by visual sighting."

Jeremy pursed his lips. "In other words, you have to see a black bomber against a black sky before you can shoot it?"

"In a nutshell."

"That's what we're working on now," Cunningham cut in with a small laugh. "How do we physically *see* them? We can't sit and wait for the system to be perfected—they bombed our cities for fifty-seven straight nights, and they're still doing it. Some of our technique will have to be developed during our attacks on their raids." He chuckled again. "We hope to see the glow of flame coming out of the bombers' exhaust."

"That sounds a little doubtful," Jeremy replied. Nevertheless, a stirring of cautious excitement gripped him against the emptiness he had felt upon arriving at the dispersal hut to face the reality that his comrades had gone away. Finally, he asked, "May I see this 'magic box' in action?"

Anderson and Cunningham exchanged glances. "Of course," Anderson said, "but one other thing you should know: we're very selective, out of necessity. If you join us, you're our first recruit, meaning there's just the three of us and our operators. We hope to have another three crews trained by year-end."

Once again, Jeremy stared. "And that's all there is?"

"That's all." Anderson smirked. "You're getting in on the ground floor."

"Against all that the Luftwaffe sends?"

"Aside from our anti-aircraft guns."

That night, standing behind the pilot's seat with Cunningham at the controls and an operator in the turret, Jeremy flew in the new aircraft, a Beaufighter, and witnessed the potential of its radar. The next day, he bid a sad *adieu* to his squadron leader and his beloved Spitfires and joined 604 Squadron.

2

November 11, 1940
Off the coast of the isle of Cephalonia, Greece

Rear Admiral Arthur Lyster, in charge of carrier operations for the British Mediterranean fleet, leaned against the rail on the steel island of aircraft carrier *HMS Illustrious*, watching as twelve Swordfish biplanes revved their engines and moved into taxiing position. He had wanted to attack three weeks earlier on October 21, Trafalgar Day, which celebrated Britain's triumph in 1805 over the combined French and Spanish fleets near the end of the Third Coalition of the Napoleonic wars. That victory had terminated the French emperor's dreams of invading Great Britain. Now, another tyrant with similar dreams must be stopped.

A fire in the hangar of the *Illustrious* had obviated the ability to launch on the preferred date. Lyster hoped the calamity was not an omen.

Once again, the British Isles faced the threat of an invading force, this time from the Third Reich, an enemy made more ferocious by their modern weaponry and more

fearsome from a demonstrated sadistic nature. Led by Adolf
Hitler, the Germans had annexed Austria and invaded
Czechoslovakia, Poland, Norway, Denmark, Holland, Belgium,
and northern and western France, as well as small nation
states scattered among the European countries. Frustrated by
Prime Minister Winston Churchill's refusal to negotiate a
peace treaty, Hitler vowed to bring Britain to its knees and had
bombed and strafed Britain's towns, ports, cities, factories, and
churches.

His campaign against the British Isles had begun with an
attack aimed at destroying Fighter Command to gain air superiority. When Churchill's famous Few, the RAF's fighter pilots,
repulsed the *Luftwaffe* by sheer wit and tenacity, the German
dictator resorted to nightly bombing raids lasting as long as
ten hours and delivering tons of incendiaries and explosives
on a battered but resilient nation.

Such was the success of the RAF's response against
Germany that the air superiority crucial to Hitler's strategy
had been denied him far into the autumn months when the
waters in the Channel became too treacherous to attempt a
crossing in strength. He had been forced to postpone Operation Sea Lion, his planned invasion.

Lyster hoped to further inhibit German capabilities by
blunting Italy's naval reach here in the Mediterranean. The
two countries had been formal allies since June. He sighed. *It
would have been fitting to do this on Trafalgar Day, but I'll take the
fight to the enemy whenever opportunity presents itself.*

Several weeks earlier, he had flown to Alexandria, Egypt,
and briefed his proposal to Admiral Andrew Cunningham,
Commander-in-Chief of the Mediterranean Fleet. "Italy tries
to dominate this sea using a 'fleet in being' strategy," he said.
"They threaten our ships just by the presence in Tobruk and
Taranto."

Cunningham had studied the map of the Mediterranean hanging on the wall. "That's a given," he said, "and their warships are fast and deadly. Their fleet was already bigger than France's, and after we destroyed the French fleet in Toulon and Algeria, ours is the only one that can counter them. What do you propose?"

Lyster grunted and pointed out three places on the map. "Most of the territory on either side of the Med was friendly only six months ago, but now that's all changed. Since Italy joined Germany in their Axis Pact, all we've got now is Gibraltar near the mouth of the Mediterranean, Alexandria protecting the Suez at the east end, and Malta halfway between as a good but vulnerable re-supply/re-fuel depot. If we lose any one of those three points..." He let the sentence hang.

"Our ground forces are planning an operation next month to seize this port," he went on, indicating Tobruk, Libya. "If they succeed, that will ease the pressure on defending Alexandria, but we must keep Alexandria if we hope to maintain control of the Suez and our supply lines from the Far East. That leaves our Royal Navy to deal with the threat with only four battleships, nine cruisers, and two carriers. One of the carriers, the *Eagle*, is ancient."

He moved his finger diagonally across the Mediterranean to the northeast over Taranto, Italy. "Meanwhile, the Italians stationed six battleships, twenty-one cruisers, and a bunch of destroyers here. They sit in port while we incur wear and tear on our ships and burn fuel over long, vulnerable supply lines. Until we get the Italian ships out of that port, we'll be forced to conduct any operation as a full fleet to avoid an ambush. That would keep us from doing more than one operation at a time.

"From our Maryland-bomber fly-over reports, we know their six battleships are moored at Mar Grande in the Taranto harbor, with seven cruisers and twenty-eight destroyers in the smaller adjacent part of the harbor, Mar Piccolo."

"Back in September," Cunningham broke in, rubbing his chin, "I tried to draw Italy into a major sea battle, but they declined to show up. Now you intend to destroy them in Taranto, at anchor?"

"In simple terms, yes. If they come out of port, they could overpower most convoys coming through the Med in short order, and the rest of our British fleet is spread thin, protecting the homeland and our Atlantic supply lines. Without those supplies, we can't feed our people, much less conduct a war. We must take Italy out of the equation here on the Mediterranean, or at least weaken them for the near term."

Cunningham leaned back in his chair. "I read your preliminary summary, and I agree. From his experience as first lord of the admiralty, the prime minister understands your view perfectly. He won't disagree with your assessment.

"As I understand the first part of your plan, you want the entire fleet to pretend to escort a convoy from Alexandria to Malta. Before arriving there and under cover of darkness the night before your attack, the *Illustrious* and *Eagle* will divert and take up positions off the coast of Cephalonia. Your raid would stage from there.

"That part I'm fine with, but I have some doubt regarding how you'll meet the objective with the rest of your plan. Explain it to me in detail."

Lyster did, and when he had finished, Cunningham exhaled while shaking his head. "The Swordfish? You're expecting a lot out of a machine that's nicknamed the 'Stringbag.' It was obsolete before we entered the war."

"My view is different, sir. The plane arrived in service only four years ago, it's sturdy, with a metal frame, and it's highly maneuverable."

"It's a cloth-covered biplane." Cunningham quelled exasperation. "It's slow, and you need speed for an attack."

"If I had a metal plane with similar capabilities, I'd use it, but I don't. One advantage of the cloth skin is that we can repair holes easily. We can do it in the ship's hangar with a needle and thread. That's why it's nicknamed the 'Stringbag.' But it's stable and needs very little distance to take off or land, so it's perfect for carrier operations. And it's the only plane we have that can haul a torpedo off the deck of an aircraft carrier."

Cunningham heaved a sigh. "You've got me there."

"And as you well know," Lyster pressed on, "not every plane can drop a tube and put it on target. How the missile hits the water is crucial—it can't be slanted up or down when it immerses. It's got to hit the trough of a wave, not the crest, and the aircraft must stay over it for a few seconds to ensure its proper orientation via a wire that then drops away. That maneuver dictates slower aircraft speed when it launches the torpedo. The Swordfish's stall speed is fifty miles per hour. That gives us plenty of room to drop the tubes with the required attitude. We don't have another aircraft to match that capability."

Cunningham closed his eyes in thought and then re-opened them. "Suppose we approve this plan. What will our pilots face? What are the Italian defenses at Taranto?"

"They're tough," Lyster admitted grimly. "The numbers I provided are estimates, but we think they're close to accurate. The Italians have thirteen gigantic electronic listening devices that can detect our aircraft out to thirty miles, so surprise will be mitigated. But at top speed, we can close that distance in about twelve minutes."

"And you're *relying* on surprise," Cunningham interrupted with raised eyebrows. "Go on."

"As near as we can tell, they have ninety barrage balloons surrounding the ships—"

"You're going in at night?"

"Yes, sir, under moonlight."

"The cables that anchor those balloons can shear off a wing."

"We'll pick a date with a good moon. We need it to be fairly bright." Lyster grimaced inwardly at Cunningham's expression of skepticism. "Shall I go on?"

"Of course. We must consider every option."

Lyster breathed in deeply. "We estimate that the Italians have twenty batteries of heavy anti-aircraft guns there as well as four automatic cannons, and over one hundred machine guns. Our pilots will have to dodge twenty-two search lights intended not only to spot them but also to blind them; and every ship is armed with anti-aircraft guns."

He paused for breath.

"Anything else?" Cunningham inquired.

Lyster nodded. "Besides what I've mentioned, the fleet is surrounded by over four thousand yards of anti-torpedo nets down to twenty-four feet below the water's surface. We've configured the torpedoes to run at thirty-one feet."

Cunningham sat quietly, deep in thought. "God help our pilots if we do this thing," he said at last.

"Don't forget, sir, that we've practiced the type of tactics we'd employ, and we took out the French battleship *Richelieu* back in July with a Swordfish-launched torpedo. So, the question isn't can we do it, but can we breach those defenses."

Cunningham shook his head in doubt. "The *Richelieu* was in Dakar and lightly defended. As you just pointed out, our chaps will run a gauntlet."

"And if we don't do this raid, our shipping will most certainly run a continuous gauntlet, one we might not be able to protect against, and that will cost even more lives." He pointed to a sheaf of documents on the conference table. "You'll see in there that I intend to confuse the enemy by having every British naval ship in the Mediterranean put out to sea on execution day, and we'll even have empty merchant convoys steaming through. Those elements of the plan should preserve the surprise a while longer. The listening devices are not like our radar—they won't know the launch point or intended destination until the planes are nearly on top of them."

Cunningham nodded and raised his hand in a placating gesture. "I get your point, Arthur. I really do, and I tend to agree. But I must feel confident with the details before I approve the plan. It's complex despite the simplicity of the objective. Let's go over it again a few times, shall we?"

Admiral Cunningham had given his approval reluctantly, specifying only that the battleships be hit with torpedoes and the lighter ships with bombs. Since then, the pilots had pored over maps and aerial photographs relentlessly until they pictured in their sleep the Taranto harbor and its ships; and they practiced maneuvers to the same degree.

Now, hearing the roar of the Swordfish engines and watching the planes move into position, Rear Admiral Lyster felt the same reluctance. His stomach churned, his throat grew tight with a lump, and his eyes teared. *These are my chaps going into a firestorm, and fifty percent probably won't return.*

Even before plan execution, problems had arisen significant enough to imperil the mission. Lyster had planned for thirty planes to make the attack. However, the *HMS Eagle* was supposed to have lain nearby to launch fifteen of them. Unfortunately, the carrier had sustained battle damage in previous engagements. Its fuel system completely broke down, so it could play no part in the raid. The *Illustrious* could accommodate only five of *Eagle's* planes, so the number of available Swordfish had reduced to twenty, and the *Eagle* had limped away with the remainder. As a result, the aerial assault force that lifted off was down a third from its intended firepower, reorganized into two flights with eleven fighters in one and nine in the other.

The pitch of the engine on the lead biplane, tail number L4A, raised to a smooth hum. Looking frail and rickety, the aircraft positioned itself on the deck, and the flight operations officer glanced at the admiral. Lyster nodded, the signal was relayed to the crew, and the Swordfish started down the deck, gained speed, and quickly bounded into the sky. It twisted slightly against the wind, banked right, and began a steady climb.

Lyster glanced at his watch. "That'll be Hooch and Blood," he muttered, referring to the pilot, Flight Commander Kenneth Williamson, and his navigator/observer, Lt. Norman Scarlett. "Off at 20:35 hours. God be with them."

"Sir?" the watch officer standing nearby inquired, thinking the admiral had spoken to him.

Suddenly feeling very old, Lyster half-turned toward the man and shook his head. "It's nothing." He turned back and watched eleven more of the tiny, open-cockpit biplanes launch into the cold November sky illuminated by an almost full moon over a glimmering sea. Strung along each of their undercarriages was a torpedo, eleven feet long, eighteen inches in diameter, with three hundred and eighty-eight pounds of TNT.

As they lifted into the night air, Lyster muttered the names of the pilots and wished them Godspeed. When the last one had departed, he made his way to his quarters and closed the door.

An hour later, he returned to the same spot on the aircraft carrier's island to watch the second flight prepare to take off into the night. Then, as two were raised via a huge elevator from the deck below, their wings became entangled. While repair crews scurried to resolve the situation, the other seven Swordfish flew into the dark sky. One of the two remaining aircraft was quickly fixed and sped after the flight. The other kite would take longer to mend.

Once more, Admiral Lyster watched them go, repeating the names of the crews and commending their lives to good fortune. The ship's captain approached and stood beside him. "Are you all right, sir?"

Lyster turned to face him with a grim frown. "I am, thanks for asking." He took a deep breath and peered through the moonlit heavens in the direction the Swordfish had gone. "I've never become accustomed to sending good men into harm's way." He closed his eyes, took a deep breath, and added, "I hope I never do."

3

Hooch hunched his shoulders against the wind and scanned to his left and right. They had been in the air for over an hour. He flew at the center of the formation. By the light of the silvery moon, counting the planes in his squadron was easy: five out to his left and five more to his right. Ahead was a bank of clouds, but it did not appear particularly threatening or large. He saw little reason to divert around it, a maneuver that would use up time and fuel.

Behind him in the cockpit where the navigator/observer normally sat back-to-back with the gunner, Blood scrunched against the fuel tank that had been added for greater range. He scanned the sky and made out the other planes in the squadron, then glanced down, seeing nothing other than the vast, sparkling sea.

They flew through the cloud bank with little turbulence and emerged on the other side to a clear sky. Once more, Hooch checked left and right, and his gut dropped. He pressed the switch on his intercom and called back to Blood, "Are we missing one?"

Blood whirled back and forth, rising in his seat and

stretching his neck for a better view. Then he dropped back down and leaned his head against the back of his cockpit. "We are," he called. "Only four on the left. We're missing L4M."

Hooch groaned. *Lieutenants Swayne and Buscall.* Both good men. He had trained with them since entering flight school and had led them through other engagements. Fingering his radio button momentarily, he shook his head. *Can't break radio silence. I hope they either pressed on or made it back to the ship.*

———

An hour behind Hooch and his squadron, Lieutenant Commander "Ginger" Hale, piloting L5A with Lieutenant Carline in the navigator's seat, took stock of his undersized squadron. He was supposed to have left the ship with nine kites but saw quickly that only seven had made it into the air. An hour later, L5Q with Lieutenants Morford and Green peeled away, apparently with a mechanical problem, and returned to the *Illustrious*. That was disappointing, but by then, they were nearing the target area.

Hale grunted and pursed his lips. *We're down to six to do the job of fifteen.*

———

Back on the deck of the *Illustrious*, Lieutenants Clifford and Going, the pilot and navigator of L5F, the second Swordfish that had been damaged on the elevator, scrambled to complete repairs. Several of the struts between the top and bottom of the right wing had broken. The two lieutenants had assisted the repair crews in lowering the plane back into the hangar, removing the damaged parts, and installing the new ones.

A half hour after their chums had departed, their aircraft trundled toward the end of the ship, gaining speed. Watching it take off, Lyster shook his head in wonder at the courage of the young pilot and navigator as they lifted alone into the moonlit sky.

Lieutenant Swayne, piloting L4M, scanned the coastline anxiously. "Can you confirm that is the right location?" he called over the intercom to Lieutenant Buscall in the observer's seat.

"I've checked the maps and charts," Buscall replied. "We're in the right place."

"Where is everyone?" Swayne circled back out to sea. "Keep your eyes peeled for our mates. Taranto knows we're here." Recalling the briefings about the listening devices, he expected that the Italians had heard their approach at least ten minutes earlier and had jumped into immediate battle stations. Already, searchlights probed the night sky, arcing back and forth, and a few anti-aircraft guns had shot flak, evident by their mid-air explosions and distant booms.

Swayne had not expected that L4M would be the only aircraft to have arrived at the Taranto harbor. "Keep the target area in sight," he told Buscall. "I'll fly out of range and orbit a while. If we go in alone, we'll have every gun in the place aimed at us. It'll be a suicide mission."

"Roger. I'll let you know if we're getting too far out."

While he flew, Swayne tried to think through how he could have arrived before everyone else. He had seen enough to know that the big battleships lay untouched, and nothing indicated battle damage to the harbor itself. So, he concluded, the rest of the squadron had not arrived.

When the whole unit had flown into the clouds, Swayne had not been concerned. They were wispy and intermittent, barely enough to be called a mist but sufficient to obscure his view of his mate, and for most of the time, the aircraft to his right had been in sight. He had experienced some buffeting, nothing worrisome, but when he emerged from the clouds, no other plane was in sight. Fearful that he might have fallen behind, he had opened the throttle.

"I think we got here early," he called on the intercom.

Over the coastline in the target area, searchlights continued to sway back and forth across the sky, and mid-air flak explosions had become almost non-stop.

"I think you're right. Surprise is blown. We've awakened the beast. But one good thing I can see is that there aren't nearly as many barrage balloons as we'd been expecting. I'd say around thirty. That's a little relief."

"A little," Swayne agreed.

Roughly two and a half hours after takeoff, Hooch and Blood in L4A, with the squadron abreast, saw the coastline in the distance. They also saw searchlights beaming into the night sky and puffs of smoke and bursts of flame from flak over the target. While they had expected the listening devices to alert the Italians that something threatening was on the way, they had not expected to find the enemy's ground defenses wide awake, fully prepared, and already shooting a barrage skyward.

As they closed the distance to less than a mile, Lieutenants Kigell and Janvrin, in L4P, veered off, circled the southern harbor, Mar Grande, from the southeast to the northeast, and dropped magnesium flares that lit up the sky, illuminating the Italian battleships lying at anchor.

Lieutenants Lamb and Grieve followed in L5B; however, seeing that the whole area was already well illuminated, Lamb held back on dropping additional flares. Meanwhile, the other Swordfish swooped low, lined up on their targets, and skimmed the waves. As they closed the distance, the Italians ceased firing for fear of shooting each other.

Hooch and Blood led the way, wheeling over destroyers *Lampo* and *Fulmine*, taking aim at battleship *Conte di Cavour*, and splashing their torpedo. Lieutenants MaCauley and Wray in L4R circled to the north and attacked the same target from the opposite direction. MaCauley's tube missed but Hooch's hit, ripping a cavernous hole in the side of the ship.

As he banked away, Hooch's satisfaction was short-lived. He climbed a bit, and then heard plinking as a barrage of bullets rained on his aircraft. It crashed into the water.

Swayne and Buscall had rejoined the squadron by then and zeroed in on the front of battleship *Littorio* from the southwest while Lieutenants Kemp and Bailey attacked the same ship in L4K from the northwest. Both Swordfish scored hits, tearing massive gashes in the ship's hull. Flying low and close to the vessel, Swayne gulped and pulled up fast, barely clearing the ship's mast.

E4F, one of the Swordfish transferred from the *Eagle* with Lieutenants Maund and Bull, flying with the last torpedo of the first wave, winged as low as possible from the west into Mar Grande, heading for the *Vittorio Veneto*. It dropped its torpedo, but to the pilot's and observer's disappointment, it ran aground without hitting its target.

The Swordfish carrying bombs fared no better. Lieutenants Murray and Paine in E5Q dropped their load on *Libeccio*, but none exploded. Lieutenants Sara and Bower in

L4L could not get a clear shot at their target, so they dropped their bombs on a seaplane base, but saw no explosions. Forde and Mardell in L4H, after opting not to drop their flares, skirted the harbor and flew back to the southeast corner, where they set a field of fuel tanks ablaze with their bombs before heading home, dropping flares as they went to confuse the Italian gunners.

Just past midnight, the second wave, led by Lieutenant Commander Hale, flew in over the Taranto harbor to add to the destruction and confusion. One Swordfish that left the *Illustrious* late had caught up, so Hale attacked with seven of his nine aircraft.

Immediately, L4F with Lieutenants Skelton and Perkins, followed by L5B with Lieutenants Hamilton and Weekes, diverted to drop their flares on the near side of the harbor and continued to strike the fuel-tank field again. To the north of the harbor, Hale and Carline lined up on the *Littorio* to their south. On their right, Lieutenants Torrens-Spence and Sutton flew abreast in L5K; and on their left, Lieutenants Bayly and Slaughter flew in E4H.

Suddenly, Bayly and Slaughter cut across the flightpath of the other two Swordfish. Then their aircraft exploded in a ball of fire and plummeted into the water.

Steeling themselves against the tragedy they had just witnessed, the pilots of the other two planes pressed on and splashed their tubes almost simultaneously. Moments later, the *Littorio* was hit for the third time, but by which torpedo, no one could tell.

Behind them, Lieutenants Lea and Jones in L5H bored in on the *Caio Duilio*, dropped their torpedo from eight hundred yards, and saw it hit its target. To escape, Lea then flew so low between the *Zara* and *Fiuma* that the Italians found themselves shooting each other while attempting to kill L5H; but with good fortune favoring the Brits, Lea and Jones escaped over the open sea.

While the other planes were delivering their munitions on their targets, Lieutenants Welham and Humphreys in E5H had circled to the north and descended, heading south. Their kite had been riddled with bullets in its flight but remained aloft and operated without difficulty, so Welham continued his mission. Flying low over the city, then back out over the harbor just above the water, he lined up on the fleet's flagship, the *Vittorio Veneto*, and released his torpedo, missing his target. Then he flew through a gauntlet of gunfire on his way out to sea, heading for home.

The guns around the harbor at Taranto had fallen silent and the searchlights had switched off by the time that Lieutenants Clifford and Going, in their repaired and late-departing L5F, arrived at the battle scene. They circled, heading for the cruiser *Trento* in the northern part of the harbor, Mar Piccolo.

Re-awakened Italian defenses concentrated their fire on the lone aircraft, but it pressed on, dropping its load of bombs on the *Trento's* deck. With dismay, Clifford and Going watched the bombs bounce on the steel deck—without exploding.

Three days later, the two admirals met again in Alexandria. "That was a magnificent job, Arthur," Cunningham greeted Lyster. "We could not have asked for a better result."

"You weren't so complimentary on the first day after the mission, sir."

"We didn't have the full battle damage assessment," Cunningham said, looking chagrinned.

They sat in comfortable armchairs in Cunningham's office and shared a brandy. "Thank you, sir. Our chaps deserve the praise."

"What they did was remarkable, and you're owed a great deal of credit. I'm just sorry we lost two good men and two aircraft. By the way, we just received word that Hooch and Blood survived and are POWs. Did I get their nicknames right?"

Lyster smiled grimly and nodded. "You did, sir. That's good to know, thank you." Then he shook his head. "Losing Bayly and Slaughter was painful. The men felt it. They had trained hard together. Their courage and skill were tested and proven, not mine."

"That's a healthy view. I'm getting all the attention in London, and our country needed a victory, but all I did was say yes to your plan." Cunningham shuffled some papers on his desk. "The damage assessments are impressive. Unbelievable, really. The largest and most modern navy behind our own—since France left the equation—was defeated by twenty-one cloth-covered biplanes that almost everyone, including me, thought were obsolete."

He brought a document close to his eyes, frowned, and then exclaimed, "My word. It seems that my only contribution to the plan was an utter failure."

"Sir?"

"The bombs. I insisted on the bombs for the smaller ships, and they all failed. Every one of them."

"Not all, sir. The ones that hit the fuel-oil fields did extensive damage."

Cunningham nodded and tossed the paper on his desk. "We'll have to do something about that. We won't win this war with non-exploding bombs, will we? I should think not." He looked up brightly. "Well, we sank three battleships. Who knows at this point if they can be repaired? We also damaged three cruisers and three destroyers; and intelligence informs us that battleships *Vittorio Veneto* and the *Giulio Cesar* have been ordered to Naples for safekeeping. That removes them as a threat for the time being."

"Hmm," Lyster mused. "This should put to bed the argument of the primacy of carriers over battleships."

"I think so. Your pilots in their Stringbags set naval precedent. Carriers extend our projection of military might well beyond what's possible with battleships." He picked up another document. "Here's what I wrote in my official report. 'Taranto, and the night of 11–12 November 1940, should be remembered forever as having shown once and for all, that in the Fleet Air Arm, the Navy has its most devastating weapon.'"

"I agree completely." Lyster shifted in his seat. "What do you hear from the home front? Is anyone doing anything about that *blitz* Hitler rains on our cities?"

"I have a little insight on that, but nothing to share right now. I'll just say that Chief Air Marshal Dowding is an acquaintance. He's under huge pressure to 'do something' about those nightly raids, and the argument between him and 12 Group's Air Marshal Mallory continues over the merits of the 'Big Wing' strategy versus Dowding's approach. I'm with Dowding on that. Having planes burning fuel and incurring wear-and-tear while orbiting and waiting for the rest of their formations to rendezvous makes no sense to me. What Dowding's developing will affect our operations in the not-too-distant future, and I feel confident that it will alleviate that situation at home."

He sipped his brandy. "As for the night raids, I think Hitler miscalculated again. He thought he could defeat us by demoralizing our people, but he only makes them angrier and more resilient. He can't bomb us forever. He's stretched across the Continent and North Africa, and I suspect that he still wants to go after the Soviet Union, his treaty with them be damned. I'd wager he wants to do that more than he wants to conquer Great Britain.

"Subduing the Bolsheviks was always in his plan; invading England never was until Churchill refused to make peace. That Austrian corporal is using up raw materials, equipment, fuel, food, his soldiers... He doesn't have an infinite supply, and one of these days he'll wake up and realize that."

Lyster listened intently. "So, what is Dowding doing to end that hell?" He took a deep breath. "We both have families and friends in the middle of the *blitz*. Some have buried loved ones."

"Yes," Cunningham said, slowly and sadly. He locked his fingers and rested his chin on them. "I can't say much because I don't know much. But I'll tell you what was told to me. Think Chain Home in miniature, installed on fighters; and the Germans still don't have the large version."

Lyster drew back, wonder in his eyes. "Are you serious? That would change everything. The implications are enormous."

"My thought exactly. You presented us with one game changer. We could use another."

4

November 14, 1940
Bletchley Park, England

Claire Littlefield took a deep breath and knocked on Commander Alastair Denniston's office door. Though she had no notion of why she had been summoned, her relations with the head of the intelligence facility at Bletchley were cordial, even friendly.

Bletchley's employees had been sworn to secrecy about its existence, given its status as Great Britain's greatest military secret. Claire had crossed a protocol line once by discussing one of the facility's secrets with someone not authorized to know them. That the person was an intelligence officer in another part of MI-6, Bletchley's parent organization, had made no difference, nor did the fact that Claire's actions had helped to save a French Resistance network in northern France. The added fact that her brother, Paul, was the other intelligence officer had probably made things worse and jeopardized his career as well, but the net effect of their conversation was that the Resistance network was saved.

Later, Claire had redeemed herself by discovering an opportunity to recruit a spy in Field Marshal Reichenau's German 10th Army headquarters in Dinard, France, the very unit and commander responsible for planning Operation Sea Lion, the *Wehrmacht's* planned invasion of the British Isles. Although she had received no direct feedback as to the value of information received from that source, she had to believe, based on messages she had decoded originating in Dinard, that her spy was successful.

Claire had also sensed from those messages that Reichenau's staff was becoming agitated that Britain seemed to know German moves before making them, and the locations of key facilities in France that the RAF then bombed. Such knowledge, the Germans seemed to conclude, must have come from within their own headquarters.

What the Germans did not know, and the reason why Bletchley was such a closely guarded secret, was that it housed a German encryption machine and a group of highly educated and specialized people who had broken Germany's military codes and could read their messages almost as fast as the intended recipients. Thus, while the *Wehrmacht* was correct in deducing that it might have a spy in the Dinard headquarters, they did not know that much of what British intelligence knew came from Germany's own radio messages encrypted with code that they perceived to be unbreakable.

Claire heard Denniston call to her to enter. When she did, he stood behind his desk in uniform, a fit man with an elegant manner and boyish good looks that included dimples on each cheek, although he must have been nearing fifty years of age. A hint of gray hair around his temples gave him away.

"Come in," he greeted, and waved her to a seat in front of his desk. "Seeing you is always a pleasure." Despite his warm demeanor, she noticed that he seemed unusually distracted, concerned.

"Thank you. Likewise, I'm sure."

The commander took his seat, taking note despite his preoccupation that an air of world-weariness seemed to have overtaken Claire. Lines creased the corners of her eyes, and circles had formed around them. "Are you all right? You look a little tired."

"No more than anyone else, sir. The war wears on us all, particularly with the incessant bombing."

"You're right, of course." He regarded her with concern. "How are your brothers?"

Involuntarily, Claire's mouth quivered, and she felt tears rising at the corners of her eyes. She took a deep breath and fought back the emotion. "I don't want to burden you with my problems. You sent for me. How can I help?"

Denniston ignored the question. "Have you found out where your POW is yet?"

Claire pulled a handkerchief from her sleeve, touched it to her nose, and nodded. "That's Lance. He's in Colditz."

Denniston's eyes narrowed as he stared at her. "I'm sorry to hear that. Isn't Colditz the special prison for POWs who make frequent escape attempts?"

Claire nodded. "That's my understanding, from messages we've seen come through here."

"Hmm. Germany is still observing the Geneva Convention by and large. Can you take comfort from knowing that Lance is alive and still using his wits?"

"I do, sir, but I worry that he'll get himself shot. He can be a handful to deal with on occasion."

Denniston chuckled. "That seems to be a family character-istic." Without waiting for a reaction, he asked, "What about Paul? Isn't he the one you got in trouble with?"

"Hmph," Claire replied, fighting down agitation. "Your ability to find out about him is probably greater than mine. All I know is that he's off on some secret assignment that might last for the duration of the war. I don't *know* where he is. I haven't seen him since September right after the last big daylight raid on our airfields. He could only tell me not to worry and that he would be safer than any of us here. I wish I could believe that."

"That surprises me. I know nothing of it." He studied her a moment longer. "Tell me about Jeremy, the famous brother. Is he still convalescing at your house?"

Claire shook her head. "He's back flying again, but he can't tell me what or where. He's not in Spitfires, which surprises me, and his American friends transferred to another squadron, so I know no more about him than any other member of my family."

"Your parents? Are they coping all right on Sark?"

At mention of her parents, Claire's reserve nearly broke. She could not stop the tears, so she turned to hide her face. "Excuse me, sir..." Her voice convulsed and she could speak no further.

"I apologize," Denniston said, rising and coming around the desk. "I didn't mean to pry. I thought you might have good news about some of your family."

"It's all right," Claire said, composing herself. "How can I help you?"

He sat down behind his desk and leaned back while gathering his thoughts. "I'll get to the point. I believe you decoded some of the messages coming out of Berlin concerning the raid on Taranto a few days back."

"Yes, sir. I did."

"What do you make of them?"

Claire chuckled and lowered her eyes. "Sir, if you'll recall," she said, raising her gaze to meet his, "I've been admonished twice by your boss that I'm a decoder, not a translator or analyst."

Now Denniston laughed and leaned forward. "Yes, that's right, but your analyses were correct both times, and if not for your language ability in both French and German added to your dedication, we would have missed them."

"Thank you, sir. I appreciate the compliment. How can I help?"

"I'll get to the reason I called you in here shortly, but first, I'm interested in your impressions of what you've seen in those messages."

Claire settled back into her seat, thinking. "I can start with what I read." She summarized the attack. "The Germans are upset that our Mediterranean fleet successfully raided and nearly destroyed roughly half of the Italian navy using obsolete aircraft. We've trumpeted our success, and the Japanese sent their military attaché from Berlin to Taranto to study what happened."

"Those are the facts as I know them," Denniston said. "Do you draw any conclusions from them?"

Claire pursed her lips. "I hadn't given that aspect much thought and I don't know much about Japanese military capabilities, but if I had to guess, I'd say they're thinking of launching a similar attack somewhere."

Denniston sucked in his breath. "Those were my thoughts too, but I wanted to bounce them off someone who was not close to the day-to-day analysis. Japan just joined the Axis Powers two months ago, so the question becomes when, where, and against whom?" He rubbed his eyes. "Thank you, Miss Littlefield."

She started to rise. "Will that be all?"

"Excuse me? Oh wait, no. The main reason I brought you

in is that we'd like to offer you a promotion. The idea arose while we were discussing those messages about Taranto in a senior staff meeting. I mentioned that I'd like to get your take on it, and Director Menzies asked when I was going to promote you into our analysis section. He said you'd already demonstrated the ability, and the promotion was past due."

Claire stared at the commander in amazement. "MI-6 Director Menzies said that? He's the one that scolded me so sternly."

Denniston laughed. "That's his way. He's uncompromising, and he has a tough job, but he recognizes talent and accomplishment. Are you interested?"

While he spoke, Claire's mind went to the series of messages she had decoded several months ago that led her to identify the potential for recruiting the spy in Dinard. She had even identified the lady by name, Jeannie Rousseau. Claire had brought the information to the commander with the suggestion that Jeannie might be open to recruitment. Claire suspected that the idea had been pursued successfully, because the alternative explanation for Jeannie's employment in the headquarters was that she was a collaborator. If that had proved true, the intelligence Claire had supplied would have been enough for the local French Resistance in Dinard to execute Jeannie. The thought had horrified Claire.

"Well?" Denniston prodded. "Would you like the promotion?"

"I'm flattered—"

Denniston frowned with disappointment. "You're going to turn me down. Is that because of Timmy? No one knows his story more than those of us that work with you—"

"No, no," Claire protested. "Our nanny does a wonderful job of caring for him when I'm not there. That's not the reason at all."

"If it were, we'd accommodate—"

"Thank you, sir, but the reason is—how do I put this? I was coming to see you on a different matter. Do you remember the conversations we had about Miss Rousseau?"

"Of course." Denniston looked chagrinned. "I told you I'd get to you with feedback, and I haven't."

"That's fine, sir. We're in a highly classified program. I wasn't expecting any, but I've followed her progress in the same way that I became aware of her in the first place, via the messages I decode."

"I see. So, what's the issue?"

"I think someone in that headquarters is on to her, or at least suspects her. I think she might be in danger. If she is, I feel responsible. I wouldn't want to make a move away from decoding until I know she's safe."

Denniston leaned back, surprised. "That's admirable, but you don't even know her."

"Sir, if she's in danger, I caused it. I couldn't live with myself if something happened to her, and I hadn't done everything possible to save her."

The commander studied Claire. "You are a rare human being," he said softly. "If the world were like you, we wouldn't be in this war." He paused in contemplation. "How about this? I'll run it up the staff to see if there's a rescue option, and we'll speak again about moving you when we have a resolution."

"That works, and I'll stay where I can monitor until I know she's out of danger."

"Thank you for coming, Miss Littlefield."

Claire started to rise and depart, but on impulse, she settled back on the edge of the chair with her hands on her knees. Denniston glanced at her inquiringly.

"Sir, dare I ask about the communications concerning the

Luftwaffe's Operation Moonlight Sonata, its plan to bomb Coventry?"

The commander sat up straight in his chair and regarded her sternly. "Miss Littlefield, are you forgetting yourself again?"

Taken aback by the severity of his reproach despite half expecting one, she met his glare with wide, concerned eyes. "But sir, this attack is going to be monstrous even by recent standards..."

"Miss Littlefield," Denniston tried to interrupt, but Claire pressed on.

"...of what's been dropped on London. Hitler himself ordered it. Coventry will be destroyed. Shouldn't the city be warned?" Urgency and anxiety infused Claire's tone. "It's only forty miles..."

"Miss Littlefield." Denniston's voice rose.

"...from here, and members of our staff have family and friends who live there." Claire's insistence matched his stern voice.

"Miss Littlefield!" the commander called grimly, and took to his feet abruptly.

Claire also stood, her eyes fixed on his, her cheeks red. "And I know that Mr. Churchill has been informed."

Silence.

"Sit down, Miss Littlefield." Denniston's stern command pierced Claire's senses. She stared into his eyes as realization of her rashness sank in. Slowly, she settled back into her seat.

"I'm sorry, sir. I overstepped again."

Denniston stood silently observing her a moment, and then came around to the front of his desk. "I want to tell you that the offer for your promotion is still open, but it's good that you'll have time to think about it."

He stood, rubbing his temples while he searched for

words. "You're in the unfortunate position of not only decrypting messages from blocks of meaningless letters into German words but also understanding their content. That's giving you a very narrow view of events, like looking through a straw. Given incidents such as the threat to the Boulier network; the nature of the camp where your brother is a prisoner; or, in this instance, the devastation to Coventry on schedule for tonight, each one of them seems like it should take priority."

He closed his eyes, massaged the back of his neck, and let out a long breath. "You are not the only person to feel the pain that comes with advance knowledge of horrors arising out of compromises we make."

Chagrinned, Claire apologized again. "I didn't mean to presume—"

The commander nodded. "You need to think about what you'll be exposed to if you take the promotion. Coventry will represent neither the first nor the last time that agonizing decisions will be made in which we could have saved lives by giving warning—and for the record, Coventry will receive the standard forewarnings issued to every community under threat, but nothing more."

Claire listened with rapt attention. Watching Denniston's face as he talked, she saw the pain behind his eyes stemming from what he must know.

"We make such decisions every day, and each time, what we do at Bletchley must be protected. If Hitler ever learns that we read his communiqués almost as soon as he does, he'll change his codes, we'll lose this war and our country, and I suspect a lot more people will die prematurely in horrific circumstances."

He circled back to his seat and grasped the back of it. "If you join our analysis group, you will get a much broader picture. You'll see a multitude of situations, each of which, taken in isolation, should be earth-shattering; but such is the scale of this war that it is another calamity within a universe of terrible, inhuman catastrophes.

"I don't say that to be callous or uncaring. On the contrary, I believe we would betray our people by *not* making those judgments." For a fleeting moment, he looked exhausted, haunted. "Such is the wickedness of the demon in Berlin."

He pulled his chair out and took his seat. "Claire, you'll need to assess whether or not you can deal with those realities. The evaluations of German communications in the analysis section inform our national leaders all the way to Winston Churchill about the facts, assumptions, and courses of action that shape those decisions. That's what you'd be getting into."

All that night, Claire heard the rumble of bombers passing overhead, reminding her of the terrifying first night of the *blitz* when she and Amélie Boulier had found refuge with hundreds of other people in the basement of a department store in London near the docks of Dog Island. For ten hours, they had sheltered while the seemingly endless bombing raid continued, with nowhere to run as each explosion seemed to come closer, bringing a terrifying sense of helplessness. And then they had narrowly escaped being burned alive.

Claire shuddered. That, or something worse, was the ordeal that Coventry faced.

Timmy cried out in fear from his bedroom. Claire rushed to him, brought him to her bed, and curled her body around him protectively.

A few days earlier, she had seen *Luftwaffe* message traffic regarding a new radio navigation system referred to as the *X-Gerät*. It was the latest in a series of German ranging technologies that markedly increased bomber accuracy. As a result, being nearly forty miles from Coventry, Claire suffered little fear of bombs dropping on her home. Nevertheless, she anguished through much of the night over what Commander Denniston had revealed and what the people in Coventry must be suffering. Because their city resided in a low area typically blanketed by mist at night, they had believed that German bombers were unable to identify it. The *X-Gerät* had demolished that myth.

Claire had often visited the beautifully quaint city. Founded in medieval times, it had transformed into an engineering and manufacturing center that had increased in importance to the war effort. As a result, the *Luftwaffe* had taken particular interest, and it became an obvious target. Hour after hour, the bombers flew over, and Claire heard, burying her sorrow in her pillow.

The news reports the next morning offered no relief. Claire read them in anguish, seized with guilt. The raid had lasted for more than ten hours with over five hundred enemy aircraft. So vicious was the attack that heat from incendiary bombs melted the lead roof on Coventry's fourteenth-century cathedral. The liquified metal ran through the streets like a stream of molten lava, spreading noxious gases.

The foray had laid waste to the city, systematically destroying it with over two hundred and fifty fires and killing five hundred and sixty-eight people, that figure still rising from another eight hundred and sixty-three badly injured. Yet another three hundred and ninety-three unfortunates sustained lesser injuries. Further casualties had been limited by the practice of large numbers of Coventry's citizens, after previous raids, to trek to nearby villages each night to sleep there in relative safety. People who sought refuge in air raid shelters had seen few deaths or injuries, but over five hundred homes and two-thirds of the city's buildings, particularly its factories, had been destroyed.

With a heavy heart and heavier steps, Claire trudged into work at Bletchley the next morning. She intercepted some messages and started work on them at her desk but found concentration difficult. Commander Denniston's words from the day before rang repeatedly in her ears: "If Hitler ever learns that we read his communiqués almost as soon as he does, he'll change his codes, we'll lose this war and our country..."

With an expression more resolute than she felt, Claire left her desk, made her way to Denniston's office, and waited until he returned from a staff meeting. He finally appeared, looking haggard, and cast a glance at her that seemed cautiously pleased.

"I want to apologize again," Claire said, "about yesterday."

"No need. We won't speak of it again."

"I want to say, sir, that I appreciate your patience, and that, once we know Jeannie is safe, I'll be honored to join the analysis group. If you'll still have me."

Denniston smiled tiredly and stretched. "Miss Littlefield, that's the best news I've had in a while. We'll keep a seat warm for you."

5

November 19, 1940
South of Leicester, England

Compared to flying the nimble Spitfire, piloting the twin-engine Bristol 156 Beaufort night fighter was like the difference between racing the country lanes in a Maserati sports car and driving a late-model sedan on a straight road. Not that Jeremy had ever steered a Maserati, but he had been a passenger in one a few times when driven by one of his better-heeled aristocrat fellow fighter pilots, and Jeremy was already an ace from dogfights in Spitfires and Hurricanes against German *Luftwaffe* Messerschmitt 109s and 110s.

To be fair, this kite's got nearly triple the power of a Spitfire, and it maneuvers well. The twin 1600-horsepowered Bristol Hercules engines were each more than a half-time larger than the single one that powered the iconic fighter through aerial battles. It lacked the sleek lines, the agility, the sense of having strapped on wings to fly, characteristic of the Spitfire. But the blunt-nosed "Beaufighter," as pilots had dubbed this new aircraft, was a heavy fighter built for killing aircraft with a barrage of firepower, speed, and long-range flight capability.

The original production model had carried a pilot and gunner. The model Jeremy flew had been modified, its gun removed from the turret to make room for the new Air Intercept Mk IV air-to-air radar equipment, affectionately called the "magic box." Further, the cockpit and fuselage had been shifted backward to adjust the center of gravity to accommodate the added weight. The result lent the plane a hulking appearance, with its pilot ensconced in the nose. Despite being wedged between the two giant engines, the aircraft provided a wonderful field of vision, with only the feathering-capable propellers protruding in front of the pilot.

As they lifted into the night sky, Jeremy's magic box operator, Sergeant Farlan Pirie, sat in the turret behind the pilot's seat. Jeremy felt fortunate to have him. He was older than Jeremy by a few years, but by how many, Jeremy did not know. Farlan had been a mechanic in Cheshire before the war but had volunteered while the so-called "Phoney War" played out in France. Trained as a radar operator, he had found himself an untrained rearguard infantryman during the evacuation from Dunkirk, like Jeremy. He too had evaded overland in France; and farther south, he had managed to escape on one of the last remaining boats to England.

Having been exposed to radar technology, Farlan immediately grasped its potential and embraced the opportunity when offered the job on the Beaufighters. He worked hard to improve his skills and had proven adept at spotting target planes on the magic box during training exercises.

Jeremy often wondered about the men who rode in turrets on bombers and fighters. They experienced every toss and turn of the aircraft, yet they had no ability to affect any of their twists, rolls, direction, speed, or any factor that determined where the plane would go or in what manner. That was particularly true in a Beaufort that could ascend or dive vertically and execute barrel rolls or any other maneuver to gain an advantage over a foe, and in the case of the Beaufighter, the operator did not even have a weapon with which to shoot back. In this job, his responsibility was to stare into a pair of glowing cathode-ray tubes at the most critical moments.

Jeremy fingered his array of trigger mechanisms and had to grin. *What I lose in maneuverability compared to a Spitfire, I make up for in hellfire.* This Beaufighter could train devastating firepower on enemy bombers and fighters with four 20 mm Hispano Mk II cannons in the nose; six .303 Browning machine guns in the wings, four on the starboard side and two to port; and eight RP-3 130-pound rockets in the fuselage. With a range of fifteen hundred miles and a top speed of three hundred and thirty miles per hour, the aircraft posed a lethal threat to the *Luftwaffe*.

So versatile and effective was the base-model Beaufort that further variants, the so-called Rockbeau and Torbeau, were being discussed. The former was designed to provide close support for ground troops by firing volleys of rockets from the wing, and the latter to drop torpedoes against enemy shipping from a distance. Jeremy mused momentarily how such aircraft might execute their missions, but then returned his thoughts to the present.

He peered through the darkness blanketing the countryside. The massive radar system along the eastern and southern coasts of Britain, codenamed Chain Home, had spotted yet another huge horde of hostile aircraft massing to attack across the English Channel with the apparent target being in the midlands near Leicester, east of Birmingham.

For reasons unknown, instead of being controlled by their usual station at RAF Sopley near Bournesmouth, control of

604 Squadron Beaufighters had been passed to RAF Tangmere under II Group headquarters, which had vectored them
east. He climbed into clouds, wincing as a jab of pain in his
shoulder reminded him that he was not yet fully recovered
from his wound. The controller, callsign Boffin, then turned
him south over the Channel where he broke into a clear,
moonlit sky over silver waters.

No one expected that Germany had ended its assault on
the factories and airfields across Great Britain. But since
October 31, the last day of heavy German targeting of RAF
airfields, German strategy had altered, sending Hermann
Göring's bombers almost exclusively to drop tons of incendiaries and explosives on the hapless British population, tipping
cauldrons of fire, destruction, mutilation, and death on the
inhabitants of London, Manchester, Liverpool, Sheffield,
Southampton, Birmingham, Hull, Glasgow, and Coventry,
with more cities sure to receive similar blistering onslaughts.
Beginning in mid-August, Germany had dealt their carnage in
attacks almost unopposed, striking at dusk with incendiary
munitions that created furnaces, which in turn acted as
beacons for heavy bombers, summoning them in the dark of
night to deliver their deadly cargoes.

Jeremy had read newspaper reports about the air raid over
Coventry and the devastation there. The plight of the city
highlighted Britons' justified demands that Winston
Churchill's government "do something" to stop the nightly
incursions. More specifically, the prime minister looked to Air
Chief Marshal Sir Hugh Dowding to augment his wide-area
ground-controlled air interception network that had so
successfully countered Adolf Hitler's daytime attacks on the
RAF's airfields and Britain's ports and factories. *Tonight, we'll
see how Dowding's response works.*

Using other aircraft as targets, Jeremy, Anderson, and

Cunningham had practiced night maneuvers extensively over the past month, but this was no practice run. Once his Beaufort had left the ground, a controller vectored him toward the enemy, and as he closed with it, Farlan, in the turret behind him, watched for green blips on the cathode tubes to guide Jeremy into attack position.

Then, it was up to Jeremy to see and engage a dark phantom against a dark sky.

A crucial element of maneuver nagged at Jeremy, one that had not been mastered, and as yet, no solution had been developed. The concept of attacking the enemy called for fighters to ascend at an angle from below and behind their targets. The radar showed where the bombers were within three miles to a minimum of a hundred feet, but the operator would have to estimate the closing rate between the target and the pursuing Beaufighter from watching how fast the blips on the cathode tubes closed.

Since the fighters flew faster than their targets, acquiring that final view had proven difficult in practice, and therein lay the danger: overshooting the target at best, or ramming it at worst. But only after visual sighting had occurred could firepower be unleashed. And so far, the Beaufighters had not shot down a single nighttime bomber.

Despite himself, Jeremy's mind wandered. During the weeks that he had trained with 604 Squadron, he had not mingled socially with other pilots. He missed his comrades from the 609th, to be sure. Additionally, as had many pilots since the war moved into the skies over Britain, he had remained aloof simply because losing friends had become so frequent and painful that distance was a common defense for maintaining equanimity.

Then for a fleeting moment, stirring thoughts crossed his mind of Amélie, the French beauty who had rescued him at

Dunkirk. "Not now," he muttered, jolting himself back to awareness. His eyes darted across the black emptiness, searching where the coastline must be—the guns there would be first to engage the German bombers as the leading edge of the attack crossed the shore. Flashes of light from midair anti-aircraft explosions would give warning that the bombers' thrust toward Leicester was imminent.

Boffin called over the radio, "Hallo, Blazer Two Six. Orbit, orbit. Bandit coming your way at Angels II."

Throttling up, Jeremy radioed back, "Okay, Boffin. Orbiting." The mammoth sleeve-valve engines growled deeper as the Beaufighter responded to his touch. Scanning his instruments, he called back to Farlan, "I'm going up to fifteen thousand. We need height."

"Weapon ready," Farlan called back, referring to his magic box.

Jeremy puffed up his cheeks and blew the air out, his mind going to his squadron leader, John Cunningham. Over the weeks that Jeremy had been with the squadron, he had learned much about the pilot. At twenty-four years of age, he was a quiet, unassuming man who dodged limelights. A handsome chap of average height with a firm jaw, he had apprenticed with de Haviland Aircraft Company on completing secondary school, and he had participated in designing two new planes, the T.K.2 racer, and a touring and training aircraft, the Moth Minor. Simultaneous with joining the company, he had been accepted into the Royal Auxiliary Air Force with 604 (County of Middlesex) Squadron. Proving to be a remarkable pilot, he had remained with the squadron for several years, and had recently been promoted to squadron leader, probably the youngest pilot in the RAF at this point to achieve that position.

Shortly after meeting him, Jeremy had asked Cunningham

if he was related to the famous admiral in the Mediterranean. Cunningham had shaken his head. "Only by name. I come from rather lowlier roots."

"The admiral's a hero now, after what his fleet pulled off in Taranto."

Cunningham had agreed, adding, "With what our Beau-fighters carry, they'll make an equal mark on history."

Jeremy also respected the commanding officer, Michael Anderson, a slender fellow with light skin; but the two had not spent as much time together. Anderson had left Jeremy's training to Cunningham while he sought out more recruits for the night fighting squadron. However, to have occupied such a sensitive leadership position at such a young age, Jeremy figured that Anderson must be a pilot of unusual skill and judgment.

Boffin's voice broke through the drone of engines. "Hallo, Blazer Two Six, contact imminent. Flash your weapon."

"I heard," Farlan called. "Magic box switched on."

Jeremy felt a rush of adrenaline as he throttled up to full power. He gulped in air and twisted slightly in his seat while glancing down at his instruments with a grim smile. "You won't get away clean tonight," he muttered to his unseen foe. "If you're lucky, you'll limp home."

After these weeks of training on the Beau, he felt confident that he had in his grasp a combat multiplier that could tip the balance in favor of the RAF, and more importantly, the people of Great Britain.

Boffin's voice broke through the rush of wind. "You're closing on a big boy. Maneuver into firing position."

Once more, Jeremy glanced through his windshield at the darkness and saw nothing. Many times, he had flown near the tall towers of the Chain Home radar system that had alerted Fighter Command that an attack was inbound. He had thought idly a few times how nice it would be to have such a system inside the plane capable of making enemy aircraft visible to the crew at night and from a distance. He had not dreamed that it could exist within the span of this war.

Yet behind him on Sergeant Farlan Pirie's screen was the manifestation of the electronic apparatus, and tonight, that compact air intercept system would perform in its first combat deployment.

Behind Jeremy, Farlan sat still, watching his magic box intently.

Subsequent radio traffic from Boffin gave Jeremy a mental picture of the situation: the German bombers lumbered through the night sky over the Channel and heading north on a line west of Leicester, apparently headed toward Birmingham. Boffin vectored Jeremy on a wide curve that brought his Beaufighter behind their leading formation.

"Closing in," he muttered to himself. "Remember tactics. Their gunners can't see you. When you hit, watch for falling debris. Dive and veer off but keep your general direction until clear. Pay attention to the controller. Return to airfield, reload, refuel. Do it again. The night is your friend."

"You have contact ahead," Boffin called.

Farlan heard and swallowed hard. Success now rested on him to guide Jeremy into position dead astern of the tail. "Modify course two degrees port." He watched the blip crossing his screen at an accelerating speed. "Increase climb rate and angle."

Jeremy brought the Beaufighter's nose up slightly and nudged his throttle.

"Steady," Farlan called. "Steady. You should see him at any moment."

Suddenly, far out to his left, Jeremy saw flashes that he recognized as coming from the muzzles of Hispano cannons, followed by tiny white flashes of light from high explosive rounds impacting against a hard object. And then, tracers flew in the opposite direction as the gunner on the German bomber returned fire.

For a second, Jeremy wondered if the historical significance of the moment had been impressed on Anderson or Cunningham as it had on him. One of them had just scored, and Jeremy had just witnessed the first use of air-to-air radar to engage an enemy aircraft.

Scarcely had the thought entered his mind when more flashes farther away in the dark sky signaled that yet more Hispano cannons had been fired by another Beaufighter, but no telltale signs indicated any hits.

Suddenly, right above Jeremy, a deeper black appeared against the starlight of the night sky. Acting on instinct, Jeremy jammed his stick forward and to the left, stepped on his corresponding pedal, and dove. Too late. He heard the wrenching of metal on metal as his tail scraped along the belly of his German target.

The mood in the dispersal hut was muted when Jeremy trudged in with Farlan after limping his kite back to RAF Middle Wallop. Cunningham had downed a German bomber, but his natural modesty precluded overt celebration. Jeremy's calamity contributed a dampening effect.

Fortunately, although his stabilizer had been bent and twisted, it had provided sufficient aerodynamic constancy that, with persistent manipulation of the controls, allowed him to land the aircraft safely. Shining his torch on it after climbing down from the cockpit, he shook his head in wonder at the impossibility of what he had just done.

"Cunningham proved that the concept works, but we have more work to do," Anderson said after Jeremy reported what had happened to his aircraft. "He hit one, but the collision nearly cost us dearly. Judging the closure rate and getting that visual contact are crucial." He addressed Cunningham. "Tell us what you did. How did you get visual sighting and engage the target?"

Cunningham reached over and nudged Jeremy. "Glad you and Sergeant Pirie are still with us, mate."

Jeremy smiled bleakly in acknowledgment.

"First off," Cunningham began, "what I did is replicable. We can train others to do it. Initially, I saw ground searchlights swarming across some clouds, so I figured the bombers must be passing over in that vicinity. That aspect alone is one we should pass along to our chaps on the ground. That was an immense help. As we got closer, my operator, Jimmy, locked onto the blips on his screen and fed me estimates of speed, distance, and height.

"One thing I can tell you that we anticipated wrongly is the notion of looking for the glow around their engines. It's not that they don't exist but that we are searching the skies for something specific.

"Jimmy first spotted the aircraft from about twelve thousand feet behind and above the bomber. I lowered my landing gear, using them as airbrakes to decelerate and descend below him. Jimmy continued to feed me course, altitude, and attitude corrections until I saw a patch of sky that was darker than the rest. I'm not sure that's the most accurate way to describe it, but that patch didn't have any stars. As we closed in, it grew wings and a tail, and I knew we had our target, and when we were about three hundred feet below it, we even identified it as a Heinkel HE III. We could tell by its elliptical tail.

"We cut loose with all of our weapons, including some of the rockets, but then the pneumatic firing device failed, and about that time, the wretched man in the gunner's cupola started firing back at us." He laughed. "We saw our tracers hit, but the bugger wouldn't go down. We followed the bomber as it turned before reaching its target and descended as it headed out to sea. That is one tough aircraft. We saw the hits, and at first, they seemed to have no effect. We were out of ammunition by then and running out of fuel, so we took it on in. As a result, we can claim only a probable kill, but our technology and tactics worked."

Everyone in the group had listened, mesmerized. Then Anderson turned to Jeremy. "We need to analyze what went right and what went wrong. Don't feel bad about what happened to you." He grinned with empathy and clapped his own chest with a gesture of futility. "I thought I saw our target. I fired. I missed. Just tell us how your collision came about."

Jeremy nodded. "Besides seeing the bandit, I think the hardest part is gauging how fast we're overtaking it. We're flying faster, and we want to hit them from below, which means we're coming at them nose up. We have to keep that attitude until after we've fired.

"My error was in not seeing the target in time to shoot and dive. I undershot. What Cunningham just said about not searching for something specific in a night sky, like engine glow, is brilliant. That glow is so low intensity that we'll probably rarely see it.

"Farlan zeroed in on my target perfectly. I saw it, too late, while I was looking for the glow. So, we need to practice coming up behind the target without flying or shooting in front of it or colliding with it."

The next morning, Jeremy picked up a newspaper someone had left on a table in the dispersal hut. Its headline read, "Liverpool Blitzed." Pictures of a gutted downtown took up the middle section, with relics of tall buildings reduced to rubble, smoke rising from blackened ruins, and people huddled together, many of them injured. Blankets covered many human forms.

Jeremy shook his head sadly and was about to put the paper back on the table when another smaller headline below the fold caught his eye. "Beaufort Night Fighter Brings Down German Bomber." The subheading read, "Flight Lieutenant John 'Cat's Eyes' Cunningham Shoots Down Target in the Dark."

The article extolled the heroism of three pilots of 604 Squadron racing through the night to Leicester, and highlighted their incredible night vision, in particular Cunningham's.

"If they only knew," Jeremy breathed. Anderson had informed Group Headquarters, Fighter Command, and the Air Ministry of the night's success, and the government was making the most of the attack's propaganda value. Jeremy was well enough acquainted with Cunningham to know that the man shunned celebrity status. But Jeremy also perceived a method to the madness in the publicity: Britons needed winning heroes, and Germany might realize a vulnerability that could become a deterrent.

6

Marseille, France

Madame Marie Madeleine Fourcade called Henri Schaerrer and asked him to send Phillippe Boutron to meet with her that afternoon. "I'd like to come along," Henri said.

"I'd prefer you didn't," she replied.

"We can discuss that when I arrive," he said. "Phillippe will come later, depending on the outcome of our discussion." His voice was pleasant, and she knew him to be a genuinely friendly person, so his pushback came as a surprise, but she also understood that Phillippe was the best man on Henri's teams. She had already used the former French naval officer in a highly sensitive operation once before without informing Henri of the details. She had a hunch that Henri was not willing for her to do so again.

She was a small woman, highly intelligent and well educated, with a thin face and smooth skin, pretty with rounded eyes and a square chin. Her short, straight hair changed with tactical demands, and she melded into crowds

at a moment's notice. Few would suspect that she helped organize and run a Resistance network.

When she and Henri met on the veranda of her villa overlooking a grand view of the sparkling blue Mediterranean, he
immediately launched into the issue. "I stipulated that if I
recruited my former naval colleagues into your Resistance
organization, that I would run that part of the organization.
You agreed to that."

"No argument," Fourcade said, "but the mission I have for
Phillippe is a continuation of the one he executed last
summer. What we need him to do is even more crucial. I don't
spell out the details to you for operational security reasons. If
anyone associated with the mission is caught and breaks
under interrogation, good people will die, networks will be
blown, and if the Gestapo traces it back to here, our entire
organization could be lost."

Henri regarded Fourcade with a doubtful look. "Am I
always to be kept in the dark? We had an agreement."

Fourcade reached over and touched his arm. She liked and
trusted Henri as much as anyone she had ever known, and she
disliked making him feel distrusted. Swiss by birth, he was tall
with a strong build, dark hair, and a ready smile. Having wanted a
naval career since childhood, he had taken a commission in the
French navy where he gained wide acceptance and respect
among his peers. After the French had capitulated and disbanded
most of its navy, he had joined her Alliance group of the French
Resistance and recruited many of his former colleagues.

"I've lived up to our arrangement in every respect
including Phillippe's operation. I discussed it with you and
secured your permission before acting, as we had agreed that I
should." She pulled back and watched him fondly. "Henri,"
she entreated, "I think so highly of you that I got British intel-

ligence to send Jeremy Littlefield here for the sole purpose of convincing you to bring in your former navy comrades to join us."

He sat eyeing her without speaking.

"Do you trust Phillippe?" Fourcade asked.

"With my life," Henri replied without hesitation.

"Do you trust me?"

He nodded reluctantly. "You know I do. I think maybe you don't trust me."

"Let's put that to rest. Before today, I had not considered you might think that. Talk to Phillippe. Ask him if he thinks the security arrangements around this operation should stay the same. If he says you should be read in, we'll do it. Otherwise, we go forward as things are. Agreed?"

Rising from his seat, Henri took a deep breath. "We can resolve that right now. He's waiting down the road."

Five minutes later, Henri re-joined Fourcade on the terrace, bringing Phillippe with him. She explained the dilemma.

Phillippe had been a gunnery officer aboard the French dreadnaught *Bretagne* as part of the French fleet anchored in Algeria when British warships destroyed the ships to keep them out of Nazi hands following France's surrender. That action embittered French naval officers toward the British. Convincing them to join the Brits in supporting the French Resistance had been no easy feat.

Phillippe had been furious and ashamed that France surrendered to Germany, especially after only five weeks. Fiercely patriotic, he had railed against his leadership to the brink of insubordination when it refused to either scuttle their fleet or surrender it to the British to keep it out of German hands. He had been the first among Henri's colleagues to urge joining forces with Fourcade.

Now, he listened quietly as she disclosed the dilemma about how much Henri should know about Phillippe's operation, and then remained silent for a few moments with his own thoughts. When he spoke, he directed his first comments to Fourcade. "I think the difficulty lies in who is taking the risks." He gestured toward Henri. "We are out among the population, actively recruiting and already carrying out sabotage operations. In combat, you trust and fight for the person to your left and right. If that trust is broken..." He shook his head. "I understand my friend's reluctance."

Fourcade shoved aside a sudden surge of annoyance. "I see your view," she said, addressing both men. "I'd like you to see mine." She focused her attention on Henri. "You two have done a marvelous job of building your organization, but yours is not the only one that traces to me, nor is it the only one that we recruit for.

"We have a school-age girl living with Maurice and his family. You know her, Chantal Boulier, and she is not attending school because the risk is too high, so we must hide her during the day. Her father leads a major network in the north. Her sister, Amélie, as you know, is active in another part of the Resistance. Just having Chantal with us could draw unwelcome attention.

"That's only one of our many vulnerabilities. Maurice is constantly recruiting, but as opposed to your activities to bring in former known colleagues, he's often dealing with and trying to vet friends of friends—people he doesn't know, including criminal elements with valuable skills, like forging identification and travel documents. And that's only one of several organizations we work with.

"All of those threads lead back to me. I have to be ready to move myself and my immediate staff to safety at a moment's notice, and we are in frequent radio contact with London, which adds further jeopardy from detection by signal-direction finders. My point is that we are all in constant danger, which is why operational security is a must." She caught herself. "I'm sorry. I didn't mean to prattle on."

She turned to Phillippe. "You know the nature of the mission and the stakes. I trust your judgment. Should Henri know the details of the operation you went on or not? The issue is important now because there's more to do. You know the lives at risk."

Phillippe stared at Fourcade, his eyes narrowed and hard. "Is Swan in danger?" he asked.

"Yes, and British intelligence's SOE desires that we alleviate the situation."

Phillippe leaned back as he contemplated what to say. Swan was the codename for Jeannie Rousseau, the spy inside the German 10th Army Headquarters in Dinard. He had helped establish communications with her after Amélie Boulier had recruited her for the Resistance.

An incredibly intelligent young lady with high education and gifted with a photographic memory, Jeannie was also elegant and beautiful. Known for treating everyone with courtesy and respect, she had gained the attention of the German command in Dinard as a capable interpreter and translator, being fluent in five languages, including German. Deliberately coquettish, she had charmed her German masters into revealing military secrets. Through first Amélie and then Phillippe, she had shared what she learned with Fourcade, who passed the information on to British intelligence.

During their last meeting, Jeannie had delivered to Phillippe detailed maps, sketches, lists, and tables drawn from memory of documents she had seen and conversations she had overheard inside the headquarters. Taken together, they detailed troop strength, headquarters locations, ammunition storage dumps, staging sites, schedules, contingencies, and all manner of detailed information regarding Operation Sea Lion, the impending German invasion of England. Based on information she supplied, RAF Bomber Command had carried out raids on key military installations along the French Atlantic coast.

On that day when he last met with Jeannie, Phillippe saw plainly the toll her activities took on her psyche. To add to her discomfort, a particular German SS officer, Major Bergmann, seemed to suspect her. Phillippe had offered to "take care" of the major or otherwise help her leave the area, but she had declined, re-stating her duty to help in any way she could to defeat the Nazis. Apparently, the danger had intensified.

Phillippe turned to Henri. "You are my friend," he said. "I pledged to follow your orders for our Resistance. Tell me you need to know these details, and they're yours, but hear me out first. We're military men. We share everything about our lives, but sometimes we possess critical security secrets we cannot divulge, even to each other.

"This is that kind of secret. It's got to be kept among the fewest number of people, and the identities of those people must be protected." He cupped a hand behind Henri's neck and spoke, eye to eye. "I know you care about the people in our organization; you feel responsible for supporting and keeping them safe while they do dangerous things. Sometimes, you must keep your hands off and trust the individuals. This is one of those times. If I'm killed fighting for France, I can't ask for a more worthwhile death."

Henri listened without interruption while Phillippe spoke. He regarded his friend solemnly for a few moments, and then turned to Fourcade. "We're in this fight together. I leave the mission and Phillippe in your hands."

He started to leave, but Fourcade stopped him. "Please

wait. There's more for us to discuss once I've finished with Phillippe."

After Fourcade and Phillippe had conferred, they met again with Henri long enough for goodbyes. "You made a wise choice," Phillippe told his friend. "I must go. I'll see you when I get back."

They grasped hands, clapped each other's backs, and Phillippe departed. Fourcade started to lead Henri back out to the terrace, but he stopped her. "I apologize," he said. "I hadn't considered your danger. I make matters worse by being here."

Fourcade tossed her head. "You're here because I welcomed you here."

Henri bowed his head slightly in acknowledgement, and the pair walked to the terrace. Two men waited there whom Henri recognized, Sergeant Derek Horton and Maurice. They rose to greet Henri and Fourcade, and then the four sat down together.

Before Fourcade could open the discussion, Henri preempted her. "I just learned about security concerns surrounding Miss Fourcade and this villa," he said. "It's an intolerable situation. She's at the center of our brain trust. I volunteer my organization to establish an invisible perimeter around the villa with procedures for coming in and out and an early warning system, in case Pétain's secret police make moves against us."

"Thank you, Henri," Fourcade exclaimed. "I'm touched."

"I should have thought of it sooner," Henri returned. "If any of the people you meet with all the time are exposed, they'll put all our lives at risk. It's a gaping security hole, and every day, Pétain acts more like his Nazi idol and clamps down harder. He's already identifying Jews for roundup like in Germany and Poland. Just because the German army stopped coming south doesn't mean their methods won't impact here." He turned and spat. "Pétain is their willing puppet."

Henri shifted his attention to Maurice. "You have concerns about vetting people to avoid recruiting collaborators. We can help with that."

The other three studied him. Maurice was the first to speak. "I blame myself," he said. "We take precautions in the field. I hadn't thought about securing the villa, but we have to do it, and without drawing attention."

"I'll take some of that blame," Horton quipped, speaking in fluent French. "I don't want to be left out." He grinned and the others laughed. "I don't mean to make light," he said, becoming serious. "We tend to think of being able to handle ourselves in the field with our weapons and our mates watching our backs, but Miss Fourcade is here undefended."

"I have a pistol," she said, pulling it out from the folds of her dress.

"We have to fix this," Henri scoffed, viewing the small weapon and turning to Maurice. "Do you have enough men and women with arms to watch over this place? My people can train them."

Maurice nodded. "I'll work out the details with you."

"Good," Fourcade said, "and thank you. Now, let's get down to why I wanted to meet today. We know where Lance Littlefield is, in Colditz, a town on the other side of Germany. It's beyond our immediate reach. But that doesn't mean we can't help him, or any prisoner." She turned her attention to Horton. "You have a special affinity for Lance—"

"I should say so. He saved my life, he did. Up at Dunkirk and all the way across France. Ten of us. I wouldn't be here now but for him."

Fourcade smiled at the stocky British noncom. "I understand. As I was about to say, your regard for him is what brought you back to France after your escape to England. You've been officially transferred to SOE to be my liaison, but you had established good relations with Major Crockatt at MI-9, is that right?"

"I don't know where you're going with this," Horton said with a comical expression, "but that sums things up."

Fourcade laughed. "Here's the issue. MI-6, MI-9, and SOE all belong to British intelligence. Their missions are similar but different enough that at times, they could be in conflict. I've been in touch with MI-6 since before the war because I saw it coming, so I know their workings better. They're set up to run spies quietly. They don't want attention. On the other hand, SOE, Churchill's Special Operations Executive, is intended to run missions that will draw a lot of notice by blowing up things, like those fuel storage-tank fields you exploded at Saint-Nazaire." She patted Horton's arm.

"Don't think I did that all by myself," Horton cut in, his eyes wide with mock-seriousness. "I was just one of the participants. Lance organized it."

"I understand," Fourcade said, chuckling. "That brings us to MI-9. It's still organizing, but its main objective is to help downed pilots, separated soldiers, escaped POWs, and anyone else fleeing the Nazis, to get them out of the country.

"The way I see things is that we're at the fulcrum of all three of those British intelligence sections. We don't care which of them we're dealing with; our aim is to free France." She chose her next words carefully. "That might at times put us at odds with one organization or the other." She spoke directly to Horton. "And that's not anything they need to hear over there."

"About what?" He grinned. "I ain't heard anythin'. I'm here to liaise, not be a diplomat."

"All right, then, let me get specific. SOE will be funding us. They'll send agents, money, equipment, arms—things that will help us raise a partisan force." Fourcade addressed Henri directly. "Obviously, we want to keep them pleased, and with your network of former military officers, you're perfectly placed to assist." She turned her attention to Maurice. "Networks are forming in other parts of the country specifically to help POWs escape and soldiers and airmen evade capture. Two of them, codenamed Prospect and Comet, are already up and running. We need to contact them, compare notes, and establish how we help each other."

"One thing on that," Maurice interrupted. "Those escape lines run well west of here to the northern border of Spain where it meets France. Generally, evaders work their way through the Pyrenees, go west to Bilboa, south to Madrid, and then down to Gibraltar."

Fourcade nodded. "We've helped the Boulier network all the way up in Dunkirk, and we've participated in operations in other parts of France. One that comes to mind is getting word to Lance that we're on the watch for him. Our main advantage is that Marseille is still a relatively safe zone. Our ability to communicate and maneuver is greater than in the occupied zone. If we can help, we will. If not, we'll stay out of the way. But we want to be active in finding the need. We had several British soldiers come this way after Dunkirk, and we were able to get some across the sea into the French territories in North Africa, and from there they made their way home. All avenues must stay open.

"I'll discuss specifics with each of you, but another point to make is that the Resistance is going to become more difficult to build, not less. As Pétain increases his grip and Hitler terrorizes our people in the Occupied Zone, we're going to find fewer people willing to help. And we'll be betrayed, that's assured. Bribes, terror, and blackmail will be used to expose us."

"Greedy people will help the Nazis, and so will starving and terrified people," Henri interjected. "We can't show mercy to collaborators. People should be as afraid of betraying us as they are of the Nazis. On that note, I received a report about the French woman in Saint-Louis near the German border who led the *Wehrmacht* to re-capture Lance. She will never betray anyone again, and her friends and neighbors are well advised along the same lines." He did not expand his comments further.

Fourcade sighed and nodded. Then she pushed back from the table. "Let's get to work."

7

Dinard, France

"You look tired, *Mademoiselle*." Major Bergmann's voice acquired a crooning, taunting tenor when he addressed Jeannie Rousseau. With her back to him, she forced a flirtatious smile before turning to face him.

"Aren't we all," she said, rubbing her temple. "I imagine *you* most of all must feel the strain with the heavy responsibility you carry. I don't know how you do it." She held a sheaf of papers in front of her lips while batting her eyes shyly, twice.

Bergmann regarded her coldly. Reaching for the papers, he tore them from her and perused them. "These are classified. What are you doing with them?"

"I'm filing them, sir, as I was directed to do by the field marshal. Am I doing it incorrectly? Each document has the proper cover so all I can read is the document title, and I'm cleared to do this."

"A mistake in judgment, in my view."

From the other side of the room, *Wehrmacht Oberst* Meier

watched the exchange. He strode across and stood in front of Bergmann, arms crossed, his face challenging. "Is there a problem?"

For a moment, no one spoke, but then Jeannie brightened her smile and flashed her eyes. "I don't believe so," she replied. "The major was worried that I might not be getting enough rest and that I might be misfiling these documents."

Bergmann glared at her and turned to Meier. "I am concerned that *Mademoiselle* Rousseau is in this room at all," he said, barely concealing his contempt for her or Meier. "Having someone from the local population translating for us and working in our security vaults makes no sense."

"That's not your call, Major," Meier retorted sternly. He turned to Jeannie. "Will you excuse us, please?" His voice took on a menacing undertone. "I need a private chat with the major."

Without a word, Jeannie hurried away. As she turned to go into a nearby restroom, she glanced back at the two officers. The *Oberst*, a tall man, leaned over the major, who stood at attention. Meier thumped Bergmann's chest with his index finger, and his face creased with anger.

Jeannie hurried inside the restroom and closed the door, locking it. Then she leaned over the sink, breathing hard. Moisture had beaded on her forehead, and when she looked in the mirror, she had turned ghostly white. Stumbling to the toilet, she closed the lid and sat on it, buried her face in her hands, and calmed herself. *No tears. I can't have red eyes.*

"You listen to me," Meier growled at Bergmann. "Your insolence and lack of judgment got our men killed in Dunkirk, and I won't have your careerist hostility causing havoc in this headquarters. *Fraulein* Rousseau was doing exactly as Field Marshal Reichenau directed. You're in charge of security, but I run the operations staff, including you. If you have a problem with one of our workers, you bring it to me. Am I making myself clear?"

Bergmann snapped his heels and hissed out a terse, "Yes, sir."

"Dismissed," Meier said.

Once more, Bergmann snapped his heels, flung his right arm high, palm up, and delivered a sharp, "Heil Hitler."

Meier only stared back through narrowed eyes and walked away.

In the restroom, Jeannie had recovered her composure. She stood again in front of the mirror. Some color had returned to her face. She dampened it with cold water and then dabbed it dry with a kerchief. Straightening and regarding her reflection in the mirror, she practiced a bright smile. Then she flushed the toilet, lifted the lid to its normal upright position, and opened the door.

When she emerged, *Oberst* Meier waited for her across the room. "I apologize for the major's bad behavior. I expect that it will not happen again."

Jeannie waved her hand in a dismissive gesture, graced Meier with her smile, and shook her head. "It was nothing. I understand that he must do his security job, including the safety of documents. I'm not offended, but I appreciate that you came to my rescue. Shall I continue with the task?"

"Of course. The field marshal directed you."

Later that afternoon, alone in her parents' house, Jeannie heard a knock on the door. Peering through a peephole, she saw a workman standing on the other side. He was above medium height and slender, and he wore a black beret pulled low over his forehead.

"Who's there?" she called.

"You called for an electrician?" the man said.

Jeannie hesitated. She recognized the voice. With an unexpected release of tension, her body shook even as her heart leaped with excitement. Taking a deep breath, she regained her composure and slowly opened the door.

Phillippe stood there. "I received a message that your electrical problem had returned. If you like, I'll take a quick look."

"Yes, please," Jeannie replied while checking both ways along her street. She saw no one else. "Come in."

Closing the door, she swung around, threw her arms around Phillippe's shoulders, buried her face against his chest, and shook while fighting back tears. "I'm so glad to see someone I can talk to," she gasped. "I've been terrified, but I can't show it, and I can't speak with anyone."

"Hold onto me as long as you like," Phillippe said. "That's why I'm here. I won't leave again until you're moved to safety."

For several minutes they stood in the foyer, embracing. Then, finally, Jeannie pulled away and led Phillippe into the sitting room. "It's so good that you're here," she said, her voice just above a whisper.

"I was sent to get you out," he said. "I hear that the danger is increasing."

Jeannie regarded him, puzzled. "How could anyone know that?"

Phillippe chuckled. "Honestly, I don't know how. We understood at the outset that the pressures on you would be immense, but we've learned that you might be under suspicion and that this Major Bergmann is becoming an increasing threat. Somewhere, you've got a guardian angel watching over you who keeps us informed."

Jeannie closed her eyes, exhaled, and nodded. "Just this afternoon, I was filing some classified papers. Bergmann came up behind me. I think he must have seen me scan them before putting them in their files because he accosted me about them right there. They had classified covers, and if anyone else had seen me, I would have done like I have in the past and explained that I was double-checking the documents against their file numbers to make sure I put them in the right place.

"He started to dig into me, but then our new chief of staff, *Oberst* Meier, appeared out of nowhere. I was surprised at his reaction because Bergmann had just begun speaking to me when Meier confronted him. Bergmann told him that hiring locals to work in classified areas was a mistake." She giggled nervously. "I guess I prove his case."

"Was there anything worth knowing in those files?"

Jeannie nodded. "There were schedules of ammunition transfers to the barges along the Atlantic coast for the invasion, including their pick-up and delivery points."

"I thought that had been canceled."

Jeannie shook her head. "Only postponed. A final decision will be made in the spring. Also, the order of march has been developed, at least tentatively, with units designated for specific tasks; and the plan for coordinated air support."

Phillippe sat back in amazement. "You were able to get all of that?"

Jeannie smiled wryly and tapped her head. "It's all here. I'll reproduce it for you."

"Good. That's all valuable, including the fact that there is a new chief of staff."

"I should have specified that Meier is the operations chief

of staff, but Major Bergmann reports through him." She tilted her head and gazed toward the ceiling as a thought struck her. "That interchange between those two men was strange. Meier apologized to me afterward, and I don't think he had salacious intentions—he's not a womanizer. He's too businesslike, and his apology was for Bergmann's conduct. But he was so fast to intercede when the situation had not escalated to requiring him to do that. Meier stood Bergmann at attention and pounded his finger into the major's chest while scolding him. I think there's a history between the two of them."

"Maybe we can get London to research both of their backgrounds." He gave Jeannie a long, searching look. "We need to talk about getting you out of here."

Jeannie stood and paced while pressing her fingers against her mouth. Then she set her jaw tightly. "Not now. Not yet."

Startled, Phillippe stared at her. "Why not? You've done more than anyone could have expected. Continuing to risk your life makes no sense."

Jeannie shook her head firmly. "Everyone's in jeopardy until this war is over. Suppose I get to safety. What becomes of my parents or friends? We agree that I need to leave, but only after suspicions about me alleviate."

She crossed the room to a desk, pulled out a pad and pen, and started writing. "I'm jotting down information I saw today so you can take it with you. And then you need to leave. You've been here too long already."

"Will you be all right?"

"I will. Thanks for coming. You gave me a tremendous boost. Tell London that I'm going to scale back my activities unless something very pressing pops up. Come back in a week. Meanwhile, I'll start thinking through how to extract myself from this. When you return, we can refine the plan. Meanwhile, I'll deal with Bergmann."

8

November 25, 1940
Bletchley Park, England

"You made a good call." As Commander Denniston paced behind his desk, he looked more pressed than the last time Claire met with him. She had been startled to receive his summons, and further surprised to receive his request that she research as much as she could from past decoded messages that mentioned two officers at the German 10th Army head-quarters, *Oberst* Meier and Major Bergmann. He instructed her to bring the results with her.

"Our young lady in Dinard is in danger. Grave danger, and the information she's supplied to us is immense. Through her, we know now that Operation Sea Lion was only postponed and the active buildup for it continues despite that the troop-carrier barges have been moved from their launch sites. Signals we've intercepted and decoded tell us that the barges intended for the invasion have been put up in storage, but she says a final decision won't be made until the spring, so we can't let our guard down. That's valuable information."

"How can I help?"

"For the moment, Jeannie Rousseau won't leave the head-quarters, but one of these two officers I asked you to research, Major Bergmann, seems to suspect her. From direct reports received through MI-6, we know that he's ruthless—"

"I recall that a Captain Bergmann was at Dunkirk. He was the executive officer in one of the lead companies that entered the town. His commander was killed in combat. He took command but promptly transferred to the SS. If memory serves, he was the officer that went after Ferrand Boulier and his network."

"Good memory. That's the one."

"I could hardly forget him. If Boulier and his daughters survive the war, Ferrand is likely to be my brother's father-in-law."

Momentarily distracted, Denniston cast a piercing glance at Claire. "Ah, yes. That was the issue that caused your hubbub with the director of MI-6."

"That's the one."

Denniston took his seat behind his desk. "Well now, this Bergmann is a threat to Miss Rousseau. If she's taken in for interrogation, the damage to other networks could be immense. What do you have on Meier?"

Claire shuffled through the stack of messages she had brought. "He was Bergmann's boss at Dunkirk. Meier was a lieutenant-colonel then, commanding one of the lead battalions on the thrust down through Belgium into northern France. He's a favorite of General Rommel, and thus has somewhat of a protected status with Hitler. That was a good thing because shortly after Bergmann's transfer to the SS, Meier fired him."

"Any idea why?"

Claire looked through more messages. "What information

I have is scant, but I gather that Meier was upset with the way Bergmann carried out his investigation into the death of a German soldier. That soldier was believed to have attempted to rape Boulier's youngest daughter, Chantal. Bergmann accused Boulier of murdering the soldier out of revenge. In the process of searching for the old man, the major executed several citizens at Dunkirk while trying to coerce information. In retaliation, partisans attacked and killed some German soldiers. Meier apparently was infuriated by Bergmann's actions, ordered him out of the command, and sent him back to Berlin."

Denniston had listened intently. "Hmm. A principled German officer. I wonder if he could present opportunities. What brought him to the headquarters in Dinard?"

Claire looked through her papers again. "He seems to have been wounded. I don't see how or to what extent, but he was hit badly enough to have given up command, and he convalesced for a while. He's been promoted and is now the chief of staff in the operations section in Dinard, and..." She looked up, chuckling. "As I said, Bergmann once more reports to him."

Denniston broke an involuntary laugh. "Small world." He sat quietly in thought for a few moments. When he spoke again, he did so pensively. "I'd like for you to monitor message traffic for anything to do with Jeannie Rousseau and those two officers. I wish she would get out now, but I gather she's worried about repercussions to her family. Let me know of the slightest hint that she's in immediate danger."

"Yes, sir. I will."

9

Marseille, France

"The visit with Jeannie was good, but when I go back to Dinard again, I'm staying until we pull her out," Phillippe told Fourcade.

She stared at him blankly. "I don't have a problem with that, but if she gets more intelligence that's critical, we'll need to pass it along to London quickly."

"I've thought of that, but we can't just leave her unprotected. She shouldn't have to handle the stresses alone. A few months ago, you sent an SOE radio operator to the Boulier network near Dunkirk. That area is fairly quiet right now. Maybe Boulier can lend her to us until we get Jeannie out. If something significant transpires, we can radio London directly."

Fourcade sat back and gazed at Phillippe while she thought. "That's an idea," she said slowly, "but I'm disturbed that you know about the radio operator. That's not information you should have had access to."

Phillippe regarded her with slight agitation. "Look," he

said, "we're a tight group. *You* sent Jeremy Littlefield to convince us to join your Resistance network. We know his story, and therefore that of Amélie and her father. We also know what happened to his brother, Lance, and the steps you've taken." His lips widened in a slight smile. "We're not the enemy. We talk among ourselves. We hear things."

Fourcade sat very still before responding, closing her eyes. "I worry, perhaps too much. I'm not the right person to be reminding naval veterans about operational security. I've never been tortured, but I doubt that I could hold out very long. That's not to say that you can't or that..." Her voice broke and she paused a moment. "I worry."

Phillippe gazed at her with a softening expression. Then he reached across and took her hand. "You're right, and we've already had partisans captured who gave up information. We need to be more careful. I'll remind the others."

Fourcade smiled. "Thank you. Now, back to the present. Your idea is a good one. You should take Amélie with you. We can put her SOE and MI-6 training to good use and she can fill you in on the Resistance members. You'll have to take back-roads, and you can travel as husband and wife—"

Phillippe chuckled. "She's attractive, but a bit young for me, and I wouldn't want a misunderstanding with Jeremy."

"All right, she can be your sister. She'll provide you instant vetting with Jacques and her father, and going there will give her a chance to see them. We'll have Maurice get new travel documents forged."

"How about if we go by train until we're near the dividing line between the occupied territory and Vichy France? We can use Henri's network to move us across the boundary at night in a sparsely populated area, and then travel backroads the rest of the way. Doing that will cut down on travel time and we can avoid a few checkpoints."

Fourcade agreed. They discussed how they would make the move to Dinard and set up. "Coordinate your final plan with Jacques and Ferrand Boulier. They've already established their network to a degree in Dinard. We sent Amélie there ahead of you to make initial contact with Jeannie. Her father didn't know she was the one going, but his network made the arrangements for where she stayed."

Phillippe exhaled and shook his head. "What a war this is. We send a girl into harm's way, get her father to make the arrangements, and he doesn't know it's her." He drummed his fingers absentmindedly. "I want to find out more about this *Oberst* Meier. His anger at Major Bergmann was unusual. I've heard that the *Wehrmacht* doesn't care much for Hitler. Maybe we have an opening with him?"

"Good point." Fourcade reached into a pocket within the pleats of her skirt and removed a folded piece of typing paper. "This report came in from London this morning. It's about Meier. I have no clue how British intelligence got the information, but it's included with the response to what we provided from Jeannie." She cocked her head. "You know, it's almost as if they have people listening in on the Germans, but I don't know how they would do that."

Phillippe had taken the paper from her and now studied it. "This is incredible. It says that Meier is a favorite of General Rommel, and—"

Suddenly, Fourcade banged her hand on the table. Startled, Phillippe looked up. Fourcade gazed at him with bright, excited eyes. "I don't know why I didn't think of this earlier. We have a woman right here who can give you the best insights. Anna, Ferrand's sister-in-law. We brought her out at the same time we rescued Ferrand. She worked in Meier's headquarters in Dunkirk and saw the interaction between him and Bergmann. She says that the two men hated each other. I'll arrange for you to speak with her to get more detail."

"All right, but this mission is growing. We might need more than a radio and operator. We're not only talking about watching over and protecting Jeannie, but also about exploring if we can contact Meier. What do we call him, a potential resistor?" He chuckled and rapped his knuckles on the table. "And you realize that we might have to take out this Major Bergmann, don't you?" He mimicked shooting a pistol.

Fourcade fixed her eyes on his face. "I know you won't hesitate, and you might even be eager, but if that becomes necessary, put some thought into how you'll do it. Jeannie is still there because she worries about her family. You won't solve her problem if you shoot Bergmann; the Germans retaliate by executing people. Her parents could become their victims."

Phillippe nodded grimly. "Point taken."

"I'll get Anna. You can talk with her here."

Anna was as good as her billing. She was a frail woman, advanced in years, and very thin. The color of her watery eyes had faded, but her mind was intact.

"That Bergmann is a bad man. A bad man." She spat on the ground and repeated, "A bad, bad man. He accused Ferrand of killing a soldier, and everyone at the headquarters knew that the soldier abused people and brought his death on himself. But Bergmann executed civilians and threatened to kill more."

She rubbed her bony hands together while gathering her thoughts. "Meier is a good man. He was always civil to me, and he would not tolerate criminal behavior from his soldiers.

When Bergmann transferred to the SS and then came back to the headquarters like a peacock, he thought he could throw his weight around. *Oberst* Meier clipped his wings very quickly." She laughed and thrust her fingers in the air with a scissoring motion. "I hope that someday Bergmann gets what he deserves."

Phillippe's eyes hardened into a glint. Then they softened as he gazed upon the old woman's lined and wrinkled face. He patted her hand. "Rest on that hope, Madame. It might not be an idle one."

***

Fourcade smiled broadly as her terrace filled with people she had come to care for. Phillippe and Anna still conversed at one end of the table, and then Maurice arrived, bringing with him the Boulier sisters, Amélie and Chantal.

He was a huge man who had been Fourcade's friend for many years. When she and an officer on Marshal Pétain's intelligence staff had first perceived that war was inevitable and imminent, she had contacted Maurice. She and the officer, codenamed Navarre, had set Maurice up in a vegetable vending and delivery business in Marseille that catered to high-end hotels and fine restaurants, their belief being that he could circulate and recruit among employees in places where conversations could be overheard and intelligence gathered. Further, the enterprise could help finance a local Resistance unit.

When the war came and millions of refugees flooded south and east ahead of the German *blitzkrieg*, Fourcade and Navarre's prediction had proven correct—many French people, including members of the wealthy and aristocratic classes, had descended on Marseille, an obvious place to seek refuge. The city had a history and culture of independence and was positioned on France's Mediterranean coast midway between Italy and Spain. Germany had already spread its forces across northern and eastern Europe, and with an air war still going on with Britain and ground combat in North Africa, Germany's military resources were stretched thin. Therefore, the possibility of Germany thrusting its army this far south in France anytime soon remained in doubt in the minds of Fourcade, Maurice, and many of their countrymen. That was particularly true since General Pétain, iconic hero of the Great War and now titular head of Vichy France, had become the Nazis' willing marionette.

Maurice's size, his bulging eyes, and his lumbering gait could be intimidating, but his gregarious manner and warm smile disarmed people instantly. As a result, the notion that he could build an organization to eavesdrop and report on conversations in high-society establishments rarely crossed anyone's mind. But he proved adept at doing so, and he had also recruited from the underworld, bringing in members with special skills, such as forging documents and breaking locks. "The Germans will come eventually," he told them. "You're loyal Frenchmen. We must be ready."

The effort had already paid dividends as groups of British, Dutch, Belgian, Polish, and French soldiers, abandoned after the debacle at Dunkirk, had evaded south, acquired counterfeit travel permits, and made their way into Spain and Gibraltar or across the sea into colonies still held by Vichy France, and from there to Great Britain.

From Marseille, Fourcade's network had organized and staged raids into German-occupied France along the southern end of the Atlantic coast, blowing up bridges, ammunition dumps, and fuel-storage tanks, among other targets. When Henri and his former French navy-officer comrades joined her, Maurice had quickly supplied many of them with the forged documents they needed.

Fourcade watched him fondly as he approached the table. "I got a message that we should talk," he said quietly.

She nodded and rose to kiss his cheek. "Yes, but today the weather is so beautiful, and the sea is sparkling blue, I thought we could make it an afternoon with friends, eat good food and drink wine. I've invited Horton, Kenyon, and Pierre, and I told Henri to come and bring as many of his compatriots as he wants to. We can talk this evening." She gestured with her chin. "I'm sure Anna will be happy to see you, and Phillippe will have some business for you when he gets here."

As Maurice went to greet his friends, Fourcade turned her attention to Amélie and Chantal, who waited patiently behind him. They were both petite, Chantal an inch or two shorter than her sister; both had auburn hair and honey-colored eyes and were beautiful.

"Ah, my two favorite nieces," Fourcade said, putting her arms around both at once and squeezing. "I hope I'm not presumptuous. We've become family, you know. I haven't seen either of you in weeks. Let me look at you." She stepped back to observe them. "Chantal, you're changing so fast and looking so mature." Her expression changed to one of playful scolding. "Don't grow up too fast. When this war is over, you'll need to make up for all the fun you missed." She tilted her head toward Maurice. "He tells me that you're becoming quite the accomplished observer, drawing sketches of possible targets, taking notes of approaches and escape routes, checking for choke points, etcetera. You weren't supposed to enjoy doing it so much."

Chantal blushed, and her smile spread across her face beneath sparkling eyes while she twisted back and forth on her feet.

Fourcade laughed and hugged her again. *War is hell. She's still a little girl. She should be shopping with her friends.*

Amélie, waiting patiently beside them, nudged Fourcade's arm. "Is there any news from Jeremy?"

Fourcade pursed her lips in a sad smile and shook her head mournfully. "I don't have any. I'm sorry." When Amélie's face dropped in disappointment, Fourcade added, "The bad news is the war is still on, but the good news is that we have no bad news about Jeremy." She laughed softly and hugged Amélie. "If we get word that he's coming here, it'll be for a covert mission that could be dangerous; and if we don't, he's probably flying fighter combat patrols. So, for the moment, let's wish for no news."

Amélie smiled glumly. "I know. I can't help hoping, though."

Fourcade placed both hands on Amélie's cheeks and pulled her face close to her own. "Stick with hope. It'll get you through this mess. Jeremy will survive all right. I'm sure of it."

Amélie sniffed, threw her arms around Fourcade, and held her close. "I'll be fine," she said, straightening and wiping her eyes. "I want him safe. That's what matters."

"You need to stay busy," Fourcade said. "We've got another task coming up for you."

Chantal's head snapped toward them. "Where is she going?"

Mentally scolding herself for the lapse, Fourcade patted the side of Chantal's face. "We'll go over all that later. Look, more guests have arrived."

She stepped away to greet Horton, Kenyon, and Pierre. Chantal darted in front of them and tugged Horton's sleeve. "Have you heard anything about Jeremy's brother? Do you know where he is?"

Horton laughed and looked into her bright, expectant

eyes. "Well, aren't you the plucky one," he said. "And yes mum, we know where Lance is, but we don't know much about the prison aside from its name, Colditz. That means 'dark forest' in Serbian."

Chantal pulled back in teenage shock. "He's in Serbia?"

"No mum, he's on the east side of Germany in a place that once belonged to Serbia. Seems like *les Boches* have broken the commandment about not envying your neighbor's stuff for a long, long time."

Fourcade and Amélie had joined the group and listened in. "Why don't we know more about Colditz," Fourcade mused aloud.

"Well, mum, we just—"

"I'm serious. We provide all sorts of information to London and risk our lives getting it. We should know what comes in about the prison camps. I'm going to ask."

Henri appeared at the periphery of the group and gestured to Fourcade. When she greeted him, he put his mouth close to her ear and whispered, "We need to talk."

"Can it wait?"

"I don't think it should."

She excused herself from the others, and they moved to a secluded part of the terrace. "What is it."

Henri dropped his head, shamefaced. "I'm not trying to ruin your party. I think it's wonderful that you thought to have everyone here. God knows we could use a release of tension."

"What is it? Tell me."

"First, to let you know, our security plan is in place. We have people watching the villa now. They know what to do if something looks strange."

"That's great, Henri. Thank you."

"Here's the part I wish I didn't have to say. I think having a party like this is a bad idea. It draws attention."

Fourcade drew back in some disbelief. "I understand the concern, but I don't agree. This is Marseille, not northern France. If we suddenly stopped our social lives but had people coming in and out of here all the time—that would attract attention."

Henri stared as if the thought had not occurred to him. "Good point, but I'd still urge caution. Maybe avoid loud music—"

"We don't have any, but if we danced to music on the radio, that wouldn't be unusual. But I understand your concern. We'll keep things low tone and let people know to leave early."

"I'm sorry, Madame." Henri was obviously chagrinned.

Fourcade stood on tiptoes and kissed his cheek. "Don't be. That was good advice. Having you around will keep us alive."

When most of the guests had left, still seated around the table were Amélie, Fourcade, Maurice, and Phillippe. Henri had already departed, and Chantal stood at the end, hands on hips, red-faced and annoyed.

"This won't take long," Amélie chided her. "We just need a short conversation and then we'll leave. All I've asked is that you wait for me on the other side of the terr—"

"All you've done is treated me like a child," Chantal broke in. "Again." Her eyes sparked with anger. "I'm no longer fourteen. I'm fifteen now."

Startled, Amélie stared. "You've had a birthday. I forgot—"

"Yes, while you were in London for those three months." Chantal glared. "That's fine. We're at war. I didn't expect anyone to remember. But that's the point, isn't it? I'm in the war too. I can't go to school and Maurice tries to make me feel important by sending me on those 'courier' missions so the two of you can talk with Fourcade."

Her expression softened, then she laughed and turned toward Maurice. "I'm sorry, but when I get to where you send me and we take the 'coded' message out of the handlebars of my bicycle, the person I deliver it to throws it away without looking at it. Anyone could figure out what you were doing."

Maurice pursed his lips, attempting to hold back a shame-faced grin. "I'm sorry, little one—"

"No, no," Chantal cried, wiping tearful eyes, "you're all protecting me. I love you for it, but I'm growing up in a war, and I don't have a choice about that. But I can choose how I spend my time." She faced Amélie. "I told you that if you don't let me participate in the Resistance, I'd leave and find a group that will put me in the fight." She lifted a fist with the thumb and index finger extended and barely apart. "I'm this far from doing that."

Amélie started to respond, but Chantal stopped her with an open palm. "Wait. I'm not finished." She took a breath. "I fled across France with you and millions of refugees. I've been in the secret Resistance locations." She gestured toward Maurice. "I've ridden with him for hours, loaded his vegetables, and seen what he does and how he does it." She held back laughter with a hand cupped to her mouth. "So, being fifteen isn't far from being fourteen. I know that. But the little girl who woke up one morning like every other morning five months ago and then heard bombs falling and exploding and watched the British evacuate in front of her house at Dunkirk, and then was nearly raped..."

Tears rolled down her cheeks and she choked out her next words. "That little girl is gone. I wish that weren't true, but it is. And now, I have to help win this war like everyone else."

Silence weighed, with all eyes on Chantal. Amélie rose to her feet and rushed to hold her sister. "I'm sorry—"

Chantal shook her head, and with one arm around Amélie's back and still wiping away tears with the other, she faced the group. "I know you're sending her out again, somewhere dangerous. I can help." She indicated Maurice. "Ask him. He'll tell you. I learn fast, I keep my mouth shut, I do as I'm told, and I'm good at improvising."

Maurice nodded his big head. "She does all of those things, and more. If the German army ever comes here, or if Pétain tries to crack down, he might find a fight he never expected because of how good she is at reconnaissance, surveillance, and sketching."

Chantal's eyes brightened. "I can even act like a child when it's helpful." She laughed, pressing the fingers of both hands against her cheeks and raising the tenor of her voice to illustrate her point. Then her eyes took on a determined look. "I'm alive because my sister stopped my rape. I'm going with her, or I'll leave. I won't sit and wait to find out she's been killed."

Amélie gazed at Chantal in a new light. At the opposite end of the table, Phillippe stirred. "I'll be leading this expedition," he said. "I expect to have final say." He peered sternly at Chantal, studying her.

She held her breath.

"We'll take her."

November 29, 1940
London, England

Captain Paul Littlefield rubbed sleepy eyes as he entered Winston Churchill's lair in the prime minister's bunker-basement war office at Whitehall. His flight from New York City had been long, and he had slept little. Ahead of him were Bill Stephenson, codenamed Intrepid by Britain's quintessential prime minister, and US Brigadier General William Donovan, commonly known among his colleagues and friends as "Wild Bill." President Roosevelt nicknamed the pair "Little Bill" and "Big Bill," respectively.

Churchill looked up from his desk with his normal pugnacious expression as they entered, seizing a cigar stub from his mouth. "Come in, come in, gentlemen, find a seat." He stood and looked about the cramped room. "We should have enough chairs."

Churchill appraised the three men briefly: Bill Stephenson, physically small, in his mid-forties, and with a full head of brown hair over intense eyes that gave away nothing; Bill

Donovan, somewhat larger, in his fifties, having a high fore-head but otherwise a full head of white hair, a piercing glance, and a square jaw, and was obviously a dedicated athlete; and Paul, above medium height, also athletic, and looking very much like his siblings, with sandy-colored hair, brown eyes, and a straight nose.

"I am so pleased that President Roosevelt won his third term," Churchill said. "Of course, I called to congratulate him back on the fifth immediately after his victory was announced. But for that electoral result, all the groundwork we've laid would have gone up in smoke." He took a puff on his cigar. "Roosevelt met with the head of our purchasing mission in Washington, Arthur Purvis, two days after winning the election to discuss what weapons and supplies we're needing, but he can still sell arms to us only on a cash-and-carry basis due to that damnable neutrality act."

His exasperation escaped. "He can't even let me have the aircraft we've already paid for with cash."

The prime minister shook his head and shot a sly glance at Stephenson. "We'll figure a way to handle that, won't we? We must have American industry to win this thing."

Paul took in the prime minister's statements. He had observed the US election campaigns with detached interest, and he knew of the close working relationship between the two heads of state via Stephenson, but he had not considered how drastically the path of the war might have changed had Roosevelt lost. The neutrality act was something he had heard about but did not fully understand.

The prime minister peered over his glasses as he extended his hand and half-smiled at Paul. "Did you settle in New York all right, Captain? You'll tell me if Intrepid works you too hard, won't you? I hear he's a slave driver."

Struggling through travel-induced brain fog, Paul shook

the prime minister's hand and said simply, "He treats me well."

Churchill grunted. "Sorry you won't be in London long enough to visit anyone. I know your brother and sister would like to see you, as would that WAAF officer. What was her name?"

"Ryan Northridge, sir. Thank you for keeping us in touch."

"Rubbish. I sent a courier. Anything that came afterward was between the two of you." He turned his attention to Donovan, forming a statement into a question by his tone of voice. "I understand that the president will name you his communications coordinator, per my suggestion, by the end of the year."

"Yes, sir. And I'm already at your disposal. I managed to get out of Washington without anyone noticing."

While the two men exchanged greetings and with his alertness returning by degrees, Paul looked around Churchill's office with interest. He had been in it once before, when he was offered the assignment to work as Stephenson's aide in New York. It was then even more dimly lit. This time he could see a bit more of the room. The prime minister's desk took up most of the width of it, so that squeezing by was an imperative to get around to the prime minister's seat, particularly for a man of his size. Behind it was a large wall map. Chairs were set on either side of the narrow room, and beyond them, each wall also bore large maps of the European war theater. At the other end of the room was a bed Churchill used for his famous catnaps and frequent overnights, complete with a chamber pot at the foot.

Having greeted all three men, the prime minister brushed his left hand over his balding head. "Let's get right to it, shall we?"

Before they could sit down, he turned with his back almost

facing them. "Take a look at the map. Gather round." He returned his cigar stub to his mouth.

"I've never been convinced that the non-aggression pact between Stalin and Hitler would hold," he began, "and we've been seeing far more German troops and materiel moving east than he needs to guard the oilfields in Romania or train their army. He's put eighteen divisions there, many times over what he needs for that purpose."

He waved a dismissive hand. "The Nazi is too wedded to his hatred of Communist Bolsheviks. Their treaty was an artifice to give *Herr* Adolf a free hand against us, and when he realizes he's botched things up here irreversibly, he'll push north to Moscow. He wants their oil and their industry, and more space for the Aryan race to proliferate."

As he spoke, Churchill removed the cigar once again, and still holding it, swept his palm across the map from Berlin to the heart of the Soviet capital. "It won't be the easy battle he expects, but it might be less difficult for him than *we* think—unless we prepare the field."

He brushed his wide-open hand along the lines and colors depicting the remaining officially "neutral" countries of eastern Europe: Hungary, Romania, Bulgaria, and Yugoslavia. "This," he announced, "is the next battlefield *before* the German surprise assault on Soviet territory." He pointed out Greece. "With Italy invading there from Albania at the beginning of the month, we have some opportunities, but Greece is such a mishmash of politics, what with their civil unrest and all. The best we can say now is that the people are fiercely patriotic and anti-fascist, they've put their politics aside, and they fight like their very existence depends on it, which it does.

"But—" Churchill's tone dropped to conspiratorial. "Italy mucked up its assault on Greece and is calling for German help. Three weeks ago, Hitler ordered an operations plan to be drawn up for that purpose." He chuckled. "The Greeks will never give up, and we do have an ace—Turkey warned Bulgaria that it will attack if it joins Italy in their invasion of Greece. That relieves pressure along Greece's northeastern border."

He ambled back to his seat and sat down, facing his audience of three with the defiant glare that had become so famous worldwide. "Since Stalin won't listen to our warnings, we're in the strange position of having to save the Bolshevik from himself and arrange the outcome we must have."

"Sir," Stephenson asked. "Do you think Stalin really believes that Hitler won't attack?"

Churchill's fixed glare shifted to him, and then softened through passing moments. "I don't know," he said at last. "He has his own intelligence sources, but he shows no hint of disbelieving Hitler. Regardless, we cannot afford for the *führer* to win against the Soviets and then turn the full combined industrial and military might of the Bolsheviks and the Nazis against Britain, which he most assuredly would do. Therefore, we must devise a plan to stop him."

The moment hung in the air, and then Churchill abruptly stood, returned to the map, and trailed his fingers along the horizontal blue swatch representing the Mediterranean Sea. "Thank God, Admiral Cunningham's chaps secured these lanes for us—and with 'outdated' fighters, no less. The 'Stringbag.'" He gestured toward Paul and chuckled. "Let that be a lesson for you, lad. When does something become obsolete?"

Taken aback from being addressed so directly by the prime minister and not sure that a response was expected, Paul grasped for words. "When it's overtaken by better technology, I suppose."

"Well, I'm glad our chap Admiral Lyster didn't think your

way," Churchill responded. "No, he didn't, and a good thing too." He stuck his cigar back in his mouth and searched Paul shrewdly. Then he turned to Stephenson. "Have we got the right man on this job?"

"Oh, don't be so rough on him, sir," Stephenson said, laughing. "He's still learning and might not yet understand when you say things in jest. Besides, he was the pick of the litter."

Churchill harumphed and cast another appraising glance at Paul. "Something is obsolete when it no longer serves a useful purpose. Our 'antiquated' Swordfish took out nearly half the Italian navy and all its 'advanced' equipment. That fighter isn't nearly done yet, mark my words. It will make yet another significant strike for us." He returned his focus to the map.

"Here's the issue. We now possess, courtesy of Bletchley Park, proof positive regarding Hitler's intentions for Stalin, in the form of his full Directive 21: Operation Barbarossa." He shook his head and muttered, "The cheek of that man knows no bounds and will be his undoing. Barbarossa? The Austrian corporal forgets himself."

He flung another comment at Paul. "Hitler sees himself as the medieval pirate turned admiral of the Ottomans who added Algeria and Tunisia to their empire. If you don't know about the man, Barbarossa, read up on him, and you'll see why this is laughable." He shook his head in disgust. "The codename also hints that Hitler is leaning into his superstitious nature.

"Anyway, as I was saying. The *führer* is obviously not a student of history, although he fancies himself a brilliant military strategist in a league with Napoleon and Alexander the Great. No doubt, he's studied their victories, but he'll be brought to ruin by his fascination with the occult, and because he obviously has not studied the errors of his human idols.

"He's counting on Stalin's belief in the steadfastness of their non-aggression pact and his weak preparedness for war. Comrade Joseph doesn't seem to realize that a major impetus for the agreement from Hitler's view is that Germany didn't want to take on Great Britain with hostile Soviets at his back. The *führer* perceives them to be militarily weak, particularly after the long time they took to bring Finland to heel.

"Unfortunately, we can't show Stalin our proof for these conclusions. Coming from Bletchley, we'd have to expose the secret of our codebreaking capability, and that would amount to giving up the farm." He chuckled. "The fact is, pertinent points of Hitler's communiqués are telephoned to me almost as fast as he sends or receives them, and he appears to have drastically underestimated the mobilization Stalin pulled off in modernizing his heavy manufacturing plants. They can be converted to produce tanks and fighters rapidly.

"So, we'll keep whispering in the Russian bear's ear, goad things along, and be ready to pounce when the time is right."

The prime minister paced the edge of the map before re-taking his seat behind the desk. "Sit, sit, gentlemen. General Donovan, do you have any messages for me from the president? I should have asked when you came in."

As they sat down, Donovan nodded. "I do, sir." He took a slender document from his jacket and handed it to the prime minister. "He sent this along with his good wishes. He understands the outline of what you intend, and he wants me to explain your plan to him when we've hammered out the details."

"What's in the envelope?" Churchill asked.

"Confirmation of Operation Barbarossa from an independent source."

Churchill was opening the envelope but stopped and raised an eyebrow. "Can you fill me in?"

"Are you familiar with *Hauptman* Fritz Wiedemann of the *Wehrmacht*?"

"Of course. Some reports have him as Hitler's commanding officer in the Great War."

"That's him. They were in the same unit, and Wiedemann was an officer, although what the line of authority was that ran between him and Hitler, I don't know. In any event, he became an enthusiastic supporter. More recently, Hitler sent him to the US on a diplomatic mission. Not to get into the weeds too much, but he's suggested that he's disenchanted with Hitler and wants to get away from him. We've had our doubts about his sincerity, but he's vouched for by a German informant we rely on and by one of our own men, Sam Edison Woods, our engineer turned diplomat who brought you and Mr. Roosevelt news of Hitler's grand plan for purifying the races."

Churchill had begun scanning the document. Now he looked up, his expression deadly serious. "Of course I remember. From Texas. He's the one saying to believe Wiedemann?"

"He is, sir."

"Then we should believe him." He returned his attention to the document, muttering, "And it's good to have corroboration."

Donovan watched Churchill a moment. When he spoke again, he enunciated his words slowly and carefully. "Keep in mind, sir, that Yugoslavia has the largest and best equipped army in what remains of 'neutral' Europe. It could block our plans. However, what's outlined in Wiedemann's document is a trap to pull Hitler into a war he cannot win and lead to his ultimate defeat."

Churchill leaned forward and concentrated on the document. Minutes ticked by. Paul had listened, mesmerized. Now he watched with equally rapt attention. Stephenson sat calmly observing, saying nothing.

At last Churchill looked up. "It's time to get down into those proverbial weeds, gentlemen. I'd like you to go somewhere where you won't be disturbed and thoroughly analyze Hitler's Directive 21 and this document provided by Wiedemann, and then let's meet again, say after the first of the year, to lay our plans. What say you?"

"We'll be here, sir," Stephenson said.

As the men started rising to leave, Churchill's telephone rang, and he glanced at Paul as he answered it. "Yes," he replied to his secretary in response to a query, "we're finishing up. Please make that call now and put it through in here."

He rose from his chair. "I think we've concluded our business. I'll show you out. Uh, Captain Littlefield, remain in here a moment. A call will be coming through on my phone." His eyes gleamed with mischief. "Would you take it, please? It'll be for you."

Paul watched in shock as Churchill ushered Stephenson and Donovan through the door. The phone rang again even before they had closed it. Gingerly, he stepped to the desk and lifted the receiver. "Captain Littlefield speaking."

"You certainly have a unique way of courting a girl," came the reply.

Momentarily speechless, a boyish grin broke across Paul's face. "Ryan? How did—? How are—? Where are you?"

"As if you don't know. It's not every WAAF officer who gets a call from the PM's office and is told to stand by. Everyone in the bunker is staring at me." She laughed musically, the way that had captured Paul the single day they spent together at Fighter Command's II Group bunker in Uxbridge, north of London. Air Chief Marshal Dowding had sent Paul there to observe operations for a report compiled for the MI-6 director. Ryan had been his escort for the day.

That had been a terrible day, one of the worst in Hitler's attacks on Great Britain. On that day, Germany came closer to delivering victory to the tyrant than he could ever know. All of Britain's reserves were committed, and only a few more hours of fighting would have brought her to her knees.

Looking back, the two good things that had come of the day were that Great Britain had survived, and for Paul personally, that he had met Ryan.

"I'm so pleased to speak to you—"

"Ooh, so formal," she teased.

"But I didn't place the call. It was a surprise..." Paul stopped talking, and then rolled his eyes at how ridiculous he must sound.

"So, you didn't want to talk to me?"

"Of course I did. I've loved your letters. I live for them." His neck and cheeks flushed hot, and he knew he must sound giddy, like a schoolboy.

"Are you in London, then? Can I see you?"

Just then, the door opened. Churchill peered in, grinned, and shot him his famous "V for victory" sign. Then he tapped his watch and left once again, closing the door behind him.

Paul returned his attention to Ryan. "I want to see you for certain, and yes, I'm in London. We flew in this morning, but we're flying out again straightaway. I'm already getting the high-sign." He stumbled over his next words. "I think of you all the time. Your image in my head gives me... Well, I like it."

A short silence followed, and when Ryan spoke again, she struck a mournful note. "I feel the same," she said quietly. "Please take care of yourself, whatever you're doing. I know it must be important."

When Paul hung up, he leaned forward and rested his

hands on the desk. His short reverie was ended by the door's reopening.

"Come along," the prime minister chided. "The war won't wait." As Paul passed by him on his way out, they shook hands, and Churchill added, "You should call your sister from the airport."

11

December 2, 1940
Rockefeller Center, New York City

"The president is safely ensconced in Jamaica," Stephenson said, looking up from a newspaper he was reading in his office as Paul sat across from him. "The press is reporting that he's combining an inspection of US naval bases in the Caribbean with a vacation. He should be sunning himself by now, giving the impression that the war is the furthest thing from his mind." He continued scanning the article.

"Donovan is already on his way to Bermuda under the alias 'Donald Williams.'" He chuckled. "And the newspapers are reporting—with glee, I might add—that 'America's Secret Envoy Flies on Mystery Mission.' He gave them the slip in London. They're frustrated that they don't know his destination. They pointed out that his 'weak' disguise was undone by his having carried his own luggage with his real initials, WJD. That leaves me free to travel unnoticed."

Stephenson stood. "I should be off, then. I'll see you in Bermuda at least by tomorrow, I expect. Bring your swimming trunks if you like, although I wouldn't expect either the weather or our schedule to allow much time for the beach. Analyzing Hitler's Directive and that other document will take all of two weeks."

December 15, 1940
Bermuda

"Our gambit is working so far," Stephenson told Donovan, chuckling while scanning a newspaper. "The US press is complaining that they've lost track of this 'foreign emissary who causes difficulties for the foreign service.' That would be you."

Paul sat quietly listening to the conversation. For two weeks, he had read Hitler's stunning Directive 21 over and over to the point that he could almost recite it. The three of them had pored over its details and those of Wiedemann's document, analyzing them against a large map of Europe hanging on a conference room wall; and they had discussed a blinding number of alternatives to thwart Hitler with limited resources.

"I leave tomorrow on another presidential assignment," Donovan replied, "and I'll take every opportunity to enhance my growing reputation as an inept international vagabond. I'll arrive back in London on the 24th, and then the three of us meet with the prime minister on January 2.

"So, let's get to the nubs of the issues. Both Finland and Romania have a bone to pick with Stalin for territory he seized and absorbed into the Soviet Union. They'd like to have it back. Hitler's concept is to have the Finns pin down the Russkies in the north while the Romanians do it in the southeast, preventing a strong military response when he launches his 'greatest deception plan in the history of the world.' His words. Does that describe things in a nutshell?"

"With a few refinements," Stephenson said. "Yugoslavia and Greece are key to securing Hitler's southern flank, and he needs the Romanian oil fields to meet the huge demand he'll create when he invades Soviet territory. Air superiority is imperative for Barbarossa's success, but Hitler's used up only a fraction of the *Luftwaffe* in battling us, and now he has the resources from all the countries Germany's conquered."

"Roger that. So, Yugoslavia and Greece become key to our mucking up his plans, which we aim to do with virtually no resources."

"That's what we'll present to Mr. Churchill."

"I have other business to attend to in London, so I'll see you there on the 2nd. What's on your schedule?"

"There's another program we're working with Canada," Stephenson replied. "I mentioned it to you. Camp X. We have some preparatory work to do on it. We'll take a trip up there soon, and I'd like to have you along.

"I'll fly to London on the 1st." He looked at Paul with a smile. "Our young captain will already be there, because he'll be home in time for Christmas."

Taken by complete surprise, Paul whirled around. "Sir?" He held his enthusiasm in check and straightened up. "Thank you, but that's not necessary. I'll be wherever you need me to be."

"Which is at home. You've earned it. I'll be resting a few days too, so no need to fret. Come back ready for work."

12

December 24, 1940
London, England

The international news media picked up Donovan's trail
quickly when he landed in London. On spotting him, a
reporter called out, "Where've you been? Why did you resort
to your Douglas Williams alias? Your initials on your suitcase
gave you away."

Donovan kept walking through the airport, waving a hand
over his head and glancing down at his luggage as if surprised.
"Ah, you caught me."

"What are you working on? Can you tell us?"

Donovan smiled obligingly. "I'd rather not. Mum's the
word, as they say on this side of the pond, and if you trip me
up too many times, I'll get canned."

"The word's already been leaked," the reporter persisted.
"Purportedly, you're here for a few days of conferences, and
then sometime in the spring you'll go on a tour of British facilities, particularly in the eastern Mediterranean and the
Baltics, to assess for President Roosevelt whether or not the

British can hold out for any extended time; and you'll meet with French commanders in North Africa to reach a new understanding with Vichy France. Can you confirm that?"

Donovan laughed as he saw other reporters heading his way. "If that's what your papers report, then it must be true," he replied, and then dodged into an embassy sedan waiting for him outside the terminal. "Whitehall," he told the driver.

A block away from the War Office, he saw that another gaggle of reporters had gathered at the main entrance. "Let me off here and get someone to drop my suitcase in my room at Claridge's," he instructed. Then, carrying only his valise, he strode toward the door, anticipating the rush and clamor of journalists anxious for scoops. As they trooped toward him, he threw his arms in front of him as if to avoid their attention as much as possible.

"Please don't make me mysterious or important," he pleaded. "I'm here on a mundane task that I can't mention but you all seem to know about. As some of you have pointed out, I'm not someone the president would trust with something earth-shattering."

He stopped outside the entrance to engage the press, answering routine questions. "No. I don't know how long I'll be here."

"Will I disappear again?" He shrugged. "I might."

"I'm sure the prime minister has far more important matters to deal with, but if I see him, I'll pass along your concern."

"The US is a neutral country. The president made that perfectly clear. If he changes his stance, you'll know about it before I will, as you've demonstrated regarding my current mission. If that happens, I'm sure Congress will have something to say."

After breaking through the gaggle, he found Paul awaiting

him inside the enormous, stately entry of the War Office. Here and there, Christmas was celebrated with bits and pieces of paper in holiday colors, and last year's banners and lights festooned the balustrades. The two men stood to the left of a grand marble staircase leading to a second-floor mezzanine, but neither spent time taking in the magnificent interior or its trappings.

"A little bit of a somber Christmas," Donovan noted, and then nudged Paul. "Good job leaking the news of my arrival. When did you get in?"

"Not even an hour ago. I got your message to meet you here just before I boarded the airplane."

"Good. I needed that charade out front to go well. Now, for the rest of the show."

"Do we need to see anyone here at Whitehall?" Paul asked.

Donovan shook his head. "No. This is a pass-through. I'll hang out for an hour or two, look up some old acquaintances, and then have a car take me to the hotel. I'll see you again on the 2nd with Stephenson and the prime minister."

"Any changes or new information?"

"Nothing pertinent. My job is to appear intent on a mission, which means attending several do-nothing meetings and social events, and yours is to not be publicly identified with me. Your time is your own. Enjoy yourself, take a break." He started to walk away, then turned back, his eyes twinkling. "I almost forgot. I'm expecting to meet a WAAF here, Flight Officer Northridge, I believe. She's my escort."

Paul gulped and glanced about, his heart suddenly throbbing. "Are you sure you've got the right name?" he asked anxiously.

"I'm sure. She was instructed to meet me here at the bottom of these stairs." A questioning look crossed his face. "Is that the name of the WAAF officer you—"

Then they heard a woman calling, "Paul? Is that you?"

When they turned, Claire stood there, her hands covering half of her face. She stared wide-eyed as tears brimmed. Then, rushing to Paul, she threw her arms around him.

Next to them, Donovan watched in amusement. "I neglected to tell you that your sister was coming too."

Just then, a WAAF officer approached in a blue uniform that matched her large eyes adorning a face with smooth skin, full lips, and an upturned nose. Her dark hair was pulled back in a bun. She stared at Paul questioningly as Claire continued to hold him and then stepped toward Donovan. Extending her hand, she said, "General Donovan? I was instructed to meet you here to escort you."

Donovan took her hand. "My pleasure. Flight Officer Ryan Northridge, isn't it? And now your instructions have changed." He gestured toward Paul. "You're free to spend as much or as little time with Captain Littlefield as you care to for the next two days, courtesy of Mr. Churchill, and you can use whatever leave you're allowed after that. Then you'll return to normal duties."

Standing almost at attention, Ryan alternated an astonished gaze from Donovan to Paul and back. Then she glanced at Claire, who had let go of Paul but still dabbed tears from her eyes with a kerchief.

Donovan stepped next to Ryan and leaned close to her ear. "That's his sister," he whispered. "They haven't seen each other in a while." With that, he turned and disappeared into the passing stream of people.

Claire observed Ryan and then Paul, understanding dawning on her face. She drew in her breath. "You must be Ryan Northridge," she said. "How wonderful. Paul mentioned you in his letters. I'm so happy to meet you. He's never shown such interest in anyone before."

Ryan's face grew red. Paul's eyes widened, and he stared at her.

Claire laughed. "Sorry," she quipped. "I didn't mean to embarrass either of you." She shoved her shoulder into Paul's arm. "Go on," she pressed. "Hug her. You might even try a kiss. You know you want to, and she wants you to." She looked around at the Christmas decorations around the great hall, and then pointed. "Look there. Mistletoe." When both hesitated, she laughed. "Don't waste time. There's a war on, you know."

She stepped forward, grasped Ryan's elbow, and started edging her toward a branch with deep green leaves and small white berries. "Of course you'll stay at my home for the next two days—that is unless you have other Christmas plans. I have a spare bedroom and Paul can sleep in Timmy's room. I'll make sure he behaves, but that's really up to you, and anyway, he's always such a gentleman.

"It's so good to see Paul. I've lost count of the months, but I hadn't expected to see him again until the war's end. I can't believe he'll be here for Christmas." She sighed. "But with the war on—"

Claire caught herself and went on. "There's no reason to stop for your things. You look about my size, so you can borrow whatever you need."

Still looking dazed, Ryan allowed herself to be steered, glancing back uncertainly at Paul. Claire followed her gaze. "I'm so excited that Paul has finally met a girl he really likes, and so pretty too."

Bewildered at the unexpected turn of events, Paul scratched his head. Then, he grinned as overwhelming excitement seized him, and he hurried to catch up.

13

L'Orme, France

Ferrand Boulier traveled only at night and only on backroads and lanes unknown to the *Wehrmacht*. He skirted checkpoints, slept in barns, and approached households where the inhabitants were known and vetted. The routine was difficult for a man in his mid-sixties, but his practices had kept him alive since fleeing his home with Amélie and Chantal six months ago. Thin by nature and habit, he had grown thinner, his clothes hanging on him, and he now wore an unkempt beard that matched his hair in color and condition. Usually fastidious, his appearance bothered him, but he tolerated it as a means of hiding his identity. In public, he walked slowly, bent over, with a cane. Out of sight of all but friends, he straightened up and walked energetically with the gait of a much younger man.

Tonight, he was going to an unknown farmhouse in this rural community a few miles from Dinard. He had been opposed to this trip of over five-hundred kilometers each way to an area not familiar to him, but it had been specifically requested by Hérisson, codename for Madame Fourcade. She had been instrumental in saving his life and restoring his network, so he was reluctant to refuse. Then, when he resisted, she persisted, and when he pressed back harder, she told him, "Go, Ferrand. You'll be glad you did."

Also traveling to L'Orme in pairs by diverse routes were his brother, Claude; his nephew, Nicolas; the MI-6 team leader, Jacques; the courier, codenamed Théo; and the radio operator, codenamed Brigitte. They converged with Ferrand on the farm after dusk and rendezvoused in a stand of trees well back from a barn. He sent Nicolas and Jacques forward to reconnoiter.

Waiting for them in the darkness and with the passage of time, Ferrand stemmed anxiety. When they returned, Ferrand noticed that his nephew barely concealed unexplained excitement.

"Come on," Nicolas urged. "It's safe."

Ferrand and the rest of the group followed Nicolas and Jacques through the darkness into the unlit, cold, damp barn. There, Nicolas turned on a flashlight and led them to one of the far corners, then stooped and lifted a section of flooring to reveal a dimly lit staircase. Urging caution with a gesture, he led them down into a small room lined with empty shelves. Behind them, Jacques lowered the trapdoor back into place.

"Follow me," Nicolas said in a low voice. "The farmhouse here is ancient. It has an underground tunnel that connects to the barn."

He went to the opposite side of the room and pulled on a section to reveal a hidden passage. Gesturing for the group to follow, he turned on a flashlight again. The tunnel was not long, but the other end was blocked by a wooden panel. Nicolas knocked lightly, and from the other side came a thump, the sound of voices, and a knob turning.

The door swung open into a wine cellar illuminated by dim lights along the wall. Ferrand followed closely behind Nicolas. On emerging into the room, he looked about in wonder at the huge vats lining each side.

A man approached him. "I am Phillippe," he said. "Two people here are anxious to see you."

Phillippe stepped aside, and there, with shining, tearful eyes and broken smiles, stood Amélie and Chantal. They rushed to their father and flung their arms around his neck. Phillippe and the rest of the group moved quietly to another part of the cellar to allow the Bouliers a private visit.

After the initial shock of seeing his daughters, Ferrand stood back to look at them. "You're both maturing so fast. Chantal, look at you. You're becoming a young woman." He drew her head close to his chest while his eyes searched Amélie. "And you," he said, his voice wavering. "I can see in your eyes that you've aged—too much."

He wiped his eyes and hugged her again with his free arm. "You shouldn't be here," he muttered. "It's too dangerous."

"None of us should be here," Chantal said, looking up at her father's face while holding his embrace. "We should be in our homes, safe and living our lives."

"But you're still a child."

"She's grown up, Papa," Amélie interjected. "Faster than we would have liked, but as she points out, that's the reality of this war."

"I'm going to fight, Papa," Chantal said. "I told them that if they wouldn't let me come that I would join another Resistance group."

"You should hear about the things she's been doing," Amélie said. She related all that Maurice had taught Chantal and the surveillance she had carried out.

Ferrand put both arms around Chantal and swayed back

and forth with her. "This is not right," he said, "this is not right. You should be in school. You're still *my* little girl."

He turned to Amélie. "What are you doing here? Neither of you should have come."

"Papa, I have some things to tell you." When Amélie had finished describing her previous trip to Dinard to establish contact with Jeannie and then her training with SOE and MI-9, he once again held her close. "I'm so proud of both of you," he whispered, "and so scared for you." He pulled back to look at them again, rubbing moist eyes with the back of his fist. "And I could not ask for a better Christmas."

Everyone slept on cots in the cellar that night. The next morning, they ate breakfast brought to them by an old man and his wife who lived in the house above them. The couple greeted each person, and then returned upstairs.

Nicolas cautioned the group to enter and exit from the barn and to go into the house only for food and personal hygiene. "Our hosts are determined to help the Resistance," he said as they ate, "but there's not much they can do besides let us use this space. We contacted them through our Boulier network, and they're tied into a local group that's pulling security around the farm. The location's good because it's not far from Dinard, and the area has been in decline for several years, so *les Boches* don't pay it much attention.

"When coming or leaving through the barn, we have good concealment into the woods. From there we can make it to roads unobtrusively."

"Let's be clear," Phillippe said when they had removed the breakfast dishes. "We have three primary things to do. The first is to extract Jeannie. Secondly, to do that, we will have to dispose of Bergmann one way or another, and we'll have to do it in a way that does not start an investigation. And finally, we want to find out if Meier is approachable. Is there a German resistance, and is he working with it?"

Startled, Ferrand snapped toward him. "Could there be such a thing?"

Phillippe shrugged. "We don't know for sure, but there is friction between Hitler and his generals. They can't be happy with where he is taking Germany. They might not see working against him as a betrayal of their country." He paused. "We can hope."

Ferrand contemplated the thought. "Do we have a timetable?"

Phillippe shook his head. "I'll visit Jeannie this afternoon and find out how things are now. The latest word from London is that she's under increased threat from this man, Bergmann." He spat out the name. "She confirmed that to me a week ago."

"The threat is real," Ferrand growled. "The bastard is relentless, and he likes taking down innocent people to get what he wants. If he's after her—" He gestured toward Amélie and Chantal. "He's the one who drove us from our home."

"I heard the story," Phillippe said.

"Are we going to kill Bergmann?" Chantal blurted.

All eyes swung to her, and she was suddenly self-conscious. "Sorry. That popped into my head." She squirmed and giggled nervously. "I just don't see any other way of stopping him."

"We shouldn't be talking about these things in front of one so young," Ferrand protested. "Can't she go somewhere else while we have these discussions?"

"No!" Chantal's voice rang fiercely, and she half-rose to her feet. She turned to her father. "You must stop thinking of me as a child. What happens if some or all of you are killed? Will the Nazis go away? You know they won't, and the war will go on, and young, untrained people will have to fight it." She pushed a loose strand of hair from her face. "You don't like it, and I don't like it either, but we're in it, and I need to know what's going on. I'm staying." She leaned over and kissed Ferrand's cheek. "And I love you."

He heaved a sigh and nodded with eyes closed. "I just dislike planning a murder in front of my daughters."

"It's not a murder, Papa," Amélie broke in. "If he gets his hands on Jeannie, he'll torture her, and many other people could die. She can't count on Meier's protection indefinitely. I don't see that we have a choice. Remember our friends that he executed trying to find you. The moral failing would be not stopping him by whatever means."

"I don't disagree," Ferrand said in a tired, faraway voice. "I just wish my daughters were not involved. Your mother—"

"Would be proud of how you raised us, protected us, got us to a safe place, and organized the Boulier network. You're guilty of nothing but goodness, Papa, and many people already owe you their lives—" She paused as her voice broke, and tears formed. "Including Jeremy."

Ferrand smiled softly and put his arm around Amélie. "Ah, Jeremy. He's a good man. A great man. He came back to save *my* life." He chuckled. "If he asks you to marry him, you have my permission, but I want to be there."

Amélie blushed. "Stop, Papa. He's already proposed. I told him he had to ask your permission, and I wouldn't do it while this war is on."

Ferrand smiled. "Don't put that condition on yourself, my sweet. Who knows how long this war will go on or who'll be alive at the end of it?"

For a time, everyone remained silent. Then Phillippe said,

"Your daughters are right about Bergmann, Ferrand. He has to go, but it has to look like a bona fide accident."

Ferrand sighed. "All my life, I've believed in doing the right thing, of abiding by the law. I've tried to do that and to teach my daughters the same. Now, our government is dissolved, we have no police, no courts, an enemy rules us, and we are left to protect ourselves with few weapons." He heaved another sigh, and his eyes expressed painful regret. "I'm sorry to say that I agree with you, but—" He turned his attention to Amélie and Chantal. "Know this: if fair law and true justice ever return to our beautiful country, I will never agree to go outside of it. I hope you feel the same way."

He paused and then said to Phillippe, "Indulge me a little. I agree with you concerning Bergmann, but whatever action we carry out, I'd like to think that we followed some form of legal procedure. Therefore, I propose to try him in absentia right here, right now."

Surprised, Phillippe frowned as he contemplated Ferrand's suggestion. "I guess we could do that. We have no judge, no witnesses other than you and your family, and he has no one to defend him."

"We have to be better than them," Ferrand urged. "Bergmann summarily executed our friends and neighbors. Out of respect for them and future generations, we must preserve the idea of law that treats everyone fairly and equally; and that we follow a legal procedure to reach decisions and carry them out."

Phillippe nodded. "All right then, let's do it."

———

The trial took a day. The old man who owned the house acted as the judge. Two members of the local Resistance with legal backgrounds performed as prosecutor and defense respectively, and a jury formed from the same group.

"This cannot be perfunctory," Ferrand warned. "If we are to preserve the law for the benefit of France, then we must conduct this intending to find truth and justice. If we go in with a pre-conceived outcome, we will defeat our purpose."

He, Amélie, and Chantal testified to the events that occurred at their house the day that Bergmann's soldier attempted to rape Chantal and the subsequent interrogations, arrests, reprisals, and executions. Cross-examination took place, with the prosecutor and defense delivering lively closing arguments. The jury deliberated in seclusion, and the verdict rendered: Guilty. Sentence: Death.

After the trial was complete and sentence meted, Phillippe once again focused attention on next steps. Meeting with his group again around the table in the wine cellar, he turned to Brigitte, the radio operator. "Make sure your signal is strong with London and Marseille and keep transmissions short. When I go this afternoon, I'd like to give Jeannie a way of communicating with us in an emergency. She won't be able to call us. She has no courier—"

"I have an idea," Amélie offered. "When I came here to make first contact with her, I sat in a café across the street from the German headquarters. She got the waiter to give me a note telling me how to meet with her. I remember that he was nervous about giving it to me, but he did it, so he's probably sympathetic to the Resistance."

"That's good," Phillippe said. "Work out the details with me before I go into Dinard." He turned to Jacques and Nicolas. "I have no reason to distrust the security around us, but I don't know the people in that group. Check them periodically but in a friendly way. If you see anything strange, let us know right away." They both nodded.

Then he turned to Ferrand. "This is your network but my mission. Are you all right with that?"

Ferrand chuckled. "You're the military man. I'm an amateur, a troublemaker."

"You're an inspiration," Phillippe said. Then he looked around at the rest of the group. "We're all risking our lives, and we're working things out as we go along. We'll develop a plan when I get back." He paused. "If I *don't* get back—"

Chantal gasped.

Phillippe glanced at her. "If I don't return, Amélie knows how to find Jeannie, and you'll have to develop a plan without me. Amélie, since Bergmann knows you by sight, you'll need a good disguise. You should do that anyway. Dye your hair.

"You too, Chantal. But Jeannie must get out of there. She's too valuable, and she knows too much, not the least of which is that there's a network growing in Marseille."

Amélie added, "She also knows it's connected to the Boulier network in Dunkirk."

Dinard, France

Jeannie could barely conceal her mixture of anxious thrill at seeing Phillippe when he knocked on the door that afternoon. She met him with her normal outward charm and poise, but she glanced up and down the street as she greeted him.

"You called about the electrical problem again?" he asked in a slightly raised voice for the benefit of anyone who might overhear them.

"Yes. I don't know why it's happening. Maybe because the house is getting old." She let him in, closed the door, and led him into the living room. "Bergmann is closing in," she said

before they had even sat down, her voice steady but with a
tone of anxiety. "He's always around, peering at me. I told you
I'd curtail my activities, but now I have no choice. He leaves
me no room even to breathe."

Phillippe studied her face. Classically beautiful as she was,
she verged on being uncharacteristically frantic, the effect of
months under enormous pressure and her only outlet being
his infrequent visits. He took her hand and kissed it. "We have
people here to get you out. When we develop the plan, I'll be
able to tell you only your part of it—"

"Of course." Jeannie turned her big brown eyes on him. "I
understand that. Just tell me what to do and when. But my
parents—"

"They will not be implicated." Phillippe rubbed her hand.
"Our priority is your safety and theirs. Right now, tell me
about Bergmann. What are his habits?"

Jeannie winced. "At the moment, his chief habit is
watching me. I don't know how he gets any other work done."

"When does he get to the office and leave, and where does
he stay? Does he have any favorite off-duty activities you know
about? Where does he go to eat?"

Jeannie rubbed her eyes and shook her head. "I wish I
could tell you, but I try to stay out of his way. I've heard him
say that he likes to run along the cliffs by the sea in the
evenings. There's a path that goes along them above the shore.
It's splendid, but I can't imagine that he goes there to enjoy the
beauty. He's rather proud of his physique, always wearing his
uniform well-fitted to show it off. Otherwise, he just works.
He's there when I arrive in the morning, and he's still there
after I leave."

She paused to process a thought. "He's going on a two-
week leave in a few days. That will be a welcome break. I don't
know where his home is, and to be honest, at this point, I don't

want to look it up." She sniffed. "I bring my lunch now just so he won't follow me to local cafés. I've stopped phoning friends for anything, to avoid dropping something inadvertently. In effect, I've become a prisoner of this job."

"You've done amazing work, Jeannie. You've saved lives. Now we have to save yours. What about Meier?"

Jeannie let out a relieved sigh. "He's my savior. I'm sure that if he were not around, Bergmann would have had me stretched on a rack and interrogated weeks ago."

"I told you that Meier's a favorite of Rommel's, who is a favorite of Hitler's. That makes him a de facto favorite of Field Marshal Reichenau. How deep that goes with the field marshal, I don't know, but as long as Hitler likes Rommel, Meier is safe. But the colonel is brazen in his disgust for the SS, the Gestapo, and Nazis in general. My sense of him is that he's a military professional who loves his country. I'd say he's from the 'ours is not to reason why' school, but the philosophy is wearing thin with him."

"Could he be reached? Is it possible he's part of a German resistance?"

Startled, Jeannie pulled back and stared at Phillippe with wide eyes. "I don't know. The thought had never crossed my mind that there could even be such a thing, much less that Meier would be a member." She let the thought settle. "If there is a German resistance, I could see him being part of it, but my sense right now is that he and Bergmann despise each other for personal reasons, and those are the nubs of the issues between them."

Phillippe studied the face of this unusually gifted, intelligent, poised woman. "Will you be safe for a while? We're only a few kilometers away, we're armed, and the force is not large, but it's capable." He thought of the two old brothers, Ferrand and Claude; the two young and untrained but eager men,

Jacques and Nicolas; the two young sisters, Amélie and Chantal; and the courier and radio operator, Théo and Brigitte.

Jeannie sniffed and nodded. "I need to get through the next few days. I'll pester Meier for things to work on and do extra things for the field marshal. He likes when I do that, and I always smile big and flash my eyes around. I'll continue that for the next few days, and then Bergmann will be gone for a while, and I won't have to see him until several days after New Year's."

"Can you leave while he's gone? Can you resign?"

"I don't think that's a good idea. Bergmann is not shy about his suspicions of me. He knows where I live. If I leave while he's gone, I'm sure he'll intensify his investigation. He's probably already coordinated with the Gestapo to surveil me."

They sat silently for a few minutes, then Jeannie stirred. "You shouldn't come here anymore," she said. "I'm not being rude. It's just that it's dangerous for both of us. For all I know, Bergmann has my house watched; and how often can I have the same electrical problem?" She chuckled. "The neighbors will think I'm having an affair, but the major will correctly think something else is going on."

"Agreed. We'll set up a system to watch over you." He thought a moment. "Do you still go to that café on the other side of the street from the army headquarters?"

Jeannie nodded.

"Do you have a regular table?"

"Yes, if it's available."

"You gave a note to a waiter who passed it on to Amélie. Is he still there, and can we get him to help?"

Jeannie stared at him wide-eyed. "We can. He's a friend. I wouldn't want to endanger him."

"We won't. Do you have a favorite scarf or hat you've been seen wearing before?"

"I have a scarlet hat like a beret. It's the only one I have in that color."

"Good, carry it with you. Do you have another one, or maybe a scarf in a different color?" He explained his purpose and took the scarf with him.

Fifteen minutes later, as he was about to depart, Jeannie kissed his cheek. "Thank you for coming. I feel better knowing others are looking out for me, even if I don't know who they are."

Phillippe hugged her and then went to the front door. Opening it, he stepped onto the stoop, then turned, touched his cap, and said in a loud but conversational tone, "I'm sorry that electrical issue is causing you so many problems, *Mademoiselle*. Maybe I fixed it this time. If not, give me a call. Otherwise, I wish you a Merry Christmas and a Happy New Year."

"Oh, and the same to you. I'd almost forgotten that the holidays are on us." With that, she closed the door.

As Phillippe turned onto the sidewalk, he noticed a car far down on the opposite side of the street. It was parked over a rise and around a gentle curve so that only its windshield and roof showed. As he walked toward it, he heard the engine crank, and it pulled away from the curb. It was a large, low-slung, black Mercedes sedan, and moments later, it passed him. The driver and passenger made no pretense of not noticing him. On the contrary, they slid by slowly, staring.

14

Stony Stratford, England

"This is such a grand place," Claire declared, taking off her gloves and coat as she looked around at tinsel, brightly colored lights, fir boughs, and stockings hanging from the mantel above the fireplace inside The Bull. "We've made such good memories here."

"Yes, we have, milady," Red Tobin said in his best Texas twang. "An' I hope we make a lot more." At six inches over six feet, he was easily the tallest man in the room. That all by itself would have garnered much attention as he led Claire to their regular table at the back of the tavern, but his red hair would have been enough to gather equal notice. Already seated at the table were Andrew Mamedoff and Vernon "Shorty" Keough, two close friends of Red's and Jeremy's that Claire had grown fond of.

"Where's Jeremy," Shorty asked.

"He'll be along. I spoke to him a little while ago. He said he doesn't have to get to the airfield again until late tomorrow."

"Lucky him," Red said, grinning. "We're due at the

dispersal hut at first light. How did your no-good brother get that kind of a pass?"

"He asked for it, I suppose?" Claire shrugged. "I know he tries to get time to be with Timmy whenever he can"—she rolled her eyes— "which is not very often these days. I imagine he'll stay the night at my house and spend the morning playing with him."

"What about Paul and Lance. Have you heard any news of them?"

Claire's face darkened. "I hear Lance is safe. He's in a POW camp called Colditz. That's about it." She pursed her mouth and sighed. "I don't know where Paul's assigned. We had lunch together right here just before he transferred. He came to tell me that he had to go away, perhaps for the rest of the war. He said not to worry, that he would be safer than all of us."

Suddenly, Claire's face brightened with excitement, and she burst into laughter.

The pilots stared at her.

She dropped her face into her hands. "I'm terrible at keeping surprises," she said. She looked up, her eyes bright. "Paul is here, in London. He arrived this morning. But Jeremy doesn't know. He'll come into the pub after Jeremy arrives. And there's more."

"That's great," Red exclaimed, followed by similar expressions from Shorty and Andy. "How long can he stay?"

"Until just after New Year's." Claire's face took on a conspiratorial expression, and she whispered, "He has a girl-friend. That's so exciting. He's never had one before; not a serious one. She's a very nice WAAF officer. Ryan Northridge. Strange name for a girl, but she says her father wanted a son and stuck with the name when she came out. Very pretty. She'll stay with us for a couple of days."

She caught her breath and drank some water, then plopped her elbows on the table and smiled at each man in turn. "So, tell me, how are my three persona-non-grata American RAF fighter pilots doing. You look so handsome in those RAF uniforms. I haven't seen you since September in the hospital at Andover when Jeremy was shot down."

"The Duke of Kent stopped by the 609th for a visit back in August," Shorty piped in, laughing. "I asked some of the Brit pilots if I should call him 'dook,' but they insisted that 'sir' would do. He shook everyone's hand, but he had to bend down a ways to reach mine."

"He looked tired," Red said. "I'm not sure what 'dooks' do, but he must have been doin' it pretty hard."

Claire slapped his shoulder ruefully and then turned to Andy. "A little bird told me you've got a girlfriend too. What's her name?"

Andy turned red and nodded. "Penny Craven. I like her. She's pretty and very nice. Her laugh is infectious. We're going to be married."

"Penny Craven," Claire repeated, astonished. "*The* Penny Craven?"

"Do you know her?"

Claire shook her head. "I know *of* her. She's *only* one of the most eligible heiresses in England. Her family goes back generations, and for well over a century they've amassed a fortune from manufacturing and selling cigarettes that bear their name. Well done. I'm happy for you."

Andy's face turned expressionless, but before he could respond, Shorty interrupted. "You called us 'your pilots.'"

"Excuse me?" Claire turned her attention to him.

"You said we were your pilots," Shorty repeated, grinning. "And what do you mean we're *persona non grata*?"

Claire's face reddened slightly. "Of course you're my

pilots." She chuckled. "You're family. You trained and fought alongside my little brother and kept him safe. As for being *non grata*, I was poking fun at the US neutrality policy. I'm hearing that lots of American pilots are showing up now. You're all rebels—" She looked around at the other patrons. "And much loved by my countrymen."

"Those new guys are just drugstore cowboys aiming to get their pictures took," Red drawled. "We got here when the gittin' was tough."

Andy shouldered Red good-naturedly. "The fight is plenty hot. We can use all the pilots we can get." He turned to Claire. "You might have heard that the RAF activated 71 Squadron. It's all-American and they call it the Eagle Squadron. Enough of us are over here now to have our own unit, like the Poles, Canadians, and Aussies do."

"I saw the stories about it in the newspapers. That came about while Jeremy was convalescing—"

"You mean lollygaggin'," Red chimed in.

"Oh, shut up," Claire retorted. "He had hoped to join you—"

"On the basis of your stepfather being born American?" Red teased.

"Yeah, yeah," Claire said. "He'd have used whatever influence he could to stay with the three of you. But by the time he got back to the 609th, Eagle Squadron had formed, and the three of you had transferred."

"Well, we miss him," Shorty said. "He could outfly any of us. He was the first among the four of us to make ace."

"I heard that, Shorty," a voice from behind them called, and Jeremy stepped into the light by the table. "Be careful. Red thinks he's not only God's gift to women, but also that he's the best thing that ever flew in the skies over Britain. And we all know you can fly circles around any of us."

"Why would I limit those braggin' rights to Britain," Red said, chuckling. "Anyway, Shorty's pretty good, even if he has to sit on two pillows to reach the rudder bar in the Spit." He clapped the short pilot on the shoulder. "We love our Shorty."

"That's not a worry now," Shorty shot back. "We're flying Hurricanes again."

"And you're still sittin' on pillows."

Everyone at the table erupted in laughter.

Jeremy stood back and observed his three friends. "So, you got your own squadron now. How is it?"

"We miss the 609th," Andy said. "We were always in the middle of the action there. We were the first recruits for the Eagle Squadron, and when we arrived, they didn't even have kites for us. When we finally got some, they were battle-scarred beat-up Hurricanes without much life left in them. The squadron hasn't gone operational yet."

With a glimmer of sadness, Andy continued, "Of the seven Americans in the thick of fighting before Hitler started bombing at night, two of the originals were killed, including your buddy, Fiske. One opted not to be in the Eagle squadron." He chuckled. "You remember Donahue. He thought we were cowboys, and he didn't have the patience to wait around for aircraft, so he pushed for a transfer back to the 64th, where he had been."

"We were back to feeling unwanted, tolerated," Shorty broke in.

"You're always wanted here, rest assured of that," Claire interjected. "Always."

Shorty beamed. "You need to stop hanging around with that red-haired bean-pole and spend more time with me."

Everyone laughed.

"One of our Eagle Squadron pilots accidentally rammed another plane in mid-air," Andy went on. "He never flew again. So that leaves only the three of us with experience to teach the newbies." He frowned. "It's sobering."

"What about you, Jeremy?" Shorty broke in. "Are you still at Middle Wallop?"

"I'm still there," Jeremy replied. He moved behind Claire and kissed her cheek. "I haven't said hello to my big sister." Then, he announced, "It's Christmas! Let's celebrate. The next round is on me."

Another voice spoke up from behind them. "May we join this group?"

Recognizing the voice, Claire leaped to her feet and rushed around the table. "Surprise!" she cried, and pulled Paul by his jacket out of the shadows.

Elation beamed on her face as Paul emerged into the light, and she flung her arms around his neck. "I'm thrilled to have my brothers here at Christmas."

Dumbfounded, Jeremy circled the table to embrace his siblings, and as he did, Ryan stepped forward next to Paul. "You must be Ryan," Jeremy said. "I've heard about you from Claire. Good things."

"And you must be Jeremy," Ryan said. She extended her hand, and he grasped it. "Paul and I watched your dogfights from the control bunker at Fighter Command on that last day of heavy daytime fighting back in September. He was so worried for you, especially when it looked like you had gone down, and I guess you had."

As she spoke, Jeremy grasped Paul's shoulder. "We've always been very close." Then he added with a grin, "But that only works because of my great patience. I'm fairly amazed that you find him tolerable."

"Hey, look who's talking," Paul broke in, turning from Claire. He clapped his brother's arm and then hugged him. "Look at this, a family reunion of sorts."

"Minus one," Jeremy said somberly. "But since we're in a war to save lives, let's celebrate it the way Lance would want. Our parents too." He looked for a waiter. "Can we please get two more mugs over here and fill everyone's to the brim."

"This will be a somber Christmas," Claire said. "So many people having family members far away and in harm's way. And you three"—she gestured to the American pilots —"you're here instead of with your families." She sighed. "The church bells won't ring anywhere in Britain tonight because that's the signal that the enemy is on our shores. We're here in this nice pub, darkened on the outside for the blackout, and many of our fellow citizens will spend the night in air raid shelters. I was gratified to hear, though, that the entire country has united to make this Christmas as good as possible for the children.

"I feel guilty celebrating, but I think we must. Preserving our way of life is the main issue of this war, and we don't do that by giving up our special traditions, even when it's hard."

When she had finished speaking, the group was quiet, and other patrons who had overheard also maintained silence. Claire, with moist eyes, went to a piano in the corner and began playing "O Come, All Ye Faithful." Almost immediately, everyone in the pub, including the staff and manager, joined in singing. Then, while she continued playing, they sang through a series of Christmas carols.

Back at the table, Red nudged Jeremy and motioned him to follow. They stepped outside where snow had begun to fall and already blanketed the surroundings.

"You sidestepped talking about your new squadron. Any reason for that?"

Jeremy nodded. "Claire has enough on her. She doesn't need to know that I'm flying night fighters."

"Night fighters, eh?" Red regarded Jeremy through tired

eyes. "You sure do keep your plate full. Stay alert, brother. I'll tell the others not to bring the subject up again."

"Thanks." Jeremy peered at Red, noticing a gaunt look about his friend. His eyes had sunken and the long dimple on his right cheek had deepened. Lines furrowed his brow. "Are you all right, mate? You're looking unusually tired. I heard that you collapsed a while back."

"Who told you? Big mouth," Red grumbled. He forced a grin. "Just a lot of flying and patrols. I'll admit that wears thin. The doctor told me I've had a stressful year." He laughed. "It's good he told me, or I would've never known."

Red's banter did not end Jeremy's concern. He grasped the tall American's shoulder. "Take care of yourself. We like having you around."

They headed back inside. Before reaching the door, the way narrowed, and Jeremy went ahead. Behind him, Red heaved a sigh and closed his eyes momentarily. Then he re-opened them, shook off his fatigue and, forcing a smile, followed.

15

Colditz Castle, Colditz, Germany

Despite that Sergeant Lance Littlefield sat between two crack German guards, and a third soldier sat in the front passenger's seat, he enjoyed a cozy feeling of wellbeing that he had not known in months. The drive from Dulag Luft, the transit POW camp at Oberursel, had been less than ideal, but getting out of that hellhole provided a sense of relief, even if it was fleeting. His former fellow prisoner, Squadron Leader Roger Bushell, had seen to it that he left with a full belly, courtesy of other POWs who contributed from their Red Cross parcels.

As he sat scrunched in the back seat of a *kübelwagen* with the heater blasting, the drive took him through the wintry gray of Germany's peaks and valleys. He turned a sardonic grin on one of the guards but saw only a stern and unresponsive profile. Turning the other way, he encountered a similar countenance.

He stretched his legs and leaned back, crossing his arms for greater warmth as he closed his eyes, breathed deeply, and smiled. *Jeremy made it home safely. No one's shooting at me. I'm rested and fed, and I'm not hiding. Life is good.* He dozed for a while, and then sat up and took in the view. *No bombs, no airstrikes, no destruction. Just peace.*

He first saw Colditz Castle from a distance, high on a hill that dominated the landscape for miles. From a distance, it appeared as a fairy palace with high walls in a yellowish tint with steepled red and gray slate roofs and quaint dormers covered in snow. As he and his escort drew closer, the mood the edifice evoked changed from one of wonder to one of dread. Built with massive walls bedecked with a honeycomb of windows buttressed by tall towers crowned with spires, the fortress evinced impregnability. Since the year 1046, it had stood as a bastion against outside attack. Now, the Nazis used it to house *Oflag* IV-C POW camp.

The *kübelwagen* wound through the village's narrow streets, then up an inclined cobblestone driveway before turning left to enter an arched gateway and halting. Sentries checked papers, signed documents, and swung open a great portal. Inside, the vehicle turned left again and ascended a shallow rise through a short, narrow tunnel. On reaching the other end, it turned right, waited while another set of arched gates opened, and entered a quad roughly twice the size of a basketball court. More tall gray stone buildings loomed on all sides. They sobered Lance out of his sense of a life changed for the better.

The guards stepped out of the vehicle, and Lance followed. As on previous occasions when he had entered a new POW population, prisoners surrounded him, called greetings, and asked about news from home. Then, they parted, and a tall, distinguished Royal Air Force officer strode between them.

Lance came to attention and saluted. "Sergeant Lance Littlefield," he reported.

The officer returned the salute and extended his hand.

"Welcome, Sergeant. I'm Lieutenant-Colonel Guy German, the senior British officer. I hope you realize that you've arrived among the elite, and therefore the most guarded of POW escape artists."

"There are twenty-five of us Brits so far, including you," Guy said as he escorted Lance across the courtyard. "We have seventeen officers, seven other ranks, and one unfortunate civilian volunteer who was captured on a return trip to defend Finland. You're the first British army person we've seen here.

"The Poles have a rather large contingent, around a hundred and forty. Some Belgians, Frenchmen, Dutch, and even a Yugoslav are also here. Quite a mixture, and the guards try to keep us from socializing between nationalities, but I don't think that will last long."

Guy glanced around the high, imposing walls of the buildings surrounding the courtyard. "This castle is too large for the Germans to know all of the nooks and crannies without a lot of time for exploring. The place is a maze of staircases and interconnecting passages and doors." He grinned. "Time is all we have, so the various nationalities are already finding out how to visit each other. When the guards find POWs in the wrong section, they punish them, but it's becoming so frequent that soon they'll have to put all of us in the cooler. I expect that rule will go by the wayside soon."

As they walked, Guy pointed out various facilities. "We have a canteen over there—one of your fellow inmates can explain how the money works later. Just past it is our own kitchen—the German rations taste horrible; we can't wait for Red Cross packages to start arriving. The showers are two stories above it." He indicated a low, shed-like structure built against a main wall in front of the kitchen. "That's the delousing station." Then he turned and pointed in the opposite direction. "Over there is the chapel. And at the top of that building"—he gestured—"we have a theater." His face pinched in a sardonic grin. "It's supposed to keep us busy and out of trouble."

He pointed to a set of windows at ground height in the corner of one section near the clock towers. "That's where they house the *prominentes*. Well, there's only one there now, Giles Romily, but I expect there will be others. He has a special curfew, and when he's allowed out of his cell, which isn't often, he must be back in by ten o'clock at night. If not, they send an armed squad of guards into our barracks to find him, and then march him back to his cell. Guards are always posted outside, and it's fitted with a hole so that he can be seen every minute. All of those arrangements are supposedly for his own safekeeping, the implication being that the POWs could be a threat to him."

"That's odd, sir. What did you say he was?"

"A *prominente*. Theoretically, they were leaders in their countries: members of the aristocracy, mayors of large cities, and the like. People of influence or their relatives. I only know that because he's explained it to me as best he knows it. Then again, he's a journalist, and not a well-known one at that. But he's married to Winston Churchill's niece. He's kept in almost perpetual solitary, but he's allowed personal items, including a gramophone. Sometimes you'll hear his music playing into the courtyard and he can see out here."

Lance stared at the windows. "Who has the imagination to think up such things?" He took a quick look around the courtyard. It had emptied out, leaving only a few men making haste to another part of the compound against a cold wind. "The castle doesn't look crowded. How many are here?"

"I don't know exactly, and it's still filling. Nine of us Brits got here in early November right after the Poles arrived, and eight came in at the beginning of December." He pointed to a row of low, more recently added buildings near the gate where Lance had entered. "At some point, you'll undoubtedly make acquaintance with those charming places. Together, they compose punishment cells more commonly called 'the cooler,' and they're used quite often."

Prompted by this last revelation, Lance grunted. "I was in them plenty in my last POW camp." He asked his most pressing question. "And what about escape, sir? I can't imagine staying in this dreary place for the length of the war." He stopped walking and glanced at the lieutenant colonel. "And what do I call you? I imagine your last name can sometimes confuse conversation in this place."

"Right you are," Guy said, laughing. "It's a bit ironic with the name 'German' in a German POW camp, but keep in mind that the French call our hosts 'les *Allemands*.' The Poles call them '*Niemieccys*,' or whatever epithet comes to mind. The other nationalities have their own words for them, and Germans call themselves '*Deutsche*,' so my last name causes confusion only among we Brits." He laughed again. "I guess I could mistakenly take offense if I heard one of our chaps say, 'That damned German SOB.'

"Anyway, I'm commonly called 'SBO' for senior British officer. That would be like me calling you 'Sergeant.' We're quite informal, but if our Brit contingent swells, as I expect it might, more military formality might need to be imposed. Sooner or later, someone more senior than me is likely to show up. The Poles already have a general and an admiral here."

Guy turned his head, surveilling the tall gray buildings. "And our living quarters are all above ground-level."

They entered their barracks through a door midway along the back of the courtyard across from the gate. As they mounted the stone stairs to the third floor, Lance said, "I'm curious about one thing. I had expected a demoralized prison population, but that's not what I'm seeing. The men who met me at the gate didn't seem to be in despair. I saw plenty of that where I came from."

They climbed several more steps before Guy responded. "Good observation. Most POWs in any other camp will never attempt an escape. Those who try seem to absorb the notion of escape into their blood—a compulsion. They have purpose, they hone skills, they get creative. And in Colditz, you have a collection of such people who'll share ideas and methods. There's a sense of pride at being assigned here, and we all subdue our national differences in favor of frustrating our common enemy. For example, we have French prisoners here from both Vichy and occupied France, and even they keep in check whatever hostilities they might have toward each other. If you ask me, the Germans miscalculated. Eventually, some will find a way out."

"My compulsion is escape. I want out of here."

Guy laughed again. "You're as keen to scoot as a hare, aren't you? Let me show you a few more things first. For starters, you might have noticed on your way in that the German living section in the other courtyard where you first entered the castle is larger than ours. That's not for their luxury. They have more guards than POWs here, and they expect to maintain that ratio.

"We currently have three rooms. I stay in one reserved for senior officers from the various countries. Believe me, it's no more comfortable than yours. I think the idea is that if the seniors get along, our countrymen will as well. Anyway, when we get to your room, you can look outside and see the walls, which at the base are nine feet thick. There's a one-hundred-foot drop from the lowest windows, and they all have bars on them. The guards floodlight the entire place every night despite the wartime blackout, and they don't miss inside corners or around outside ones. Down below, they've put in a thick palisade of barbed wire that's constantly patrolled by sentries."

"You're saying that breaking out is going to be tough," Lance observed, and then grinned. "If they hope to hold 'escape artists,' I wouldn't expect less. What are their weaknesses?"

"Hmph. We need to qualify that bit about being escape artists. The fact is, Colditz is a bad boys' camp where they send anyone they *think* is a problem. I didn't even try to escape at Spangenburg—I wasn't there long enough. I set fire to some German propaganda magazines. I gave the guards such a hard time that they decided I had that kind of potential. They preempted me by sending me here.

"At some point, you're bound to meet Padre Platt. He was also at Spangenburg. He was captured when he helped some doctors working to save nine hundred wounded during the German advance on Dunkirk. When he arrived at Spangenburg, he had a wire in his suitcase that he used to prop up the lid. The Germans called the wire a 'housebreaking tool for escaping,' charged him with a violation, and shipped him here.

"So, you see, our stories and drives vary, but in Colditz you have people who are highly motivated, if not to attempt to escape then to help those who do."

Lance glanced sideways at Guy, scrutinizing him. "All right, SBO, sir. On which side of the line do you stand?"

Guy grinned back at him. "I said I wasn't at the transit

camp long enough to try. I didn't say I wouldn't give it a good college go.

"The Poles have become master lockpicks," he went on. "If they can get to the locks, there is nowhere they can't get into. I think the French are tunneling already, but we don't pry into each other's business."

They had come to their rooms. "The noncoms are in this one," Guy said as he turned the knob on one. "The day room is down the hall, and the privy. It's not terrible right now, but when this place fills up, it won't be pleasant regardless of how hard we try to keep it clean. Our captors' housing plan looks to anticipate one stall per forty men."

Lance wrinkled his nose and frowned at the unpleasant thought. Guy showed him his room and announced him as they entered. Several other POWs looked up from conversing, reading, dozing, and other activities. On seeing the SBO, one of them called the room to attention. As the men rose to their feet, two more men entered with lieutenant insignias on their uniforms.

"Carry on. We have a new guest," Guy said, raising an eyebrow sardonically. "Please make him welcome." He introduced Lance around to warm handshakes from his new roommates.

The space was medium-sized with four two-tier bunkbeds arranged against the walls, various dividers assembled from scrounged odds and ends to attempt a vestige of privacy, and tables and chairs in the middle area. Guy indicated an unused upper bunk near a window. "That one's probably a mite cold right now, but we'll scrounge more blankets if you need them. You might appreciate the location in the summer. I'm guessing this place gets hot then."

"I might not be here that long," Lance said. He took a quick glance outside. The impediments to escape were as forbidding as Guy had described them. Far below, the tops of black helmets on German sentries moved over a wide path between two lines of barbed wire, each with many stacked strands. On the other side, the Zwickauer Mulde River meandered past, though from this distance Lance could not tell whether it was frozen. Beyond, wide, snow-covered fields spread out below low, distant hills.

When he turned back into the room, Guy had taken a seat at one of the tables. The two lieutenants lounged against the wall behind him, and the noncom prisoners had pulled up chairs or sat on bunks across from him. "Have a seat," Guy said. He looked around at one of the lieutenants. "Do we have a stooge posted?"

The men nodded.

"A measure of security," Guy remarked. "I'm sure you did the same at Oberursel. We like to gather as much information as we can from new prisoners while it's still fresh, but we don't need the Germans listening in. If something you have to say is too sensitive, you can tell me later."

Over the next two hours, prompted by questions, Lance described entering fierce battle north of Dunkirk, fleeing across France with nine other soldiers among millions of refugees, finding himself shipwrecked at Saint-Nazaire, and subsequently being rescued and then captured. Then he told of how he had escaped, evaded recapture on the eastern side of France for several weeks, was betrayed near the German and Swiss borders, and attempted two more escapes.

The RAF pilots listened, mesmerized. "That's four attempts and several weeks of living among the enemy undetected," Guy said. "Astonishing." He chuckled. "Certainly, if anyone belongs in Colditz, that would be you. And you speak French and German fluently. That's helpful. We need you on the escape committee. It's just forming, and the idea is to pool our knowledge and resources to help anyone making an attempt. Would you mind?"

"I'll help any way I can. But you might think twice about putting me on that committee. I tried again on the first day they started to ship me here. I was originally slotted to come here back in September, but Colditz wasn't open to British guests just yet, so I was held at the transit prison until mid-November. Then I tried to escape again on the day I was to be transferred."

Seeing the shocked reactions of his audience, he shrugged. "It was a spur-of-the-moment thing. The guards left me unguarded in their *kübelwagen* for a few minutes. When they came back, I was gone." He grinned. "I took off running the same way I did the night I arrived there, across a field into some woods. They caught me the same way, with dogs." He sighed. "I think I embarrassed them. My punishment was unusually harsh. Six weeks in their cooler before being transferred here."

Guy shook his head in disbelief. "Well, you're here now, and we'd welcome you on the committee. You've been more successful than anyone here." He added, laughing, "Or we wouldn't still be here."

He turned his attention to one of the lieutenants, a tall blond man. "Pat, see to getting him on that committee, would you?" Receiving a nod, Guy said, "Pat Reid heads up our escape committee. He had some success before arriving here—"

"Obviously not enough," Pat chimed in, laughing good-naturedly. "Maybe if Sergeant Littlefield and I put our heads together, we'll figure out a way to get all the way home." The men erupted into laughter. "I'll be glad to work with you."

"I stay away from escape planning," Guy said, and added with a crooked smile, "except my own, of course. Things need to be that way so that I don't trip up in dealing with the *kommandant*." He gestured toward the other lieutenant, a darker-haired, lean, and shorter man. "Chip here is our intelligence officer."

Guy addressed Chip directly. "We need to get Sergeant Littlefield up to speed on coding techniques. Take care of that, would you?"

"Will do, sir." Chip shifted his eyes to Lance. "Have you done any? We get intel to and from London through encrypted letters sent via the Red Cross."

"Wing Commander Day and a squadron leader at Oberursel made sure I learned coding," Lance replied.

While the exchange of questions and comments had gone on, Guy had sat quietly, studying Lance. "I should inform you that we've already vetted you," he said. "We received word from Day through London that you might come this way. Your story checks out with what we already knew." He peered closely at Lance, who listened with a blank expression. "You don't seem surprised."

"I would have expected nothing less."

Guy stirred in his chair. "Fair enough. What questions do you have?"

Lance thought a moment. "How is the *kommandant*?"

Guy smirked slightly. "We're in a rather curious situation. You'll meet the *kommandant* at some point, *Oberstleutnant* Schmidt. He's from the old school of German military: stern but fair and dedicated to carrying out his orders. He treats us with respect even to the extent of telling prisoners to be at ease as soon as he enters one of our rooms or the courtyard outside, so we give him the same measure of respect. He understands our duty to try to escape. He disciplines according to the Geneva Convention, which specifies that punishment can be no greater than the most severe penalty meted out to a German officer. So far, he has not been abusive when he captures an escapee or when someone violates camp rules."

"That's different from what I've heard about other places," Lance interjected.

Guy agreed. "Or even here. Colditz was a transit prison until late October. Three of our Brits had escaped during that time and were beaten brutally on their recapture and even taken out and treated to their own fake execution for the amusement of their guards. Schmidt came in after that, and he won't tolerate such behavior.

"He has a difficult task, though. The Germans are careful about how they treat pilots because of the investment in us. They hope that we'll do the same with their captured pilots. So, the idea, as far as I can deduce, is to do everything possible to prevent and discourage escape attempts, keep us as busy as possible with activities to keep our minds and hands occupied, and otherwise leave us to ourselves."

When he grinned again, mischief played in his eyes and at the corners of his mouth. "But they've gathered here, in one place, the men most likely to attempt and succeed. Most importantly, most of these prisoners are bent on escape."

Lance smiled at the irony. "What about the staff and guards?"

"That's a curious situation. The *kommandant's* subordinates reflect his values and attitudes. Major Menz, the second in command, is purely professional, as is the adjutant. Our primary interactions are with *Hauptman* Priem and his assistant, *Leutnant* Eggers. Priem seems to be held in by the *kommandant's* attitudes while Eggers seems like a genuinely professional man."

"How so?"

Guy took a moment to gather his thoughts. "Priem

concerns himself with the administration and discipline of the POWs, while Eggers watches over security.

"Priem was here when the first permanent POW arrived, a Pole named Jedrzej. He had been here while it was a transit prison and had been held in the cooler for weeks. Priem spent a lot of time visiting him. Apparently, they talked in a pleasant way about everything under the sun. Then Jedrzej was sent away for some reason. When he came back, more Poles had arrived, Priem had been promoted from lieutenant to captain, and the two greeted each other like long-lost friends."

Lance shook his head in disbelief. "Friendship between captors and captives? Is that remarkable or deplorable."

"That's an interesting question, but it gets better. I mentioned Padre Platt—"

Lance affirmed.

"He arrived with five other POWs. Lieutenant Eggers greeted them by saying, 'Good evening, my English friends.' As it turns out, Eggers went to school in England, and later he had hosted a man studying for the ministry in Germany who had been a roommate of Platt's brother. When that was discovered within a few minutes of arrival, Platt and Eggers carried on like people who've discovered a common friend. The interaction strengthened a tone of comity that started with Priem and Jedrzej."

Guy frowned. "Make no mistake," he continued, "we and Schmidt and his staff are combatants on opposite sides in this war. If given the provocation or if ordered by Berlin, they will shoot any of us—and we would do the same if we had the means, and the circumstances warranted. However, for pragmatic reasons, while we understand each other's intentions— ours to escape and theirs to stop us—we've somehow developed a balance of respect and at least courteous tolerance that allows them to do their jobs while we do ours. So, while we annoy the guards with catcalls and jeers, we don't try to kill them or physically assault them, and they treat us with sullen indifference as long as we observe the rules." He added, "I should say that while you'll find our chaps maligning the guards quite frequently, we discourage it, and if it gets too out of hand, I take disciplinary action."

Lance locked eyes with Guy. "I don't know what to say. Does that make our job of escaping harder or easier?"

Guy chuckled. "You have a one-track mind, Lance, don't you? Our jailers would not like what I'll say next: the situation makes things easier for us. You'll be surprised at the things we can do behind these walls in darkness, and even in daylight."

He stood and addressed everyone in the room. "That wraps things up. You can all go on about your business." Turning to Lance, he said, "I have one more thing for you, if you'll step with me into the corridor."

Lance followed him while the men dispersed. Out in the hall, Guy reached into his jacket pocket and pulled out a bundle of letters. "These are letters from home. I didn't want to give them to you until we'd checked you out."

As he handed them over, Lance's eyes locked on his mother's strong cursive lettering. He suddenly felt lightheaded and leaned against the wall. Looking up, he tried to thank Guy but found that his voice had suddenly gone, and his jaw quivered.

"Are these the first letters you've had?"

Lance averted his face and nodded.

"Since Dunkirk?"

Again, Lance nodded.

Guy stepped back into the room, where he found Pat Reid still conversing with two POWs. He tapped the lieutenant on the shoulder and gestured for him to follow. "Would you please take Sergeant Littlefield to one of your hideaways where he can read his letters in private?"

"With pleasure, sir."

Lance followed Pat numbly while scanning through the other envelopes. He recognized Claire's handwriting, and then Paul's and Jeremy's and finally Stephen's.

"We're going high into the attic. When you're ready to rejoin us, just come through the false wall. I'll show you how. Be sure to replace it, and follow the passage, going down every staircase you come to until you reach the courtyard. Anyone can tell you how to get back up to the room. Take as long as you need."

———

Alone in the small space, Lance read and re-read each letter. The wrinkled paper and holes informed him that the censors had done their jobs, although the cut-out words were easily guessed, and the full meaning of any sentence should have given no reason for concern to either Brits or Germans. All his family members were astute enough not to write about anything that could not pass scrutiny, thus the main value to Lance of each letter was not their content, but the profound message they brought just by their presence, of being loved and cared for at home. He passed his fingers over each one, feeling the bond with family that they evoked.

Late in the evening, long after hunger set in, Lance scanned through the letters one more time before folding them and putting them in his pocket. Before emerging from his hiding place, he closed his eyes and pictured Sark Island with waves crashing on cliffs; his siblings, running with him across the green high plateau; his stepfather, climbing with him among the rocks; and his mother, headstrong and compassionate, watching over all of them. "I'll get home, Mum," he whispered fiercely. "I promise you. I'll get home."

16

Christmas Day

Midafternoon of the next day, Lance gazed around the courtyard in disbelief. It was coated with a fresh layer of snow. A
cold, swirling wind pierced to the bone, but what caught his
attention were makeshift decorations in greens and reds that
adorned doors and windows around the courtyard to celebrate Christmas Day. The ornaments were not profuse, just
bits of cloth and paper with splashes of holiday colors, but
they raised spirits so that even the air seemed festive. POWs
called greetings to each other and even to the guards, and at
one end, they pushed and pulled each other around in the
snow on a piece of metal they had bent into a makeshift sled.
For their part, the guards, normally implacable or severe,
smiled and nodded and returned greetings in amicable
acknowledgement of a shared tradition.

Lieutenant Pat Reid walked up behind Lance. "We're
invited to a party this afternoon," he said, clapping Lance on
the shoulder. "The Poles. They know we Brits are not getting
Red Cross packages yet, but their border is just over a hundred

miles east of here, so their parcels get here much quicker, including those from their families. With the size of their contingent, and being Christmas, that translates to a lot of food packages. The *kommandant* sanctioned the gathering."

Lance laughed. "That's big of him. Remind me why we're fighting Germany."

Pat arched an eyebrow. "Do you really want to go into that?"

"No, sir. Not here. Not now." He took a deep breath and let it out. "It's such a shame. My mother spent time in Germany long before the war. She loves the German people. When I was first captured, the frontline soldiers treated me with courtesy, even offering me cigarettes and coffee. When I was recaptured along the French border, a guard treated me decently. He's a conscript who had been born in America—in Kansas. He was raised there until he turned ten, and then his parents moved back to Germany."

He stomped his boots in the snow to warm them and his eyes took on a faraway look. "After I was captured the first time and on the forced march of prisoners across France, I witnessed a British officer gunned down at point-blank range because he dared to protect one of our soldiers who had collapsed and was being beaten by one of the guards." He closed his eyes and shook off the memory. "I've seen such cruelty and such kindness from Germans, and the divide is sometimes hard to fathom."

"I've had similar thoughts. The way I see things, you can chalk up the last war, the great one, to miscalculation and the inflexibility of mobilization plans. Once one government started moving troops to its borders in 1914, the neighboring countries felt threatened and responded. None dared to stop and pull back lest they be attacked while unprepared. So, with ordinary people having little say about going to war, millions died to make the world safe for democracy. But when the Allies won, we gutted Germany's economy, driving it into poverty. The people were punished for what their leaders did."

He took a deep breath and let it out slowly while watching the POWs make merry in the snow. "So, here we are again, and this time because an ambitious corporal with a silly mustache seized power and mesmerized the population with his rhetoric."

"He didn't do it alone," Lance rejoined.

"Sadly, that's true. And as *Herr* Hitler grew stronger, European governments pandered to him, including our own. Even the US has its Nazi sympathizers to this day."

The two men stood silently watching the activity on the courtyard. Then Pat sighed and clapped Lance on the back. "Well, we talked about the mess despite our intent not to. It's Christmas." He gestured toward the theater. "The party's begun. Let's celebrate."

"What shall we celebrate, sir?"

"Do you mean aside from the birth of Christ?" Pat rubbed his chin and looked about. "How about that we're alive, and we'll form friendships here to last a lifetime?" He extended his hand. "Merry Christmas, Lance Littlefield."

———

Lance found the Poles to be a jovial lot if a touch on the dark side. Wide-faced and beaming, they greeted their guests with all the enthusiasm of having found long-lost cousins. "Please, come in. Come in."

They had laid out a table buffet-style with food received in parcels from their homeland that included bits of pork, chicken, and beef with bread and sausages, sauerkraut, pickled cucumbers, and sour cream laced with marjoram and other spices. On another table, they had spread out plum cake; kolaches with poppy seeds; nuts, jams, and other fruit mixtures; apricot-raisin rugelach; and an assortment of angel-wing and thumb cookies.

Lance stared, mesmerized, and his mouth watered. Pat constrained him with a patient grin. "Let's say hello to our hosts first, shall we."

Polish Senior Officers Rear-Admiral Unrug and Lieu-tenant-General Pishkor stood together at the center of the room with Guy. Pat exchanged greetings with them, and then introduced Lance. "This is our newest addition."

"You're most welcome," Pishkor said. "We saw you come in yesterday." He shot a sly glance at Guy. "Word reached us that Sergeant Littlefield is dedicated to the craft of escaping and with some success. With your approval, I'll introduce him to our best and they can compare notes and generate ideas."

"Brilliant," Guy rejoined. "Lance, does that suit you?"

"I couldn't ask for more."

The chairs, normally set in rows for a theater audience facing the stage, had been rearranged so that the POWs could gather in groups for conversation while they shared their meals. Despite the circumstances, the room filled with laughter and storytelling. Then, the men pulled the emptied tables aside and re-set the chairs in their normal positions. German guards stood around the periphery and circulated through the gathering occasionally, but they remained less obtrusive than normal.

The Poles had written and rehearsed a hilarious rendition of *Snow White and the Seven Dwarfs*. The man General Pishkor introduced to Lance, Miloš, was to be in the starring role. He and Lance sat together with a mixed group of Brits and Poles.

"We'll talk later, more seriously," he told Lance in broken English as he left the group after he had finished his meal. "Time for dress-up. I must put on my tutu and makeup." He guffawed. "Enjoy the show."

Lance observed the details of the room while enjoying his new comrades. It had obviously not been intended as a theater, the stage having been built at a later time. The foyer led to the main entrance, and through a window that over-looked the courtyard from three stories up, Lance observed the clock tower at the opposite end with the German quarters on the other side of the chapel. *That means the partition behind the stage should be the outside wall.*

While the chairs were being re-set, he edged close to the stage, and at one point he backed against it, running his boot into it. *Plywood. It's hollow under there.*

Maneuvering unobtrusively, he checked out both sides of the stage. They abutted against the wall with no doors leading anywhere.

Struck suddenly with the strange sensation of being watched, he glanced around the room. From the other side, Pat observed him. The two lifted their glasses to each other and smiled. A short while later Pat sidled up to him.

"You don't rest on your laurels, do you, Sergeant?"

"Not if I can help it, sir. I'd like to look under that stage."

Pat smiled. "It's been checked out. That's the outer wall. On the other side of that plaster is solid stone. Even if you could get through it, you're facing that one-hundred-foot drop *after* you get down the three stories of this building."

Lance contemplated that. "I'd still like to see for myself."

"All right. I'll get some of the blokes to join me on stage at the end of performance to congratulate the Poles for a job well done. Behind the curtain is a cutout in the floor. The Germans haven't discovered it. I'll show you where it is. You've got half an hour at most. After that, the party will be considered over, and the guards will usher us out. If you're caught, you'll spend time in the cooler."

"Then I mustn't get caught."

17

December 29, 1940
Stony Stratford, England

"Having you here for these days has been so good," Claire told Ryan as the two women strolled down the garden path to the car parked in the driveway where Paul stood waiting. She gripped Ryan's arm, squeezed it, and whispered, "I wish you could stay longer, but it's wonderful to see Paul being so interested in you. I believe you're the first girl he's seriously cared for. He's chosen well."

"I'm flattered," Ryan replied, laughing lightly in embarrassment. "We'll see where it leads."

"If we survive this war," Claire said, chuckling, "anyone who sees you together can see where it's likely to lead. Apparently, Mr. Churchill had a hint. Paul told me how he took steps to keep the two of you in contact with each other." She elbowed Ryan playfully. "Timmy could use a playmate in the family."

Ryan blushed a deep red. "Oh, stop it. I need to keep my head on straight." She glanced furtively at Paul. "I worry about him. I have no idea where he's going when he leaves here, or what he does, but I know it must be terribly important."

"This war keeps people separated with their secrets," Claire observed. "It's a strange, strange situation."

"I envy you," Ryan said, casting a glance about the garden and then back at Claire. "I'm proud of what I do—"

"Which is another secret," Claire interrupted. "Paul warned me not to ask."

"Yes. I'm sorry about that. As I was saying, what I do is crucial and I'm happy to be doing it, but I see the carnage from a distance, and it saddens me. And of course, we're all living through this *blitz*. You're so lucky to be able to be on this estate and just take care of Timmy."

Claire smiled wryly. "I know," she said softly. "I should be doing more."

"Oh no," Ryan cried, concerned. "I didn't mean my comment that way. Our children must be cared for, and you gave Timmy a home. It's just— Well, I see things I wish I didn't."

"It's all right," Claire said. They reached the end of the garden path. "I admire you, and I'm happy for Paul that he found you."

———

"I think I just insulted your sister," Ryan told Paul as they drove off. "I didn't mean to." She told him of the exchange between her and Claire. "I didn't intend to make light of what she does. The home is what we fight for, and she's at the heart of it. That's what I meant to say."

"Don't worry," Paul assured her as he turned onto the main road. "She wouldn't feel slighted in the least, but I'll pass along your concern when I get back this evening." He started to say something, then stopped himself and added, "I can tell you only this about Claire: she's active in the war in ways she can't talk about, even to me."

Ryan stared at him in disbelief. "Secrets, secrets, and more secrets." She shook her head. "Just dealing with what you can and can't say to whom is difficult enough, and then there are the secrets themselves, sometimes too awful to contemplate that they're real." She sighed. "When will I see you again?"

Paul exhaled. "I don't know. I'll fly out within the next few days, and I don't know when I'll be back."

Ryan leaned her head on the back of the seat and closed her eyes. "So, we're back to sending notes to each other via diplomatic pouch and I can't know where mine go?"

Paul nodded. "I'm afraid that *is* the case."

"Then I want to say something to you, Paul Littlefield. I want to give my heart to you, but I won't, not now. If even your destination is so secret, then your assignment must be very dangerous, and you might not come back." She wiped her eyes as tears formed. "I won't be able to stop thinking of you, and I'll worry about you, and I'll be ever so glad to see you when you come home, but if the worst occurs, I might not even be informed, and I'll go a lifetime wondering what happened. I'll need to move on."

Dusk approached. Paul glanced at the skies. "I expect that the *Luftwaffe* will begin dropping its incendiaries for the night soon. We need to get you to your flat before that starts up."

Then he glanced at Ryan, seeing startled anguish on her face. "I'm sorry. I didn't mean to be so insensitive. You're pouring your heart out to me, and I'm talking about bombs." He took a deep breath. "I'm not good at this. Obviously, I have strong feelings for you. If times were different, I might already be on one knee in front of you, holding a little box, and hoping against hope—" He stopped talking, seemingly amazed at the implications of what he had just said. "I mean I understand what you're saying and wouldn't ask you to put your life on hold for me."

Ryan scooted closer to him, leaned her head on his shoulder, and draped her arm across his chest. "Shh," she murmured. "Say no more. I think we understand each other."

Paul reached for her hand, lifted it to his lips, and kissed it. "Just one more thing I'll say. To borrow my sister's favorite line, things will work out for the best. You'll see."

RAF Middle Wallop

Jeremy punched the starter button on his fighter's dashboard and listened to the mammoth engine on his right sputter as the propeller began a slow rotation, gained speed, and settled into a roaring whir. He repeated the sequence with the left engine.

"Are you settled in?" he called back to Farlan.

"Our magic box is humming," Farlan replied. "I'm ready when you are."

Jeremy completed his pre-flight checklist and contacted the tower. Moments later, his Beaufighter lifted from the end of the runway as the rim of the sun sank over the horizon. He cleared the airfield at Middle Wallop and established radio contact with his combat controller at RAF Sopley, call-signed "Starlight." Then he told Farlan over the intercom, "Our daytime fighters have already engaged Nazi bombers along the eastern coast. The Germans are heading for London.

"We're the third fighter in flight from our squadron. The pilots in the three coming up behind us are inexperienced at night fighting. This is their first patrol with us, so keep a close eye out for anything that strays into our vicinity that we're not specifically pursuing. Let me know about it and be ready for immediate evasive action. I'm sure Starlight will keep us well apart, but extra caution won't hurt."

"Blimey," Farlan said, a trace of irony in his tone, "I think I can handle that."

"A bit touchy tonight, are we?" Jeremy shot back, grinning. "Listen," he said, setting banter aside, "Starlight informed me that the incoming formation is very large. Its aircraft are spread out, so sighting them will be difficult. They appear headed for London. Starlight said that the leading elements are dropping their incendiaries on the historic district around St. Paul's Cathedral."

Darkness settled in rapidly, and from his high vantage at fifteen thousand feet, he saw from an orange glow visible out this distance that the *Luftwaffe* had already reached London and dropped tons of incendiaries.

"The bombers that follow will use those fires as beacons to drop their heavy munitions," Farlan muttered over the inter-com. "Bollocks! Can't they be satisfied with slaughter? They've got to take down our national symbols too?"

"St. Paul's is an easy target," Jeremy replied. "I'm surprised they didn't go for it sooner. If the goose-steppers have in mind to destroy our will by destroying our symbols and culture, that target is an obvious choice."

"And we'll stop them," Farlan replied grimly.

Jeremy orbited, awaiting instruction from Starlight. Far to the northeast, mid-air bursts originating from anti-aircraft guns outlined the coast and marked a corridor parallel to the Thames as German heavy bombers flew inland. Sporadically, machine gun tracers and cannon fire marked an engagement between the last British daytime fighters and either bombers or German fighters still engaging before braving a dark sprint back to the coast and across the Channel to their airfields in France.

Anderson and Cunningham had taken off in their Beauforts before Jeremy and were therefore closer to the targets designated by their controllers. Jeremy reflected briefly on the natures of the two men who complemented each other so well. Anderson primarily concerned himself with selecting recruits and planning missions while Cunningham focused on training new pilots.

Prior to the advent of Beaufighters, squadron leaders flew at the front of their formations until they ordered "tally-ho." With the inability to see each other during night flight and the dangers of winging near each other even during daylight, normal formations were impossible in the dark, and thus mandated that night fighters fly out at staggered intervals. Leadership manifested in understanding pilots, selecting recruits, training them to the utmost, and then trusting their skills, experience, and judgment. Only combat-tested veteran pilots would do.

Because so few British pilots flew at night, Fighter Command assigned a controller to each aircraft, and in that way, the Beaufighters were kept out of each other's way. The concept of airborne-air intercept scopes on fighters being guided to designated targets by combat controllers had been proven. Using Cunningham's methods, Anderson had downed a Heinkel two days after Cunningham had. Both pilots had scored again in the intervening weeks, and Jeremy had succeeded in bringing down his first night target a week ago.

The public, thirsty for deliverance from their nightly hell at German hands and thrilled with the exploits of John "Cat's Eyes" Cunningham, soaked up news of him, building up his aura to mythological stature. However, with still only six trained crews including Anderson, Cunningham, and Jeremy, the Luftwaffe remained relatively free to romp across British skies almost unchallenged.

The controller from Tangmere interrupted Jeremy's thoughts. "Blazer Two Six, your target is crossing from the south at Angels 29 on a heading of three five zero. Alter your course ten degrees south, and I'll guide you around behind him. Expect contact in two."

"Okay, Starlight," Jeremy called as adrenaline coursed through his limbs. Despite the number of times he had gone in pursuit of targets whether in daytime or at night, his body tingled with expectancy. He leaned forward, pushed back in his seat, and checked his oxygen, those actions accomplished automatically and within fractions of a second. "Target identi-fied," he called to Farlan. "We're in the hunt."

"And here I was readying me'self for a nap," the sergeant called back.

18

London, England

Paul looked anxiously at the sky. He had lingered with Ryan longer than he had expected and would have to cross London during blackout conditions. The rumble of German bomber formations had alerted them that he should be going, and as the day cast its last shadows across the city, he started his trip.

Leaving Ryan had been more painful than he could have imagined. Each time that he had begun to depart, she had either refused to let go of him by holding him tightly or he had turned back after taking a step away, and he once more embraced her. The thought of not seeing her for a long time—or worse, never seeing her again—seared his mind, plunging an ache into his chest. But his commitment to his assignment with Stephenson in New York had been for the duration of the war, which seemed to be still in its very early stages.

As he steered the car from the curb, he steeled himself to concentrate on the road ahead of him. With the overhead glow of the day's last light, he made out the edges of the street and the vehicles ahead of him. City of London authorities had thoughtfully had the street curbs painted white to assist drivers and pedestrians navigating the thoroughfares under blackout conditions.

Those measures helped, but they held the speed of travel for motor vehicles to a pace that would embarrass tortoises and snails. Headlights had been dimmed, and although they aided in avoiding oncoming traffic, they did little to illuminate pedestrians crossing the streets, particularly elderly people with hearing impairments or anyone who chose daring over caution. In any event, within a few minutes, vehicular and pedestrian traffic had disappeared as people sought shelter.

Roughly thirty minutes after starting his journey, the roar of bombers grew, and Paul realized that a formation of them must be passing over his head. Strangely, they dropped no bombs, and he decided that they either must have already fallen elsewhere or were headed to another city. By this time, full night had fallen, and he wondered whether he should seek refuge. He was not familiar with this part of town and had no idea where to find a bomb shelter. He imagined that people must be hurrying to them, probably even forming queues to get in, if he could just see them.

Carefully pulling to the curb and stopping, he stepped out but saw no one; and above the low hum of aircraft high over-head, he heard no one. As he was about to get back into his car, he noticed an orange glow in the eastern sky, growing rapidly.

Paul watched, transfixed, as he considered what must be happening. The planes that had passed over him had indeed dropped their cargoes, incendiaries that made little sound compared to the concussion of bombs, but they hurled propellants over wide areas that immediately burst into flame. With thousands of them landing on rooftops of homes and businesses as well as on the ground, conflagrations erupted and spread. More insidious, the bright flames served as beacons for the next wave of bombers carrying high-explosive bombs.

Standing next to his car and caught in a trance while deciding what to do, Paul heard a man and a woman calling, apparently to him, since he saw no one else. They hurried from the direction he had been traveling, arriving next to him out of breath.

"Can you help us?" the woman panted. "We need to get into London. Your car seems to be the only one on this street right now and we can't find a taxi. We barely saw your head-lights, they're so dim."

Startled, Paul gave up scrutinizing the pair after only a second, a useless pursuit in the dark. "You want to go *into* the city?" he asked, incredulous. "Have you looked at the horizon?"

"We need to get there," the man interjected. "I'm a reporter from America. We were doing a story on 11 Group at Uxbridge, but I got a call that the bombers are hitting London's historic district. Apparently, their target is St. Paul's Cathedral. We heard confirmation of that on the BBC."

Paul listened in amazement. "That's not where I was going," he said, opening his door to have a little light by which to see the pair.

"We'll pay you," the woman said. She reached for her purse.

"No, no," Paul replied. "It's not that." He tried to see her face through the darkness. "There must be horrific things going on over there."

"Which is exactly why we need to be there," the woman insisted. "If you won't take us, can we take your car? If it's wrecked, our employers are good for it."

Paul almost burst out laughing. "I don't even know that

you're really reporters," he said. "You could be a couple of brilliant con artists."

"He's right," the man cut in. "Look." He reached for his wallet while telling Paul, "If we were crooks, we'd hardly have called out to you when we could have snuck up and banged you on the head." He stretched his arm out, wallet in hand. "Here are our credentials. I'm Bill White with *The Emporia Gazette* and *Reader's Digest*." He gestured at his female companion. "This is Marguerite Higgins. She reports for the *New York Herald Tribune*, and she got out of Paris just ahead of the Nazis. She's covering the war from London and helps Resistance forces here. Our organizations are collaborating on our story."

Paul took the press card and studied it in the dim light while Marguerite fished hers from her purse and handed it to him. "All right, I'll take you. It's a government car, so if you're feeding me a line, your employers will get to reconcile the loss with our government. Where specifically do you want to go?"

"As close to the fire as we can get. I'm guessing we'll find streets closed off, so the route will be circuitous. We'll just have to aim for the center of that orange glow and keep taking whatever streets are available."

"Get in," Paul said. Bill took the front passenger seat while Marguerite piled into the rear. "I'm Paul Littlefield." Before he started the engine, he turned to face them. "Are you sure this is what you want to do?"

"That's our job," Marguerite replied. "Thank you for being so courteous."

"Thank me if you live through it," Paul said. "If you don't, I might never forgive myself."

"Before we came out on the street, we made calls to acquaintances in the area that's being hit," Marguerite said. "They told us that the formations seem inordinately large tonight. The incendiaries fell like huge raindrops, thousands of them. The flames engulfed whole neighborhoods and commercial centers in minutes."

"What makes you think the target is St. Paul's?"

"We could be wrong, but if we are, so is the BBC. They're basing their conclusion on the pattern of the falling incendiaries. The bombers keep concentrating in that vicinity, and some incendiaries have landed on the cathedral, but so far, firefighters have kept the flames at bay. I'm guessing the stone walls and dome must be keeping the propellant from leaking inside and spreading the fire there."

"You might be right," Paul said grimly, "but I hate to think of what's happening to the poor people living in those neighborhoods and the workers still in those commercial sites." He turned slightly to Bill. "What's your interest?"

Bill let out a deep breath. "I told you, we're reporters. There's a huge debate going on inside the US about whether America should be in this war. Frankly, I think we should, and Marguerite agrees. We've formed our opinions from what we've witnessed. If Hitler wins here, he's not going to stop. He'll take a breather, gather his forces, and in no time, New York City will look like London does now.

"I believe that, but we have to keep our personal opinions out of our reporting. So, we go where the facts are, report them, and let people form their own opinions. It's hard to see that they'll come to any other conclusion." He laughed. "If they believed Orson Welles' *War of the Worlds* radio broadcast two years ago, they ought to at least consider the possibilities. Then again, he might have blunted our effect."

"This is a new type of warfare," Marguerite said. Paul had sensed that she had a spirited personality, but right now, her tone was urgent and serious. "The people on the streets are the targets, and if one of your spotlights manages to shine on one of the bombers, they can see the aircraft trying to kill them and watch the deadly cargo falling on their heads. And those bomb shelters are not always going to withstand direct hits. Hundreds of people will die tonight."

Her voice caught, but she pressed on with increased resolve. "Americans need to feel the danger viscerally before it reaches them. The United States is the only remaining country strong enough to stop the Nazis."

As the small car puttered through city streets, not a single window light or streetlamp broke the darkness, but as they drew closer to London's center, the wail of sirens rode the air, bringing with them the acrid smell of smoke.

And then Paul steered around a corner. Immediately to their front, not a block away, a wall of fire danced across their path, rising several stories into the sky, the ferocity of its flames casting debris all about.

The trio slid out of the car and stared in disbelief, and as their gazes climbed higher, they saw spotlights swaying back and forth across the smoke-blackened sky. The beams criss-crossed and then parted, and as they watched, a shadow appeared in one. Several other beams converged around it, illuminating what appeared to be a swarm of black flies streaming through the lights.

Almost immediately, the raucous noise of heavy anti-aircraft guns overrode the sirens with *thumps* and *whooshes*, and moments later, the air around the bombers filled with flashes of fire and the dull sounds of distant blasts as time fuses on projectiles released the kinetic energy of their munitions.

But the formation flew on, inexorably. Trying to take in the whole of their effect, Paul saw that the orange glow over the city had grown to epic proportions.

When Jeremy had flown close enough to London to see the extent of the incendiary-induced fire overtaking the city, he gaped in disbelief. "Starlight," he called to his controller, "London is ablaze. We must stop this. Put me on a target."

"We're hearing reports, mate, but keep your head. We won't do any good by throwing caution into the fire as well. Stay on your last course and make a shallow climb to Angels 28. Orbit there, keeping clear of the corridor from the coast. We don't need you to become a casualty of our own AA guns."

"Roger, maintaining course. Climbing to Angels 28." Jeremy took a deep breath to control his breathing.

"Blazer Two Six," Starlight broke in. "You should see targets at any moment. Flash your weapon."

Seconds later, Farlan yelled, "I have a solid contact. He's less than a thousand feet ahead of us on this trajectory and five hundred feet up." He whistled into the mic. "I hope Starlight gives us better notice in the future."

Jeremy squawked his radio. "Starlight, we have a firm contact." He flipped his commo switch again. "All right, Sergeant. Guide me in."

"We're closing at a good pace. Keep your trajectory. He's about eight hundred feet out, dead ahead. Slow down a bit and go nose up."

Keeping his anticipation in check, Jeremy glanced out the top of his cockpit, trying to ignore the distant sight of London in flames. He found mind-boggling the notion of being invisible to hundreds of enemy bombers flying only a few hundred feet above him while they were plainly tracked for airspeed, direction, and altitude.

He dropped his wheels to act as airbrakes and throttled back to slow the aircraft. Immediately, the engines' booming roar changed to popping noises as the Beaufort descended under control.

For a fraction of a second, visions of his desperate flight across the beach at Dunkirk flashed through his mind. Was that really only six months ago? Since then, he had escaped across France, survived a shipwreck, flown Hurricanes and Spitfires in the Battle of Britain, and been shot down three times. And now, here he was flying almost within reach of the enemy, invisible to them. As he brought himself back to the present, the roar from hundreds of engines vibrated through the Beaufort's skin, and the backwash from their props buffeted his aircraft.

"Check port," Farlan called from his perch in the gunner's seat. "Closing on six hundred feet."

Jeremy took a deep breath as excitement and anxiety collided. He made the correction and trailed his fingers along the triggers, checking to ensure they were unlocked. Curiously, far to his front in the target area, a black hole appeared in the middle of a wide circle of flame.

He scanned the sky above again, searching for the dark blob that he knew must pass across his view for him to have a viable target, but all he saw were stars. And then, there it was, a dark void moving against the throng of the heavenly darts of light. As he watched, it took shape with an elongated body, a nose, wings, and a tail.

"I see it," Jeremy called back, barely subduing his excitement. And now he saw that elusive tell-tale sign, the dull red glow of engine heat.

"Passing through five hundred feet," Farlan said. No emotion tinged his tone. "Lift the nose a notch and increase speed a tad."

Jeremy complied, retracting his wheels.

"On target."

Jeremy's excitement grew. "Roger. Keep reading me proximity numbers."

"Passing four."

Sweat formed on Jeremy's forehead and streamed down into his goggles. Unable to wipe it away, he blinked his eyes to ward off stinging.

"Three hundred." For the first time, Farlan's voice sounded tight, anxious. "Are you going to fire?"

"Hang on. The ride's going to get rough." Jeremy pressed the triggers, firing a stream from his cannons and three two-second bursts from his machine guns.

Before he had fired the third volley, flames shot into the sky above him. Immediately, he shoved his nose down, pulled the stick to the left, and pushed hard on the pedal. Simultaneously, he called his controller.

"Starlight, this is Blazer Two Six. Target found; target hit. Get me out of here and find me another big boy." As he pirouetted away, he rolled into a U-turn so that, looking through the top of his cockpit, he saw where he had come from marked by flaming wings and a fuselage falling through the air. Its nose plunged, and it exploded in a ball of fire on the ground, well short of London.

19

Hot wind fanned the flames through the street toward Paul and his companions. Too late, they realized that they had no time to dive into the little car to reverse course. As one, they turned and raced through the darkness, driven by self-preservation and a wave of heat that threatened to suffocate them, and seeing only the white lines painted on the curbs as a guide toward possible escape. Behind them, they heard an explosion, and scanning over their shoulders, they saw the sedan lifted into the air and dropped where it had been, fueling the cauldron.

They came to a wall. Having no idea what its purpose was and being unable to make out any of its dimensions, they dove behind it and huddled together, listening to the roar of flames and the crashing and moaning of bending metal structures.

Amazingly, the flames receded. The trio edged from behind the wall and stared at the inferno.

"What happened?" Bill asked. "We're not in the bomb area."

"Must have been a stray release," Paul said. "What now? I left my torch in my car." He pursed his lips. "That's gone."

"I have one," Marguerite volunteered while fumbling in her purse.

"I do too," Bill said. "I still plan to get as close to the center as I can. Marguerite?"

"I'm going with you. We still have a story to do."

"You're welcome to come along," Bill told Paul. "Sorry about your car. We'll have to hoof it."

Paul heaved a grim sigh. "If by that you mean we'll have to walk, no problem. We have no choice, and I'll come with you for the time being. I'm sure we'll run into rescue squads and fire teams needing volunteers. I'll stay with them and you two can go on." He looked about, trying to see landmarks to give him a sense of direction. "We were traveling east when we ran into the wall of flame. I suggest we go south toward the Thames and then cut along as close to the river as we can. At least that way, we might have a puddle of water to jump into if the fire gets too close again."

As they made their way through the streets, Paul became aware of how the war must be affecting his people. In New York, he had walked the streets with no fear. Now, with the drone of aircraft overhead, he found himself acutely attuned to other sounds around them. They occurred infrequently, the quiet being deafening aside from the distant German bombers, but they added a heightened feeling of imminent danger from any direction, and thus to his sense of hearing. He found himself reacting to any disharmony that broke the night, no matter how small.

An hour later, he and his companions trudged past Covent Garden and then Leicester Square before turning east. Minutes later, they found the Savoy Hotel, and as they drew near, they saw to their surprise that it was open and doing business. Smudged, dirty, and reeking of smoke, they entered, hoping to quench their thirst.

Inside, they were astonished to find life continuing as though nothing of consequence were going on. Music played. Well-heeled guests moved about in their evening finery. The concierge gave the three a disapproving look as they passed by him, and staff members went about their tasks with only passing glances in the direction of far-off explosions as they occurred.

"Is this for real?" Bill remarked. He led them to the restaurant, where the maître d' objected to their entry.

Paul stepped forward. "I don't think you want to refuse us," he said. "You know me. I come here often with my sister, Claire Littlefield. I'm Paul. But in any case, tonight of all nights, you shouldn't be refusing anyone."

The maître d' stepped back and scrutinized him. "Ah, yes. Mr. Littlefield." His eyes traveled the height of Paul's body. "I didn't recognize you. You look like you've been through a bit of a wringer."

"The city's been through the wringer." Paul took a breath to keep his annoyance in check. "We're tired, we're hungry, and we're thirsty. Will you please show us to a table? We'll be staying only long enough to rest a little and then we'll be on our way." He glanced around at the disapproving looks from patrons scattered about the foyer and the restaurant. "We have no wish to scandalize your guests," he seethed, "so give us a table out of the way."

When they were seated, Paul noticed Bill and Marguerite eyeing him curiously. "Who are you?" Marguerite asked. "You've got influence here, and that's not easily acquired." Her brow furrowed. "Paul Littlefield. The name sounds familiar, but not quite. Littlefield." She squinted as she reached back into her memory.

"You've probably heard of my brother, Jeremy Littlefield. He was in the news a few months back."

"Yeah, I remember," Bill interjected. "He saved that kid from the shipwreck. Very heroic. And your parents are on Sark Island, right?" He stopped talking as Marguerite elbowed him. "I'm sorry. That was senseless of me. You've been good to us. We won't turn this into an interview, I promise, but I'm curious about your brother. What's he doing now?"

"He's a fighter pilot, but God only knows where. For all I know, he could be up there now with the night fighters going after the *Luftwaffe*. I'm afraid our family has been fragmented by this war and keeping up with each other is difficult."

"I can imagine."

While they waited for a menu, Paul observed his companions. Until entering the hotel, he had not been able to see them clearly. Marguerite was trim, with an oval face, dark eyes, and light brown hair. She bore a serious yet playful expression, but her demeanor left no doubt that she could be assertive if need be. She dressed professionally in a brown skirt with a matching jacket and low heels. Paul imagined that their walk across town must have been agonizing, but she made no complaint.

Bill was tall with a muscular build, broad shoulders, a strong chin, studious eyes, and full, dark hair. He wore a business suit, although he had loosened his tie. Both he and Marguerite appeared around Paul's age, and they interacted with each other as though from long and friendly association. "Let's eat and be on our way," he said, signaling to a passing waiter.

20

"Blazer Two Six, this is Starlight. We have fresh formations crossing the Channel. I'm going to vector you south and bring you around behind them, but first go to Angels 35 and orbit until I call you."

"Okay, on my way." Jeremy switched to intercom. "Sergeant, are you seeing anything?"

"Negative," he replied, clipping the word with an irritated tone.

Surprised, Jeremy called back to him, "Is something wrong?" When Farlan did not immediately respond, he repeated the question.

"You're the pilot, sir, and I follow orders. But must you get that close to pull the trigger? A few more seconds in that last attack, and you'd have rammed that big boy. I'm here to kill the Hun, not offer up a sacrifice."

Stung, Jeremy took a few moments to gather his thoughts. "Sergeant Pirie, I appreciate your experience and skill, and that you're up here risking your life. What you're not seeing is what I'm seeing, and that's precious little in this blackness.

Below us, the capital of the country we cherish is on fire. We're told that the target is St. Paul's Cathedral. I don't know if that means anything to you, but to Anglicans worldwide, and particularly those living in Great Britain, it's a symbol. If it falls, the result could be a catastrophic blow to our countrymen and others who hold it dear.

"Further, to hit the target, I must see it. I can't just think I see it or guess that it must be in front of me or pull my triggers on a hope and a prayer. When I flew in the Battle of Britain, the most successful fighter pilots were the Poles. They accounted for better than fifteen percent of German hits but made up less than three percent of the total number of pilots. Their secret was that they pushed to within two hundred and fifty feet of the target while our doctrine had us firing from six hundred and fifty feet. And do you know why they were so daring? They learned it in Poland, fighting to save their country. And now, we're fighting to save ours, and our doctrine has changed.

"I'll make just one more point, and then you can say whatever you like. When we approach a target, I must and *do* rely on you. I don't question your skill or your judgment. Those were affirmed when you were recruited.

"If you had told me to keep flying at full speed in the direction we were headed, I'd have done it without question. Now we're getting ready to go around again and engage another big boy. If you're not up to the task, tell me now, because as we get closer to the target, I don't want a single doubt in my mind that you're giving your best to our mission."

Silence.

"Sergeant Pirie?"

"You're right, sir," Farlan muttered. "I'm embarrassed."

"Don't be. We all have our moments."

"Blazer Two Six, Starlight here. We have your target."

Paul and his companions, having refreshed and rested, walked out from the main entrance of the Savoy. There, to their amazement, they found taxis providing service, even as the distant explosions gave notice that the raid was still ongoing. They approached one and asked to be taken closer to St. Paul's.

"Like hell I will," the driver said. "The fire between here and there is a furnace. You're bonkers, the lot of you."

The second driver they queried expressed a similar sentiment albeit in more base terms. However, the third was exuberant. After they presented their credentials, he declared, "Of course I'll take you. There's a route open by the river, and they keep a street open going north from there for emergency vehicles. I'll take you as far as I can, but the coppers will probably stop me before we get all the way in."

"Do you know anything about how the church is faring?" Paul asked as they made their way through the dark, smoke-filled streets. He sat in the front passenger's seat.

"It's a strange thing," the driver replied. "Almost all the neighborhoods and commercial centers around it are in flames, but so far, the cathedral seems untouched. I haven't been allowed close enough to see for myself, but I can tell you that over a hundred parishioners refused to be turned away and showed up at the front door. They told the dean that they needed the comfort of the church and wanted to pray for its safety." He laughed. "The dean couldn't very well say that he doubted the power of their prayers, now could he? I should think not."

In the back, Marguerite leaned against her seat. "I think we're going to the same destination, Paul. That's where we'll get our story, and that's probably where your volunteer service might be very useful. I'm not questioning prayer, but I'm betting there's at least an earthly reason why that cathedral still stands."

21

Starlight called to Jeremy, "Blazer Two Six, you should be seeing your bandits at any moment."

"We have contact," Farlan called from the rear.

"Roger, Sergeant. Break." Jeremy flipped his switch from intercom to radio. "Starlight, Blazer Two Six. We have firm contact. I'll call back when it's over."

"Roger. Starlight out."

"Guide me in," Jeremy called back to Farlan.

"He's a thousand feet ahead of us. Nudge to starboard and raise the nose a tad. Maintain speed."

Jeremy complied, his heart beating rapidly and his hands already becoming clammy. His confrontation with Farlan came to mind, and he set it aside. *No time to think about that now.* But the essence of the sergeant's concern persisted. Had Jeremy flown too close on the earlier engagement?

"Eight hundred," Farlan called.

"Okay." Slight frustration settled on Jeremy. He had seen the previous target from five hundred feet out. That was four hundred and fifty feet closer than doctrine had been before changing it, and plenty of bandits had gone down at that range. With only six night fighters in the sky against the hundreds of bombers flying over London carrying thousands of tons of incendiaries and highly explosive munitions, every shot had to meet its mark. The Germans had to be shown that the RAF had weapons to punish them at night, that they could no longer attack Great Britain with impunity. What was it his father had told him about the battle at Bunker Hill during the American Revolution? Then he remembered. William Prescott, an American officer holding out against an overwhelming British assault force and knowing that every lead musket ball must count, ordered his men, "Don't fire until you see the whites of their eyes."

Same situation. Going against overwhelming forces. Every shot must count.

"Four hundred."

"I see him. Closing in from below, straight ahead. I see the engine glow."

"Three hundred."

Once again, Jeremy pressed his triggers, and once again the Beaufort trembled and shook as it sprayed cannon and machine gun rounds into the dark shape of the enemy bomber.

Once again, fire erupted on the bandit, but this time it neither exploded nor fell out of control. Its nose dipped, and it began a slow descent to its left. Obviously, Jeremy had disabled the aircraft, but he had not put it completely out of commission. The pilot still had a modicum of control.

"He's down but not out," Jeremy called back to Farlan. "Keep tracking him. I'm going around to get behind him again. He's flaming enough that I can keep a visual on him. Break." Jeremy flipped to his radio. "Starlight, we wounded the big boy, but he's still flying. How's the air around me? I'm going after him. Looks like he's still headed to London."

"Okay. You have plenty of room and the air is clear at your altitude and for ten thousand feet above and below. Remain south of the Thames. If you don't have him by then, let him go, or you'll fly into our own anti-aircraft barrage."

Jeremy acknowledged and pulled his stick back and to his left while stomping on his pedal. The fighter responded, screaming into a tight turn while Jeremy searched the sky for the burning bomber. "Do you still have him on your tube?" he called to Farlan.

"Affirmative. Hold your turn a bit longer. I'll advise when to straighten out, and when you do, drop your nose. He's descended a ways. We'll come down on him from above."

As Jeremy executed the maneuvers, he contemplated the sergeant. The way that Farlan had addressed his concern about how close Jeremy came to the first target before shooting had been in bad form. Then again, with no control over the aircraft, and that being Farlan's only complaint in a terrifying situation, Jeremy had to appreciate the tenacity to speak his mind to his superior officer while staying within the bounds of respect. *Not an easy task under the circumstances. And he corrected immediately.*

"Roll out now on a northerly heading," Farlan said. "I'll feed you corrections."

"I see him now, down about ten degrees," Jeremy replied.

"That's him."

"He's burning brighter now. He'll jettison his cargo soon if he can. How far to the Thames?"

"About two minutes."

"Feed me proximity numbers. We've got to take him down. He's heading straight for the dark spot within the ground fires. I'm guessing that's where the cathedral is."

"We're out two thousand feet from him now."

Jeremy rolled out of his turn and set his nose to center on

the flaming bomber, clearly visible against the dark sky. Well beyond it, past the docks lining the Thames, he saw plainly the fires raging in London's historic district; and at their center in a straight line, he saw the dark area where St. Paul's must be.

He thrust the throttle open wide and the fighter responded, ripping through the sky at maximum speed. The distance closed, but not fast enough, and the Thames grew closer and closer.

"I'm going to try something," Jeremy yelled back to Farlan. "Hang on, this is going to get rough. Keep that target in your tube." He dropped the nose into a forty-five-degree dive and checked his throttle to be sure it was full open. Air speed accelerated, and he closed the horizontal distance rapidly, but at the point that he pulled his stick back to climb, the vertical distance was considerable, and the g-forces immense. He remembered to push his chest forward against his knees to control his breathing.

"You still have him?" Jeremy yelled to Farlan. "Lock me in on him."

"Come to your right five degrees and lift your nose a tiny bit. That's it. A bit more. There. You'll have a straight shot. He's still fifteen hundred feet out."

"We won't reach him in time," Jeremy called. "I still have my rockets, but the cannons are empty, and my machine gun ammo is low. I'll empty my magazines on him before he crosses the Thames, but they will be long shots. Maybe they'll jam his bomb bay doors."

Thirty seconds later, short of the river, Jeremy leaned forward in the cockpit, gritted his teeth, and pressed his triggers in two-second bursts, doing his best to correct onto the target between successive shots. The Beaufort bucked through the sky as rockets and machine gun bullets streamed forward.

Whether or not he hit anything was difficult to see from this distance. Some rockets flew past their target as, undoubtedly, so did some machine gun fire. Small flashes of high explosives hit the plane's belly, but whether they caused damage, Jeremy could not tell.

The bomber's nose fell as it flew on, and its descent accelerated. Jeremy followed, but then, short of crossing the Thames, he rolled into a turn away from the river in such a way that he could still see the bomber through the top of his cockpit.

"He's dropped incendiaries. The fire outlines them," he called back to Farlan, "but I'm not seeing any bombs." As he continued to watch, the bomber flew past the dark area within the fire and then plunged into its outside perimeter nearly a mile further on. There, flames from multiple explosions reached high into the night sky.

———————

Later, as they walked together into the dispersal hut at RAF Middle Wallop while waiting to be refueled and re-supplied with ammunition, Farlan kept glancing at Jeremy with a worried look on his face. Jeremy noticed out of the corner of his eye.

"Sir," Farlan began haltingly, "I was out of line—"

Jeremy interrupted him by clapping his shoulder. "You did brilliantly, Sergeant. Let's get some coffee, shall we, or would you prefer tea?"

22

An hour before Jeremy's engagement on the south side of the Thames near St. Paul's, and despite their frenetic flight from fire and the hike through the smoke-filled streets to the Savoy, Paul, Marguerite, and Bill were aghast at the sight that greeted them as they began their one-mile taxi ride to the cathedral. The cab took a circuitous route owing to blocked-off streets, but a quick glance provided the reason for the detour: visible several blocks away, orange flames licked tall edifices, danced on the rooftops of low buildings, and leaped across streets to the fodder of yet more structures that fed the fiery, blistering beast. Even at this distance, they heard and felt the wind created by oxygen rushing in to replace that already consumed and heard the groans and shrieks of bending and collapsing frames as dwellings, factories, and storefronts cascaded in on themselves amid thick, black smoke.

Having departed the Savoy traveling east on The Strand, and with the ever-present drone of bombers overhead, their taxi drove past King's College and took one of the side streets south toward the Thames. It worked its way parallel to the river for most of the way and then wound north through back streets and alleys, thick with smoldering ash, until they reached a corridor established by the police along Sermon Lane leading to Ludgate Hill and the great cathedral.

At first, constables regulating permissible traffic into the passageway refused their car entry past a checkpoint they had established. Bill and Marguerite showed their press passes, arguing that they must report to their US readers the extent of the damage to London; but only after Paul produced his army identification did the constables step aside and wave the taxi through.

"We hit the jackpot when we ran into you in the dark," Bill muttered. He gazed about at the roaring flames. "I recall that last year, a German newspaperman bragged that the London docks and the older parts of the city could be burned off like patches of weed. He was talking about right where we are now, and that seems to be the *Luftwaffe's* intent tonight."

Heat from opposing conflagrations on either side of the street parched their skin, causing their eyes to water and hindering their breathing. As the taxi crept through even more dense smoke, lines of exhausted firefighters struggled to aim heavy hoses and brass nozzles spouting thick streams of water along the base of the buildings and into the lower stories to hold back enormous walls of flame. Emerging through the fire and smoke intermittently with their emergency lights flashing, police cars and ambulances passed the group traveling in the opposite direction.

Then the taxi drove past the flames and through several blocks of buildings that, although blackened by soot and showing signs of having been hit by bombs, were relatively untouched. As they progressed, they noticed a heavier presence of firemen. Thinner smoke cloaked the ground, and the air became less oppressive. The heat dissipated and the sounds of fire and crumbling buildings abated, replaced once again by the incessant low hum of German warplanes passing overhead.

They crossed Carter Lane, and then the tall columns, the grand Baroque façade, and the dome of St. Paul's rose in front of them in ghostly white splendor. They paid their taxi driver, bade him farewell, and mounted the steps of the south transept.

Entering the building, the trio found that chaos had turned the stately interior to one of gloom. Smoke had penetrated inside, leaving a black film on the walls and statues, and obscuring the ceiling of the rotunda with its dark clouds. People huddled below, speaking in low, anxious tones. Others had moved into the nave to pray.

"This is where we get to work. I suggest we interview people," Marguerite said to Bill. Turning to Paul, she held out her hand. "What's it been, five hours since we met? And the bombing goes on. Thank you for your help. We might not have made it without you. I hope we meet again."

Paul shook her hand and then Bill's and watched as the two journalists began approaching people. Then he cast about to learn where he might volunteer.

A man hurried by with a worried look. Paul moved swiftly to walk alongside him. "I'm sorry to bother you. I'm Captain Littlefield. I've come to help. Tell me what to do."

Without stopping even for a second, the man glanced at him. "I'm on my way now to see the dean. I'm sure he could use you."

They found Walter Matthews, Dean of St. Paul's, on the opposite side of the rotunda as he was about to go through a small door. "I've alerted the firefighters that we're nearly out of water," the escort told him. "They promised to do what they can to get more in here, but they didn't offer much encouragement." Then he introduced Paul. "He's an army officer, and he came to volunteer. I thought you might use him upstairs. Our architects are nearly exhausted. Surely he could replace one of them."

Matthews, a man of average height and build with a shock of thick brown hair over a determined countenance, eyed Paul briefly. "Shouldn't you be out on the front somewhere? Maybe in North Africa?" He turned to the door again and gestured for Paul to follow. "I'm in a bit of a hurry."

"I'm home on leave, sir," Paul said, going after him. "We didn't expect this calamity."

On the other side of the door, they entered a narrow, short hall, and at the end of it, they mounted a winding stone stair-case lit with lanterns and candles. Matthews kept talking as he climbed them. "I don't know why you wouldn't have antici-pated this bombing. Hitler hit London for fifty-seven straight nights before a single one of reprieve, and he shows no sign of letting up. Where are you stationed?"

"I don't want to be rude, sir, but I'm not allowed to say."

The dean eyed him dubiously and then sighed. "I apolo-gize. We're doing all we can to save the cathedral and I've become tired and a little impatient. The man who introduced us is correct. Our architects could use a break."

"I'm not an architect, sir."

Matthews laughed involuntarily, a full belly laugh. "Thank you for that comic relief. I'm becoming a bit punch-drunk." He paused on the stairs, panting for breath. "I'll explain. These architects volunteered here as firemen. They've come every night since the *blitz* began because they've studied the blueprints and they know where the vulnerable places are."

He started ascending the stairs again, and Paul followed. "This church's record for surviving fires is not a good one. It's burned to the ground twice in its thousand-year history. We're rather challenged in trying to keep that from happening a third time, but we must."

His voice took on an urgent timbre. "This isn't just a building. It's a symbol to millions around the world about their belief system, and that's particularly true here in London where people see it every day and where we've suffered the nightly bombings. Whether the building survives or succumbs to the shelling will affect the morale of both sides of this war enormously, which will in turn affect the eventual outcome."

His voice took on an even more grim tone. "Losing St. Paul's might shorten the war, but we would not like the result. Churchill knows that and that this is tonight's Nazi target because all their incendiaries and bombs fell within a square mile of here.

"He called to let me know that the cathedral must be saved at all costs, and that he would send whatever aid was necessary for that purpose. The fire department was so instructed, which is why they've concentrated on dousing the flames surrounding the church."

Paul listened attentively as he huffed and puffed his way up the stairs, wondering how the dean could do it so easily while talking. All that Paul could think to say was, "I understand, sir."

"We're almost to the top, which is three hundred and sixty-five feet above ground level," Matthews went on. "I'll show you how precarious our position is and what must be done, and by the way, we have another volunteer team led by my wife below the cathedral. They're preparing refreshments for the volunteers. Down there is where the crypt is for Admiral Nelson, the Duke of Wellington, and Sir Christopher Wren. If you don't know, Sir Christopher was the architect for this rendition of our church."

They emerged onto a landing. Paul gaped in amazement as the dean shined a torch at various beams built into a framework immediately under the vault.

"This is a ready-made furnace," Matthews breathed, staring about as he moved his light across the structure. "People think St. Paul's dome is made of stone, but it's not. Rather, it's a lead shell resting on an intricate wooden lattice that Sir Christopher designed. Lead itself has a low melting point at which it becomes flammable and releases noxious gas. That's another danger we face. And these timbers have been here since the church was erected two hundred and thirty years ago. That should tell you that they are very dry and if ignited in flame..." He shook his head to let Paul deduce the conclusion, and then added, "And below are many items to fuel a flame.

"When the raid first started, we got hit almost immediately with thousands of incendiaries. They were bouncing off our roofs onto the ground, and some penetrated through the lead onto the timbers in the lattice and ignited. Our chaps were out there climbing around on the beams, in the dark, to put them out." He paused and wiped his eyes. "Extraordinary, really."

The two stood in silence, taking in the courage already demonstrated and the enormity of what still faced them. "We must stop every incendiary that hits our dome and our other roofs or that penetrate and fall below," Matthews said. "So far, we've been successful, but we're running out of water and our team is getting tired, so having you come in is a big help. Maybe we can put our chaps on a rest-rotation schedule. Do you have any questions so far?"

"I'm overwhelmed with what your people have already done. I'll do my best to hold up my end."

Another figure approached them through the shadows. Matthews introduced him. "This is Mark. He leads the team in this section. He'll show you to your post." The dean then explained to Mark how Paul had come to be there. "And now, I must go on about my errands."

After Matthews left, Mark told Paul, "It's good of you to come. Let me describe what you're looking for. Fire, obviously, but the incendiaries are small, round projectiles, tubes really, with fins on one end and a small, flat explosive device on the other to bore a hole in a roof or whatever it hits and light the magnesium powder that's inside. It's maybe two inches wide and eighteen inches long, and when it hits, it makes a popping noise. The magnesium ignites and spreads immediately, setting everything around it on fire."

Paul listened almost in a daze. He was tired himself from spending the day with Ryan, driving her home, and then trekking across London through smoke and fire. But the danger was unfathomable. The idea that the enemy was so close, right overhead, and intent on killing him, Mark, the dean, everyone within the cathedral, those in proximity, and, in fact, anyone and everyone within the City of London was beyond comprehension, which made this task an immeasurable challenge.

When he had finished explaining, Mark asked, "Do you have any questions?"

Almost numbly, Paul shook his head.

"Then I'll show you where your station is and what to do in case of a strike."

Sitting in the dark, Paul listened to the distant, continuing roar of German aircraft and the far-off thud and concussion of high-explosive munitions. He wondered absently how many casualties would occur that night, how many children orphaned, and how many mothers and fathers left childless.

He also wondered about how St. Paul's had been spared amidst the destruction he had witnessed all around it. Then the thought occurred that perhaps, if the first fires in or near the church had been quickly extinguished and the *Luftwaffe* used the incendiaries as location beacons, then as the fires raged in other places but the area around the cathedral became dark by comparison, the bomber pilots might have been fooled into releasing their bombs away from the church. Apparently, no one had queried the German chain of command about the dark area amidst the orange and yellow blaze.

As he mulled the thought, Paul became aware of a higher pitch within the cacophony of the overhead drone of engines. The errant sound grew louder and deeper and Paul knew what it must be—an aircraft approaching the church, possibly at a lower altitude. And then he heard the engine coughing and sputtering. It passed overhead, and he heard another sound, one that Mark had described to him, that of heavy raindrops falling on the metal roof. He knew what they must be: incendiaries.

He looked about wildly. The sound disappeared as quickly as it had come, and then was followed by another, a clattering noise as incendiaries landed on and rolled from the roof and then made a plopping noise as they fell to the ground. And in the distance, Paul heard another explosion, this one longer, louder, perhaps closer, but it was followed by additional explosions with similar qualities. Then they fell silent, and once again, the monotonous hum of the bombers resumed with the thud and boom of farther-off explosions. *Did the bomber that flew overhead go down?*

The thought lifted his spirit, but his hope was immediately

dashed by a peculiar smell and then a hiss barely heard above the din. Scanning his section of the dome anxiously with his torch, he saw a dark spot appear on the lead shell. It deepened and grew larger, and then turned into a bright, sparkling light casting tiny shards of flame in all directions. Within seconds, the incendiary had burned through and dropped to one of the smaller crossbeams to Paul's front, where it continued to burn.

A small flame ignited.

Jumping to his feet, Paul felt his way along the outer rim of the frame supporting the leaden dome. With his other hand, he shined his light across the network of beams, looking for the one that would provide him adequate support to climb out to the incendiary. Meanwhile his mind worked to determine how he would put it out.

The tube had landed on a smaller horizontal beam on the opposite side of a vertical timber. To get to it, Paul would have to mount onto a main beam several feet below the one where the device now blazed, raise himself over two more intermediate supports, and pull himself out to the upright, reach around it, and somehow manage to douse the incendiary, all while it spewed hot magnesium powder toward him.

Keeping an eye on the live flame that had started to grow, he shoved the end of the torch into his mouth and mounted the first beam. Below him, he saw nothing but darkness.

Mark yelled from behind him, "Take this," and stretched out over the cavity to hand Paul a large piece of canvas. "We're out of water, but in any case, we couldn't get it up to you. You'll have to use the canvas as a shield to get close, and then cover the tube and pound it out with your hand. Double the cloth over to make it as thick as you can."

His heart pounding, Paul took the canvas, shoved it in his belt, and continued across the beam. He reached the first upright and climbed. With his breath coming in short gasps, and heaving for oxygen amidst still prevalent smoke, he pulled himself to the next horizontal beam. Steadying himself, he started for the third.

And slipped.

Throwing himself fully at the vertical support, he caught it, pushed upright, and steadied himself.

He glanced at the flame. It grew higher with each passing second, but fortunately, the magnesium had all but burnt out.

One more time, he reached for the next horizontal beam. His muscles screamed in protest and the filthy air made him lightheaded, but amidst much groaning and panting, he pulled himself firmly onto the third beam and edged toward the obstructing upright. It was thick, perhaps eight inches square, and had itself begun to smoke on the side away from him for being near the growing flame.

Not daring to look down, Paul pulled the canvas from his belt and reached forward to feel the side of the upright closest to him. It was warm, but just barely. Reaching around to the other side, he tapped it gingerly. It was not yet too hot to touch.

He pulled himself against the upright, and leaning against it for support, he reached around it. In doing so, he had to twist his head to the side to keep his torch out of the way but miscalculated and knocked it against another timber. The action wrenched the torch from his mouth and sent it clattering against the framework into the void, finally coming to rest far below on the attic floor.

Paul leaned his head against the upright and took a moment to steady himself. The flames had grown into dancing demons and threatened higher crossbeams. The upright was too large for Paul to reach around to throw the canvas over the fire with any certainty of success. Instead, he wrapped the cloth around his right arm and, holding on with his left hand, leaned out and around the upright, extended as far as he could, and directly pounded the flames.

The fingers on his left hand shook as they supported most of his weight, and Paul wondered for a fraction of a second if he would have the strength to pull himself back. At first, the fire showed no effect from his effort, but as he continued to beat it, the fire became smaller, and smaller, and finally flickered out.

For a time, Paul hung where he was, the pain in his left arm and fingers excruciating. When he tried to pull himself back, he found that fatigue and smoke inhalation had overtaken him. He was too weak. His fingers started slipping.

23

December 30, 1940
Stony Stratford, England

Early the next morning, Claire paced her living room floor while Timmy played. Minutes ticked by and she glanced out the front window again for the umpteenth time. The phone rang, and she raced to pick it up and greet her caller.

Her shoulders slumped as she heard Ryan's voice. "No. Nothing yet," she said. "I'm sure Paul's all right. We'll just have to wait. I'll call if I hear anything."

"You won't be able to," Ryan said. "I'm on duty. Access to outside phones is limited. I'll call you as I can."

Claire recognized the worry in her voice. "That will be fine. I'm sure Paul will try to reach you at first chance as well."

"Thank you. I must get back to work."

As Claire hung up, a taxi turned into the driveway and proceeded over crunching gravel to the garden path and parked. She stepped to the window and watched as the rear door opened and Paul appeared. When he straightened, his clothes were rumpled, he appeared haggard and dirty, his hair was disheveled, and his eyes were sunken. She hurried to the door, opened it, and ran down to meet him, seeing then that his left hand and right arm were bandaged.

"What's happened?" she cried. "Did you get caught in the raid?" She started to hug him but held back as he appeared to be in pain.

Paul nodded and smiled as best he could while limping stiffly. "I'm afraid I did. It was silly, really. My own fault. I'll tell you all about it."

"I'm due at work in thirty minutes. Ryan's been calling. I telephoned her when you didn't come in last night, and she told me you'd left at dusk. We've been beside ourselves. I'll instruct the nanny to let Ryan know you're home safe the next time she calls. Meanwhile, you should get some rest."

At that moment, Timmy appeared at Paul's knees and reached up, pleading to be held. Paul bent down and scooped him in his left arm, being careful not to scrape his bandages. Seeing them, Timmy pointed and turned his face to stare into Paul's eyes curiously.

"You're hurt," Claire said, alarmed.

"Nothing serious. I scraped my hand and burned my arm. I'll tell you the whole story later when you come home."

That evening, Claire's eyes widened in astonishment as Paul told her of driving the journalists, Bill and Marguerite; of their trek on foot through London after the car blew up; the goings-on at the Savoy; and the taxi ride to St. Paul's. "I met some very dedicated people last night. They made me proud to be British." He told her of the parishioners who gathered inside the church, and of the dean and the architects working furiously to save the cathedral, and the priority Churchill had given it.

"But how did you get hurt?" Claire asked.

Paul heaved a sigh. "I'd really rather not say."

"But you will, or I'll march right down to St. Paul's and ask Dean Matthews for myself. I'd rather hear the story from you."

Paul smiled ruefully. "You are, after all, Claire Littlefield, aren't you?"

He told her, and when he came to the part of having lost strength sufficient to save himself, he confessed, "I thought I was done for."

"What happened?"

"There was this fellow, Mark, one of the architects. He oversaw my section. When I was up in the rafters and had put out the fire, that's when I became so weak. And then I heard Mark. He had climbed up behind me. He grabbed my wrist and said, 'I've got you,' and pulled me to safety. We rested there for a time, and then he helped me climb down. I couldn't have survived the fall. He saved my life."

Claire stared at him and then went to sit beside him. "Paul, Paul, Paul," she said. "You're always crediting everyone else and never seeing the good that you do. Yes, he saved your life. And you helped save the cathedral and the city. I couldn't be prouder."

She wrapped an arm around his back and leaned her head on his shoulder. "I know we don't get to have you here much longer. When do you leave?"

"On January 2. When is that? Three days?"

Claire bit her lower lip and nodded. "That includes New Year's Eve. Let's make the best of it, shall we?"

24

December 31, 1940
Sark Island, English Channel Isles

"It's New Year's, darling," Stephen Littlefield said, "and you look ravishing."

"Oh, rubbish," Marian retorted. "Don't flatter when it's obvious that's all it is." She had dressed up, and so had Stephen, despite that they had no place to go, but now she stood in front of her bedroom mirror and observed critically the skeletal figure meeting her eye. The dress she wore hung on her, barely concealing her protruding collarbone and knobby elbows. "This is really pathetic. How much more can the Germans cut our rations? It's comical when you think about how much emphasis they put on 'maintaining goodwill.'"

Stephen crossed the floor and stood behind her. "Beauty is in the eyes of the beholder, my dear, and you're as beautiful now as the day we met."

Marian tossed him a skeptical glance and chuckled. "I think you mean that as a compliment, but I'm not sure it worked. If I looked like this the day we met, then I'd seriously question your judgment in having anything to do with me. Now, what shall we do this evening to celebrate a new year of occupation?"

"We could build a fire. We still have a doorframe or two that are yet untouched. They won't burn long, but perhaps long enough to warm up the parlor. Or, if you prefer, we can light them in the kitchen stove and hopefully boil enough water so that you can take a semblance of a bath."

Marian turned, laughing, and caressed his face. "Are you saying I need one?"

"Hardly, my dear. I still value my head. But I remember from times past that you enjoyed them so. I couldn't get to the store to buy you a Christmas gift, so I thought this might make up for my negligence."

Marian turned full around and embraced her husband. "Oh, Stephen," she whispered, "I do love you so. How can you be lighthearted in such times?"

"Only with practice, my dear, I assure you. Only with practice. But you'll soon tire of me if all I bring is gloom to add to what the *Wehrmacht* so ably spreads about."

She pulled back and stared into his eyes. "You know, for a man who was born American in New Jersey, you sound an awful lot like a thoroughbred Englishman."

Stephen let out an exaggerated sigh and arched his brows. "Well, I've been around almost no one but Englishmen going on twenty-two years. But I can turn on American if you prefer."

Marian laughed and then gazed into Stephen's eyes sadly. "Let's just say what's on our minds. Our children." She let go of Stephen and buried her face in her hands. "Will we ever see them again? We were so happy together, and now they're scattered to the wind. We've heard nothing from Lance. Paul seems to have disappeared from the earth, and Jeremy tells us nothing about what he is doing. Claire does her best to bring us news, but even she is short on detail, so I get the impression that they're all involved in things they can't mention. I'm sure they've been able to decipher a hint of how conditions are here and neither want to worry us further nor say something that could be valuable to the Germans, damn their censors to hell. And now I'm rambling."

Her body shook as she fought back tears, so she leaned into Stephen, who wrapped her in his arms. He held her, rocking gently while her sobs subsided. After a time, she wiped her eyes and stood back again.

"I'll be fine," she said. "Our sons and Claire need for us to be here when they return home after all this, this wickedness, is done. And our people look to us for strength. As much as I don't feel up to it, that's the way it is."

Stephen gazed down at her, and then turned and offered his arm. "Milady, our feast is served in the dining room. With some imagination it can be whatever we want it to be in whatever sumptuous portions."

"To what shall we toast with our empty wine glasses?"

"Why to the new year, in the blessed hope that it is better than the last one."

"And when we're done pretending that our stale slices of bread are French éclairs, we can play bridge."

Colditz, Germany

Lance shivered in the cold, but he recognized the quiet that often heralded the fall of heavy snow. For most POWs, escaping ahead of a snowstorm might seem like folly, but Lance trusted his fluency in German and French and in his proven ability to adapt to changing situations and meld into crowds. Tonight, he would also count on the mental numbness that descends on people contending with freezing weather and icy surfaces.

He had been warned that his accent might give him away. "Nearly every village in Germany has its own dialect," he had argued. "With the *Wehrmacht* drawing recruits from across the country and reassigning to places regardless of origin, an accent that's slightly off won't automatically trigger anything. It's the rest of an escaped prisoner's behavior that can draw attention."

In the week since arriving at Colditz, he had become an accomplished thief, stealing any and every part of German army uniforms that came unguarded within inches of his deft hands. Other prisoners had donated bits and pieces of German regalia, and a Pole had adjusted the outfit to him with needle and thread. He had thus acquired a full set that fit him at least as well as those of most German soldiers, complete with lieutenant's insignia and a great overcoat. He then set about acquiring warm civilian clothes, snitching them from workers allowed in the camp for work and pleading for items of clothing from other prisoners who harbored visions of escape but knew they would never make the attempt. One of the noncoms who had worked leather in pre-war life fashioned civilian shoes out of bits and pieces of several pairs of boots so worn that they had become useless in their original forms.

Soon after his arrival, Lance sneaked into the Polish section, and there, with Miloš' help, he sought out a prisoner known to be an excellent forger and bartered for a set of travel documents. His side of the deal was that he would take Miloš with him.

"My plan is simple," he told Pat in the lieutenant's capacity as escape officer. "I've watched the guards when they leave at the end of their shifts. Instead of walking all the way out along the main entrance, some turn right through a small gate at a right angle to the road at the mouth of the arched tunnel we came through on arrival. I intend to walk out that way." He had not been able to acquire good intelligence on what lay beyond that point, but he had to believe that a path into the village must intersect somewhere down there. "There must be another security checkpoint that we can't see from our POW quarters. I just have to get a way down to the main ramp leading out from the castle."

Pat had not been warm to Lance's plan at first. "You're going out in the dead of winter, you have no way of getting down to that walkway, and if you succeed in doing that, you won't know the password, which is a number that changes daily."

"I'm going in the dead of winter precisely because no one will expect that. Look, the Germans take roll call by counting us, not by name. They're usually half-asleep when they do it. We'll have one of our men play like a rabbit after he's counted, by ducking low and running to the end of his line to be counted again. If we do that, the guards will take longer to see that I'm gone."

"Good idea, but what about the password."

Lance told him his plan.

"Hmm, that might work," the SBO said, arching his brows. "I guess it's worth a try, but if you're caught, you'll spend time in the cooler. It could be worse than that since you'll be wearing a German uniform."

"I've done cooler time before," Lance replied with a gritty grin. "I survived."

"But you still don't have a way down to that walkway. I won't approve until you show me how you can do it with relative safety."

"But I do have a way, sir. I told you about the grate I found against the back wall under the stage in the theater."

"Yes, so?"

"I managed to nip a hacksaw blade and saw off the bolts. Inside was a horizontal ventilation duct. It was tight, but I crawled through it about twenty feet to another vent that opened in the ceiling of a room below the theater." Lance's eyes glistened. "Sir, that room is unused. It overlooks the arch over the road that the guards use to walk out. It has an exit onto a stairway leading to a path that connects with that road." His excitement now infected Pat. "From the window in that room, I can see the path. It has a chain across it that says

'*Verboten.*' We can walk right out onto the road, big as you please, and take that side exit the guards use."

"We?"

Lance stared anxiously. "Me and Miloš. That's the deal I made to get the documents done up quickly."

Pat glanced askance at Lance. "I like the Poles, but they can be shy on attention to detail in executing their plans. One of theirs had an intricate plan. It incorporated a route that went out windows, over rooflines, had stooges in place with signals to coordinate their movement... It worked marvelously until the final stage of getting out of the castle. His rope was too short. I believe that was Miloš."

Lance sighed. "I know, but I'm not going to discount Miloš or the lot of them because of an oversight that any of us might have made. Just how would we have measured how long the rope should have been?

"Look, we've rehearsed for hours on how to interact with the guard at the gate. I'll do the talking. His German is broken. Mine's fluent."

Pat agreed reluctantly. "And from there you'll go to the train station?"

"We'll change into our civilian clothes and split up. He'll look for a labor group traveling east that he can hide in, and I —" Lance grinned. "I'll be going to wedded bliss." He pulled out a photo and showed it to Pat. "My fiancée." He laughed. "I'm headed to Switzerland to get married. That's my story."

"Who is she?"

"I haven't a clue, but I'm sure we'll be very happy."

The two laughed together, and Pat went through several more points with Lance. "Shouldn't you be carrying a suitcase? Most people traveling on trains in Europe do. Without one, you'll stand out, particularly traveling alone."

"I'll snatch one."

At last, Pat said, "All right. I'll approve your plan, but on one condition. Someone must go with you into the theater and replace those bolts in the grate. And you have to lock that unused room after you exit. We might be able to use that route again, and I don't want to expose it to the Germans."

"I've already thought of that. If we're recaptured, we'll say we went out with another shipment of old mattresses. That's been tried before, and the escaper was caught, so they already know about it."

When Lance had completely briefed Pat on his plan three days ago, the escape officer's enthusiasm had almost matched his own. "Good luck, old boy. When will you go out?"

"New Year's Eve, sir. The celebration party will be the diversion."

Pat had raised an eyebrow. "It's good that Red Cross packages finally started arriving, and on Boxing Day, no less. We can reciprocate some of the Poles' hospitality, however meager, and you'll have rations to get through the first day or so."

"And the *kommandant* approved an extra half-hour before lights out, so no one will be looking for us during that time. With any luck, by the first roll call, we'll be long gone."

Getting through the ventilation duct had been more difficult than expected. Before when Lance had crawled through it, he had stripped down to his skivvies, but he had only taken a single tool with him. This time, he not only had to push his bundle of clothes ahead of him, including the uniform and his civilian garb, but he had to help Miloš coming behind him. The exertion was such that, despite the icy air, sweat ran in rivulets over his forehead, stinging his eyes and soaking the rest of his body.

After much grunting and pushing, he had emerged into the abandoned room, dropped his bundle, lowered himself to the floor, and stood on a chair to help his companion. Then, quietly, they had stood a few inches back from the window and peered outside. Below them, the cobbled driveway led to the main entrance.

Two guards passed below. They walked a few yards past the bottom of the arch by the side of the road, turned sharply, and descended out of sight on a set of stairs.

Lance and the Pole nudged each other and grinned.

By the ambient light streaming through the window, they wiped from their faces the streams of mud formed by their own sweat mixed with dust. Within minutes, they had put the uniforms on over their civilian clothes, and while the Pole had picked the lock, Lance fixed the grate back in place with glue. He hoped it held in the freezing temperatures.

A cold breeze blew through the room. Miloš whispered gleefully, "It's open."

Lance hurried over. Peeking out and finding his way clear, he stepped onto the landing.

Snow fell in flurries and wind whipped his ears. Behind him, Miloš re-locked the door. Then together, they crept into underbrush around the stairs. Stooping, they sat and listened.

The wind abated a bit, and for a time, all they heard was the soft whisper of falling snow onto the blanket that had already accumulated. Then, they heard the crunch, crunch, crunch of footsteps breaking through the crystalline white, and two more guards ambled along the road toward the main gate.

Lance and Miloš waited until the sentries were sufficiently

far away before hurrying to the corner of the building where they could check the back trail. It was clear.

Quickly, they stepped out onto the road. They waited a few moments to allow more distance between themselves and the guards, and then started a meandering walk roughly seventy paces behind them.

The sentries continued past the side path. Then they stopped and turned. Lance thought they must have heard his and Miloš' own crunch in the snow, but instead, one reached into a pocket and pulled out a pack of cigarettes. He turned his body to shelter his hands from the wind and struck a match. As he did, he caught sight of Lance and Miloš.

"Happy New Year!" he called in German as he lit his match. It burst into flame, and he raised it to his cigarette.

Lance's breath caught. They could not stop. "Happy New Year!" he called back as he and Miloš continued their slow trek through the snow.

"Do you want to walk with us?" the other one called. "We're going into town to celebrate. Have a party."

"Thank you, no. I just finished a double shift because Fritz was sick. I want to get into bed. Anyway, we're taking the path down the hill."

"You have a place to stay in town? Lucky you."

"It's my girlfriend's place. She's working tonight, so I'll get some sleep before she gets home in the morning."

"Ha ha! You *are* lucky. What about your friend?"

"His girlfriend won't arrive until the day after." Lance guffawed. "We'll make him sit outside while Helga and I get reacquainted, if you know what I mean." He delivered his best lascivious laugh.

By this time, Lance and Miloš had neared the path at the turnoff and were within twenty paces of the two sentries. "Happy New Year again," Lance called.

Suddenly, one of the guards stiffened and nudged the other. They both snapped to attention and saluted. "Sorry, sir," one called, "we couldn't see that you are an officer."

Lance returned their salute. "Not a problem, my fine soldiers. It's a cold night, we should be celebrating, and instead we're trudging through snow far from home. Enjoy your evening."

When Lance and Miloš had descended the short run of stairs onto the lower path, they both breathed a sigh of relief, but neither spoke. The path sloped downhill, took a ninety-degree turn to the right, and continued down. A hundred feet out, they saw a lone sentry moving about outside the guard hut, pulling his coat around him, kicking his toes against the side of the hut to keep circulation going to his feet, and otherwise trying to ward off the freezing cold.

Lance's heart beat faster as they approached, and he imagined that Miloš' must be as well. The guard looked up and brought his rifle to port arms to challenge them.

Lance and Miloš continued their leisurely pace, and Lance said a few things in German in a conversational tone. The Pole grunted and threw his head back to laugh.

"Password?" the sentry challenged.

Lance swung his head forward, fixed his eyes on the guard, but continued walking without responding.

"The password," the soldier said again, an insistent tone in his voice.

Lance turned to Miloš and said something in a low voice before looking up sharply at the guard.

"The password," the soldier repeated, this time sternly, bringing his rifle forward.

Lance did not hesitate. He walked brusquely up to the guard. "You dare threaten me?" he growled menacingly. "Who is your commander, and since when do you not salute officers." He strode forward and thrust his face to within inches of the hapless guard's chin. "What is your name, unit, and service number? Consider yourself on report. I shall take the matter straight to *Leutnant* Eggers."

While the sentry stuttered through giving his identity information, Lance retrieved a pen and paper from his coat pocket. "Do you even know what the challenge number is?" he demanded. "Well, let's hear it."

His eyes wide with consternation, the soldier obliged.

"That's correct," Lance barked. "It's good that this weather has not frozen your brain."

He stepped back, took a breath, and regarded the soldier with a more compassionate expression. "Perhaps I've been harsh. It's New Year's Eve and you're stuck out here while everyone is celebrating." He looked into the man's eyes. "Have you learned your lesson?"

The man nodded rapidly. "Yes, sir."

"Good, then." Lance wadded up the notepaper, threw it into the snow, and clapped the soldier on the shoulder. "In that case, let's call it a night, shall we?"

"Thank you, sir."

As Lance and Miloš resumed their escape toward town, they heard more footsteps crunching in the snow behind them.

26

January 2, 1941
London, England

Prime Minister Churchill pulled the cigar from his mouth and exhaled a ring of smoke. "Gentlemen, I've read your analysis. I see no flaw in it. What you've outlined, among other things, is that the pompous schizophrenic, *Il Duce* Benito Mussolini, can't decide if he'd rather restore the Roman Empire or emulate Germany's mustachioed curmudgeon. He has neither the resources, the military organization, nor the skills to meet his ambition.

"The Greeks established a defensive line in Albania last month, from Vlorë to Pogradec, and it's holding. Mussolini can't improve his situation without German help, and in effect, he's turned his country into Hitler's dependent client-state. So, his war is even more pointless. He's angry with me because I've pressured Greece to allow Britain military airfields and cut exports to Italy, but our air forces are aimed at threatening German control of Romania's oilfields, not Italian forces. So, his real reason to be in this war is his ego. Benito wants to be another Adolf."

He stared at the map on the wall behind his desk. Stephenson, Donovan, and Paul sat in their familiar places in front of it, remaining quiet while Churchill ruminated.

He passed his hand across the map over Hungary, Romania, Bulgaria, and Yugoslavia. "Since these 'neutral' countries are governed by pro-fascist regimes, Hitler thinks he'll negotiate them into his so-called Tripartite Pact with Italy and Japan. That's how he expects to protect his access to Romania's oilfields, give him control of southeastern Europe, and let him dominate the Mediterranean via Yugoslavia and Greece—whenever Mussolini manages to finish off the latter country, which he never will. So, I agree that we should pin Germany down on the southeastern flank in Yugoslavia and Greece. The Finns in the northwest won't be as much of a problem for Stalin as Hitler thinks, so we can let that flank take care of itself.

"Once the invasion starts, which Comrade Joseph still discounts, the Soviet factories will go into full-steam war production, and I should think that the Russian people will man the battlements in defense of Mother Russia just as they did when Napoleon made his unwelcome entry."

He took another puff on his cigar. "If Hitler dares to attack Moscow, then he should do it in the winter snows, just as Napoleon did, and his army should meet the same end." He turned and faced his small audience with his best pugnacious expression. "Our task is to bring that about."

Paul listened in shock. He wondered if the enormous implications of the prime minister's last statement had registered on Stephenson and Donovan the way it had on him. With Britain's ground forces already reeling from defeats and casualties across North Africa, the RAF still engaged in fending off nightly bombing raids the length and breadth of the homeland, and the Royal Navy defending supply lines throughout the Atlantic and the Mediterranean, an objective of causing such an outcome seemed far beyond possibility.

For the next forty-five minutes, Paul observed, intermittently astounded, as the prime minister, Stephenson, and Donovan developed the outlines of a plan. "We need to provoke Germany to come to Italy's aid in Greece," Churchill said. "That will divert a massive number of troops, and it won't be a quick skirmish.

"I can order an expeditionary force into Greece to support its fight in Albania. Bulgaria made noises about entering the war in that area on its western border in support of Italy but held back because Turkey threatened to attack if they did so. If we enter here on Greece's east coast"—he indicated a small seaside village on the map—"that should incite Germany to ward off Turkey and invade Greece from the east. The Greeks will be forced to divert forces from their defensive line in Albania, and Germany can then descend into the country from the northwest."

"You're suggesting giving up Greece," Stephenson interjected gravely.

"Only temporarily. I'm talking about keeping Hitler's troops occupied so that they miss their launch date for Barbarossa, and if we can bog them down in the Balkans, so much the better. Every day that we delay him gets us closer to winter. Then the arctic blast of Russian blizzards becomes our weapon."

Stephenson took on a cautious look. "I understand your logic, but that's a compromise with the devil. Thousands of civilians will die."

Paul studied his face, looking for any indication of emotion. He observed none, and then he watched the prime minister's eyes fix on Stephenson's.

"Tens of thousands will die regardless of what we do," Churchill retorted, his face flushed with passion. "We limit what we can, but assigning such concern the highest priority is a losing proposition, and defeat plunges the world into slavery with far more innocent deaths. Painful ones." His eyes flashed. He bolted to his feet and shook his cigar across the desk. "Mr. Roosevelt's ideas about lend-lease would be very helpful about now, but Congress is dead set against them, and the American public has no stomach to enter the war.

"We can count on this: if we do nothing, then on May 15, the German *Wehrmacht* will invade the Soviet Union on three fronts using its *blitzkrieg* tactics. If it succeeds, Hitler will attack us with the combined military and industrial might of Germany and the countries he's conquered, including the Soviet Union. He'll romp over Britain, and then the United States becomes his main target."

He paused for breath, his eyes boring into Stephenson's. "So yes, our plan is the compromise you so artfully described, but if Hitler invaded hell, I should make at least a friendly reference to the devil in the House of Commons."

To Paul, the air seemed suddenly thick, oppressive. For moments, no one spoke.

Donovan had sat quietly listening and studying the map during the discussion and Churchill's outburst. "That won't be enough," he broke in, his voice as solemn as Paul had ever heard it. "The forces Hitler would use in Greece are not enough to have the effect we need on his invasion into Russia. We need his army bogged down in Yugoslavia too, and that's one of his potential fascist allies."

Churchill leaned back in his chair, puffing his cigar, then swiveled and scrutinized the map again. Stephenson propped an elbow on the desk and squinted as he also studied it.

"There's a man in Yugoslavia, a communist," Churchill said. "Our MI-6 has been reporting on him. His name is Josip Broz, and he goes by Tito. He spent time in Moscow, but the Party didn't treat him well, so he's disenchanted with them. He hates fascists, including the regime in Belgrade, and he leads the largest guerrilla fighting force in the country by far." He chomped on his cigar as he thought. "He could topple that government and effectively fight the Germans. We need him on our side."

As the discussion neared its end, Churchill asked Donovan, "You must succeed with the ruse detailed in our plan. When will you go?"

"Next month," the general replied. "Winter will be at its coldest, and it's bitter in northern Greece and the Baltics. I'll be able to move around those countries without much interference." He chuckled. "Tricking the press isn't difficult. They already think they outwit me. They'll outsmart themselves and help us in the process." Then he gestured toward Paul. "Maybe I could use our good Captain Littlefield here to assist? We can put him on an American passport to lessen his odds of being captured."

Churchill regarded Paul with a sideways glance. "That would give him a chance to get out of the office, so to speak, and see how things work."

Startled, Paul sat up straight and probed the faces of the other three men. He sensed a familiarity between them that he did not yet enjoy, and that he was being offered an opportunity to enter their small circle of history makers.

"What do you say, Intrepid?" Churchill asked Stephenson.

"It's a thought," came the reply. "Various people can cover for Paul while he's out. If our plan works, a young person should witness it. He can tell the story while we're haggling with St. Pete about the toll at Heaven's gate." He turned to Paul with a glint in his eyes. "You'll have to keep your lethal pills in close reach."

On impulse, Paul reached up to the pocket on his chest and felt the small box containing the deadly capsules.

Donovan eyed him gravely. "This is an intricate project, and I haven't discussed Paul's potential involvement with him yet. Let's let the idea simmer. I'd like to explore it." He looked at Paul. "If you're open to it."

Feeling a mixed twinge of excitement and dread, Paul nodded. "Of course, sir. I've said I'd do whatever is needed to win the war."

Stephenson regarded him through squinted eyes. "That might require more than you'd imagine," he said quietly.

"Then we'll explore the option," Donovan said. He stood abruptly, walked to one of the maps on the side walls, and peered at it closely. "Prime Minister, are you certain that Hitler will invade?"

"Nothing is certain," Churchill replied. "But you read and analyzed Directive 21."

"I did," Donovan replied. "My firm wish is that he would not execute Barbarossa."

"He always wanted to subjugate the Bolsheviks. He thought Germany and Britain together would go after them. His attacks on us and his plan to invade the Soviets came out of revenge because we upset his grand strategy, and we didn't surrender. I don't think he will cancel Barbarossa. He hates the Bolsheviks more than he wants revenge against us."

Churchill shoved away from his desk and took to his feet again. "He will invade. Of that, I am positive. We can't stop him, but we must limit the field and set the timetable for his launch. That's within our power."

27

January 5, 1941
Rockefeller Center, Manhattan, New York

Stephenson stared through his spectacles at Paul. "What bothers you about what we're doing? You're here to observe and remember, not analyze, recommend, or do anything that you are not ordered to do. As I told you at the outset, we recruited you to be our institutional memory in case of my demise. That's all. Memories *are*. They don't *act*."

"My involvement in Greece next month broadens the job description a bit, I think." Paul dropped his eyes while fighting off anger that he was sure could be detected in his flushed cheeks and the redness up the back of his neck. He had tried to stifle it in his tone of voice but was not sure he had succeeded. "We're proposing to shape American public opinion, sir," he said with some vehemence, adding, "and their president is currently our country's only ally. I'm still coming to terms with the idea that we're running British intelligence from downtown New York City with his sole knowledge and consent among American officialdom."

"I'm proposing nothing. I'm executing precisely that action, and I make no apologies," Stephenson replied. "This is war, and we won't win without the industrial might of America. We can't wait for US public sentiment to catch up to reality. You know how close Hitler's fingers are to atomic weapons. If we lose, you'll go home to goose-stepping guards at the gates of Buckingham Palace and black swastikas hanging outside of Parliament. We won't be far behind on this side of the pond either. Our world will descend to its darkest place in history."

Stephenson scrutinized Paul's face for a hint that his words had an effect, and then continued matter-of-factly. "The notion that Britain is alone in this war is inaccurate, irrespective of the president or the American people. You forget that Britain is still an empire. Whether its power emerges intact when this war is over remains to be seen, but I'll remind you that degrees of independence were granted to various countries in the late 1800s, including the Dominions of Australia, Canada, India, the Irish Free State, New Zealand, and South Africa, which are bound to each other and Great Britain for defense and other purposes by the treaty that created the British Commonwealth in 1926. Those countries sent pilots, troops, and materiel to fight for us." He chuckled. "I was part of Canada's contribution." Then he grew serious again. "But their combined resources and manufacturing capacity don't match those of the US, and we need ships, tanks, fighter aircraft, bombers, bullets, food..."

He continued evenly, "When you come up with a better plan for gaining the support we need before the British people starve or our defense forces run out of bullets, I'll support it with all vigor. Until then, we'll do things my way."

Frustrated but uncertain of where the moral high ground lay, Paul retreated from the discussion without further comment. "What are my instructions?" he asked simply.

A hint of a smile lifted the edges of Stephenson's lips. "You were a good choice, Captain. By questioning me, you increase your understanding of our dilemmas."

"Mr. Churchill placed me in your charge," Paul replied, his expression indicating that despite acceding to higher authority, he had not conceded the point. "My duty is to follow your orders."

"Yes, well, there is that," Stephenson said with a low laugh while viewing Paul over the tops of his spectacles. "Maybe there's something to be said for having a mite of tyranny. Now listen to me. Obviously, you were chosen for your intellectual ability, so I won't insult you by expecting you to hear and not question.

"One of the difficulties of war is that moral absolutes become indistinct. 'Thou shalt not steal or kill' are two of them. When the Germans bomb us, they rob our people of life, the means of production, shelter, food, water. We bomb them with the intent to stop them, depriving their people of the same basics. Their intent is to conquer; ours is to prevent. Do we have the moral high ground? The results are the same: civilians die.

"People look to their leaders to protect them, and ours accept that responsibility. Where should they draw the lines of ethical behavior in war when we face an enemy that recognizes no rules or the sanctity of human life?

"Mr. Roosevelt knows the danger Hitler imposes. That's acknowledged in his allowing us to operate here in his country, but he has a problem. Half of his citizenry does not understand the threat to them, and he has to coax public opinion along until it's ready to join the war. He knows that to best protect America he must take the offensive overseas. The pacifist part of his populace doesn't see things that way, believing that the oceans on either side of their continent will protect them. Thus, he lies by omission in not divulging the true nature of our presence in Manhattan; not to his cabinet or staff, or even key members of Congress, though I should point out that the Ten Commandments forbid bearing false witness against one's neighbors but say nothing about lying. I take that as recognition that on occasion, a good lie is necessary.

"Our problem is that the war rages, our ordinary citizens, soldiers, and airmen are killed, our materiel is used up, and the president's effort to get US public sentiment behind the war, even just to re-supply us, is like pushing a wet noodle. Americans don't believe our plight is serious, or they think that, somehow, we'll muddle through.

"This new intelligence operation that you abhor is a catalyst to spur US entry into the war. Wild Bill Donovan will have a part to play later.

"Now if you don't mind, it's time to move on from theory to practice. We have news of a British seaman at the port selling information to the Germans regarding the positions and schedules of British convoys. Two FBI agents will take us downtown to see the evidence. We leave in five minutes. Remember that they believe this is the British passport office."

Even after three months in New York City, Paul hardly knew how to characterize it, particularly after surviving through the night of the bombing raid on St. Paul's Cathedral. This city was rumbling, loud, and clouded with exhaust fumes from streets crowded with cars. He realized that the same could be said of London in daytime despite the war, but there was a qualitative difference that at first, he had difficulty identifying. The cars in the British capital were square and boxy, while here they were rounded and muscular; but that aspect did not quite describe the essential difference beyond the massive size of this city, which, in any case, he could not see from ground level in the financial district of Manhattan.

A horn blared as he and Stephenson crossed a street, and then he put his finger on the issue. In both cities, traffic moved, but in London, they proceeded in well-ordered straight lines while here cars seemed to maneuver all over the thoroughfares depending on where they could continue forward most rapidly. In both cities, pedestrians packed together on sidewalks and dispersed at intersections to venture in fits and starts to navigate to the opposite side of a street.

Stephenson had already introduced him at his swank business club, The Stork, where the elegance of high-class living was pronounced compared to the noisome tumult on the streets. In the cool, refined atmosphere of cozy camaraderie, Paul had become aware that his mentor was not a newcomer to either the city or the back rooms of America's business elite. In fact, he learned, the Rockefeller family allowed Stephenson and his British Security Coordination organization to occupy two stories in their tower essentially rent-free. *They wouldn't do that for a Johnny-come-lately.*

"Here we are," Stephenson said, stepping toward a dark sedan that swung to the curb and stopped in front of them. He opened the back door and slid to the other side. Paul clambered in beside him.

"Where are we going?" Stephenson called out.

The front-seat passenger turned. He was a stern-looking man with a thin face, but his shoulders were broad. He removed a cigarette from his mouth. "Good to see you, Bill. Who's your sidekick?"

"This is Paul Littlefield. He's on loan from the British army, an aide, so to speak."

The man scrutinized Paul. "Why would the British passport office need a British soldier over here, and why isn't he wearing a uniform?"

"He's a captain. If you must know, we're supposed to be rounding out his training. I'm not sure how that works. I'd guess the British government would like to track any unsavory characters who might do us harm, like the one we're checking out now. I requested an aide, and this is what I got. Don't be too rough on him. He seems like a good sort."

The man searched Paul's face, and then extended his hand. "Sorry. I'm suspicious by nature. I'm Special Agent Bernardi and this is Special Agent Thompson."

The driver grunted while Paul shook Bernardi's hand.

"What do we know about our quarry?" Stephenson asked.

"Not a lot yet," Bernardi replied. "We got lucky. On a fluke, one of our special agents overheard part of a transmission while scanning radio stations. He thought he heard German, so he tuned back to the station. We keep an active presence in the ports, and the bad guy was careless. We nailed his identity in about fifteen minutes."

They arrived in an alley off a back street near the docks. "He's not here now. He doesn't know we're on to him yet, but we have him under surveillance. We already have a warrant based on our transcript of the broadcast we overheard."

After parking the car, the two special agents led the way through a back door of an apartment building, up dimly lit stairs, and to a green wooden door that already stood open. "Two of our guys are in there," Bernardi said. "They're securing evidence, dusting for fingerprints, and so on. When he comes back, we'll arrest him."

"What happens then?" Stephenson inquired.

"We'll take him to our offices and hold him. He'll be arraigned tomorrow, or at least within a few days. He won't be offered bail because he's engaged in espionage. Your people are really the ones who have a beef with him, so I imagine your embassy will be notified and request extradition. That'll take time. Several months down the line, we'll ship him back to Britain, and your guys will deal with him."

Stephenson glanced askance at Paul and then returned his attention to Bernardi. "All of that for a man who's been caught dead to rights carrying out actions that will kill British citizens. There must be a more expeditious way of dealing with the issue."

Bernardi shrugged. "That's the system. He's entitled to due process, and we'll have to prove our case in court before we turn him over to your government."

Stephenson hid his disgust and circled the room silently with Paul in tow. Bernardi handed him some papers. "This is what we've transcribed so far." He pointed to a section near the top of the first page. "This shows the ships in port, what's being loaded onto them, their departure schedules, destinations." He turned the page. "Here you can see when and where they'll join their convoys, and their expected progression across the Atlantic." He turned another page. "This shows the same information for ships already at sea."

Stemming his anger, Stephenson pointed to a photograph stapled to the top of the first page. "Is that him?"

Bernardi nodded. "We pulled his record from the ship's files."

Stephenson studied the document and thrust it at Paul. "Read this," he said, his voice marked by contained anger. "This is what we have to contend with. He's directing German U-boats to our ships with the most militarily significant cargoes. Most of them also carry food that our people are desperate for and everyday products they need to survive." He jabbed a finger at the photo. "This criminal would have our sailors killed and see British people starve to line his pockets. The authorities on both sides of the ocean will coddle him for months and use up the king's legal resources and treasure to try him, and in the end, he'll meet a hangman's noose. There should be a way to shorten the process, bring him to justice, and save the money."

While Paul scanned the papers, Stephenson continued to examine the room. It consisted of a bedroom, bathroom, and kitchen with a tiny area for a breakfast table. A two-way short-wave radio with microphone rested on the table.

Stephenson studied the equipment without touching it. "It's powerful," he told Bernardi. "How long has the man been here?"

"Not long. The manager says he rented the room three days ago. That jibes with when his ship came into port." He rubbed his forehead. "I just got some news. It's not good news, but it's not terrible. Our men lost track of him. He went into a crowded train station, and we didn't have enough people to keep him in sight. He has to come back here, though, unless he's abandoned his radio."

"Why didn't you grab him when you had the chance?"

"We were hoping to see who his contacts are." He lifted his palms in a chagrinned gesture. "So far, nothing." The agent heaved a sigh. "The guy ought to be given the chop."

"Maybe I'll do that," Stephenson said, blandly arching his eyebrows.

"Sure you will." Bernardi laughed while shooting Stephenson a nervous look.

"I've seen enough. Please take us back to our offices."

Paul and Stephenson arrived back at Rockefeller Center shortly before lunchtime. Stephenson had been unusually quiet on the ride back, his eyes fixed on an indefinite point ahead of him. On entering their reception area, he walked into his office without a word and closed the door. Paul went to his own desk just outside.

Thirty minutes later, Stephenson emerged brusquely. "I have some errands to run. No need for you to accompany me. I'll be back before close of business."

True to his word, Stephenson strode into the office suite shortly before nightfall. To Paul, he seemed less agitated than he had been that morning, even perhaps pleased with himself. "Anything concerning happen while I was out?" he asked as he passed by Paul's desk.

"Mr. Bernardi called a little while ago. He sounded urgent but wouldn't leave a message." He handed Stephenson a note with a telephone number.

"Maybe they've found their spy. I'll call him right back."

A few minutes later, Stephenson emerged, smiling Sphinx-like. "It seems someone saved the British and US governments a lot of trouble and expense. Our spy was found in the basement of his apartment building with a broken neck. I suppose he was not universally loved." Swinging his right hand down and striking the edge of it into his left hand, he chuckled and said, "I said I might give the guy the chop."

Paul's head popped up. With a strange sense of inexplicable dread, he stared into Stephenson's eyes but said nothing. He did, however, notice a hard glint in the Canadian's eyes that he had not seen before.

Stephenson returned the glance. "Did you know I was a champion boxer?" He saw Paul nod and went on without waiting for further response. "Yes, strictly amateur. That was before I flew for the RAF in the last war." Stretching, he took in a deep breath and exhaled. "Well, Bernardi's call settles that situation. Back to work. As we discussed earlier, this war leaves no time for mulling over moral dilemmas. We need to get cracking on that project we discussed this morning."

He peered at Paul, studying him. Then, without a word, he disappeared into his office, reappearing a few moments later with a thin booklet. "Read this tonight," he said. "I've under-lined a passage. Pay particular attention to it."

Paul tossed in his sleep that night. *Did Stephenson admit to murder?* He went over the Canadian's words again and again: "I said I might give him the chop."

Did he do it?

And what of the notion of misleading the American public —Stephenson's new intelligence operation—to maneuver events that might sway public opinion to support America's entry into the war. Paul's mind went to the meeting he had attended with Claire in which MI-6 Director Menzies had scolded them both for breaching Bletchley protocol.

The director had railed, "We've acquired information through our Enigma decoding machines telling us that our convoys are headed into ambush and certain death, and yet we do not warn them. And do you know why? Because if the enemy learns that we've broken their codes and can read their messages at will, they will simply change them, and we will fight blindly against overwhelming force. We'll suffer more casualties; we'll lose the war; and our people will be enslaved like those in Europe." He had even used the same words that Stephenson had uttered this morning. "I make no apologies."

Paul sat up in the night, wide awake. He had already read the pamphlet Stephenson had given him. He pulled it out again and flipped to the underlined passage. The booklet was Shakespeare's *King Henry V* play, and the highlighted section read, "He which hath no stomach in this fight, let him depart... But we in it shall be remembered. We few, we happy few, we band of brothers... For he today that sheds his blood with me shall be my brethren..."

Regarding himself, Paul was sure that the part Stephenson intended most was, "He which hath no stomach in this fight, let him depart..." Under the circumstances, Paul was not sure he wanted to be "brethren."

He ambled to the window. The room where he had been quartered was in a penthouse belonging to one of Stephenson's friends. The luxury was beyond any Paul had ever experienced; certainly, it was far greater than the *Seigneurie* on Sark Island.

Paul had not met his host, but Stephenson had shown him the room, handed him the key, and assured him that there was no difficulty with his staying there. "You have the run of the place. My friend is a good chap. He knows Great Britain is up against bad odds and he wants to help."

"Does he know what we're doing?" Paul had asked, surprised.

Stephenson's smile in response had been one of those that would go unnoticed by anyone not paying strict attention, a slight turning up of the corners of his lips below hooded eyes. "Do you mean assuring that our countrymen's passport concerns are handled efficiently? Of course."

The city was laid out in an array of twinkling lights as far as Paul could see in any direction. On the streets below, the taillights of innumerable cars and delivery vehicles streamed between an unbroken string of bright greens, yellows, and reds of neon signs. If not for the events and conversations of the day, Paul could easily feel a sense of grandeur from this perch. And then he recalled the pitch-dark blackouts of London.

What have I got myself into? The meetings at Whitehall with Churchill, Donovan, and Stephenson had been unnerving, even surreal. *Is Stephenson a churl or a patriot?*

"We're at war," he muttered, admonishing himself. "I'm not an investigator. Stephenson made no confession. Without one, or without any other evidence, he's presumed innocent. His comment could have been pure jest. And even if he did kill that man, what's the difference between what he did and what soldiers do every day? They go out and kill the enemy.

"As for the disinformation project: Mr. Roosevelt is responsible for his own intelligence. My loyalty is to Great Britain, and my job is to obey the orders of those in authority over me, which now is Bill Stephenson."

He went back to bed, switched out the lights, and fell into restless sleep, rising at dawn with still cascading, conflicting thoughts of Stephenson's implied action, Shakespeare's passage, and the realities of this war. *Are we acting in the best interests of Great Britain?*

28

January 8, 1941
Dinard, France

"Happy New Year, Mademoiselle Rousseau."

Jeannie stymied a gasp and managed a big smile that she hoped contained traces of friendliness as she glanced up at Major Bergmann's taunting face. He walked to her desk and leaned over it.

"Happy New Year to you," she said. "Did you enjoy your leave?"

"It was very good," he replied, clipping his words. He glanced down at the papers in front of her. "What are you working on today?" Without waiting for an answer, he cocked his head around for a better view and then picked them up.

"They're translations from French to German that the field marshal wanted. He has a team going through French doctrinal manuals to see if there's anything useful."

"'Learn from those you defeat with no fight,' I always say," Bergmann muttered with thick sarcasm. "That makes sense to me." He tossed the documents on the desk, scattering them.

Jeannie looked down and started gathering and arranging them.

"I hear that you've had electrical work done in your parents' house. Is your electrician good? I need some work done in my room, but my men have been unable to locate the one that you used. Maybe you can call him?"

Stung, Jeannie steeled herself to be calm. She continued straightening the documents while she looked up with a shrug. "I can try to find him if you like. He was referred by a friend. I'll have to ask for his contact information this evening. Will that be suitable?"

"Major Bergmann!" *Oberst* Meier commanded from across the room. "Do you have business with the *fräulein*?" As he spoke, he strode toward her desk.

Bergmann straightened and turned, the back of his neck turning red. "I was performing my duty as security officer to check the classification of the documents she is working on."

Jeannie looked rapidly back and forth between them. "He kindly conferred a New Year's greeting," she said brightly, "and asked if I might refer an electrician."

Meier glanced at her for a second without emotion, and then turned to Bergmann. "She is in a secure location cleared for classified documents, and she is authorized to read those at the lowest level of classification."

"And I was checking to ensure that the ones on her desk were not above that level—"

"Those above her classification are in a vault." Meier's voice had turned hard and angry, and his tone had dropped low, menacing. "You are harassing her. I saw you pick up those papers and toss them down, scattering them. She told you that the field marshal ordered the work she's doing. Do you wish to question him?"

Bergmann straightened to attention. "Not at this moment, but I do need to conference with you. Is now a good time, sir?"

Jeannie's heart dropped into her stomach.

Meier peered at Bergmann through squinted eyes. Then he glanced at his watch. "You have fifteen minutes, and you'd better not waste my time."

Jeannie watched them walk down the hall. Despite raw nerves, she waited a minute, picked up her bag, and headed for the restroom. Instead of going in, she checked to see if anyone looked her way, and then darted toward the exit. She had several corridors to navigate, but she managed to reach the foyer with no one stopping her for conversation.

"Are you taking an early break?" the security supervisor asked her at the entrance.

She smiled and winked. "I need real coffee," she said in a mock conspiratorial whisper, "not *Wehrmacht* poison, if you know what I mean. Would you like me to bring you some?"

"That would be great, *Fräulein*," he said, laughing.

"I'll be just a few minutes," she said, while putting on her coat.

As soon as she was outside, she removed her scarlet beret from her bag and put it on. She walked briskly, ostensibly against a cold January wind blowing off the sea, but she was also in a hurry. Along the way, she met people that she normally saw, and she did her best to give her usual friendly greeting, but fear darkened her spirit.

At the first intersection she came to, she entered the crosswalk and trotted across to the café. Her regular waiter greeted her with a smile. Then his eyes rolled up to her hat and he blanched before forcing another smile. "Your regular table, *Mademoiselle*?"

"No thank you, not today. I think I want something a little

farther away from the door. This weather is biting to my bones."

Struggling to remain calm, the waiter showed her to the table. "I'll get your coffee," he said.

"Can you bring one that I can take with me? I promised it to the guard at the security checkpoint."

"*Bien sur.* I will bring it right out." He hurried to the kitchen, where he placed a phone call. "I cannot take delivery today," he said. When he hung up, he leaned over to catch his breath and then hurried to get Jeannie's coffee.

Meanwhile, she kept a close eye on the entrance. She had taken a cosmetics case from her bag and checked her makeup. *I could use a touchup, but now's not the time.* She had only brought it out to have something to do to keep her nerves calm while she waited for her order. To add reality to her ruse, she daubed her nose with powder.

Other customers came and went but the hour was still early for lunch, so foot traffic was sparse. Then she saw Phillippe. He was bent against the wind, and he had grown a beard, but she recognized him by the gray janitor's overalls he wore, along with a blue work cap. He lumbered into the café. If he saw Jeannie, he gave no indication. He went to the counter, ordered coffee, and took it to another table.

Presently, two more men entered. They too ordered hot beverages and went to a different table.

The waiter emerged with her order.

"Oh, I'm so sorry. I won't have time to drink it. Let me have both in paper cups."

The waiter obliged, placing the cups carefully in a paper bag. Jeannie took it, paid him, and headed for the door.

Before she reached it, Phillippe moved ahead of her. "Allow me," he said, "your hands are full."

"Thank you, *monsieur*," she said. As they emerged, he

moved ahead of her. Behind them, the other two men took up their rear.

Just as they reached the curb, the peculiar alternating high-pitch low-pitch whines of European sirens sounded. Jeannie whirled around, fighting panic. Other people along the street also looked about.

Tires screeched at the corner by the café. Two black Mercedes sedans slid to a halt, and a man jumped out of each one. They ran toward Jeannie, one confronting her, the other posting himself behind her. She looked about frantically. Neither Phillippe nor the two men who had been at her back were in sight.

The men from the two Mercedes produced credentials. "Come with us," one barked. "Gestapo."

Phillippe rushed down the stairs below the barn's trap door, his face a mask of fury. When he reached the door at the end of the tunnel, he pounded on it, and when it was opened, he pushed through. Neither looking at nor speaking with anyone, he went to a side table holding several bottles of various liquors provided by the group's hosts. He poured out a double bourbon and downed it in one swallow.

Amélie, Chantal, and the others watched him wide-eyed. Jacques and Nicolas had trailed behind him in the tunnel and now stood against the wall, arms crossed, heads drooping.

Amélie looked back and forth between the men. "What happened?"

"They took her," Phillippe roared, slamming his glass down on the table so hard that it shattered in pieces, sending shards flying across the room. "The Gestapo took Jeannie."

Amélie looked anxiously at Nicolas, who nodded. He

motioned her over with his hand. "We received the emergency call from the waiter in a house close by," he told her, frustration lacing his voice. "The system worked perfectly. We were in the café within three minutes. We ordered our coffee and took our seats. Phillippe was already there. Jeannie ordered hers to take with her. When she left, Phillippe went out in front of her, and we followed behind. We had a car waiting around the corner. Once we had her in there, we were supposed to go pick up her parents, but by the time Jeannie got to the sidewalk, the Gestapo was there and arrested her. We could do nothing."

While he explained, Chantal had retrieved a broom and dustpan from another part of the cellar and started cleaning up the glass. Phillippe watched her, still burning with anger. Then, his expression softened. He walked over and touched her shoulder. "I'll do that," he said, and took the implements from her.

"What do we do now?" Ferrand asked when they had assembled around the oak table.

Phillippe, seated at one end with both elbows on the surface, ran his hands over his head. He held them there, interlocking his fingers, and leaned the chair back while scanning the anxious faces searching his own. "I don't know. When they took her so quickly, they blew all our contingency plans for getting her out of there. We expected more time. One minute later, and she would have been sitting here with us right now, and her parents too." Then, in quiet exasperation, he added, "She had the waiter change her order to takeout. If she hadn't done that—"

He turned to Brigitte. "Get a message to London telling them what happened." Then to the others, he said, "I'm taking Jacques and Nicolas with me back to the house where we kept surveillance near the café.

"Ferrand, ask the local group to keep up their watch and report anything unusual. Also, tell them to get word to the waiter to do the same thing. He'll be scared. We'll pay him if we need to.

"The rest of you, stay low. Regardless of what happens to Jeannie, we still have one other mission to accomplish." He gritted his teeth and spat out his next words. "We are going to get that Major Bergmann. He's at the back of what happened this morning, I'm sure of it." Turning to Ferrand, he growled, "Tell the locals to get me that bastard's habit patterns. I want to know how often, what time of day, and what part of the cliffs he runs on. We also need their three toughest fighters, preferably some who've been blooded in battle."

Sitting across from Ferrand, Amélie and Chantal glanced at each other. Amélie's eyes were full of concern. Chantal's shone with anticipation.

29

"You did what?" *Oberst* Meier nearly sprang from the seat behind his desk, then caught himself and stood, his anger burning. "On whose authority?"

"On my own as chief security officer," Bergmann replied, matching Meier's tone. "I need no one's permission at this headquarters when the matter is safeguarding state secrets, and I imagine that war planning for the invasion of England is a primary secret at the moment."

"Your notion of the scope of your authority is grandiose beyond reality. You preempted me, my boss, the chief of staff, and the field marshal himself. You had no right to report anything to the Gestapo without clearing it through me, and I would have sought higher guidance."

Bergmann regarded him coolly through hooded eyes. "I reported nothing. I merely mentioned to the head of the Gestapo in Dinard, who is a friend of mine, some of the things I've seen, and I asked what he thought about them. His actions after that were his own. I made no requests."

"You manipulated the system," Meier roared. "Stand at attention." He came around his desk and leaned over

Bergmann, bringing his face close to the major's. "You're a petty little man who enjoys stepping on people. That girl has worked for our army since before this headquarters located here back in July. She's never been a problem, except in your paranoia-ridden mind. You're seeing threats where they don't exist. You did the same thing at Dunkirk, and you got our soldiers killed."

Standing at attention, Bergmann held down his own rage, and his eyes became molten voids. "I do my duty, sir." He enunciated each word. "May I speak?"

"You'll speak when I'm ready to listen, Major." He walked over to his window and viewed the sea in the distance beyond the cliffs. "This is a beautiful place, not spoiled by war so far. It would be nice to think that when the fighting is over and we have won, that we have not destroyed the land and its cities to the point that they are uninhabitable, or that the people are so hostile that they continue fighting and killing us by other means.

"The Roman Empire figured out that it could not fight its subjugated populations forever. It lasted for centuries by sending out teams to learn about these far-flung cultures and allowing a measure of autonomy."

"Rome didn't last a thousand years, as the Third *Reich* surely will," Bergmann said tersely.

Meier turned from the window and observed the major coldly. "Study your history better, Major. The lifespan of Rome depends on when you start counting. It became a republic early. An argument could be made that its demise began as power transferred from the people to their rulers and the quest for empire began."

"Are you questioning the *führer's* mode of governing, sir?"

Meier smirked. "Not at all. I just made a historical observation. Now, getting back to pertinent and current details, isn't expanding the living space for Germans one of the *führer's* objectives, and isn't the French occupation zone already designated for that purpose?"

Bergmann said nothing.

"I asked you a question, Major."

"I thought your question was rhetorical."

"It was not."

"Then you are correct, sir. We're expecting to start moving German families into France soon. And the French will be moved out."

"Ah yes, 'to the conqueror the spoils.' I suppose you think that migration will happen peaceably?"

"No, sir, I expect implementation of the plan to require extreme force."

"And where do you expect to get that force in the near term, Major. Germany is spread out over three continents and the Atlantic Ocean. Keeping the people pacified for the moment might be a good thing, don't you think? Or have you joined the *führer's* strategy planning team and thus have greater information."

Bergmann glanced at Meier, uncertainty in his eyes. He hesitated before responding. "I hadn't thought that far ahead—"

"Which is why you're still a major, Major." Meier started toward the door. "Come with me. We're taking this upstairs. Now."

"Sir."

Meier whirled on him. "What is it?"

"When I asked to speak to you, it was to tell you that the Gestapo was on the way to arrest *Fräulein* Rousseau."

Meier's eyes opened wide, and he stared at Bergmann in disbelief. Then he closed the distance to the door, yanked it open, and stared down the hall to Jeannie's desk. It was empty.

"You," he snarled at Bergmann. "Stay here. That's an order." Ignoring pain in his wounded leg, he strode through the office section to Jeannie's desk. "Does anyone know where Rousseau is?" he demanded of coworkers at nearby desks.

"I saw her leave for the restroom several minutes ago," a clerk volunteered. "Maybe she went for coffee. It's a little early for that, but she might have decided to take a break after—" She stopped speaking and glanced uneasily toward Meier's office, where Bergmann could be seen in profile, still standing at attention.

Meier followed her gaze. Then he returned to his office. "Come with me," he snapped at Bergmann. As the major came through the door, Meier said tersely, "You stay with me until I release you. That's an order."

"Yes, sir."

Meier turned to his secretary seated just outside his door. "Let the operations chief know that I'm on the way and it's urgent, concerning a Gestapo matter. Then call the field marshal's chief of staff. Let him know that I need to see him, and the matter is pressing."

He stepped inside his office momentarily, summoned Bergmann to follow him, and set off through the halls at such a rapid pace, despite limping, that the major was challenged to keep up. At the operations chief's office, Meier left Bergmann waiting in the foyer while he briefed his boss. The brigadier followed Meier to his door and scowled at Bergmann.

"Keep me apprised," he told Meier.

Moments later, the *oberst* repeated his actions at the office of the 10th Army's chief of staff. "I'll let the field marshal know we've discussed the issue and that I'll be there shortly. We can't have the SS and the Gestapo pushing us around or we'll cease to be an effective fighting force."

Meier set out again, through more corridors, with Bergmann in tow.

"*Oberst* Meier," the major said with a mocking quality to his tone. "Do you think the matter of one translator should be elevated to the field marshal?"

Meier spun in front of him so abruptly that the two nearly collided. "So now she's just one lowly translator." He pointed a finger in Bergmann's face. "You exalt yourself, Major. You preempted the field marshal's authority, and you questioned his judgment as well as that of the chief of staff and the full operations leadership, including mine. Did you think we would let you run over us?"

Bergmann did not respond.

When they arrived at the foyer for Reichenau's suite of offices, Meier swept past the secretary. "He's expecting you," she called after him.

The field marshal stood by his office window when they entered. "Explain to me what's going on, *Herr Oberst*. It sounds serious." He regarded Bergmann with distaste and turned back to Meier. "The chief of staff mentioned something about the Gestapo?"

Meier gesticulated toward Bergmann. "This SS officer sent the Gestapo to arrest *Fraulein* Rousseau. He said in so many words that we are underestimating a serious security risk. She might already be under arrest."

Reichenau glared at Bergmann. Then he strode to his desk, lifted the receiver, and dialed his secretary. "Get me the Gestapo chief. I want to speak with him immediately." After he hung up, he spun on Bergman. "You've overstepped your bounds, Major."

At that moment, the chief of staff arrived. While Meier provided him more detail, the phone rang, and the field marshal took the return call from the Gestapo head.

"I hear you might have *Fraulein* Jeannie Rousseau in custody," Reichenau snapped into the phone. "If that's true, I want her brought to my office immediately—

"I'm not asking. I'm ordering. If she is not in my office within fifteen minutes—

"You will *not* search her home, her desk, or anything else belonging to her until someone I designate is there to supervise. And you'll make it clear to your agents that her house and belongings will not be ransacked. Is that understood?

"Good. Then I'll see you, the arresting officers, and *Fraulein* Rousseau in my office in fifteen minutes."

He slammed down the phone. Spinning toward Bergmann, he demanded sternly, "Now, tell me how my judgment and that of my staff is deficient, and why you, a major, feel entitled to exercise my authority without informing me or requesting approval." He took his seat behind his desk and motioned for the other officers to sit. When Bergmann started for a chair, Reichenau barked, "Not you. Remain at attention. Explain yourself."

Not having expected this turn of events, Bergmann looked around at the hostile eyes peering at him. "Sir, I've voiced my unease about Rousseau for some time. This is not a new concern."

"You're obsessed with her," Meier broke in, "with no reason."

Reichenau quieted Meier. "Let him speak. I want to hear what he has to say."

"As the *oberst* pointed out to me," Bergmann continued while glaring at Meier, "Rousseau worked as a translator even before our army set up this headquarters, and she continues here to this day."

"That's no basis for your suspicions."

"I won't dispute that, sir, but confidence in her has been elevated over the months—"

"So, we should torture and prosecute her because she does good work for us?"

"I'm saying that the level of trust accorded Rousseau gained her access to an incredible amount of secret information."

"Have you heard her inquire for more depth on anything?"

Bergmann shook his head.

"Has she queried about material that she should not have? Have you seen her reading any classified documents she shouldn't?"

Bergmann shook his head. "She only speaks to me when spoken to."

"And why would that be?" Meier asked sarcastically.

Reichenau shot him a castigating glare and continued with Bergmann. "So, on what basis do you suspect her."

Bergmann took a deep breath. "Sir, she's present during sensitive discussions. Many times, the documents left lying around that she can see have higher classifications than she is allowed."

"So? They have properly marked protective covers."

"Sometimes those covers are folded back."

"Have you seen her reading them? Do you think she can take a glance at a document, read it, and comprehend its content enough to communicate it intelligibly elsewhere? I assume since you took this to the Gestapo that you must have had her house watched. Did anything turn up from that?"

Bergmann shook his head. "She had an electrician come by shortly before Christmas. He had been there a week earlier and several weeks before then. The thing is, we can't trace him."

"Did you ask her about the electrician?"

Bergmann nodded. "This morning. She said she would get the contact information for me this evening."

"Then what's the problem? The man is probably somebody's cousin's cousin who does unlicensed work. You know how things go with electrical and other household repairs. If that's all you have to go on—"

Bergman took a deep breath and exhaled. "Sir, if I may, we've been very frustrated in this headquarters because of British success in pinpointing and hitting our ammo dumps, motor pools, troop encampments, convoys, railroad shipments... The list goes on, and it's not just the locations; it's also the schedules. How can they know those things?"

"Is it possible that Great Britain has developed other ways of gathering intelligence?" Meier cut in. "What are those tall towers along their coast for? And are you suggesting that a translator in our headquarters can predict when and where our bomber and fighter escort formations are going to attack and get those details to British Fighter Command in time to meet them?" He tossed his head in exasperation. "Maybe you should be concentrating your efforts more broadly instead of zeroing in on one girl."

Bergmann's face gave way to chagrin momentarily, and then morphed into one of stone. Reichenau's expression changed to one of allowing for the possibility of what he was hearing. "You both make good points," he said, directing his attention to Bergmann. "You're proposing that of all the people who work in this headquarters, the security concerns come down to one girl, as the *oberst* pointed out. Why? Because she's pretty and charming?"

"There was a French girl in Dunkirk you liked very much," Meier cut in again.

"Who did not work for us, sir," Bergmann retorted.

Reichenau scrutinized the major and sighed. "I appreciate

that you're trying to do a good job, but you overstepped by getting the Gestapo involved without running it up your chain of command first. And have you given any thought to the notion that you might be giving Rousseau too much credit? She's a *girl,* and one with no life experiences. She couldn't possibly put all the data, schedules, and logistics together in any meaningful way and communicate it. Have you seen any radios or evidence of any?"

"No, sir."

"Then what is your justification for detaining her?"

Bergmann took another deep breath and looked about the room as if searching for a vestige of support. "It's a feeling, sir. She's always there, at the files, in the documents, helping out at meetings, smiling at everyone, and never becoming flustered or angry when challenged—"

"Well by all means," Reichenau said, chortling, "we should arrest all the nice, hardworking people of the world who give us no problems."

"Sir—"

Reichenau lifted his palms in a placating manner. "Your job is security. I understand that. I have no wish for friction with either the SS or the Gestapo, and I won't fault an officer in my command for being thorough." He rubbed his eyes. "When *Fraulein* Rousseau gets here, I'll ask the questions. I'll allow her house and personal items to be searched under my conditions. If you find any real evidence, like documents, communications equipment, weapons—nothing conjured up or planted—you can take her away. Otherwise, she goes free. Is that clear?"

"Yes, sir."

Jeannie and the Gestapo arresting officers entered. Reichenau, Meier, and the chief of staff watched, horror-struck, as she made her way in. Absent was the confident, pleasant, charming person who had graced the German 10th Army headquarters and had been so helpful for months. Her normally well-coiffed hair was disheveled, eye makeup smudged her cheeks, and tears had streaked them. She hunched her shoulders and walked with small, uncertain steps while looking around fearfully.

Bergmann watched her stone-faced.

Reichenau squirmed in his chair. "Would you like to freshen up, *Fräulein*?" he asked gruffly. "You may use my private lavatory."

"Thank you, sir, I would, but I don't have my bag with my things." Her normally musical voice was soft, almost timid.

Reichenau turned impatiently to the Gestapo escort. "Have you gone through her bag?"

The officer in charge, *Oberleutnant* Lukas Bauer, nodded.

"Did you find anything?"

Bauer shook his head.

Annoyed, Reichenau growled, "Well then give it to her, and get her some drinking water, for heaven's sake."

As Jeannie made her way to the lavatory, Reichenau addressed the chief of staff. "Send Bauer's three Gestapo men and three of our senior staff officers to the *fräulein's* house. Make sure ours are combat veterans with instructions to take no guff. Let the Gestapo search, but—" He turned to the agents. "My officers will watch each of you. You will not tear up Rousseau's house or personal belongings. If you do, I'll charge you for failing to obey my orders. Now go."

When Jeannie returned from the restroom, her hair had been put in place, her face cleaned, and she had straightened her shoulders. A chair had been set in the middle of the office in front of the field marshal's desk. Looking around uncertainly, she went and sat in it.

"I'll do the asking," Reichenau said pointedly, with a scathing look at Bauer. He turned his attention to Jeannie. "Do you know why you're here?"

She looked at him, her eyes doleful, holding back tears. "No, sir, I really do not. Something about stolen documents, but I don't have any. You can look anywhere."

"And I'm sure they will," Reichenau said with a glare at the remaining Gestapo man. Then he continued with Jeannie. "I'm told you left very suddenly this morning after Major Bergmann confronted you. Why did you do that?"

Jeannie took a deep breath, closed her eyes momentarily, and re-opened them. "I could see that the major was angry with me, but I had no idea why. I needed a moment to settle down. I go for coffee at the café across the street quite often, but usually later in the morning. I decided to go then. It was an impulse."

"Did you plan on coming back?"

Jeannie lifted her head with a quizzical look. "Why wouldn't I? I had promised to bring a cup of coffee to the security manager at the entry checkpoint. I even had the waiter change my own order so that I could bring it to him while it was still hot."

Reichenau glanced between Jeannie and Bauer. "Did you tell them that?"

She nodded.

The field marshal glared at Bauer. "Did you check out that detail? If you tell me no, I'll have my own officers double-check her story."

Bauer nodded.

"Did the waiter at the café and the manager at the checkpoint confirm her story?"

Again, Bauer nodded

A collective groan went up in the room. Reichenau sat back in his chair, obviously disgusted. Then he sat forward and pointed a finger at Bauer. "This young lady is no longer in your custody. She's in mine and will remain so until we hear the results of the search. If your men find anything, I'll return her to you. Otherwise, she will be free to go."

Bauer stepped forward. "I must protest—"

"Protest what? That you get her back if you find evidence?" He turned his glare on Bergmann. "You've wasted nearly two hours of my time and that of my senior staff. I won't have witch hunts in my command."

"Let me remind you, Field Marshal," Bauer growled, this time in a menacing tone, "that I support your command, but I don't report to you. I need a word with you privately, and I'll need Major Bergmann with me."

Stemming anger, the field marshal indicated a side door. "*Fräulein* Rousseau, please wait inside my conference room." Turning back to Bauer as Jeannie exited, Reichenau added, "My chief of staff and *Oberst* Meier will stay for this 'discussion.'"

Bauer, still standing, acquiesced, but said, "I'm here to detect and stop any internal threats to the Nationalist Socialist Party."

Reichenau stared at him, seething. "I know your job. Are you threatening me?" Without waiting for a response, he went on. "Maybe one way to protect the Party is to avoid making enemies where they don't exist."

He paused, choosing his words carefully. "I was hand-picked by the *führer* to lead the *Wehrmacht* through Holland, Belgium, and into France. Apparently, I did a good enough job that he asked me to lead the planning and invasion into Great Britain.

Are you suggesting that your judgment in selecting me is superior to his?"

Bauer blanched momentarily, but he recovered quickly.

Reichenau continued. "You interfere with my staff and operations based on what? Spurious instinct?" He glared at Bergmann, who sat listening in silence. Turning back to Bauer, Reichenau said, "So far, all you've provided are suppositions from a pompous SS major with no specifics and no evidence."

He placed his hands on his hips, lowered his head, and glared at Bauer. "If you are questioning my loyalty," he said, "then our next meeting will be with *Reichsführer* Himmler, and then, if need be, with the *führer*. Do I make myself clear?"

"Perfectly," Bauer said, appearing far from acquiescing.

30

Bletchley Park, England

Claire hurried through the mansion to Commander Denniston's office, knocked rapidly on the door, and dropped her hand to the knob. As soon as she heard him respond, she burst through. "Sir, something is going on at the headquarters in Dinard. You asked me to let you know if Miss Rousseau was in danger." She took a breath. "She was arrested by the Gestapo."

Denniston stood with a grave face. "Fill me in."

"The coders all over the German headquarters in Dinard were abuzz. We're intercepting and decoding many messages from there. Apparently, Bergmann confronted Miss Rousseau. That resulted in a big meeting in the field marshal's office. Somewhere in the middle of all of that, she was arrested. I don't know of any resolution."

"So, it's come to that, has it?" the commander said. He saw the anxiety on Claire's face. "I know you feel responsible for her." He thought a moment. "I'm aware of some things I can't speak about. Let me just say this. Keep in mind the old phrase, 'things are never as good or as bad as they seem.'"

Startled, Claire fixed her gaze on him. "Exactly what is that supposed to mean, sir?"

Denniston chuckled. "If I could tell you exactly what it meant, I wouldn't be speaking in riddles, would I? No, I wouldn't." Sensing her hidden frustration, he continued, "Look, I'm trying to give you hope without crossing a line. But I appreciate your coming to tell me. I'll put the information through to where it might do some good."

Puzzled and not mollified, Claire left the office.

As soon as she closed the door, Denniston called Major Crockatt at MI-9 and relayed the conversation. "You still have that radio operator up at Dunkirk, don't you, codenamed Brigitte?"

"We do," Crockatt replied, "and we've been in contact regarding this matter. She and the rest of the team are in Dinard now, and Rousseau's rescue is their objective."

"Had you heard that Rousseau's been arrested by the Gestapo?"

"We received an emergency message informing us a little while ago from Brigitte. I don't think there's anything we can do from here, particularly since Rousseau is in Gestapo hands. The Alliance group in Marseille thinks highly of their man leading the operation. He's one of the former officers recruited from the French navy. At this point, I think we leave it in their hands. Have you clued in SOE on the situation yet?"

"That's my next call."

"I'll ring up Lord Hankey, if you like," Crockatt offered. "I think he's still there, although he's supposed to hand his reins over to someone else when SOE is finally up and running."

"Yours and Hankey's are the action units," Denniston

responded. "It's better if you talk to him, and if you need any more information, I'll see if there's any to supply."

Crockatt hung up and called Lord Hankey.

"I had not heard," Hankey said after Crockatt advised him of the situation. "What a shame. She's so young, and she's supplied such good information."

"Right. Well, I called to see if you had any ideas about how to help the rescue. If she's tortured during interrogation, she could blow a hole in both the Boulier and the Marseille Resistance groups. That would set us back quite a bit."

"The difficulty is that the work Miss Rousseau has been doing is normally run by MI-6. The team that's with the Boulier network was put together by SOE and MI-9 on the fly, so to speak, because both organizations were fledgling. The operation inside the headquarters at Dinard involving her was a target of opportunity that fell into our laps, but it's not been run the way MI-6 usually does business."

Crockatt sat up in his chair. "I'm not sure I understand. We've had a very effective operation going on in Dinard for months. What's the problem?"

"I'll spell it out for you, old chap. I'm not saying I agree with what I'm about to tell you, I'm just letting you know the way things are. Although Director Menzies is fine with the setup, some in his MI-6 are not. They feel they should have been running that show. I'm not sure *we* could do anything to save her now, but if there was a way, we could not count on MI-6 for help."

Stunned, Crockatt stared at the receiver. "So, we have a young woman in harm's way who's given incredible service to our country and her own, and we can't help her because of turf jealousies?"

"I'm afraid that sizes things up. Now look, don't take the pessimistic view on this. As you've described it, the young lady is well thought of by German leadership in the headquarters, and if, as reported, the matter has been escalated to the field marshal, he wouldn't get involved unless there were mitigating issues.

"Besides that, you have a proven, motivated team in place. You didn't ask for my advice, but I'll give you one piece, free of charge: maintain contact with the relevant players as best you can, but otherwise, keep out of their way. And don't underestimate Miss Rousseau's ability. She's proven quite adept at taking care of herself, and she might surprise us again."

Dinard, France

Reichenau glared at Bauer. "I need to confer with my staff. You and Major Bergmann can wait in the foyer." He saw Bauer glance toward the field marshal's conference room. "Don't worry, *Fräulein* Rousseau will be safe with us, and she won't go anywhere."

After Bauer and Bergmann had left, Reichenau joined Meier and the chief of staff in his seating area. "You were right to bring this to my attention," he told Meier.

The chief of staff stirred. "I'm worried that we might have kicked a hornet's nest," he said. "The last thing we want to do is rile up the SS and the Gestapo against us."

"Agreed," Reichenau said, "but if the *Wehrmacht* is to win Germany's wars, it needs a free hand in battle without looking over its shoulder for internal police surveillance. If it starts with this translator, where will it end. We employ local people everywhere we occupy. And if the SS and Gestapo can construe threats based on their 'instinct' concerning any employee we hire, and further question the judgment or loyalty of *Wehrmacht* members all the way to senior leadership, then no one is safe from capricious findings. We must stop this type of activity, and we must do it now. We can't give in to them."

"Beyond that, Bergmann is a malicious person," Meier interjected. "At Dunkirk, he pursued Ferrand Boulier and his family relentlessly, executed locals at his whim, and grossly violated the limits of his authority. I ordered him out of my command. If I could have, I would have court-martialed him."

Reichenau turned to the chief of staff. "Do you have further comment?"

"Only that if you let her go, this might still not be the last you hear from the Gestapo and the SS. Your stance will certainly be reported higher."

The field marshal nodded. "So be it. They're not going to find evidence against *Fräulein* Rousseau, I'm sure of that, so after I hear that finding, I'll release her as I said I would. But Bergmann will want to keep pursuing her. We need to placate the Gestapo on this situation without giving in to them. Here is what we are going to do."

31

Amid blank stares and people moving out of her way, Jeannie made her way on wobbly legs and uneasy feet through the corridors of the headquarters. At the security checkpoint, she smiled weakly at the manager whose coffee she had purchased a few hours ago. He did not make eye contact, but as she passed, he cast her a surreptitious, sympathetic glance. She stopped at the door only long enough to pull her heavy coat around her and place the scarlet beret on her head. Then she walked out into the cold.

Crossing the street, she once more made her way into the café. The waiter greeted her warmly but nervously and inquired about which table she wished to occupy. She indicated one different from her regular favorite.

The calamity she had just experienced seemed surreal, something from a nightmare spanning centuries, but when she looked at her watch, she saw that only a few hours had passed. As would be the case on any midafternoon, the café currently served only a few customers, joined at one point by another lone woman and a few minutes later by two young men. No one took notice of her.

Feeling forlorn and vulnerable, senses that had usually been alien to her and never to the degree she felt them now, Jeannie sipped her coffee slowly, savoring its flavor as a small relief from her ordeal. She shifted her eyes to view the street, hoping to see Phillippe, but saw only normal vehicular and street traffic. Across the street, uniformed personnel and civilians entered and exited the checkpoint in an irregular flow.

"I won't have to go there again," she muttered in an undertone to no one. Despite the situation, the thought provided a sense of relief.

She prepared to leave. The waiter brought the check. As she glanced at it, she gulped on seeing a note scrawled on it. "Follow me. Amélie."

Stemming a rush of emotion, she glanced about. The young woman who had entered alone sipped coffee and watched traffic go by. She was petite and still wore her winter coat with a dark scarf tied over her head and brown hair protruding at the side. The face belonged to Amélie, complete with honey-colored eyes, and the scarf was the one she had given to Phillippe.

Jeannie sucked in her breath involuntarily. Her heart leaped.

Moments passed, and then Amélie stood and pulled the long strap of her bag over her shoulder. Then, instead of heading toward the front door, she disappeared into the hall leading to the restrooms.

Uncertain at first of whether to follow or wait for Amélie to return and leave through the front door, Jeannie decided that being out of sight was the better option. She rose to her feet and walked into the hall. In her peripheral vision, she saw the two young men fall in behind her just as had happened that morning.

Amélie stood at the back door past the restrooms. She waved wordlessly and exited. The door opened onto an alley.

Turning right, Amélie walked at a methodical pace, neither fast nor slow.

Jeannie followed, and behind her, so did the two men.

A car turned into the alley in front of them. Amélie crossed to the passenger side as it slid to a halt. She turned, summoned Jeannie with a wave, and held the back door open for her. The two men entered on the opposite side of the car.

"We'll be all right," Amélie said as Jeannie squeezed into the back while eyeing her with great uncertainty. "We're taking you to a safe place."

Then Jeannie saw the driver. Phillippe. Her emotions flooded.

———

When they had finally navigated the obstacles and were safely inside the wine cellar below the farmhouse in L'Orme, Jeannie wrapped her arms around Amélie and wept. Phillippe stood to one side and watched them.

"Major Bergmann wanted me interrogated," she said between sobs, "and Bauer was ready to do anything to make me talk." She stood back, wiped her eyes, and brought herself under control. "*Oberst* Meier is a wonderful, good man. But for him, I would be in a Gestapo torture cell right now."

She stopped suddenly and stared at Amélie. "What are you doing here? How did you get here?" She laughed through a sob. "And how good to see you."

She turned to Phillippe and embraced him, holding her head close to his chest. "And you, my good friend, you came to rescue me."

"We all did, Jeannie." He kissed her forehead. "Amélie, her

sister, her father, his brother, his nephew—" He laughed. "It's mostly a family affair. Then there's Jacques, Théo, Brigitte, and the old couple who own the farmhouse. London is monitoring." He squeezed her. "We weren't going to let you go, Jeannie. Not without a fight."

Jeannie's eyes moistened again amid quiet sobs. "I've felt so alone all this time. And now, I can't go home. I had to leave everything behind, including my parents. I'm a danger to them."

Through her tears, she saw a girl approach, a younger version of Amélie. Wiping her eyes, she turned to Amélie. "Is this your sister?"

Amélie nodded. "Chantal."

"And you came for me too? You're so young, still a girl. You shouldn't have."

"Of course I should have," Chantal said, hugging her. "Look at what you did for us. I'm happy to meet you."

"You'll meet everyone," Amélie said, "but how did you get out of there?"

"That was Meier's and Reichenau's doing."

Amélie led her to the long table with the others. "We were putting together a plan to raid the Gestapo headquarters, and then we got a call from the waiter in the café to tell us you were there. He followed our emergency protocol."

After all were seated, Jeannie told them of the events as they had happened in sequence, beginning with Bergmann's confrontation with her and the meetings with Meier, the chief of staff, Reichenau, and the Gestapo. "The field marshal is a powerful man," she said, "and he won't be bullied. I don't know why he and the army staff stood up for me, but they did." She smiled. "I know they could not believe that I would spy on them, but there was something beyond that. I could see in my last meeting with all of them that Reichenau had put the fear of God into the Gestapo and Major Bergmann. Anyway, he got them to drop their investigation of me in exchange for ordering me out of Dinard and anywhere else along the Atlantic coast." She sniffed. "I quite like the town. I'll miss it." She shrugged. "But Bergmann is not done with me. He won't stop."

"You're right," Phillippe said, glancing first at Jeannie and then at Amélie. "He sounds vindictive."

"You stay here and rest," Amélie told her. "Several of us have another task this afternoon."

"Can I help?"

Amélie shook her head. "We have enough people, but I do have a question. We've observed Bergmann run along the cliffs. Do you think he'll be out there today?"

Jeannie laughed involuntarily and shrugged. "He runs most days, particularly when he's frustrated, and today he's very frustrated. He saw me slip from his grasp. Rain, snow, sunshine. It makes no difference to him. He's obsessed with keeping that Aryan physique in shape. The path he takes will be clear. He'll run."

Amélie glanced at the others. "We don't have much time. We should go."

32

Oberst Meier watched Bergmann closely as Jeannie left the field marshal's office after being dismissed. He had seen her jaw clench and her fists tighten when Reichenau told her that charges against her would be dropped, but that she would be required to leave Dinard.

Major Bergmann burned with anger. The agreement by which Jeannie had been set free had been made over his head without anyone asking his opinions or concerns. His eyes followed her with malevolence as she disappeared through the door. He waited only moments before he excused himself and left the room.

Meier had let him go to see what he would do, and shortly after, the *oberst* followed. Predictably, the major went straight to Jeannie's desk. She had not stopped there, her co-workers told him. She had gone straight through toward the exit. Bergmann then hurried through the halls. By the time he reached the security checkpoint, she was nowhere in sight.

When he started back toward his office, he was surprised to see Meier there, watching him.

Meier advanced on him. "Major Bergmann, let me be clear. The issue with *Fräulein* Rousseau is closed. She is no longer your concern, and I direct you here, now, to turn your attention to securing the vulnerabilities of this headquarters, to include exploring the suggestions I mentioned in our meeting. That's a far more productive contribution to the *Reich* than pursuing one lone translator."

Simmering with hostility, Bergmann snapped to attention. "Yes, sir. Will that be all?"

"No. I will be watching you closely. I expect you to conduct yourself professionally. You may go."

"Yes, sir." Bergmann clicked his heels and raised his right arm in a Nazi salute. "Heil Hitler."

Meier too enjoyed the finger of land enveloped between water at the northern tip of Dinard. The area was sparsely populated compared to parts above other cliffs rising from a cove on the opposite side of this narrow outcropping that jutted into the English Channel. He walked a path near the edge of the precipice regularly to strengthen his wounded right leg. The bullet that had ended his command had gone deep and severed an artery. The quick work of an enlisted medic had saved his life, but he had lost a lot of blood, required several hours of surgery, and a month of hospitalization and therapy before the doctors would release him back to duty.

His mentor, General Erwin Rommel, was rumored to be leaving for Africa to take command of the Afrika Korps, and Meier was anxious to rejoin him and assume another combat command. His leg needed more strengthening to eliminate his limp.

On his walks, he had seen Bergmann running along the cliffs several times and had developed a grudging respect for his determination. Meier sensed that the man lived and breathed Nazi dogma and did everything possible to live up to Party expectations. That extended to keeping in good physical form, although Meier had noticed that neither Adolf Hitler nor Herman Göring exemplified that ideal.

Today was a good day for running or walking, with a sunny afternoon and a temperature of forty-two degrees. Shortly after beginning his jaunt, Bergmann loped past him in athletic attire, his jersey barely concealing a small pistol strapped to his side as he headed toward the farthest point on the small peninsula. Bergmann acknowledged the *oberst* with a curt salute but otherwise said nothing and continued along the lane. Meier watched him go, envying his physical ability.

Bergmann had seen Meier ahead of him. He loathed the *oberst* and enjoyed the sense of superiority that came from running past him in top physical form. Meier was known for strength and stamina, but his wound had relegated him to limping along. The major attributed Meier's fast pace through the headquarters this morning to a burst of adrenalin stemming from anger. *Maybe his annoyance with me will drive him to a heart attack. If not, sooner or later, I'll trap and arrest him for being an enemy of the state.*

He took a quick look over his shoulder and saw that Meier was no longer in sight. Putting on a burst of speed, Bergmann reveled in his athletic ability and the landscape unfolding before him. To his right, the sea broke against massive boulders far below at the base of the cliffs. In front of him, the trail wound uninterrupted, aside from a few houses spread far apart to his left on this small peninsula.

After some minutes, he reached the end of the finger and stopped to take in the magnificent sun in its final moments before settling over the horizon. He heard footsteps and turned to see an old man plodding his way from the other side of the outcropping. The man was thin and white-haired, and he walked with a cane and was bent at the waist. A girl walked beside him, and another young woman trailed behind them.

Bergmann took notice of the man, but quickly returned his attention to the waning sun. As it dipped, and while rays still thrust into the sky, he turned for his return run back to headquarters. Then he heard the old man call to him.

"Major Bergmann."

The major peered at the man who, standing with his back to the golden horizon, he could see only in silhouette.

"Do I know you?" Bergmann asked.

"You searched for me hard enough," the old man said. "You executed our friends and neighbors. You even thought I was dead, and you hung wanted posters for my daughters in the headquarters."

Bergmann peered through the dusk, and in that instant, he recognized the voice. "Ferrand Boulier? That's you, isn't it?" He laughed. "You're being brazen as hell confronting me like this."

"We know our limitations," Ferrand said calmly.

Bergmann shielded his eyes and scrutinized the three figures coming toward him. "And with your daughters? Amélie and Chantal, as I recall." He peered at the younger sister. "You've grown and filled out," he said mockingly. "Your father must be so proud."

An uneasy pang formed in his stomach. Mindful of an

ambush that had taken place the last time he went after Ferrand, he looked around warily. "Why are you here?"

"You've been tried and convicted in absentia for the murder of nine people. We're here to carry out sentence."

"You what?" Bergmann's tone changed to one that mocked. "You're a lunatic old man."

"And you're alone," Ferrand said. "We're not." As he spoke, six heavily armed men rose from both sides of the path, blocking the way. Two of them, Phillippe and Jacques, moved in front of Ferrand and his daughters to protect them from Bergmann.

The major searched back and forth warily, taking in the group arrayed against him. He smirked. "You're going to execute me?" he mocked. "Do you know the retribution that the Gestapo will take against the people of Dinard?" As he spoke, he glanced over his shoulder to gauge his proximity to the cliffs. Far below, roaring waves crashed against jagged rocks.

Ferrand stepped in front of his protectors and approached to within a few feet of the major. "You've guessed your sentence. I'm here to—"

In a flash, Bergmann lunged toward Ferrand, knocking him to the ground. They rolled together. No one fired for fear of hitting Ferrand. When they stopped, Bergmann held his pistol at Ferrand's head.

"If I go, old man, you do too," Bergmann growled. To the others, he yelled, "Drop your weapons and back away, or this old man dies right here, right now."

Amélie gasped.

Chantal screamed, "Papa," and took a few steps forward.

Phillippe stopped her with an outstretched arm. "You'll die too," he called to Bergmann.

"I'm dead either way," Bergmann snarled. He jammed

262LEE JACKSON

the barrel of the pistol into Ferrand's temple. "Now put those weapons down and back away. I won't repeat myself again."

Frustrated, Phillippe glanced at his men and nodded. Then he slowly lowered his rifle to the ground and backed off as the others did likewise.

"Chantal," Bergmann bellowed. "Collect those weapons and put them in front of me. Carry them by their slings." He raised his voice to a shout. "If anyone moves toward me, Ferrand is dead, and Chantal is next."

Cautiously, fearfully, Chantal complied while the others watched, and when she had finished, Bergmann called to her again. "Bring one here and set it next to me. Then stand close by." He glanced at Amélie and instructed, "Stand next to your sister." Then he called out, "If anyone comes near, both girls get it."

To Ferrand, he said, "We're going to get up. Slowly. If you so much as twitch the wrong way, I'll shoot you in the head and then kill your precious Amélie and Chantal. Do you understand?"

Ferrand nodded, and together, the two men rose to their feet, with Bergmann holding Ferrand tightly in front of him facing Phillippe and his group. Behind them, the sun's last rays shrank over the sea.

Suddenly, with a loud roar, Ferrand shoved backward. He dug his feet in, pushing with all his strength.

Surprised and knocked off balance, Bergmann struggled for footing, but could not recover from Ferrand's relentless drive across the few remaining feet to the cliff's edge. And then at the last moment, as Ferrand's daughters and their security escort watched in horror, the major spun, thrusting Ferrand over the precipice and into the dark void.

"No!" Chantal shrieked. She rushed Bergmann, hurling

herself against him and then falling to the ground with her head and shoulders protruding over the brink.

Once again off balance from the force of Chantal's attack, Bergmann teetered on the edge, terror on his face, and then plummeted to the rocks and the pounding waves where his dying scream ended abruptly.

Amélie dashed to Chantal, helping her away from the brink, while the men surrounded them and gently backed them away to safety. There the sisters dropped to their knees, holding each other in grief.

Twilight faded; night descended. *Oberst* Meier had wanted to reach the tip of the rocky finger before sunset, but he still could not walk fast enough, long enough. He was about to turn around when he heard voices in the distance that sounded distressed, with loud cries, yelps, and then a long, terrified scream, followed by women sobbing.

Continuing through the shadow of dusk, after several minutes he reached a place by the edge of the cliff near its northernmost point. By the glow coming off the sea, he found a man with two women, girls really, who were in obvious grief.

"What's the problem?" he asked sternly.

Phillippe stared up at the man standing before them. Having heard his approach, the other three men, Nicolas, Jacques, and Claude, had moved into deeper shadows.

Meier's French was passable, but his accent immediately identified him as German, and his bearing signified that he was probably military. "I am *Oberst* Meier. Who are you?"

Phillippe recognized the name as that of the officer Jeannie said had saved her. He rose to his feet and approached Meier. "My name is Armand," he said, making up the name on the fly. "We were walking here to enjoy the sunset—myself, these two sisters, and their father. Some fool was trying to climb the cliffs, and he put himself in grave danger. Their father went to help, and both fell to the rocks below." His head drooped. "I don't think either one could have survived."

Meier tried to peer through the shadows to see who else might be around. Besides Phillippe, he saw only the two girls. He took a deep breath, wondering who had fallen. *Bergmann? I didn't see him return along the path.*

He went to the girls. "Your father must have been a brave man," he said, grasping their shoulders. "I'm sorry for your loss."

Amélie and Chantal continued holding onto one another, their bodies shaking as they sobbed quietly.

"We called for them," Phillippe said, "but we heard no response."

"We should get the women back into town. We'll have to make a police report. Do you know if the second man, the fool climbing the cliffs, was German or French?"

"He cried out to us for help in perfect French but with a slight German accent."

"More than likely one of ours. We'll have to get the military police involved. But for now, let's get the sisters to safety where they can comfort each other."

"Thank you, sir. I met someone recently who knew you from the headquarters and said you were a fair man."

"I try. That's hard during a war. What was your name again?"

"Armand."

"And the friend who knew me?"

"I wish I could tell you. It was a conversation in a bar."

Meier remained silent for a while. "Well," he said, "let's take care of these women, shall we?"

The four of them walked together back along the path the way they had come. Following far behind, Jacques and Nicolas did their best to console Claude over the loss of his brother without alerting Meier to their presence or that of their other companions.

"You're limping, sir," Phillippe said.

"A recent war wound. I'm afraid I'll slow you down a bit."

"I see that. I'll take the women ahead to get them situated, and we thank you for your courtesy."

Meier took a deep breath. "I should warn you that if we can't find you tomorrow, you'll be a fugitive."

Startled, Phillippe pivoted in the path to stand in front of Meier. "You're a good man, *Oberst*, and there aren't many of those on your side in this war. I trust our paths will cross again."

"I can't see what you look like in this darkness, and I don't know your real name."

"Ah, but I know what you look like and your name." Phillippe extended his hand. "May we both work toward better times."

In the light of the stars and an ascending moon, Meier grasped it. "That's a good thought. We can share it without either of us being traitors to our countries."

As Phillippe was about to release the *oberst's* hand, Meier took a firmer hold. "Tell the sisters that if their father's body is recovered, I'll make sure to deliver it to a safe place so they can bury him properly." Then he released Phillippe's hand.

Disconcerted, Phillippe was momentarily at a loss for words. "We're grateful. Thank you." He hesitated to ask one more question. "How will we know where that will be and that they'll be safe?"

"You have my word of honor that they won't be harmed. They will be able to come and go freely for the ceremony, and no one will follow them. I'll get a message to you about location and time."

Dumbstruck, Phillippe stepped closer to Meier, trying to see him in the dark, but all that was visible were reflections of moonlight in the *oberst's* eyes. "How?"

"I have ways." Meier took a deep breath and let it out. "Just one final thing before we part ways."

"Yes, sir."

"Please give my regards to *Fräulein* Rousseau. I wish her only the best."

Nearly an hour later, Meier entered through the security checkpoint at the headquarters. Most of the lights were out and the number of people working was small. He limped through the halls and stopped at Jeannie Rousseau's desk. Then he continued, passing his own office to the headquarters' main bulletin board.

In the upper right corner, portraits of Amélie, Chantal, and Ferrand Boulier stared out at him from Major Bergmann's wanted posters. He studied them for a few moments. Then he reached up, removed the tacks holding them in place, and took them down.

On returning to his office and taking his seat behind his desk, he continued studying the photos. "You raised two fine daughters, Ferrand Boulier. Rest in peace." Then he lifted the receiver on his phone and dialed the military police. "This is *Oberst* Meier," he said when his call was answered. "I need to report two probable deaths." He described the location. "You won't be able to get to the bodies tonight. Also, you'll need to call in the local police. They might have been civilians." He remained silent a moment as the person on the other end of the line asked a question.

"I don't know their identities. I was on my evening walk and saw them fall just after sunset. Apparently, one had been climbing and got into trouble, and the other tried to rescue him. Unfortunately, they both tumbled, and that's the last I saw of them."

33

January 15, 1941
Marseille, France

Phillippe sipped coffee opposite Fourcade at the table on the veranda overlooking the villa's dormant gardens and the sea. Although beautiful, the day's winter chill had compelled them to wear their coats.

"The Boulier sisters are exhausted and grief-stricken," he said. "Traveling over back roads under threat from Dinard was difficult enough, but doing it while grieving the death of their father was more than anyone should have to suffer. They're resting at Maurice's farm. Jeannie is with them. She comforts them, although she also worries about her own parents, wondering if she'll ever see them again."

"Those poor girls, all three of them. What this war is doing to individual lives is unconscionable. Were Amélie and Chantal able to bury Ferrand?"

Phillippe shook his head. "The Dinard police couldn't find his body. It must have washed out to sea. Bergmann's had been tossed against the rocks to the point of making him unrecognizable. That German officer, *Oberst* Meier, identified him. He had promised that the Bouliers would be able to bury their father unmolested, but obviously, that became impossible. Anyway, no one from the *Wehrmacht's* 10th Army headquarters seemed bothered over the loss of the major. His passing went without a ripple. No accusations of malfeasance, no retaliation against the public. Nothing."

"And what of Meier? Tell me about him."

Phillippe thought a moment before responding. "He's an interesting character." He related the strange conversation between him and the German colonel in the waning daylight over the cliffs of Dinard. "I will tell you honestly, it was as though he knew or at least spoke based on suspicions that we were with the Resistance, including Jeannie. He warned me that if we disappeared, a search would go out for us."

"And did it?"

Phillippe shrugged. "I don't know. We stayed in the cellar below the farmhouse for two days. The old man who owns it with his wife went to the café across from the headquarters and watched from there for half a day. He also spoke with the waiter who had helped us. Neither saw nor heard anything of concern. There were no house-to-house canvasses, no extra checkpoints, no retaliation. Nothing."

"Do you think Meier is part of a German resistance? Could he be turned?"

"I don't know. My sense of him is of a professional soldier who is loyal to his country but abhors injustice. Two questions come to mind: when does the corruption in the regime he serves become intolerable to him, and how do we cross the bridge to know we can trust him?"

Fourcade contemplated Phillippe's comments. "We should find a way to monitor him."

Phillippe's brow furrowed. "I think it might be happening

already." He told her of Jeannie's question about how British intelligence could know about the danger to her. "That's a good question," he went on. "The idea to contact her came from London, and so did the information that she was in jeopardy with a request that we rescue her.

"Couple that with Meier's intimation that he knew more than he was prepared to say, a reasonable conclusion is that intelligence is reaching London about what was going on inside that headquarters beyond what Jeannie provided."

Fourcade thought a moment and added, "We need to stay on top of this. Meier has already been useful to us, and he could be again. I'll send in a request for information about him and see if anything comes back. On another subject, what will happen to the Boulier network now?"

"It will go on. Ferrand's brother and nephew were there in Dinard, and Jacques too, the man who led the SOE team. All three are capable. Jacques is young, and so is Nicolas. They listen to the older man. Between the three of them, the network should continue to be effective. They recognize that Jacques is overall in charge."

The door from the house swung open, and Horton walked out with Henri and another man. Phillippe's face lit up when he saw them, and he leaped to his feet to greet them.

"I found this chap lurking out front," Horton said with a grin, indicating Henri. "He says he came over to retrieve something."

"It's good to see you," Henri told Phillippe, ribbing him. "Madame Fourcade called to let me know you were back in town. I came to pick you up and put you to real work."

"Good," Phillippe replied, and turned to Fourcade. "Now that my mission with you is complete, can I go blow something up with these bums?"

Fourcade laughed. "Go, my friend, and thank you."

"Maybe not so fast," Henri said. He indicated the other man he had brought with him. "This is Major Léon Faye. He's a pilot in the Vichy air force and he currently leads Alliance Resistance operations in North Africa with your colleague, Navarre. He brought a plan to discuss with you. Navarre is in favor of it."

"I'm sorry, I didn't mean to ignore you," Fourcade said, rising. "I was rude. By all means, let's hear the plan."

As Faye took the hand she offered, Fourcade felt a sudden and unexpected deep stirring, one she had long ago subdued. She caught her breath and hoped no one noticed.

The officer before her stood straight and tall, with thick dark hair and an aquiline nose. Despite his perfect gentlemanly manner, a roguish spirit shone from his gray-green eyes. She found herself entranced and had to mentally shake off the feeling.

"Please sit," she said. "Tell me what Navarre is up to in Africa. This Alliance organization was his idea. I helped him organize it, and then he took off to try to turn a hundred and forty thousand Vichy troops down there to support the Resistance. Did he succeed?"

Behind a controlled smile, Léon replied, "He is still working on it, Madame, and I do not believe he will give up until he gets the job done." Then he added, "He has told me much about you. He says that the Alliance is in very capable hands."

Despite herself, Fourcade blushed. "What is your purpose here?"

Having taken his seat, Léon drew a deep breath before speaking. "I propose to dethrone that swine in Vichy."

Fourcade stared at him in disbelief. "A coup? You intend to stage a coup against Pétain?"

Léon nodded.

"I hope you dismiss that thought before it develops further."

Léon's face reddened, his brow creased, and he coughed. Clearly, the reception to his plan was not the one he had expected.

"But Madame—"

"Let's just suppose you succeed," Fourcade said with a ferocity that was unusual for her. "What do you think Hitler will do? Accept the coup as a *fait accompli*?

"The French military in Vichy is all but disbanded. We are in no way prepared to face the *Wehrmacht* across southern France. Our Resistance is still in an organizational stage with British aid without which we couldn't hope to mount much of an opposition."

As Fourcade warmed to her argument, her cheeks turned red. "How would our people survive a *blitzkrieg*? And I promise you, it would come. Hitler already plans to move our citizens out of their homes in the occupied zones. Do you think he would speed up or slow down those plans?

"I'll tell you what I think. He would move the people who would go easily and kill those who resist. He's already doing exactly that in Poland—and in France too, to the Jews, and he's pressuring Pétain to do the same thing. If he invades, he'll do it throughout all of France. Your plan accelerates our extinction as a culture and as a country."

Léon listened, stunned. "I'm sorry that you disagree so vehemently, Madame. I thought you would be more receptive. Navarre did as well."

"Navarre is in Africa," Fourcade retorted. "I'm here dealing with today's realities. I joined his Alliance network expecting to take his orders, but he asked me to lead here in France. I know he's doing important work in Africa, but since he left, I've gained formal relations and funding through SOE and put together groups that operate across most of France. Our people are on the ground and report daily, and I doubt that any of them would support such a proposal. It's foolish."

She caught herself and wiped her forehead with the back of her hand. "I'm sorry. I don't mean to be rude." She let her eyes stray over his muscular build and then spoke again, aware that her cheeks were fully aflame. "You're a man with passion for France, and no one doubts your daring or determination to defeat our occupiers, but your plan will not work."

Startled at the spiritedness of the exchange, the others had sat silently listening. Then Phillippe ventured to join the discussion. "If I may," he said, turning to Léon. "I agree with Fourcade. We have no army, we have no air force, we have no navy. What remains is outside our borders and incapable of facing a *Wehrmacht blitzkrieg*. Most of our Resistance fighters are untrained amateurs. We teach them what we can for every mission. They give their best, and quite often, they succeed. Too often, their failure is fatal. To expect them to meet and defeat a full, blooded army, well equipped and ready for combat, is to ask our people to commit personal and national suicide. I cannot support the plan."

Léon regarded him with surprise. "You are the person I least expected to oppose it. You were known within the navy for wanting to surrender French warships to Great Britain to keep them out of German hands, and you were even supportive when the British destroyed our navy at Mers el-Kébir in Algeria."

"I was, and I think I was correct," Phillippe replied. "I didn't want to allow Germany to gain the most powerful navy after Britain's. You're proposing to make the rest of France a battleground, running with the blood of our people with little to no chance for them to survive, much less prevail. We must take a longer approach, and I think the plan the madame pursues is the right one. It's in line with De Gaulle, who fights in London every day to unite and build a French fighting force to join the British when the time is right to invade and take back the Continent.

"Besides, if you're looking for support from French navy and army officers still in North Africa—particularly in Algeria —you're deluding yourselves. They're bitter about the British bombing, and they are anti-Gaullist precisely because he's in London. More importantly, they're pro-Vichy, the same government you're asking them to take down."

He turned to Henri. "You command probably the largest and most effective section of the Alliance network. Would you support Faye's plan?"

Henri looked grimly from Phillippe to Léon, then to Fourcade, and back to Phillippe. He shook his head. "No. I would not support a coup."

Fourcade stood and extended a hand to Léon. "Thank you for coming," she said. "I'm sorry that we do not see things the same way. Please relay to Navarre that the Alliance, at least the part of it in France, will not support the plan. Tell him I am confident that I speak for our British friends."

Fourcade asked Horton to stay as the other three men departed. "You gave that major an earful," he quipped as he poured a cup of coffee. "How do you think Navarre will react?"

"He'll be angry at first, but eventually he'll see that I'm right, and he'll come around. That doesn't mean that he won't try something before coming to his senses."

She changed the subject, relating her conversation with Phillippe prior to Henri's arrival with the air force major. Filling Horton in on what had taken place in Dinard, she said,

"*Oberst* Meier is the German officer who helped Phillippe and his group avoid arrest. We don't know if what he did was deliberate or inadvertent. I'd like as much information on him as we can get from London. Would you please handle that?"

"Consider it done, mum."

"There's one other thing." She told him of Ferrand Boulier's passing and the way the old man died. "Please request that they inform Jeremy. I'm sure he'll want to know."

"I'm sorry to hear about Ferrand. I'll see to it."

While they talked, Maurice arrived, bringing Amélie, Chantal, and Jeannie with him. "You can't keep sending young women to my house," he joked. "People will wonder what kind of enterprise I'm running."

His humor appeared to have had a positive effect on the girls, although all three looked tired and drawn. Fourcade noticed that Chantal's eyes regained life and she blushed when she saw Horton. She tucked the observation at the back of her mind and rose to meet her new visitors.

"I'm sorry about your father," she said, putting her arms around Amélie and Chantal. "He was a good, good man."

She held the sisters for several moments, and then, extending her hand and kissing Jeannie on both cheeks, she said, "What an honor to meet you. Your success in Dinard was astounding."

"I did a small thing, Madame, that my country needed to be done."

"Our country will be very grateful, I'm sure, and you are welcome here." Shifting her attention to include Amélie and Chantal, she said, "I want all three of you to stay at the villa for as long as you like. Rest, relax, and restore perspective." She swept her arm around to take in all of their surroundings. "Look, it's a beautiful day, a beautiful place, and you are surrounded by people who love you."

Seeing a lift in the girls' faces followed by reserved smiles, she gestured toward the table. "Sit. Maurice and Horton too. Let's enjoy the day and celebrate that people we care about are returned to safety." She looked around again with an exaggerated anxious look. "Relative safety, that is. I'll get some food brought out."

Later, as the sun warmed the day, conversation turned to chatter, and spirits rose, Fourcade sauntered by Horton. "That girl likes you," she kidded, thrusting her chin in Chantal's direction.

Horton followed her view. "Don't be silly, mum. She's a schoolgirl, and I'm three and a half years older. She's more like a little sister."

"Ah. I see you've done the math," Fourcade said, laughing quietly and moving on.

Amélie approached her, looking in better spirits but still mournful. "Have you heard anything—" She dropped her eyes.

"About Jeremy?" Fourcade finished the question for her. "I'm sorry."

"I think maybe he's forgotten me."

"Oh, my dear, no," Fourcade said, throwing her arms around Amélie's shoulders. "The war is all that stands between you two." She released her embrace, stepped back, and chuckled. "It's a pretty big obstacle, but remember, Jeremy's already proposed; and your father gave permission— that's what Phillippe told me—so the one holding back now is you." Seeing a slight smile playing on Amélie's lips below shy eyes, she added, "I'll include a direct inquiry with the next documents we send to London. I imagine our new friend, Jeannie, might give us reason to make that happen soon."

"Oh, thank you," Amélie said, looking hopeful. "Thank you." She hugged Fourcade and went to join Chantal, who had moved next to Horton and engaged him in conversation. The sergeant shot Fourcade a dismal look, like that of a cornered bear.

She observed Jeannie leaning against the railing at the edge of the veranda, taking in the beauty of the landscape and the low whisper of distant waves from the Mediterranean shore. "May I join you?"

Jeannie turned. "Madame Fourcade. Of course. I was admiring your view. This is so beautiful. Thank you for all you've done for me."

"I did a small thing that my country needed," Fourcade said, quoting Jeannie from their earlier conversation.

Jeannie laughed lightly, enjoying the reference. "You flatter me."

"No. The value of the intelligence you provided is incalculable. I can guess without exaggeration that you must have played a significant part in causing the invasion of Great Britain to be cancelled."

Jeannie blushed and turned to let the sea breeze blow over her face. "I did nothing more than the people who came to rescue me. And don't forget those others who are in the fight every day. I only did my duty."

"You are a remarkable young lady, the best of France. What are your plans?"

"I've hardly had time to think of them, but I was surprised on the way here that as we went through checkpoints, my papers were never questioned. I was very scared because I thought that surely notices would have gone out to arrest me. But there were none, I've never used an alias, and I didn't have time to get false papers."

"That was an oversight on our part. We should have taken care of that in advance. We'll add that detail to our checklist for future operations."

"Yes, that should be done, but my point is that the Gestapo in Dinard seems to have forgotten about me."

Fourcade looked at Jeannie quizzically. "What are you thinking?"

Jeannie turned all the way around and leaned against the railing. "I'm thinking that I could do this again—that is, infiltrate the German military headquarters—in Paris."

Fourcade sucked in her breath. Nothing she could say that was appropriate to the moment came to mind, so she reached over and squeezed Jeannie's arm.

Fourcade tossed and turned in bed that night. For a time, she thought of the brave young sisters who had just lost their father and the courageous young lady who proposed to spy on the German high command in Paris, and what that might entail.

Then, an image intruded on her mind of Léon Faye, the tall, handsome French air force pilot with whom she had argued over critical issues on their first meeting. Again, she felt the stirring in her chest. Try as she might, she could not dismiss him from her thoughts. Pulling the blankets over her head, she murmured, "I hate this war."

34

January 17, 1941
Oflag IV-C, Colditz, Germany

"At last, we speak," Pat Reid said. "I heard how you were re-
captured. I'm sorry."

"It happens," Lance replied with as much spirit as he could
muster. "I'm just glad to escape from that damnable cooler.
Maybe that's the object of it. You're so happy to get out that life
seems instantly better." He grinned. "The one at Oberursel
was far worse. In the one here, I could stand up, move around,
stretch out on the cot, and sit at a table. I only met Padre Platt
once before I escaped. He told me that if this is a punishment
camp, he wished he had been disciplined here before being
sent to Spangenburg. I quite agree with him, although the
meals were sparse in the cooler. SBO should really speak with
the *kommandant* about that."

"And how are you?"

"Me?" Lance patted his chest with both hands. "Never
better, and ready to get back at it. With any luck, I should be
on my way in another week. Did Miloš make it?"

Pat shook his head. "He was picked up a week before you were. He's back here now." He chuckled. "And he said essentially the same thing—he's ready for his next try."

"He's a good man. He did exactly as we rehearsed and saved me from having to take a crash course in locksmithing."

"I'm glad to see your spirits are good, but we'll take things slow for a bit. We need to debrief you thoroughly and let you know about a few changes in our procedures. The SBO wants to speak with you too." He smiled. "I believe he has a letter from home for you."

Lance grinned. "I could use one. I had all but given up on receiving another one."

Pat chuckled. "What did you expect? You hardly stayed in one place long enough for anyone to know where to send them, much less allow time for the letters to reach you. But yes, he has one. And, if you're up to it, he'd like to start your debriefing as soon as possible, with me and Chip."

"I'm up for it. Can I read my letter first?"

"Of course."

"A good letter, I hope?" Guy said after the four of them had gathered in a room cleared of other people to debrief Lance.

"It's from my mum and dad," Lance replied. He had not expected the rush of emotion that overcame him when he had read it, and the reaction threatened again. "I think they're having a rough go of it on Sark Island, but they can't say so. They sort of beat around the bush about conditions there under German occupation. They're both fighters. I can promise they haven't given in to the Jerries, but this letter is so humdrum and full of nothing. Look." He held it up. "No holes. Even the censors couldn't find anything wrong with it. If they were speaking their minds, it would be nothing but holes. They know what they're doing. This letter is to let me know they're alive and getting on."

Guy looked at him somberly. "I wanted to speak with you personally because I have two more letters for you, from your brother and sister, Jeremy and Claire."

Lance's eyes widened in surprise. "Can I have them? Where are they?"

"I'll give them to you, but I wanted to explain something first. While you were gone, we sent notes to them as if from you. They would immediately know you had not sent them because they would make no sense—referring to family members we made up and places you've probably never been. Our hope was that they would think them weird and take them to British intelligence for help. That's worked for others, and we're hoping it's worked in this case. So, I haven't read them. When *you* do, if they sound strange, they might contain coded messages, in which case I'd like you to turn them over to Chip for analysis."

Lance studied Guy's face for only a moment. "Of course, of course. May I see them?"

Guy removed them from his top pocket and handed them over. Lance took them eagerly, started to peruse one, then stopped and started on the other. Then he handed them back to Guy. "Anything to help the cause."

"I'm sorry, Lance. I hope I wasn't too presumptuous."

"I said anything to help the cause, sir," Lance replied evenly. "I don't give lip service."

"No, you don't," Guy said with an amused smile. "You certainly don't." He pursed his lips in thought. "I have another question. Do the names Horton, Kenyon, and Lancas mean anything to you?"

Lance's eyes bulged, and he leaped to his feet. "Yes, they

do," he said with alacrity. "Those two names, Horton and Kenyon, they were the chaps who went down on the *Lancastria* with me. Together, the three of us, after we were rescued, did some sabotage with the French Resistance. How do you know about them?"

Guy straightened suddenly and looked about as he smiled. "My word, Sergeant Littlefield, you are a handful, aren't you? I sent my own coded letters to British intelligence and received back a reply with those words. You'll be happy to know that your friends are fine, but I wasn't informed about their activities." He turned his attention to Pat and Chip. "Listen to me. What Sergeant Littlefield just told us stays in this room." He turned back to Lance. "Unless you want to be interrogated by the Gestapo, don't mention your activities with the Resistance again to anyone." His face softened. "But I will tell you that it was the French organization that got word through to London about your chums."

"Thank you, sir. Wing Commander Day warned me about the same thing at Oberursel. I had a mental lapse."

"Understandable under the circumstances. Just realize that some POWs would trade information about what you've done to the Germans for better treatment, and you had direct access into the French Resistance. The next slip could cost you your life, and others too. We trust only those we've vetted."

"Got it, sir."

"Let's not belabor the point. As I understand, you made it all the way to the Swiss border on this last escape attempt. What happened?"

Lance grimaced. "I'd laugh if it didn't hurt so much. There I was, standing with my papers in front of a wet-behind-the ears German border guard. I was being polite and all, and even confident because I'd been through so many checkpoints with no trouble in the least. He examines my papers, looks up at me, and nods. I thought he was letting me know that everything was in order, but when I reached to take my papers back, the chap kept them, and suddenly two other guards held my arms while two more pointed their rifles at me, and I was led away." He shook his head. "So close."

"What tipped them off?"

Lance inhaled. "The color of the travel documents had changed the day before."

Guy leaned back and stretched. "That's a disappointment to all of us. Any fixes you can think of?"

Lance shook his head. "I've thought about almost nothing else since then, but I don't have a solution. They seem to change paper colors and dates at the drop of a hat. I have no clue how they can distribute new ones so fast."

Guy looked at Chip. "Intelligence officer?"

Chip smirked and exhaled. "I'll run it through our brain trust, but I don't have any immediate solutions. It's like playing roulette."

"*Russian* roulette," Pat broke in, "but it's information we need."

They spent several hours going over the details of Lance's route. "I was lucky to be on a late train. Most people went to sleep. I nabbed a suitcase just before switching trains in Leipzig. Miloš went his separate way there. I'm glad he's safe.

"Anyway, I was on another train within fifteen minutes. The Huns are good at running the railroad on time. I was miles away by the time the suitcase went missing.

"The money you issued to me was plenty. It got me into a *gasthaus* in Gotha and kept me fed." He laughed. "We got to the train station here in Colditz much sooner than expected, so I went into one of the guard stations to warm up. They let me stay there most of the night until a train came through. I regaled them with stories of how I met my fiancée and where we intended to honeymoon, and so on." He looked at the three officers facing him as a question came to mind. "Pat said we were changing our procedures. In what way?"

Guy cleared his throat. "In several. We had an incident while you were out. An escape by some of our Brits was blown because their plan crossed with one going at the same time by the Poles. Neither knew about the other. That was an avoidable error.

"So that we don't slip up again, we agreed at the senior level that no escape plans would go forward without coordination among the nationalities. Also, that we'd establish a list. Those wishing to escape must wait their turn. All plans must be approved and coordinated at the senior level."

Lance stared at him. "Does that mean that I won't be able to—"

"Three months, at least," Guy replied, nodding. He stood cross-armed with one hand holding his chin. "That's the next available slot."

Lance stared at the floor. When he looked up again, he grinned. "I'd better start preparing, then. Three months goes fast. It's been seven weeks since I first arrived here."

Guy laughed and clapped Lance on the back. "Ah, Little-field, despite the circumstances, seeing you again, healthy, safe, and in one piece, is a delight. Welcome back."

"Is that it, then, sir? Are we done?"

Guy leaned back with a frown. "Not quite."

Lance had started to rise. He sat back down with a quizzical look. "What else is there."

"Do you recall that when you first arrived, I showed you a section of the castle reserved for the *prominentes*."

Lance nodded, bewildered. "I do. A wretched place even

by the standards we live under, but that has nothing to do with me."

Still cross-armed, Guy moved his hand from his chin to the back of his neck and rubbed it. "I'm afraid it might. Have any of our captors ever asked you about your hometown?"

Not comprehending where this line of questioning was going, Lance pursed his lips. "No, sir. I'm a junior sergeant. I'm not supposed to know a lot, so no one bothered."

"Your mother is the Dame of Sark, is she not? And your stepfather is the senior co-ruler?"

Lance laughed. "Yes, that's true. But Sark is a tiny island. My parents rule—if you want to call it that—over about four hundred and fifty people, and we call them friends. Mum and Dad consult with them before governance decisions are made, usually by a show of hands."

"I understand. However, your mother's pedigree extends back into noble families in English history. She's a recognized member of the aristocracy, and Sark right now is of much interest to Adolf Hitler. Along with the other English Channel Isles, they are his only conquests of British territory, and as such, they have high propaganda value."

Lance inhaled deeply and closed his eyes. When he re-opened them, he exhaled with a rush of air. "How does that affect me here?"

"Right now, it doesn't," Guy said, "but it's another thing to keep under your hat. If you become identified as a *prominente* —they're classifying family members of *prominentes* in the same category—then you could be moved out of here and into that section of Colditz Castle."

"Meaning my chances of escape are greatly reduced."

Guy began laughing, joined by Pat and Chip. "Lance Little-field," he gasped between breaths, "God broke the mold after he baked you. He just couldn't handle another person with such a singular purpose."

His face changed to a sober expression. "Unfortunately, it could mean more than that. There's no good reason to keep *prominentes* isolated from the rest of us. I think they're being held separately with the expectation that at some point they might be used as bargaining chips."

35

February 10, 1941
RAF Croydon, England

Dressed in US Army combat fatigues, Paul waited for Wild Bill Donovan at the main headquarters building, a nondescript two-story affair with a view of the runways and some of the aircraft. Most of them were parked out of sight, a tactic that had contributed to saving Fighter Command aircraft and frustrating the *Luftwaffe*. From where Paul stood in front of a large window with many panes, he could see inside hangars where mechanics worked busily on planes needing repair. Not so long ago, that had been an impossibility during the day because of the *Luftwaffe* raids on RAF aircraft and facilities. Those days had faded as Hitler concentrated his raids against the population at night to foment terror.

Donovan appeared down the hall, rousting Paul from daydreams of Ryan. "You made it," he said. "When did you get in?"

"Last night. I slept on a cot in a room down the hall."

Donovan scrutinized Paul's face and chuckled. "Let's go.

We've got a long trip ahead, and it'll be rough. We're flying into a small airstrip near Ioannina in the Epirus region in northwestern Greece. Our escorts will pick us up there. The Italians penetrated forty miles into Greece in early November, but they were driven back to a line well inside Albania. That's where we're going." He added wryly, "Keep those lethal pills handy."

If Donovan's intent was to shock Paul out of his daydreams, he succeeded. On impulse, Paul reached up and fingered the pocket containing them. "They're here," he said. "I'm all set. Just let me grab my kit."

"Our plane's waiting, courtesy of the United States Air Corps," Donovan called. "Make sure you've got your cold weather gear."

Paul rejoined him carrying his combat pack. "We'll be traveling partway through arctic conditions: waist-high snow in the Pindus Mountains. We're headed to a coastal town in Albania called Vlorë, but we're taking an overland route so we can see the battlefield. All the Italians have left for re-supply is one harbor in Albania, at Durrës."

Donovan warmed to his pronouncements as he continued. "Paul, the Greeks stunned the world." He spoke with controlled but intense enthusiasm. "When they took Vlorë, they secured a front extending sixty miles east across Albania to Pogradec. By rights, the Italians should have already finished off Greece. They've got the tanks, fighter planes, a blooded army with combat success—but the Greeks are defending their homes and their families, and they're doing it with archaic rifles left over from the Great War, as well as sticks, stones, knives, and even their bare hands. No one expected them to defeat the Italians. They just didn't have the equipment."

"Just those archaic rifles and their sticks and stones," Paul remarked. "That goes back to what Mr. Churchill said about when things become obsolete."

Donovan nodded. "Good point. Glad you listened. Italy attacked the Kalpaki Pass at the end of October, but they got bogged down in the snow. Their tanks couldn't make it to the border, their supply lines broke down, and they hadn't counted on how fiercely the partisans would fight alongside the regular Greek army." He looked incredulous. "The Italians penetrated thirty miles into Greece, but the Greeks mounted a counter-offensive and drove them back seventy miles. That's forty miles inside Albania."

Donovan's eyes shone with excitement, and in that moment, Paul gained an inkling into how the general had gained his nickname, Wild Bill. He was obviously eager about the prospect of heading into combat.

"How's our deception plan working out?" Paul asked.

"So far so good. I gave an interview to *The New York Times* just before leaving London, and they quoted me verbatim. I said that back in August, I had found the British to be 'resolute and courageous' and that now I'd have to add the word 'confident.' The *New York Post* led with a story that I would be heading to North Africa seeking a 'new understanding' with Vichy France."

"Are we really going to North Africa?"

"We might pop on down there. We'll play it by ear. The intelligence operations that succeed best are those that approach the truth, and the truth is that we have no interest in accommodating Vichy France at all, and I've already been to North Africa for the president."

His voice grew serious. "The flight will take hours. We can still overfly central Europe, but we'll probably take the longer route across Spain, and then skirt south of Italy." He grinned briefly. "We don't want you getting captured, what with all those British state secrets in your head. When we land tonight, the Greeks will take us forward. Did I mention that their women were fighting at the front? And re-supply from Britain isn't getting through the Italian blockade in the Aegean Sea." He shook his head with an admiring expression on his face. "But when Prime Minister Metaxas called on his people to fight for independence, Greek roads were choked with tens of thousands of volunteers. They're a proud nation with a proud heritage, and the fascists will pay hell subjugating Greece. We're counting on that to stall the German thrust into the Soviet Union."

"If I may say so, that part of the plan sounded a bit mercenary to me from when I first heard Mr. Churchill mention it," Paul observed.

Donovan studied Paul before replying. "I don't think so. You Brits broke the Italian codes as well as the German ones, and you're providing the Greeks strategic and tactical intelligence from those messages," he said. "Air support out of Crete too, so the Greeks aren't in this alone, and that's infuriating Hitler. The odds of his intervening are going up with every Italian encounter with the Brits, and that's what we want, to bog him down. We're all in the war together now, including America, whether our public wants to think so or not. Neither Germany nor Japan will leave us any other choice.

"Regardless, you Brits have to continue supporting Greece. Americans still cherish independence and loyalty and wouldn't take kindly to Churchill if he deserted Greece while asking for our help."

Paul cut in with visible annoyance to Donovan's last statement. "Then again, America isn't helping Britain much right now."

Donovan's reply was stone cold. "Tell me that again when

this intelligence operation is complete, and our young men start dying."

With the thought of the other intelligence maneuver to influence public opinion pinging at the back of his mind, Paul straightened up and faced the general. "So, we have an intelligence office in Manhattan and you're here. I get that, sir, but this war depletes Britain's hard currency reserves, yet America requires us to pay cash for desperately needed supplies and equipment so that your country doesn't appear to side with us. And you won't even deliver planes we've paid for because of that Neutrality Act. But Americans will hold us to task if we don't burn up our scarce resources more quickly by expending them in Greece?"

His own impassioned remarks surprised Paul. "I'd say Britain's suffering is at least as great as Greece's, and our demonstrated resolve is as strong as theirs, but neither they nor any other country have come to defend us. We won't win on determination alone, and neither will Greece. Germany's conquest of all of Europe aside from Greece and the neutral countries puts every bit of the continent's mining, manufacturing, food, fuel, and all its other industrial might at Hitler's disposal. Without at least equal resources, we Brits have no chance of winning the long war without America."

Donovan regarded Paul somberly. "You're getting the picture. America will come around. Our mission now is to pin down Hitler so that his Soviet foray fails.

"But regarding Italy, its senior leadership operates out of petty jealousies, undermining each other, and they don't have the resources Germany does, so they can't mount a *Wehrmacht*-style combined-arms *blitzkrieg*. And they're locked into using the same tactics over and over, ignoring successive failures, and only varying time of day between attacks. Mussolini's credibility with Hitler must be taking a major hit.

"But you need to face another reality. Your family is from Sark Island, which is isolated from the rest of Britain. And although your stepfather was born in the US, you haven't lived close enough to Americans to understand us, so I'll point out a fact that might not have registered on you: Great Britain is not necessarily considered to be our great friend, and you're asking Americans to support a war to save your country's bacon. That's the way they see it."

Paul stopped what he was doing and stared, speechless.

Seeing his expression, Donovan grunted. "Hey, my mother's parents were from an area just north of Northern Ireland where a lot of people are still not crazy about the Brits. I was born in the same century when your guys invaded the United States and burned down Washington and the White House. Probably all that saved us then was a freak thunderstorm, and that was only thirty-three years after the end of our Revolution.

"Then, a lot of your aristocracy supported the Confederacy during our Civil War. Americans are still alive who remember that, and they've told the stories to their kids and grandkids. I arrived on this planet just eighteen years after that conflict was over. Barely that much time has gone by since the last time we had to bail out Europe in the Great War. So you see, events are not as ancient as they seem, and deep wounds take a while to heal."

While he spoke, the general watched Paul's face morph from pique to confusion to consternation. He dropped his tone. "Don't get me wrong, Americans love the Brits, generally. But Americans will ask themselves why we should sacrifice the lives of our young men and our treasure to save a country that tried to conquer ours. If we do that and we miscalculate or fail to defeat the Germans before they get to us, we'll invite their invasion on the east coast and Japan's on the west coast, and our own resources will be depleted." Donovan arched his brows and smacked his lips to make his point. "Try to sell that concept to America's moms watching their sons go off to fight thousands of miles from home. That perspective is what we have to understand and overcome if we hope to succeed."

When Donovan finished speaking, Paul was at a loss for how to respond. At last, he said, "You mentioned a few aspects I hadn't considered."

Donovan stepped back quietly, observed Paul outfitted in his new US Army fatigues complete with brown boots, helmet, and combat pack, and grinned. "We're going to have to dirty you up some. You look like a fresh grunt at the beginning of boot camp."

The general's tone changed to serious again, with a cautious tenor. "Listen to me carefully. As far as the Greeks are concerned, you're an odd American with a British accent. Most don't speak English well, so they might not notice. Stick to your cover story and don't even hint that you're in His Majesty's army. If any war correspondents show up, fade into the shadows."

"I can handle that."

"A word of warning: you'll see me being apparently careless with communications to stateside. Don't let that bother you. It's part of the subterfuge. And if I poke fun at you for being a State Department puke, play along."

Paul nodded. "My skin's quite thick."

Donovan laughed. "We'll see." He glanced at Paul mischievously. "So, this girl, Ryan Northridge. Is she the love of your life?"

Paul grinned back. "We'll see."

"Fair enough." Donovan gestured toward a US Army transport plane revving its engines on the tarmac. "That's ours. Let's go."

36

Ioannina, Greece

They arrived at Ioannina as dawn broke. From the air and despite the barrenness of winter, it looked to be a gem of a town with a castle overlooking a lake, but Paul was unable to make out much more detail through his porthole window. Cast against the morning glow of sunrise, a thick blanket of snow sparkled with a fiery red and orange hue for as far as he could see. High foothills on either side of the rough runway near the north end of the lake channeled the wind, buffeting the aircraft as it descended, flared, touched down, and taxied to a stop.

Looking through his window, Paul watched a man in a very strange uniform walk toward the plane as they prepared to exit it. He wore a white jacket with flowing sleeves and matching wide skirts, and a vest of multi-colored vertical stripes over full-length white leggings. On his feet were Albanian-type slippers with turned-up tufted toes, and on his head was a red cap, like a Moroccan fez, with a thick, dark tail trailing over his right shoulder almost to his waist.

Donovan saw Paul's stare. "You don't want to mess with that guy," he muttered as the man approached the aircraft. "He's an *evzone*, a member of one of the Greek elite mountain infantry units. They won Greek independence from the Ottomans in the '20s and early '30s, and back in November, a regiment of them destroyed a crack Italian unit at Metsovo Pass. They're famous for courage and tenacity, and they have a war cry like no other, '*Aera*.' It means 'like the wind,' and their favorite tactic is to stream down the mountainside onto their enemies while screaming '*Aera!*' and then duke it out in hand-to-hand combat."

Paul glanced at the soldier with awed respect.

The *evzone* saluted as Paul and Donovan stepped down from the plane into a gust that whipped off the lake and flung glacial wind-talons at them with sharp specks of ice. "General Donovan." He spoke in perfect English, seemingly oblivious to the cold, a tall man, solidly built and lithe, and with dark skin, black hair, and penetrating eyes. "I am Major Damian Bella. My orders are to escort you and your State Department aide to the front, and along the way, to brief you on the fighting that took place.

"Vlorë is only two hundred kilometers, but due to our route and the weather, that'll take several hours. We're not running any combat operations now, but if the enemy attacks, that'll slow us down."

They left for Vlorë with a fourth man, the driver, proceeding at a normal cruising speed in a British Humber heavy utility vehicle. "The roads are clear most of the way," Damian said as they began a steep ascent out of the valley where the airfield was located. He sat in the front passenger seat with his driver. "We've had heavy snowfall this year, so the going could be slow."

"How's the fighting at the front?" the general asked.

Damian shrugged. "We're not seeing much at present. We're holding. The Italians were not prepared for our winters." He grinned, showing fastidiously kept white teeth against his dark skin. "You came when there's little fighting. It was back and forth for many weeks in November. The Italians came south as far as Metsovo—"

"I heard," Donovan said. "What you *evzones* did there only adds to your legend. The Italian soldiers outnumber you, they outgun you, and they've had a lot more combat experience."

"You speak English well," Paul interjected. "How did that come about?"

"I took my degree at Princeton," Damian said. "I intended to immigrate and become an American citizen, but I came back to defend the homeland."

As the conversation continued, Paul noticed intermittent groups of people trudging through the snow on both sides of the vehicle, all going in the same direction. They seemed in good spirits, waving at the passing Humber. "Who are those people and where are they going?"

Damian beamed with pride. "They're volunteers, and they are heading to our training camps."

Paul stared out the window at them. Most were young men, but some looked to be in their mid-thirties or approaching forty, and even a few beyond that. Mixed in with them were women, trudging with the men and waving good-naturedly, all wearing civilian clothes.

"That's remarkable," Paul said. "The divisions between your left and right were quite sharp not that long ago. A civil war was predicted."

"Hmph," Damian grunted with a stern look in his eyes. "We are Greeks, first, last, and always, and we won't let a criminal take our country from us." His face was fixed with determination. "The Italians fight because Mussolini tells them to.

They're good fighters, but they have no spirit for this war, and they're poorly equipped to fight in the Balkans. We Greeks, though, we fight for survival."

Paul started to say something that indicated empathy coming from similar experiences but caught himself, recalling that he was to give no hint of his British nationality beyond his accent. "Will they get any training?"

Damian arched his brow. "If we have time, we'll train them. Otherwise, they'll learn from our regular army as best they can. Our citizens are tenacious. Once the defensive line was established between Vlorë and Pogradec, that ended offensive operations until the spring and we could bring in and train our volunteers at a more measured pace." He flinched. "Hopefully, we'll get them ready for what's coming."

"And what about the Germans?"

"Ahh, the Germans. Who knows what is in that maniac Hitler's head today? If he comes, it won't be an easy fight."

The wind abated, but snow fell in large flakes. On either side of the road, cleared snow was piled higher than the roof of the vehicle, blocking the surrounding view. As minutes ticked by, the snow reduced to tiny flakes, floating down in such profusion that they created a haze. As the Humber wound higher into the mountains, shivering cold permeated the interior, overcoming the warmth of the heater.

"We're entering the area where most of the fighting took place," Damian said.

Paul looked about, amazed. "You fought in this? I can't see anything."

Damian pursed his lips and nodded. "Sometimes in better weather, sometimes worse. Our regular soldiers and common citizens would not give up." He glanced outside. The number of people trudging up the mountains had thinned, but some hardy souls plodded on. "When we cross this ridge and descend into the valley, we should go faster."

By ten o'clock, they had reached the crest. The sky cleared a bit, and they viewed the panorama below. The valley was deep and blanketed with snow. Traveling down the mountain road was treacherous, the sun providing little relief over frozen surfaces, but when they reached the valley floor and turned north, as Damian had said, the driving became easier. Within a short time, they entered Kalpaki.

"This was a choke point," Damian explained. "The Italians had wanted to go through here to hit our flank on the Elaia-Kalamas line on flatter ground by the sea. They hoped to avoid attacking across the Kalamas River, but we stopped them there too, and drove them back from all our defensive lines. We were outnumbered. The battle went back and forth, but we pushed them seventy miles to the Vlorë-Pogradec defensive line inside Albania."

A few miles past Kalpaki, the terrain widened, and they encountered the hulks of abandoned Italian tanks bogged down in the snow, having tipped over on the side of the road, thrown a track, or having met some other battle calamity. Donovan requested to pull over so he could examine one of the doomed vehicles.

"It's not a bad tank," he said. "Poor leadership put it here. No one bothered to study the lay of the land or the limits of this war machine's capabilities."

Damian agreed, and then pointed to the northeast. "Korçë is an Albanian town in that direction. It dominates a plateau with easier access to lower coastal ground. The tanks came through there. We took it last month, but the fighting was fierce, and losing it to Greece was a major blow for the Italians." He added, "The Albanians were thrilled to see us. They welcomed us with cheers."

"How far is it?" Donovan asked.

"In distance, about twenty miles. But in these conditions, it could take hours. If you want to go, I can take you, but my commanding general wants to see you, so we'd need to radio for approval."

Donovan shook his head. "Never mind. That was a pivotal battle. I wanted to see the site, but let's go on."

As they descended into lower ground, the landscape widened further and then turned northwest, heading toward the coast. Although snow continued to blanket the country-side, it was thinner in the flatlands and melted on the roads. Civilian vehicles were few, but military traffic increased as they continued toward the battle lines.

At Sarande, a fishing village, they turned right and traveled north along the coast road. To their left, the Aegean Sea roiled in winter tumult, its waves pounding the shore, sending spray into the freezing air.

"We're getting closer," Damian said. "Maybe an hour, maybe less."

Then they heard a sound that Paul knew well from the air raids over Britain, the high, whining grind of aircraft engines that deepened into a roar. Donovan and Damian heard it too, as did the driver.

Ahead of them, an object appeared in the sky and descended rapidly. Then plumes of snow leaped into the air on a path aimed straight at them, followed by the clipped stutter of machine gun fire. The driver jerked his steering wheel and swerved to the right just as the snow eruptions passed by them. Overhead, the combined fury of the fighter engine resounded as an Italian Caproni Vizzola F.4 fighter let loose with its two 12.7 mm machine guns.

The Humber careened into an open field, hit rough ground, and rolled over. All four men bounced around inside until it rested on its side. Paul fell down on the general, knocking him unconscious. Damian dropped onto the driver. He groaned, but the driver made no sound.

Behind them, Paul heard the Italian engines ascend into a whine once again as the aircraft climbed, and despite being in a daze, he recognized its tenor. The aircraft was looping to take another pass.

Damian heard it too and struggled to stand without injuring the driver. He reached for the passenger door, struggled to unlatch it, and threw it open.

The pitch of the engine deepened once more, and both Paul and Damian understood the pilot's intent. They heard the pounding of the machine gun while Damian managed to throw his door open. Then, with one foot on the rim of the steering wheel and his opposite knee wedged against the back of his seat, he grabbed a Sten gun that Paul had not previously seen, perched waist-high, and opened fire.

The gun jammed.

The general stirred.

Paul tried to duplicate Damian's action, resting his left foot on the top edge of the driver's seat and pressing against the back of his own, but the heavy door kept falling on him as he sought to bring his weapon to bear.

The Vizzola sprayed down hot lead, its bullets striking the trunk and the hood.

Then another fighter engine roared overhead, but this one was steady, several hundred feet above them, and speeding toward the Italian fighter now climbing to their front.

Paul felt a surge of adrenaline. He knew that engine sound from the dogfights over London. Managing to push his head, neck, and upper chest through the door, he looked up and saw the unmistakable silhouette of a Spitfire in hot pursuit.

The Vizzola pilot had seen it too. He banked out of his

loop, rolled into straight and level flight toward his lines, and then tried to climb.

Too late.

The Spitfire, already in the chase, closed the distance. Fire and smoke spat from its nose, accompanied by the rhythmic pump of its guns.

The Vizzola's engine hiccupped, and the aircraft stalled. For a moment, it looked to Paul as though it slid backward in the air, then its nose fell and it plunged to earth, smacking the ground in a ball of fire. No parachute descended.

Paul let out a celebratory whoop. Below him, he heard stirring and looked back inside to see Donovan rubbing his head and trying to climb to his feet. Paul held the door up, managed to sit on the edge of the frame, and reached inside to help the general. After lending a hand, he swiveled and lowered himself to the ground. Donovan, groggy and struggling, appeared on the car's edge. As Paul reached to help him, Damian, having climbed out of the front seat, stepped next to him, and together, they lowered Donovan to the ground, where he leaned against the undercarriage and slid down to sit in the snow.

Paul turned to Damian. "Let's help your driver."

Damian stood still, staring distantly, and shook his head.

Several moments passed before Paul understood Damian's unspoken meaning. "No," he protested. "He can't be."

Damian covered his face with his hands and nodded.

Paul ran around the car to look through the windshield. Sprawled on the door of the upended Humber, the driver stared back, sightless, his neck bent at a peculiar angle.

Damian approached and stood next to Paul, his head hanging low. He closed his eyes and murmured, "When the vehicle turned over, his neck fell against the steering wheel. I fell on top of it."

Behind the Greek, Donovan walked over on unsteady feet. He gazed through the windshield at the limp figure and then wrapped an arm over Damian's shoulder.

Numbness overtook Paul. Try as he would, for a few moments he could not tear his eyes away from the dead man's face. War had ceased to be an ethereal notion read about in reports, heard about on radios, or watched from Fighter Command control rooms. He suddenly realized that, despite *Luftwaffe* attempts to destroy the RAF, regardless of the *blitz*, notwithstanding reports he compiled for MI-6, this was the first time he knew of that a man had died within inches of him. And across the snowy field, smoke rose from the probable demise of yet another man in the Italian Vizzola.

"What's his name?" Paul murmured. He stood at Damian's side opposite Donovan and wrapped an arm over the Greek's shoulder. "We'd be dead now but for his getting off the road so fast, and I don't know his name."

"It's Elias Ariti," Damian whispered in a hoarse voice. "He was a good man. A good soldier."

Overhead, the Spitfire circled back and waggled its wings. The three men watched it, standing side by side, the British captain on one end in US combat fatigues and the American general on the other, their arms stretched between them across the shoulders of the Greek *evzone* in the peculiar uniform. Then the plane disappeared over the horizon, beyond the wide-open, snow-covered fields and the smell and pounding of the sea against the shore only yards away.

Paul turned to face the general. "Sir, we have to get you to safety."

37

February 19, 1941
Sofia, Bulgaria

Getting Donovan to safety proved to be less difficult than Paul
had expected. The Spitfire pilot called to his controller and
requested that he radio the Greek forward-headquarters and
relay that an aerial attack on a ground vehicle had occurred
between Sarande and Himarë with survivors needing aid. On
determining who had been the victims of the attack, the corps
commanding general ordered a quick reaction force to the
area, where they found the three soldiers supporting each
other as they trudged along the road toward Himarë. While
one vehicle took Paul, Damian, and Donovan into the village,
two others were dispatched to recover Ariti's body and the
wrecked vehicle.

Waiting for Donovan and Paul at the Greek headquarters
in the seaside village was a US Army Air Corps pilot who had
flown in a transport plane to a nearby airfield. He delivered a
classified message to Donovan. Dismissing concerns for his
head injury and proclaiming his mental soundness, the

general read the message, whereupon he told Paul, "Don't settle in anywhere, bud. We're on the road again."

"Aren't you going to see the commanding general, sir?" Paul's tone struck a challenging note.

"For a few minutes," Donovan replied ruefully.

"Is that all?" Paul asked, visibly disturbed.

Donovan peered into his face. "I'll give him my verbal analysis of the situation, the obstacles he faces, and the fighting abilities of his army. I'll thank him for his hospitality and that of Major Bella, offer condolences for Elias Ariti, and explain that I have orders to go elsewhere." He smirked slightly. "Don't think 'cuz you saved my life that now you can get into my knickers."

"Sorry, sir. I didn't mean to imply otherwise, and I didn't save your life. All I did was help you down from the Humber." He paused, fiddling with his fingers. "It's just that—" His face tightened. "Sir, we suffered a casualty—" His voice caught.

Donovan studied Paul's demeanor. "Was that your first one?"

Paul nodded. He took a breath, but when he spoke, his voice nevertheless broke. "The first one up close. Shouldn't we stay around to pay our respects?"

"All casualties are tough," Donovan said gruffly, "particularly the first one, and especially when it happens right next to you. When you stop caring is when I don't want you around me." He clasped Paul's shoulder. "We have a mission, soldier, and when we complete it, we'll have honored Elias Ariti in the best way we could."

Paul nodded again. "Do I have time to bid Damian farewell?"

Donovan smiled. "I wouldn't think of leaving without doing that."

"Where to now?" Paul asked when they were airborne.

"Sofia, Bulgaria," Donovan replied. "And this is where you earn your keep."

"I thought I did that when I saved your life," Paul quipped.

Surprised, Donovan laughed. "It's good to see you back up on top of your game. Next thing you know, you'll be callin' me 'Wild Bill.'"

"I'm not impertinent enough to do that, sir."

Donovan laughed again and shook his head. "You're a good man, Paul Littlefield. I'm glad to have you on our team." He leaned toward Paul. "Now, here's what we're going to do."

When they landed, Paul left the aircraft by himself. He had changed back into civilian attire, and he made his way into the commercial side of the terminal. There, he placed an anonymous call to the local office of the Associated Press, reporting in German of having seen a man looking very much like General William Donovan leave a US Army transport plane that had just landed in a secluded part of the airfield. "If it's him, I think he's trying to travel incognito, because he's not wearing a military uniform." He listened, and then responded, "Yes, he's wearing a brown fedora hat and a matching greatcoat."

After hanging up, he caught a taxi from the airport to the American embassy, arriving in time to see a gaggle of reporters around the front entrance anxiously watching the driveway. Instructing the driver to let him off a block farther on, he walked back, slipped inside the building through the consular entrance using his diplomatic passport, and made his way to the front lobby, where he expected to rejoin the general. A few minutes later, he heard shouted questions outside the entrance and knew the general had arrived to contend with the press.

"That worked," Donovan told Paul when he was safely inside and away from the journalists. "They feel like they've tripped me up again, and they'll report that I'm in Bulgaria on a secret mission for talks." He looked at his watch. "We have two hours to go over our next steps ahead of a reception with the ambassador to meet and greet Bulgarian diplomats. You can go with me or rest up. Your choice. The real show starts tomorrow when we move to Vrana Palace as King Boris' guests."

"I'd like to come, if my presence won't add to the stir."

"I'm the guest. You're my aide. The focus will be on me as President Roosevelt's eyes and ears over here. When cameras appear, you disappear, and if you need to approach me, do it from the rear and speak to me quietly with your body canted toward those I'm facing, like we practiced. You'll get the hang of it, but don't fret too much. If anyone gets curious about who you are and starts digging, they'll run into a dead end, which will probably cause whoever it is to dig deeper. By then, our mission will be accomplished, and we'll be gone. Are my 'secret' papers ready?"

"All nicely folded. I'll put them in the pocket of the dinner jacket you'll wear tomorrow night."

"Good. I'll handle things myself this evening, but when we're at the palace, keep those drinks coming. Now remember, if we get even a twenty-four-hour delay of Germany's invasion into Soviet territory, we've succeeded, and every day after that is another cherry on the pie. What you need to know is that the palace will be chock-full of Nazi agents."

Paul chuckled. "I'll remember, sir." Even as he said the words, his stomach tightened.

The drive the next day to the royal palace, situated outside Sofia's city limits on the east side, took less than half an hour. Paul enjoyed the drive along Tsarigradsko Shosé, the capital city's largest boulevard. The wide thoroughfare offered grand views between stately buildings, war monuments, and parks, but he noticed that the city seemed in decline, with needed repairs evident along the way.

Twenty miles outside the city, the car turned into a driveway. They drove under tall trees past two grand fountains and circled around in front of them below a terrace that ran the length of a magnificent, white, two-story palace with a red Spanish-tile roof. Inset along the second floor were columns and arched windows. A grand entrance graced the first floor at its center.

A Bulgarian army general met them, and after formal greetings, ushered them to their rooms. "The king will receive you privately and then you'll be seated next to him for dinner," he told Donovan. He added, with an appraising view of Paul, "Your aide may accompany you for your visit with the king and will be seated close by for dinner."

"Please, can you tell me where I can send a cable to my president? I need to let him know I've arrived."

"By all means. But we won't be able to encrypt it for you."

With a quick glance at Paul, Donovan smiled and turned his full charm on the Bulgarian general. "I don't think that will be necessary. It's just a short note."

"Then, if you like, I can take it down and deliver it to our message center, and they can send it for you."

"That will work." Donovan smiled ingratiatingly. "Just say, 'Dear Mr. President, I have arrived in Bulgaria for talks with King Boris. Will keep you apprised.'"

The Bulgarian looked up swiftly and with a slight frown. "Are you sure of the message?"

"Yes, I think so." Donovan furrowed his brow as if in thought. "That should be all. And can you provide me with a confirmation that it's been received at the White House?" He laughed. "I don't want to be in trouble with Mr. Roosevelt for failing to keep him informed."

The Bulgarian general came to attention. "Certainly, sir. It will be done."

When the Bulgarian had left, Donovan grinned at Paul. "Show's on."

Forty-six-year-old King Boris was a slender man of medium height, dark hair cut very short, a high forehead, and deep-set eyes; and he sported a heavy mustache. He stood to greet General Donovan while Paul waited at the back of the room with an orderly.

Boris had acceded to the throne when his father abdicated in 1918 after losing a great deal of territory in the Treaty of Versailles, the agreement ending the Great War. He now stood in the center of his throne room on a raised dais, bedecked in a military uniform composed of a deep blue jacket over darker blue trousers, and a grand sash crossing his chest from his left shoulder to the right side of his waist with all manner of colorful military decorations and regalia. His countenance spoke volumes of the seriousness with which he considered his position.

"Greetings," he said, extending his hand as Donovan strode forward and shook it. "I hear that Americans bow their heads to no one."

"That is correct, sir, but we don't make a big issue of it

unless someone else does. My president sends his warmest greetings."

Boris listened to Donovan, steely-eyed, and then gestured to two chairs in the center of the room. They took their seats. "I understand that you've communicated your arrival to Mr. Roosevelt?"

"I have, sir, and I appreciate your staff's services to accomplish that."

The king looked slightly perturbed. "You indicated in your cable that you were here for talks."

"Of course, sir. I wouldn't think of coming to your country without the courtesy of a sit-down. When I received your invitation to come and stay at the palace, I assumed that was your intent. If I presumed too much, I apologize."

Boris remained silent a moment, studying the general. "You just came from Greece."

"Yes, sir. I was there to observe the battlefield and the Vlorë-Pogradec defensive line." He looked around the room. "Your palace is so beautiful, and so is your country; at least what I've seen of it. I was hoping to stay a few days and see more of it." He fixed his eyes back on the king. "We can conduct business now, if you like, or we can wait. I'm in no hurry."

Boris regarded him without expression. Then he smiled and stood. "Tonight, we dine. Tomorrow, I will sign the Tripartite Pact with Germany and Japan. You may attend the ceremony if you like. We and our new allies are very pleased that the United States has remained neutral in this conflict. It's none of America's business. Land wrongfully taken from us by the Treaty of Versailles must be restored, and our access to the Aegean Sea seized from us in the Balkan War by Greece must be returned. We have no quarrel with Mr. Roosevelt or America, but we will defend what rightfully belongs to Bulgaria."

Donovan nodded. "And you *should* have what rightfully belongs to Bulgaria. I'd like to suggest, though, that you wait to sign that treaty until after you and I have spoken again. I have a message from the president, but it should be delivered when we have time to discuss it fully, and early tomorrow might be a better time, if your schedule permits."

The king nodded. "I have time. My first state obligation is at noon, and that is to sign the treaty. I can postpone whatever comes ahead of that."

Dinner was a grand affair with Donovan feted as a guest of honor. From a nearby table, Paul kept abreast of his movements, watching who came to speak with the general and taking note of who engaged him in conversation. As the evening wore on after the meal, the pronouncements, and speeches, the king retired. Then, while music played and guests danced, Paul noticed that Donovan seemed wobbly on his legs. His face grew slack, his eyes drooped, and when Paul drew close, he heard the general's speech slur.

At one point, Paul approached Donovan from his rear as instructed, and stood next to him. "Sir," he said in a low voice, "maybe you should retire for the evening."

Donovan lifted his head sharply and glared at Paul. "What? No!" he stormed, and shoved Paul backwards. "I'm having fun and making new friends." With that, he grabbed a woman by the arm and pulled her toward the dance floor. "Maybe I should have two dance partners," he called back to Paul while laughing uproariously, and grabbed another lady.

Paul watched the general, wide-eyed. The two women tried to pull away from him, but Donovan kept firm grasps around their wrists until two Bulgarian officers came and helped release them. Then Donovan emerged onto the floor and danced alone.

Late in the evening, having apologized profusely to other guests, Paul helped a stumbling Donovan back to his room. The next morning when he returned to escort the general, Donovan answered his knock on the door with bright eyes and a big smile.

He grinned at Paul. "I had visitors last night."

"They took the documents from your jacket?"

"They did."

King Boris seemed in a light mood when he received Donovan and Paul at the appointed hour. "I didn't stay through the entire festivities last night, but I hear that you enjoyed yourself immensely."

"Yes, and I must apologize," Donovan replied. "I let myself get carried away."

Boris regarded him with an edge of contempt and gestured toward Paul. "You have a very able aide. He took care to see that you arrived safely back in your room."

Donovan half-turned and glanced at Paul, who still stood near the door. "Having good help is always a good thing."

Boris' eyes gleamed. He turned and picked up something from a desk behind him. "One of my staff members found this while cleaning up the ballroom," he said, holding up the envelope Donovan had carried in his jacket pocket. "You must have dropped it last night while celebrating."

Paul frowned, and Donovan's eyes flashed. "Your staff *found* it, Your Majesty? Those are highly confidential documents. I don't suppose you read them."

The firmness with which Donovan asked the question and

the glint in his eyes seemed to have set the king ill at ease. He glanced at the envelope and then back at the general. "Well of course we read them, otherwise we wouldn't know who owned them. And they are deeply disturbing. They suggest that America might be prepared to intervene in the Balkans if Hitler goes too far."

The two men, both still standing, regarded each other from across the room. Donovan straightened to his full height. "Now seems like a good time to deliver my president's message."

Blood drained from the king's face as he stared at Donovan. Hostility crept into his voice. "Let's hear it."

Donovan pursed his lips and nodded. "It is this. If the United States comes into this war, we will be guided in policy toward Bulgaria by what you do now."

Their visit at the palace having been curtailed, Donovan and Paul departed Bulgaria within hours. On the transport plane, they listened to the BBC. No mention was made of Bulgaria having signed the Tripartite Pact.

Donovan clapped the back of Paul's neck. "We delayed that at least a day."

"How are you feeling today? You had quite a night."

Donovan leaned back and laughed. "I'm a teetotaler," he said. "I've never touched the stuff, and I didn't last night."

Paul chuckled. "I thought there must be more to the story than your having a cast-iron stomach. Where to now?"

"Belgrade, Yugoslavia. This will be a different challenge. Prince Regent Paul just came from a trip to Berlin, summoned there by the *führer*, where he was treated to the full force of Hitler's 'charm by intimidation' techniques. He was the guest of honor for a display of military power. The *führer* demonstrated his police-state efficiency and all the machinery he could bring to bear against anyone who opposes him. I'm betting we'll see evidence of Hitler's persuasiveness on the prince." He chuckled. "We're ready for him. I doubt he's ready for us."

38

February 20, 1941
Belgrade, Yugoslavia

"This country is a different kettle of fish," Donovan told Paul as their aircraft prepared to land at an airfield on the outskirts of the ancient city. "It's made up of several areas carved out of the old Austro-Hungarian Empire. The Ottomans ruled it for centuries before the Austrians and Hungarians had it. The country came into being as currently constituted by another Treaty of Versailles provision at the end of the Great War.

"They've got a boy king, Peter II, but the country is governed by Prince Regent Paul until the king reaches legal age. The regent has broad authority, but he doesn't exercise it, believing he should leave the country as it was on the late king's death. He's pro-democracy, and being anti-Bolshevik, his sympathies lie with France and Great Britain; but he's scared stiff of Germany's military power, and, as I mentioned, I'm sure that when he was in Berlin, Hitler brought to bear all of his persuasive tools and talents."

The general grinned. "Churchill describes the regent as an unfortunate man locked in a cage with a tiger, hoping not to provoke the animal while dinnertime steadily approaches. The long and short is that if the regent stays in power, Yugoslavia stays in the fascist camp."

Donovan turned suddenly and looked at Paul with a curious expression. "By the way, do you know what fascism is?"

Paul's face went blank. "I think so. It's where a strong man in a country takes over the government and rules by force and the threat of violence to impose his will."

"That sounds like a good textbook definition." Donovan shook his head. "That's what most people think, but they and that textbook would be wrong. You just described thug methods that fascists use to maintain power without regard for laws or rights. All dictators do that. But fascism is an economic system. A fascist regime is one where government and big business collude on policy for their own benefit. Their creed is immaterial except as a tool to control the masses. The government controls the means of production in partnership with big business through force, blackmail, regulation, court decisions, the police, or by whatever else works to control people's lives."

"Isn't that what Hitler does? People call him a Nazi and Mussolini a fascist."

"They're two sides of the same coin, each with his mantra, and both using the same tactics. At one time, Hitler emulated Mussolini. Now the roles are reversed. Hitler is a better propagandist and he's managed to secure far more resources. Their partnership, along with the Japanese, was forged in hell."

Paul pondered that a moment. "So, what are we going to do here?"

"Buy more time." A thump of the plane's landing gear as it dropped and locked into place alerted them that they would soon be on the ground.

"We're meeting with the prince regent?"

Donovan nodded. "And we'll make contact with Tito."

"So, who is Tito?" Paul asked as an embassy limousine drove them to the royal palace.

"He's a Serbian. He was drafted into the Austro-Hungarian army and became its youngest sergeant major. The Russians captured him during the last war, and somehow, he became enamored with them and joined Lenin's revolution in Moscow in 1917. I guess the Russians didn't like him so much because he says they mistreated him. He returned to Yugoslavia liking the Soviet economic system, but not them."

"So, he's a communist. Then, what's the difference between him and a fascist, and why would we deal with him and not the fascists?"

Donovan smirked slightly and furrowed his brow. "Ah, Paul. Stephenson told me that you get caught up in moral dilemmas. Nothing wrong with that. Resolving some of them produced the United States. The simple answer to your question is that we're in a war that we must win. If Joseph Stalin ever gets control of the resources to the extent that Hitler has, I have no doubt he would be just as horrific, maybe even worse. Look at what he did in '33 to Ukraine by creating famine, his so-called *Holodomor*. That's Russian for 'to kill by starvation.' Millions died.

"But the immediate threat for us lies in Hitler and his use of military force." He heaved a sigh and shook his head. "Once that threat is dealt with effectively, we'll no doubt have to deal with the next one, which could easily be Comrade Stalin."

"I hate to expose my ignorance, but I'm still not seeing much difference between communism and fascism. They both want to control the means of production and are willing to wage terror and slaughter to get it."

"I'm no economist, but I see the difference as semantic. The fascists claim to act on behalf of the nation, hence the Nationalist Socialist Party, or Nazis. The communists claim to do it on behalf of the people. Both end up in the same boat: exercising tyrannical power over people's lives. At least that's the way I see things."

"Then what's our strategy in Yugoslavia? You have communists confronting fascists here."

"Exactly. We'd like to see the communists engage the fascists in a guerrilla war and draw in Germany. A non-fascist Yugoslavia would threaten Hitler's southeastern flank and his access to Romanian oilfields, which in turn could subvert his drive into the Soviet Union. We're going to prod that along to help us win this war."

Paul sat back and thought through the discussion. "What will Hitler do if he sees that he could lose Yugoslavia as an ally."

"He'll invade, and that will tie up forces he needs in Russia."

"Is that what Mr. Churchill meant in saying Roosevelt would have his Coventry?"

Donovan nodded solemnly. "A lot of people will die. The open question is how fiercely will Hitler retaliate? The president knows that just like Churchill knew about what would happen to Coventry, and he still agrees with the plan to draw Germany in to fight in Greece and Yugoslavia. It can't be helped. *Wehrmacht* forces that will be used in the Balkans would otherwise be used in the Soviet Union, and no one can say if more or fewer civilians will die. All that can be said is that some will be spared in the north by those whose lives are taken in the south. Your prime minister sees the action as imperative to stop Hitler, wear his forces down, and ultimately defeat him. The president agrees with him. We can't predict how bad Hitler's response will be."

Paul blew air out through pursed lips and shook his head. "What a Machiavellian world. Megalomaniacs muck things up for everyone else. Why must they exist?"

Donovan chuckled. "When you figure that out, we'll make you potentate of the world. I have no clue what drives active greed or what pleasure some men get from slaughtering human beings. But as long as the other man's grass looks greener, people will envy his stuff, and sometimes take it by force. We're seeing that on an epic scale."

They wound through the ancient city with its stately buildings and parks. On reaching a large, wooded hill, they drove past gardens and glades along a lane that contoured its ridges until reaching the sprawling compound with the palace at its heart, a Serbo-Byzantine architectural masterpiece with arches, columns, turrets, and spires.

A welcoming party greeted them when the vehicle rolled to a stop, and they were quickly whisked into the prince regent's office. He was a man with a thin neck and shoulders supporting a large head with dark hair that had receded nearly to the middle of his scalp. He appeared perpetually nervous.

He greeted Donovan and Paul with a gratuitous smile but without fanfare, making passing mention of Paul's having the same given name as his own. Then he invited them to sit in comfortable chairs in front of his desk, and he took his seat.

"These are difficult times, I must say," he remarked, opening the discussion.

"I'll get to the point, sir," Donovan replied. "We know you're in a tough spot. I received a cable upon arrival in your city, and I must tell you, it is a splendid city."

The prince smiled benignly. "Thank you. May I know the contents of the cable. I doubt you'd bring it up otherwise."

"Yes, sir. I'll read it verbatim. It's from my president." Donovan reached inside his jacket pocket, pulled it out, and read aloud, "'Any nation which tamely submits will be regarded less sympathetically when the United States comes to settle accounts than any nation resisting the Nazis.'" He folded the cablegram and replaced it in his pocket.

When he looked up, the prince regent had turned pale. He lifted his hand as he was about to speak, but it shook, so he grasped the edge of his desk as he leaned forward with the demeanor of a supplicant. "But surely the president must realize that any move by the Nazis inside Yugoslavia would be only to secure the German flank during an attack on the Soviet Union. Hitler told me so himself."

Donovan gazed steadily at the prince. "Sir, you'll have to judge his sincerity for yourself, and I thank you for the information about the *führer's* invasion plans. The president will appreciate knowing that."

The prince regent stared—the proverbial doe caught in headlights. His jaw set, he soon ended the meeting and called an orderly to escort his visitors back to their car.

"So, now we have further confirmation of Hitler's plans to invade up north," Donovan said as he and Paul rode away in the embassy limousine. "Anyway, the prince regent seems like a nice man. I hated scaring him like that. We've been sending our cables in the clear, so he's got to know that German agents are listening.

"He's shaking in his boots, and he demonstrated exactly the mindset that concerned Churchill: that these leaders would accept Hitler's assurances regarding his plans within Yugoslavia if the country would secure the flank in his war against the Bolsheviks.

"If the perception persists and grows among the population that their fight is with the Soviet Union, they could be robbed of a reason to rise up in a Resistance army." The general paused while he gathered his thoughts. "If a mass uprising occurs, it must be in answer to Nazi violence and not in support of its Soviet incursion."

The two men rode in silence for some distance. Paul noticed that the route did not take them back to the airfield. "Where to now?"

Donovan looked at his watch. "I have one more stop to make. It's with the Yugoslav Air Force chief, General Dusan Simovic, and he's meeting me in secret, so I can't bring you along. He'll get nervous, and we need him."

"What about Tito?"

"I'll work with him through intermediaries. The message to him is simple: if his group actively resists the fascists, they will receive aid."

"And the unspoken message is that if Prince Regent Paul kneels to the fascists, Tito should lead a revolt?"

Donovan smiled. "I couldn't have said it better myself."

"Then aside from your meeting with General Simovic, we're done? This intelligence operation is finished?"

"Not hardly, Captain. We still have the British reinforcement of Greece to go, and then I'll brief the press publicly on this trip to the Balkans with my conclusions. We can bypass meeting with Vichy generals in North Africa, though. As I told you, I was already there and reported my conclusions about that region to the president.

"With any luck, Hitler's temper should be getting the best of him, and he'll invade both Greece and Yugoslavia despite his high command's more measured advice. Meanwhile, you'll go back to New York, and I'll go back to London."

39

Five Days Earlier
RAF Kirton in Lindsey, Lincolnshire, England

Red, Shorty, and Andy taxied their fighters into position abreast of each other and halted. To their left, a new pilot in a latest-model Hurricane revved his engine to speed, his face a mask of apprehension. He had joined Eagle Squadron that morning to replace Pilot Officer Phillip Leckrone whose plane had been rammed, cutting off his tail in a fatal accident while on patrol a week earlier.

The loud bell that had sent the pilots scrambling to their planes clanged almost as soon as the newbie had walked through the door. His flight leader had pointed him toward his aircraft as they ran.

"We're providing air cover on a convoy off the east coast," the squadron leader called over the radio. "Climb to Angels 30. We'll be high. Remember to turn on your oxygen. Let's go."

Twelve Hurricanes in three lines of four aircraft bounded forward, gained speed, lifted their noses, and leaped into an early morning sky of thick, rumbling clouds.

"This is not fun-flying," Red muttered as they took off. They had been patrolling over the North Sea since they had finally gone operational nearly six weeks earlier. Messerschmitts were of little concern to him this far north and out of their range. But the weather was turbulent, the clouds dark and threatening. Inevitably the squadron would have to fly through them. The threat of losing orientation due to vertigo was deadly.

They cruised north and turned east, skirting the ominous weather as much as possible. Despite the need to remain alert, Red's mind wandered. He thought of home, of a certain girl there, Anne Haring, for whom he had a fondness. There had been no commitment between them, but he liked her. Then he thought of Claire Littlefield. The two were from worlds apart, their only commonality being him.

Claire wore elegance and grace as though the concepts had been made for her, and Red had never met a more caring and friendly person. *If I ever have to choose, which one will it be? If it's Claire, would I be willing to stay and make a life in England, away from home.*

Anne was a farm girl, charming, funny, and down-to-earth. And she was at home, a place he now yearned for with increasing frequency.

His mind went to the episode late last year when he had collapsed. His friends had hurried him to the doctor for a full check-up. He was sobered by the diagnosis. He suffered from lupus, the doctor told him, and he would be increasingly fatigued, and then exhausted.

Andy and Shorty had waited for him anxiously. When he emerged from the doctor's office, they had pressed him to know the result. "Just tired," he had replied. "The doctor informed me that I've had a stressful year." They had laughed together and sought out their favorite pub.

For a moment, the odyssey he had shared with his friends that had brought them to this moment flashed through his mind. He chuckled remembering how he and Andy had fooled the FBI and slipped into Canada to meet with a British mercenary recruiting for the French air force. At a hotel in Toronto, they had run into Shorty, who was there for the same purpose. Taken aback by his small size, they had only recognized that he might be one of them because he sat waiting for the same mercenary.

Red's aircraft suddenly lurched, tossed in a violent updraft. Jerked back to the present, he checked around him for sight of his squadron mates, dropped his nose a bit, and adjusted his trim. Their course would take them into the maelstrom ahead, and looking about, he saw no break that provided a better route to their objective.

"This is Red One," the squadron leader called. "Climb to Angels 35 and spread out. Let's see if we can get above the weather. Controller, do you see better conditions?"

"Sorry, ol' boy. The clouds are thick all along the northern stretch. You'll be over the convoy in five. No enemy reported. Orbit as long as you can. Report when you depart for home."

"Roger. Break. Squadron, on my order, begin orbit."

The pilots acknowledged by squawking their transmitters. Red settled in for what would have been a boring routine, but for the weather—flying in wide circles over the convoy far below, hidden by clouds, until fuel consumption mandated their return to Kirton Lindsey. *Then again, the weather keeps the bandits away.* He grinned. *Well, that and distance.*

He looked down to his left. Andy was there and just happened to peer toward Red at the same time. They grinned and waved to each other.

Red looked in the other direction. Well below him, he saw Shorty's plane and chuckled. He always did that when contemplating the mighty small man. For pilot characteristics, no two pals could be more different. Red, tall with his shocking red hair; Shorty not quite five feet tall, and dark. And then there was Andy, the penniless White Russian refugee, who fit between them to even out the averages.

Yet no friends could be closer than this trio. "We were nearly torpedoed together crossing the Atlantic," he muttered. "We dodged panzers in France and barely got out of there before the Germans took over. We fought the British bureaucracy to let us *in* this Royal Air Force." He blew out a breath of air. "And now we're the eagles, teaching the eaglets." He wished Donahue had stayed with them. "He's a good man and a terrific pilot." He chuckled. "He thinks he's mean, but he's really more of a poet."

A voice over the radio ended his ruminations. "Eagle Squadron, single aircraft at Angels 15 headed toward convoy, origin and type unknown, at zero four five degrees, ten minutes out. Not ours. Could be lost in weather. Check out and take appropriate action."

"Okay. Break. Blue Leader, did you copy?"

"Good copy. Break. Blue Flight, we're going through the soup. We'll have to dive at full power to intercept in time. Watch your distance. Level out at Angels 20. On my command. Acknowledge."

Listening to the radio traffic and hearing the other pilots respond, Red tensed with anticipation and dread as adrenaline coursed through his system. "Yeeha," he yelled into the radio. "This is Blue Four. Roger."

"Contain yourself," came the expected reply that managed to be terse with a ring of amusement. "No time for bravado. Those clouds are wicked." He paused. "Blue Flight, dive now."

Red dipped his nose and throttled up, set his course, and adjusted his trim. Leaning forward and checking his left and right, he saw Andy and Shorty. The newbie pilot who had come in that morning would be closest to Blue Leader. The other veteran, Pilot Officer Nat Maranz, would be below and to Shorty's right.

Red's Hurricane, battered by roaring winds, creaked and groaned as it streaked down through the thick moisture. Faster it dove, accelerating as it plunged through the roiling air. For a fleeting second, Red wondered what groundspeed would have been had he been flying straight and level. A sudden vertical drop riveted his attention to his altimeter.

"Angels 30," Blue Leader called.

Moments passed.

"Twenty-five."

More moments.

"Coming up on twenty. Begin to level off. Maintain airspeed."

Red lifted his nose, re-set his trim, and scanned out and around him. The air in his immediate vicinity was wispy with dark clouds still hanging farther out. His squadron mates appeared, all accounted for.

"Blue Flight, this is Control. The target is two minutes out from you at Angels 15."

"Roger. Break. Blue Flight, follow me in fast descent to fifteen. Confirm black crosses before we engage."

"Blue Leader, this is Blue Six," Maranz called. "I see him at one o'clock low. Convoy not in sight."

"Blue Leader, this is Blue Five," Shorty called. "I see him, an Me110, and black crosses. He's seen us. He's turning."

"Tally-ho."

Immediately, Shorty and Maranz dove toward the bandit. It had executed a sharp turn to the south and sped toward more dark clouds.

Red followed, and as he did, a rare pang of anxiety struck

him. The clouds seemed to be moving toward the squadron. Now he saw the enemy fighter, nose down in an erratic, evasive flight pattern headed toward the clouds, and behind him, Shorty and Maranz in pursuit.

The German fighter flew to the bottom of the clouds, the North Sea waters churning below him. Shorty and Maranz entered the vapor in a dive about two thousand feet above him.

Dread seized Red. He entered a steep dive and leveled out at one thousand feet over the sea, screaming toward the last point where he had seen the Messerschmitt. The clouds ahead had descended to meet the violent waves. The target was nowhere in sight.

"Blue Flight, check your fuel. We're getting low."

In response, the nervous voice of the newbie sounded through the radio. "This is Blue Two. Getting low."

"This is Blue Three," Andy called. "Coming up against the margins."

"This is Blue Four," Red said. "I can make it home, but I might have to walk a ways."

"This is Blue Leader. Cut the chatter. Blue Five?"

Silence.

"Blue Five, come in. How's your fuel?"

No response.

"Blue Six, is Blue Five with you?"

"We dove into a cloud. I don't see him. My fuel is low."

"Blue Five, Blue Five, this is Blue Leader. Come in."

Red's pang of anxiety formed into a pit in his stomach. He raced over the waves toward the base of the black cloud bank.

"Blue Four, this is Blue Leader. Desist pursuit. Break. Blue Flight, reform. Break. Red One, this is Blue Leader. One lost. Inform Coast Guard that we have a probable man down in vicinity southwest of convoy. Break. Blue Flight, head for home."

⋯⋯⋯⋯⋯⋯

Red and Andy trudged from their kites to the dispersal hut at Kirton Lindsey. The ground crew and the other pilots moved out of their way as they made their way to the tiny building, eyes fixed. Their story with Shorty was well known.

For the rest of the day, the two sat and watched the runway, straining their eyes and ears whenever a hint of another aircraft passed by. Longer shadows marked the passage of the day into early evening with no news of Shorty. They sat together in the door of the hut as the end of their watch came and the other pilots departed.

Sitting at the back of the hut, the squadron leader had watched them. As twilight marked the slight interim between day and night, he approached the pair. "Let's go, chaps. If we get news, I'll bring it to you personally."

He offered a lift in his car, but they declined and tramped the distance to their sleeping quarters. Neither slept that night, and when they arrived at the dispersal hut early looking for news, they learned that as yet, there was none.

The day passed with no scrambles, news, or other events. Red and Andy passed it as they had so often in other airfields, dozing, sitting around, finding things to occupy their minds. On this day, however, nothing they did eased a shared growing anguish. The other pilots kept their distance.

"What an irony," Andy said at one point. "I'm hoping he was captured. At least he'd be alive."

Red nodded but said nothing.

Early in the afternoon of the next day, an official sedan belonging to the Coast Guard stopped by the dispersal hut. An officer emerged and asked to see the squadron leader. He carried a bundle.

Resting on two cots at the outside corner of the hut, Red and Andy saw him arrive and trail behind another pilot through the door. They exchanged anxious glances, climbed to their feet, and followed.

"...this was all we found," the officer was saying to the squadron leader. On the desk between them was a pair of very small, wet RAF boots. They could belong to only one person. Shorty.

40

February 20, 1941
Stony Stratford, England

Red met Jeremy and Claire at the door of The Bull. When they entered, Claire fought back tears, her eyes appearing hollow.

On seeing Red, Claire threw her arms around him and sobbed on his shoulder. "I'm not sure I can do this," she whispered, her words escaping through broken gasps.

Jeremy put his arms around them both, and for moments, the three held each other, oblivious to the comings and goings of other patrons. The manager quietly guided people around them, and when the trio broke apart, he cleared the way ahead of them to a table where Andy waited for them. His eyes were red, and the signs of strain on his face equaled those of the others. Claire sat next to him while Jeremy and Red took seats across from them.

"Please accept our condolences," the manager said in a low voice. "We remember your friend well."

After he had left and the group was seated, Andy said, "Thanks for coming. This is where Shorty—" He tried to say something else, but he choked, dropped his eyes, and became silent, staring down into his hands.

"We had some good times here," Claire managed in a broken voice. "I shall never forget our sweet, wonderful friend."

"I was going to say," Andy tried again, "that Shorty loved it here. He loved being with us at this pub." His voice broke again. "As painful as it is, this is the best place to remember him."

Across the table, Red had scrunched his long body into his seat with his legs curled under the table and his chest leaning over its surface. He sat with an elbow resting on the arm of his chair while holding his face in one hand, hiding his eyes. "I can't believe he's gone," he whispered, almost inaudibly. "We came over together, the three of us—me, Andy, Shorty. We—" His voice broke off.

"I loved him," Jeremy said. "He knew his life expectancy as a fighter pilot, but he—" His voice trailed off and he bit his lower lip.

Claire dropped her head forward, pulling both hands back over her hair. "You all know that you probably won't live long," she cried. "This war is insane." She looked up at each one of them. "How many of you will we lose before this is done."

Another figure appeared at the end of the table. Jeremy looked up to see Pilot Officer Arthur Donahue standing there, his face lined with sadness.

"I heard," he said. "May I join you?"

The three men stood. "Of course," Jeremy replied. "Thank you for coming."

The manager fetched another chair and seated Donahue at the end of the table. Then he remained as if he would like to speak but thought better of it and left.

The group sat in silence for a while, and the manager

returned. "May I say something?" He brought a calming presence, and the friends appreciated how he had always welcomed them. They nodded and directed their eyes toward him. "Our patrons don't wish to intrude, but they remember all of you well—the American eagles who came to fight for us. They send their condolences and their gratitude for the sacrifices you make and for the pain you suffer. When and if you salute your lost friend this evening, they would like to join you in remembering him."

Claire sobbed quietly into a handkerchief. Red stood, wiped his eyes, and thanked the manager. Jeremy also stood. "We've lost loved ones," he said. "Not just airmen, although this is the third close friend I've lost who flew with me in combat, not to mention those I was barely acquainted with when they went down; and there are many more of those. This war is chewing up our people and losing them is never easy.

"When we lost Billy Fiske—" He fought for control and wiped an eye. "He was my mentor on fighter tactics. He didn't die immediately. We, our squadron mates, waited for news of him, but he lingered, and so we went to his favorite pub and drank to him. Two days later, we lost Sandy, another dear friend, and we did the same thing. If they can look down and see us, I believe they would love to find us celebrating their lives in the places they most loved to be with us."

Struggling with emotion, he told the manager, "So, kind sir, we'll take you up on your offer. If you'll fill the mugs, we'll put an end to this sadness and remember the lively, funny, biggest little pilot who was our mate." He turned to Red, Andy, and Donahue. "We honor him best by getting back in the fight, at first light."

Mugs of ale were quickly passed out or refilled. Red toasted first. "Shorty, you were one hell of a pilot." He lifted his mug. "We'll fly the skies together again in the next life. I promise you. Happy landings in your new hunting grounds."

Andy followed. "He knew the risks. He believed in the fight." He lifted his mug. "To Shorty."

The evening drifted, customers lingered and gradually gathered around to befriend, comfort, and thank the bereaved. Eventually, someone struck a chord on a piano in the corner, and the patrons broke into singing "We'll Meet Again," followed with rounds of "Roll Out The Barrel." Late in the evening, when everyone stood and joined the Americans to sing "God Bless America" in honor of Shorty, not a dry eye remained.

Later, at Claire's house, Jeremy stopped into Timmy's room. The other pilots had driven back to their airfields. Jeremy lifted the sleeping child into his arms, snuggled him against his chest, and pressed the warm, soft head against his cheek. Swaying gently, he stayed there for several minutes. Claire stood at the door looking on.

After settling the little boy back in bed, Jeremy joined her in the living room. "Are you staying the night?" she asked.

"I thought I might. I can spend time with Timmy in the morning."

Claire sat back and regarded him questioningly. "I'm naturally thrilled, but I thought you had to be ready at first light."

"Of course, we're always in the fight," Jeremy said. "At first light, I'll go anywhere that I'm called, but as it happens, I don't need to be back until early in the afternoon."

Puzzled, Claire continued to study him until Jeremy noticed. "What is it?"

"You couldn't have taken the day off or you wouldn't need to be back until late tomorrow night."

"So?" Jeremy avoided her eyes and fidgeted with his fingers.

"You're not telling me something. I know you've left 609 Squadron because I called down there one day to see how you were doing. The person I spoke with said you'd transferred out but couldn't tell me where you'd gone."

"I just moved across the airfield to the 604th. I'm still at Middle Wallop."

"The 604th," Claire repeated. "The 604th. I've heard reference to that squadron somewhere." She suddenly leaped to her feet, crossed to a table by the front window, and seized a newspaper sitting on its surface. Scanning past several headlines, she selected an article and started reading. Then she whirled around, her eyes big and round with anger and hurt. She advanced on Jeremy.

"Oh, little brother," she cried, tears streaming down her face, "don't I have enough to weep over. Night fighting is the most dangerous flying there is. We've lost pilots left and right defending against the nighttime bomber raids." Her eyes grew wide, and her breath came in short gasps. "You must have flown on that awful night on December 29 against St. Paul's Cathedral, the longest bombing raid to date."

Jeremy climbed slowly to his feet. "I did, but it's not like you think—"

Claire suddenly rushed at him and pounded his shoulders with balled-up fists. "I'm going to lose you, aren't I?" She sobbed into his chest. "Shorty's gone, and we're going to have little celebrations of life at the favorite pubs for each of you in a row."

Jeremy wrapped her in his arms and held her until she

calmed down. Then he pressed a finger against the underside of her chin and raised her face to look into his eyes. "Look at me," he said. "Night fighting is not like you think it is, not the type I do."

"It's in the dark and it's dangerous," she insisted.

"Look at that article again. I'm flying with Cat's Eyes."

"You mean John Cunningham. He's all anyone talks about all over London. That, and the rubbish about eating carrots."

To her surprise, Jeremy suddenly let go of her and bent over in fits of laughter. "I'm sorry," he said as he fought to catch his breath. "I'm so sorry."

"Well, that's what they're saying in the papers, that the RAF selects pilots for exceptional vision, particularly at night. It fits night fighters with special glasses and feeds you a lot of carrots to maintain your vision. They even say that bowls of carrots are kept on your dining tables to make sure you get plenty of them."

Jeremy howled in fits of mirth. "Stop," he begged. "You're killing me."

"Would you please get control of yourself and tell me what is going on," Claire demanded. She crossed her arms and glared at him, with one foot tapping.

Jeremy caught his breath and straightened up. "Read the article again. They call John 'Cat's Eyes' because he's shot down a lot more bombers at night than anyone. Everyone in the squadron's shot down some. But notice our casualties."

"I didn't see anything about your casualties," Claire responded stubbornly. "I don't want you to be one of them."

"None were mentioned because we had none. We did at first, but we've improved our tactics."

Claire wiped her eyes and threw Jeremy a searching look. "Explain."

Jeremy started toward her and once again fell into a fit of laughter. Catching himself, he said, "There are some things I can't tell you. You understand that—" He took a deep breath to stave off yet more guffaws. "You know things from your work that you can't tell me, and I don't ask. Can I leave it that we want to keep our tactics a secret from the Germans for as long as possible?"

Claire stared at him in disbelief. "So, you feed a line that our night fighter pilots are eating lots of carrots so they can see the enemy better?" Suddenly, she shook with a spontaneous peal of laughter.

"Yes," Jeremy said, thrown yet again into uncontrollable mirth. "And now every mother in England is feeding her children carrots to improve their vision."

Claire joined him. "And every little boy is snacking on them for better eyesight," she cried, trying without success to hold back more laughter. "Stop," she begged, fanning her face. "I can't breathe."

"One more thing. You can't tell anyone that it's not true," Jeremy roared, gasping for breath, his face red. "That's classified."

Claire sank into the sofa and rolled, trying to recover control. "You're serious?" she said at last while wiping her eyes.

Jeremy sat on the floor with his back against the wall, took a deep breath, and nodded. "You've deduced more than you should. I know you'll hold your tongue."

Claire shook her head slowly with an air of having to believe the ridiculous. "The secret's safe with me." She took a deep breath. "They say that laugher is the best medicine. That's been true tonight." She gazed at Jeremy propped against the wall. "I couldn't bear for anything bad to happen to you, little brother."

Jeremy smiled. "I love you, sis. What's that little thing you always say? 'Things will get better. You'll see.'"

Claire sighed. "Thank you for that, but seeing sunny days ahead is becoming ever more difficult."

41

February 28, 1941
Rockefeller Center, Manhattan, New York

On seeing the lady standing in front of his desk, Paul inhaled, quashing a gasp, and decided at the back of his mind that she could be described accurately in a single word: gorgeous. She was slender with short auburn curls, smooth skin, a frank smile over a slightly cleft chin, and large green eyes that drew him in inexorably.

She extended her hand. "I'm Cynthia. Little Bill is expecting me."

Paul stared, like a child mesmerized by the wonder and joy of seeing cloud shapes. He caught himself, stood, and shook Cynthia's hand. When he did, her warmth seemed to have shot a bolt of electricity up his arm. Embarrassed, he coughed. "Mr. Stephenson told me you'd be here."

He gestured for her to precede him and escorted her through the door into Stephenson's office.

"Cynthia," Stephenson enthused. "How lovely to see you." He came around his desk, hugged her, and kissed her lightly on the cheek. "It's been too long, but you've been traveling extensively. Great work you've been doing." He indicated Paul. "I see you've met my aide."

"Not formally," she said, bestowing Paul with a brilliant smile, "but he was very courteous on my arrival."

"He's my right arm these days, or more correctly, he's the left side of my brain. Facts, figures, analysis, memory—that sort of thing, and very capable."

She turned to Paul. "Well, I'm pleased to meet you, Mr.—"

"Paul Littlefield," Stephenson responded. "He wears civilian clothes in this assignment, but he's a captain in the British army." He invited her to his sitting area with a wave of his hand. "I take it you received my message about what we have in mind."

"I did, and I'm happy to help." As she sat down, she glanced at Paul with an uncertain expression. He still stood near the door.

"You can speak freely," Stephenson told Cynthia. "Paul is our living, breathing archive, so to speak, to know whatever goes on in case of adverse events." He turned to Paul. "Please join us."

"All right then," Cynthia said when they were seated. "We're all short on time, so I'll get right to the heart of the matter. This is about the president's proposed lend-lease proposal, isn't it?"

"Exactly. He wants to lend or lease war materiel to Britain and its allies—essentially the Commonwealth countries—but Congress must approve the arrangement. Right now, the Neutrality Act mandates against it.

"Roosevelt uses the example of having a neighbor whose house is on fire. The homeowner runs to you for your hose. He doesn't want to buy it. He just wants to use it to put out the fire and then return it. Obviously, Great Britain is the burning house and America is the neighbor with the hose. The president thinks the US should be able to provide war supplies on the same basis. The British are not asking us to fight or to sell them anything. Just lend them what we have to handle their emergency."

Cynthia shrugged and alternated her eyes between Stephenson and Paul. "That sounds reasonable. What's the issue?"

"Some in Congress worry that if the bill becomes law, America would be strengthening one side of the hostilities and thus inviting the other to declare war against the US. A lot of the public feels that way too. Americans remember the ravages, casualties, and wounded of the Great War. They don't want a repeat.

"Other people see that Hitler is not going to back off, that he's allied with Italy and Japan, and they think war is inevitable. Japan gobbled up much of China and other Pacific countries the same way the *führer* did in Europe. Supporters of the bill think that if the US joins the fighting, passing the bill would give us and our would-be allies a head start. But there's a key senator who opposes it. He's influential enough to stop it."

"Senator Arthur Vandenberg. And you want me to change his mind."

"Exactly. Have you read his dossier?"

"I have, and I'll be introduced to him tomorrow evening at a cocktail party. It's all arranged."

"Magnificent. Do you have any questions?"

Cynthia smiled primly. "No. I understand the job." She stood, the men followed suit, and she leaned over to hug Stephenson again. "Working with you is always a pleasure."

Paul escorted her out of the suite and then returned to

Stephenson's office. "That was a remarkably short conversation given the expected result. Is she a lobbyist?"

Stephenson smiled blandly. "I hadn't thought of her in that term, but it seems to apply."

"Can she do it? Senator Vandenberg is one of the most powerful senators and known to be a solid isolationist."

The sides of Stephenson's mouth turned up in one of his inscrutable smiles. "If she can't, the senator probably cannot be persuaded by anyone."

"Can you tell me anything more, sir? I'm an analyst. I can't witness unusual goings-on without attempting to understand them. The implications of her success would be huge and give my country a fighting chance. As things are right now, the bombing of our cities continues and we're losing our shirts in North Africa. We could use some good news and the only thing that could be better than passing the Lend-Lease Bill would be for the United States to enter directly into the war."

Stephenson returned to his desk and sat down. "I quite agree with you." He studied Paul's face. "Then you see that achieving critical results sometimes requires unusual persuasion techniques."

Paul stared at Stephenson, doe-eyed, as an uneasy feeling crept over him. "I don't think I follow you."

"On the contrary, I think you understand perfectly. A blind man could have seen your reaction to Cynthia. Don't be embarrassed. She has the same effect on most men, and I doubt that the good senator will be an exception. She's beautiful, she's confident, she's—magic. And she knows what she's doing.

"Men first notice her beauty. Then they're drawn to her intellect and charm, and that's no accident. And then..." He left the sentence unfinished.

Paul stifled an involuntary laugh. "Are you saying that—"

"I'm not saying anything in particular, except that she works for love of country. We pay her little more than living expense.

"I told her what we wanted, and she accepted the assignment. But you're free to let the carnal side of your mind wander. As I recall from the Old Testament, Joshua's spies gained intelligence on Jericho through a member of the world's oldest profession. No mention was made about how they interacted, only that they did."

"Is that an inuendo?"

"I drew a parallel. Joshua was outgunned and used the assets available to him. Britain is doing the same thing. From a moral point of view, we would seem to have the high ground since Joshua attacked and Britain defends."

Paul let out a deep breath. "Are we saying the ends justify the means?"

"I can see how someone could construe things that way. We're in a struggle for survival, though. When your very life is at stake, you do what you must do, lashing in all directions. Would you make the argument that Britain is not so imperiled?"

Paul shook his head. "Not at all. I witnessed the Battle of Britain from two command bunkers. I was there and saw Churchill's face when the RAF had committed all our reserves, and we were hours from defeat. I experienced the night bombing and nearly lost my sister that first night. Jeremy's been shot down twice that I know of. Lance is a POW, and the *Wehrmacht* occupies my parents' home, Sark Island."

"I know," Stephenson said softly. "I'm sorry. Please keep those things in mind as we do our work here. They will help keep things in perspective."

"When do you expect that we'll know how successful she's been?"

"The senate will vote soon, but meanwhile, we have work to do on the intelligence operation you dislike so much."

"Which one was that?" Even as he asked the question, Paul knew the answer and felt tenson rise.

"I can tell from the look on your face that you know which one—as you described it, the action to manipulate US public opinion."

Paul closed his eyes and shook his head. "Is that one necessary?"

"We think it is. A necessary strike for national survival."

42

March 1, 1941
Bletchley Park, England

"Please, sit down, Claire." Commander Denniston gestured to the seat before his desk. "Thank you for coming. I have news for you, although you might already know about it."

"Concerning Jeannie Rousseau? I know she is safely out of Dinard, although I must tell you that her departure caused no small amount of angst. She's been gone nearly six weeks, and the coders there are still grumbling about it." She laughed.

"I thought you could use some good news." Denniston's face grew somber. "I heard about your friend, Pilot Officer Keough, the one you called 'Shorty.' I'm sorry. I know you had become close with some of our eagles."

Claire sniffed. "My brother, Jeremy, flew with them."

"Well, they certainly are some of 'The Few' to whom we owe an insurmountable debt. Your brother too." He let a moment pass, and then asked, "Have you heard anything unusual pertaining to Bulgaria?"

Claire furrowed her brow. "As a matter of fact, we have, sir, and I'm sure your analysis group will be receiving the translated messages soon if they haven't seen them already. Furious messages are coming out between Berlin and all the major commands. Hitler is angry because King Boris has not yet signed the Tripartite Treaty. He was supposed to have done that eight days ago. There's talk now that the May 15 launch of Operation Barbarossa into the Soviet Union might have to be delayed."

Denniston leaned back with a satisfied smile. "Then let's hope for more delays."

Claire watched him as he appeared lost in thought, then he sat forward. "Let's talk about you," he said. "We'd like to offer that promotion into the analysis group now."

Claire fidgeted in her chair.

"Is something wrong?"

"I've thought a lot about it and what I should do if offered the promotion again." She looked up anxiously. "And I'm honored to be asked."

As she spoke, Claire's mind ran through her last encounter with the commander, when she had repeatedly interrupted him and all but accused him and Prime Minister Churchill of being heartless. She also recalled what the commander had said about seeing a broader picture that might be even more difficult to deal with emotionally than what she learned about the war from decoding German messages.

"Then what's the problem. Are you worried about the bigger picture being even more bleak?"

Claire shook her head. "No, sir. It's not that. It's—Well, I seem to be in a unique position of not only understanding the Morse code, but also the German language, so I get the meaning of messages. As a result, I detect nuances in them that might escape me if I had already been in the analysis section. I don't know all the ramifications of saving the Boulier network or realizing the impact that Jeannie Rosseau had, but whatever they are, I would have missed the opportunities to bring them to light. So, I'm left wondering if my greatest contribution wouldn't be to stay right where I am. Of course, I'll do my utmost in either position."

"Hmm." Denniston leaned back in his chair and regarded Claire through narrowed eyes. "You make a good point. I hadn't thought of that." He rapped his fingers on his desk as he pondered. "How about this: you stay officially where you are, but we bring you in to the analysis group for consultation either when you spot something interesting or when we have a situation where we think your insights could help? You'll have open access to me—" He smirked. "Which you've already created."

Claire turned red. "Sorry, sir."

Denniston waved away the apology. "We'll up your status and salary to where it would have been had you taken the promotion as offered." His brow wrinkled as another thought surfaced. "You might shift some of your work to monitor Berlin, too. With Operation Sea Lion now permanently cancelled, Dinard will become less significant."

"It already has, sir. The speed barges along the French coast have been stored and much of the materiel, including tanks, fighters, and bombers, is shifting east."

"I've seen reports to that effect. They're moving in support of Operation Barbarossa, I should think." The commander shifted in his chair. "Well, what's your answer? Is my proposed arrangement with you suitable?"

"That would be lovely, sir," Claire enthused. "Thank you. I hope I don't disappoint you."

Denniston chuckled. "Disappointing me is the one thing I'm quite sure is outside of your capacity," he said. "And please try to go easy when you're scolding me. I bruise easily." He stood up from his desk. "Come along, then. We'll make this official and I'll introduce you into the group. You know everyone already, I'm sure, but they need to hear from me how we intend to work this."

Despite the sad events that had blighted her life and that of everyone touched by the war, Claire sensed elation welling up inside her as she greeted her new co-workers.

They greeted her jovially. "We've heard of you. Jolly good work. Glad to have you."

"If you need help with that little boy, we'll be happy to jump in. Give you a break."

"I heard you were caught near the docks that first night of bombing on the city. How did you ever get out?"

"Hey," one petite girl with big eyes called to her, "are those brothers of yours still single?"

For the first time in recent memory, Claire went home feeling content. She had put thoughts of her parents and siblings into a mental safe place where she kept them until moments when she was free to think of them without the war intruding, and when she could select among wonderful memories about them to relive. She had placed Shorty with loving care into that same place, comforted that good memories of him would reside with those she loved.

The afternoon was bright, the weather beautiful, and after descending from the bus that brought her to Stony Stratford, she relished the walk home among the scents of new wildflowers and a gentle breeze that touched her face.

Turning into the gravel driveway leading to her front door, she saw a government car, the same type that Paul and Jeremy had sometimes used to visit her. Anticipation quickened her step, and then accompanying anxiety settled her back down.

When she was halfway up the garden path at the top of the driveway, the front door opened, and Timmy ran out. "Gigi," he called happily in his little boy voice, throwing his arms around her knees. "Jermy here. He's here. Jermy." He jumped up and down with excitement and pointed to the house.

Behind Timmy, the nanny followed. When Claire saw her face, her heart pushed against her throat. "What's wrong?"

The nanny shook her head sadly and pointed. "He's in the back garden."

Claire hurried through the house and peered out the window overlooking the garden. Jeremy sat alone with his elbows propped on his knees, staring at the ground. An unwelcome flash of memory crossed Claire's mind. She had sat on that same bench and sobbed after saying goodbye to Paul when he left on his secret assignment.

Gingerly, she opened the back door and stepped out, closing it behind her. "What is it, Jeremy?" she asked as she approached him.

He looked up, and although no tears ran down his face, his eyes were red, and he bore a haunted look.

Claire gasped. "It's not Amélie, is it?"

Jeremy shook his head and stood.

Claire breathed a sigh of relief and wrapped her arms around her brother. "What is it, then? Has something happened to Mum or Dad or to one of our brothers?"

Once again, Jeremy shook his head. "It's Amélie's father," he said slowly. "Ferrand. He was killed in an operation in the north of France rescuing a spy for the French Resistance from the German headquarters in Dinard."

Claire stared at her brother in horror but said nothing. She buried her head against his arm and bit her lip to hold back her own tears.

Late that night, alone in her room, Claire lay face down on her bed, weeping into her pillow. Then she raised herself up onto her elbows and beat the mattress in fury. "This damned war," she railed in the darkness. "How can anyone know if you're helping or hurting." She rolled onto her back, sat up, pivoted, and dropped her feet to the floor. Holding her face in her hands, she wept quietly. "I sent the rescue team that saved Jeannie. And I sent Amélie's father to his death."

What must Jeremy be feeling? Ferrand saved his life. She wondered how Jeremy managed to get up day after day, and now night after night, to fly into the sky utterly exhausted, knowing this mission could be his last, as had happened to Shorty. Or how Paul could live isolated from his family and friends and carry on with whatever he was doing. Tears ran again as she imagined Lance in a dark cell guarded by German soldiers.

Rising from her bed, she stumbled in the dark to a small desk and turned on a lamp. A letter from her mother and father had arrived the day before, and she picked it up and read it again. It was not long, but she read and re-read a particular passage.

"This war is not pleasant for anyone. The ersatz tea is as bad now as when we first tasted it. We take comfort in knowing we raised a daughter and three sons of strong character who face challenges with courage and wisdom, and we look for the day when we shall be together again."

The next morning, having tossed through restless sleep, Claire crept out of bed and readied herself for work. When she entered the kitchen, Jeremy was there, sitting at the table and staring out the window, a cold cup of untouched coffee on its surface. She went to him, laid her head on his back, and circled her arms around him. "Did you sleep?"

Jeremy shook his head. He tried to speak but, overcome with emotion, found he could not. When he finally choked out, "Ferrand saved my life," his voice trembled. "He and Amélie together. I've never known a more caring, gentle man, and yet he was so strong. Look what he was able to pull together for the French Resistance."

"I know," Claire whispered, and then, with a sense of deceitfulness, she asked, "When did it happen?"

"Six weeks ago." Anger tinged his tone. "It took six weeks for the news to get to me."

"Why so long?" She let go of her embrace and sat in a chair facing him.

"Operational priorities, I suppose. Ferrand was a 'non-combatant,' and we're not related, so there was no formal method to let me know. I stopped in yesterday to see Major Crockatt on a social visit, and he informed me; or rather his secretary, Vivian, did.

"With the rush of war, we rarely see each other, and they thought I knew, though how I would have gotten word is beyond me. I can't imagine how Amélie and Chantal must feel." His voice shook again. "I feel like I'm going to lose Amélie. What must she think of me, not having sent condolences or anything?" He sniffed. "Vivian promised to let Marseille know that I was just informed, and I wrote a letter while I was in the office. She'll make sure to include it in the next equipment drop."

Claire reached over and squeezed his hand. "I'm so sorry." Her voice caught, sounding hollow. "I wish there was something I could say."

Jeremy shook his head and then leaned over to hug her. "There isn't. Until this war is over, suffering and sorrow are the order of the day, and you do more than your fair share of trying to make people feel better through it all. That doesn't go unnoticed."

With that, Claire broke down, her body shaking. When she had regained control sufficient to speak, she whispered, "Oh, little brother, thank you for that. I try, but the task is sometimes overwhelming."

Brother and sister held each other for a few minutes, and then Jeremy heaved a sigh and stood. "I should get ready. I have to get back to the squadron."

After he cleaned up, they spent time playing with Timmy until the nanny arrived. Then Jeremy drove Claire to Bletchley Park. She watched him drive away and then entered the facility and wound her way to the door of Hut 3, home of the analysis group. "Things will get better," she told herself as she entered. "You'll see."

43

March 12, 1941
Marseille, France

Maurice drove into the courtyard of Fourcade's villa and parked. Getting out, he hurried to the front door. His face was bright with an excited smile.

From her window on the second floor, Fourcade had seen him enter through the gate and gone downstairs to greet him. Before she reached the entrance, he burst through the door.

He stared at Fourcade with round, wide eyes and held up an envelope. "Where's Amélie? I have something for her. It came in with the equipment drop last night."

"I'm here," Amélie called from the top of the stairs. Her voice struck a fearful note. "What is it?"

Chantal appeared behind her, peering excitedly over her shoulder. "A letter from Jeremy," she teased. "That's what it is."

Amélie shoved against her in irritation and started down the stairs. Chantal bounded past her, ran to Maurice, and grabbed for it. "Let me see it."

Maurice held it away from her. "No. It's for Miss Amélie."

Fourcade watched from the side in amusement, and then the terrace door opened, and Jeannie joined them. "What's all the excitement?"

Amélie reached the bottom of the stairs, her face a mixture of elation, disbelief, and anxiety. She crossed the floor to Maurice and took the letter. Looking around as she started to open it and seeing everyone watching her, she headed for the terrace without a word.

Chantal started to follow.

"Give her some privacy," Fourcade said. "She's earned it."

Chantal stomped her foot, looking disgruntled. "That's no fun. He might have said something to me in there." But she let her sister be alone.

Amélie walked across the terrace and into the garden, which had begun to fill out with the colors of spring. She sat on the bench where she and Jeremy had spent hours together on his last trip to France before he started flying and began reading. The letter was dated a week earlier.

"My dearest Amélie, I just heard about the loss of your father. I cannot describe the anguish that causes me, and I cannot imagine the depth of your and Chantal's pain. I loved your father. I will never forget that the two of you together saved my life. Please don't think badly of me for not reaching out to you before. It was not for lack of caring, I promise you that. You are the dearest part of my life and but for the war, I would spend every possible minute with you.

The secretary promised that she'd get this to you. I believe you met her. She spoke highly of you.

Give my love and express my sorrow to your sister. I miss her too.

I don't know when this war will end, how often we'll be able to be in touch, or when we'll see each other again, but that's the day I look for. Until then, never doubt that I love you with all my heart, Jeremy."

Amélie read and re-read the letter several times, wiping tears from her face with her sleeve. Then she sat looking across the low hills to the blue sea, enjoying the breeze through her hair. After a time, she read the letter once more, and then walked toward the terrace.

Fourcade came out of the house before she reached the door. "Was it a good letter?"

Finding herself tearing up again, Amélie nodded. She breathed in deeply and then managed to say, "He just learned last week about our father."

"So, our messages didn't get through. That's regrettable, but understandable. During a war, personal notes get short shrift." She smiled. "But he still loves you?"

Amélie's face tightened, and she could only nod.

Fourcade embraced her. "He's alive, you're alive, and both safe for the moment." She looked back toward the door and nodded.

The door burst open, and Chantal charged through. "Did he say anything about me?" she blurted, running up to her sister.

Amélie laughed. "He did. He said he misses you." She laughed again. "The rest is mushy stuff."

Chantal's eyes filled with mischief. "Ooh. Mushy stuff. I want to see."

"Forget that." Then Amélie's face became serious again. "He had just heard about Father last week. He expressed his sorrow and sent his condolences."

Chantal's antics came to a halt. "Oh." She turned away and stood quietly for a moment. "I'm glad Jeremy's all right."

The door opened and closed again, and Jeannie joined them with Maurice. "Is everything all right?"

"Everything's fine," Amélie said. She held up the envelope. "It was a good letter."

"That gives us something to celebrate."

While Jeannie and the Boulier sisters conversed at the table, Maurice asked to speak privately with Fourcade. They went to a secluded bench in the garden.

"Henri's two teams that were active last night had successful missions. Kenyon was with one, and Horton with the other. These were new teams that they trained in demolitions. One blew up a railroad bridge along the Atlantic coast. The other exploded a fuel-oil storage-tank field in the same vicinity. Between our former French navy officers and these British veterans, we're training some capable fighters. I'm worried, though. There's word out that the Prosper Network has been infiltrated. Sooner or later, ours will be too."

"Is our early warning system working as we'd hoped?"

Maurice nodded. "It relies on the local population, but Pétain is becoming angrier at anti-German activity and is trying to tighten his grip. Keep a bag packed and your car's tank full." He sighed with a slight grin. "I must go. I have vegetables to deliver."

Fourcade watched the big man lumber across the terrace with affection. She was about to join the trio at the table when Jeannie left it and approached her.

"Do you have time to speak with me?"

"Of course," Fourcade replied. "What's on your mind?"

"You've been good to me, letting me stay here all these weeks, but I'm fully rested now. I can't stay. I need to get back to doing something to help win this war."

"Are you still thinking Paris?"

Jeannie nodded. "That makes the most sense. That's where the greatest concentration of useful intelligence will be."

Fourcade sighed. "That's so dangerous."

"But getting it is so necessary. I've made up my mind."

"Then let's plan when and how we do this. We don't want you left alone with no support again."

Jeannie smiled. "Thank you. I'm stronger now, and experienced, but knowing someone is at my back will be much appreciated."

"We'll do it. And right now, let's celebrate Amélie's good news."

44

Rockefeller Center, Manhattan, New York

Paul went down to the newsstand in the foyer of Rockefeller Center as he normally did. He had picked up the habit of purchasing a cup of coffee on his way into the office, and he was fixing it with cream and sugar when his eyes fell on the headlines of *The New York Times*:

"Roosevelt Transfers Ships and Planes to Britain After Signing Aid Bill;
Greece Gets a Share, Too;
$7 Billion To Be Asked for Lend-Lease Program"

Paul grabbed a copy and bolted for the elevator. Emerging on his office floor, he was surprised to see Cynthia at the entrance of the suite and turning his way as she bade farewell to Stephenson. Her eyes sparkled when she saw Paul, and she smiled mischievously. Once again, Paul sensed a schoolboy's wonder at something grand before him.

"Good morning, Captain," she said as she made her way toward the elevator lobby. "How wonderful to see you again."

Before he could return the greeting, a bell at the elevator bank announced the arrival of a car going down. Then, just before passing him, Cynthia approached and kissed his cheek. Lightning and thunderbolts seemed to have struck Paul's senses. He gazed after her as she entered the elevator and the door closed. When Paul turned back around to the office, Stephenson stood in the hall watching with an amused twinkle in his eye and his all but hidden smile.

"Is Miss Ryan out of sight, out of mind then," he called, and chuckled.

"Of course not," Paul groused, glancing again at the elevator lobby. "It's just that, she's, well—"

"Magic," Stephenson interjected. "Don't worry too much. Cynthia cranks my engine too. I just do a better job of hiding it. She won't be back today, and I don't know when we'll see her again, but you might have heard that the good Senator Vandenberg supported the president's bill the way we hoped he would."

As if checking to ensure that the vision that had just graced his presence had indeed taken the elevator down, Paul shot one more glance toward the foyer. Then, as he walked into the office suite's entrance, he held up the newspaper with the earth-shattering headlines for Stephenson to see.

"Yes, yes," Stephenson said. "Things worked out the way we hoped, but we must hurry. Wild Bill is waiting in my office. We're taking a plane ride with him today to Canada. We're starting up a new project, Camp X, and I want to see the selected site."

As the military plane droned through turbulent air, Stephenson noticed Paul scrutinizing General Donovan, who had dozed off. "Did you enjoy your forays with Wild Bill in the Balkans?"

"I did, sir. He's an amazing man. He reminds me of those lines in Rudyard Kipling's poem, 'If you can walk with kings, nor lose the common touch.' I saw him do exactly that. You told me before I met him that he's the only man in history to have been awarded the Congressional Medal of Honor, the Distinguished Service Cross, two Distinguished Service Medals, a Silver Star for courage under fire, three Purple Hearts, and to have attained the rank of a general officer."

Stephenson nodded and regarded the general with an appreciative look. "He would be a legend if more people knew about him. But he doesn't seek press coverage without purpose, so most Americans have never heard of him. We'll be seeing more of him as the war wears on and if the Americans come in with us. You're familiar with the British Special Operations Executive?"

Paul nodded. "The group charged with 'setting Europe ablaze,' to quote the prime minister. The SOE. Jeremy worked with them briefly inside France, but I think they're still setting up."

Stephenson looked impressed, a rare event for him. "I did not know that about your brother. Kudos to him."

Paul sighed and looked out the window at the passing cloudy sky. "Yes, sir. Both of my brothers are quite remarkable in their exploits. My sister, Claire, too."

Stephenson studied him. "Feeling immaterial, are you? Like you don't count?"

Paul hesitated. "A bit, sir. I'm not complaining, and so much of what I witness seems surreal—like it couldn't be happening. Miss Cynthia is a perfect example. I don't know what she did or how she did it, or even if anything she did affected anything anywhere, but the fact is, she accepted an assignment, the senator voted the way we wanted, and the implications are enormous. War materiel is already on its way to Britain. But..." He struggled for words. "I observed that situation first-hand, and I affected nothing. My whole family confronts the German threat daily, and I live in luxurious comfort in downtown Manhattan, safe from the ravages of combat and nighttime bombings."

Stephenson sat back and rested his head against the wall of the cabin in contemplation. Then he leaned toward Paul again. "Let's put things in perspective a bit." He picked his words carefully. "You're here because His Majesty personally approved our mission, and you were carefully selected."

Paul shrugged. "So I'm told."

"By the prime minister," Stephenson retorted with a stern note. "Take his word for it, if you won't take mine."

"Sorry."

Stephenson waved off the apology and gestured toward Donovan. "When the history of this war is told, most people will never hear of Wild Bill, me, or you. Forget what I do, but what the general has already done and will do in this war, his shaping of it, will be immense. But let's review the impact that *you've* had so far."

"I'm not looking for a pat on the back, sir."

"And that's not what I'm about. But seeing your effect might lift your spirits." He leaned against his seat again and gazed into space as though contemplating where to start. "If you haven't been told, then you deserve to know that when you ran the issue of the Boulier network up to Director Menzies and endured his wrath last year, your action saved the network. Doing so set in motion a series of events that resulted in our having an operator inside the German invasion-planning headquarters in Dinard who supplied target data and schedules for the invasion.

"Other information coming through that network gave warning that the spy was about to be exposed and that there was a German senior officer who might be receptive to helping the Resistance. Indications are that he helped save the life of our spy, who is now in Paris infiltrating the German high command." He chuckled. "The Gestapo in Dinard failed to inform its counterpart in the capital of this person's identity."

"You're giving me more credit than I deserve—"

"Oh, stuff the modesty. You deserve to have your work validated. We all do. My effect is easy to see. Yours is not. Let's talk about that report you wrote for Director Menzies before you left London."

"You mean that exercise in busy work?"

"It was never that. We had several objectives in assigning that task to you. Granted, it was not perceived at the outset as a necessary report. We wanted to see how diligent you were in producing it and how well you interacted with senior people under pressure over an extended period. You did well enough to have been chosen over the other candidates, and the competition was tough."

"None of us knew we were in a contest."

"Precisely. You did your assigned job thoroughly."

"It was an academic exercise."

"It might have started out that way, but your report unearthed several key elements. One was the observation that pilots complained about the unreliability of their radios. As a result, work is underway to improve them. After all, that is a chief component of our ability for our fighters to meet the enemy at a time and place of our own choosing without wasting precious fuel. That's huge all by itself, but your biggest contribution was giving the analytical basis for formalizing a change in fighter tactics."

"Sir? The issue with British fighter formations was already known. The pilots complained up through their chains of command, and some squadrons were adopting the new formation irrespective of doctrine."

"True, but your study not only highlighted the issue, it also quantified the size of pilot dissatisfaction and the casualties resulting from the old formation. It gave a data-driven basis for formalizing new air tactics patterned after German fighter formations."

Paul stretched, arched his eyebrows, and puffed his cheeks as he blew air out through them. "That's all nice to hear, but you give me too much credit. I've really done nothing more than be an observer."

Stephenson chuckled. "If you say so. I don't suppose you can shed that level of modesty, but I'll tell you that not only do I think my estimate of your contributions is accurate, but so does the air chief marshal, the prime minister, and His Majesty."

For the first time in weeks, Paul felt a surge of elation. He fought to contain it. "Seriously, sir? The king?"

"He stays abreast of high-level intelligence matters and those involved in them. And he's informed of your contributions in the Balkans as well."

Paul started to protest.

Stephenson cut him off by lifting a hand. "Granted, most of the responsibility for the actions rested on Wild Bill, but he needed someone there able to direct attention toward him or deflect it away. You did that perfectly, and indications are that events will transpire the way we want them to. Your contribution was crucial, and you braved dangerous places to pull it off. Give yourself a little credit."

"Thank you, sir." Paul leaned forward with his elbows resting on his knees and his fingers interlocked between his legs. "Do you mind if I ask you something? This woman, Cynthia—who is she? How does she move about so blithely, and how did she pull off changing the senator's mind when no one else could?"

Stephenson took his time to respond, his enigmatic smile playing on his lips. "She's an international socialite, Paul, the energetic wife of a boring diplomat who began his career in Poland. Her real name is Elizabeth Thorpe. You can probably find her photo in the social pages of the newspapers. She's helped bring about positive results in a number of places around the world, including in acquiring the Enigma machine at the heart of Bletchley's decoding operations." Chuckling, he added, "She makes a point of never knowing our own secrets so that she can never divulge any." He sighed. "Another unsung soul, but I never ask about her methods." He closed his eyes and leaned back. "She is beautiful, though, isn't she? Pure magic."

The plane began its descent. Stephenson re-opened his eyes. "Before we land, I want to tell you about what we're doing with General Donovan."

"Don't be so formal," Donovan broke in gruffly, waking from deep sleep. "You call me 'Wild Bill,' and so do all my friends. This is a small team. Paul and I have been through the muck together. He can call me that too." He turned to Paul. "Go ahead. Try it on for size."

Somewhat flummoxed, Paul said, "I'll try, sir, I mean, W-Wild Bill, but it won't come naturally. My training—well, you're a general and I'm a captain."

Donovan dismissed the comment. "You'll get used to it." He shifted his attention to Stephenson. "Now, what were you saying, Little Bill?"

Stephenson laughed and turned to Paul. "I was telling Paul that this facility we're going to is top secret. We call it Camp X. There's nothing there now, but we expect it to be built out and operational by early December. It's to be a training facility, where we'll teach ordinary people to break tyranny—a spy school, much like the ones we've established in England and Scotland to train our covert agents. It's a joint project between Great Britain and Canada, through the latter's Foreign Office. The school will be operated by the Royal Canadian Mounted Police and the Canadian army under the command of our offices in Manhattan."

"Which means you, Little Bill," Donovan intoned.

"I suppose it does," Stephenson sniffed. "Wild Bill is building an organization like our SOE. It doesn't have an official name yet, but he's been calling it the Office of Strategic Services—the OSS. When the school opens, US military intelligence and the FBI will send people to this camp for training."

Paul's eyes bored deep into Stephenson's. For a moment, he did not speak, absorbing the implications of what he had just heard. "That leads me to think that the notion of US entry into the war allied with Britain is accepted among officials as more highly probable than is generally believed."

"That's a reasonable conclusion, but the public is not yet there, which is why we have to nudge things along."

They arrived late in the afternoon under an overcast sky in a Canadian army sedan at the place where Camp X was proposed to be built. It was in a green but deserted part of Ontario along the lake by the same name, near the town of Whitby. The Canadian colonel who drove them, Josh

Lawrence, parked near the water's edge and emerged from the car. "This is the place," he said as the rest of the group clambered out and milled about looking across the empty land. "There's not much to see. But I brought the plans to show you."

"It's perfect," Donovan said. "Far from civilization. Few chances for prying eyes. No structures to tear down. Just build, and there's plenty of water."

Lawrence removed a roll of blueprints from the trunk of the car and flattened it on the hood. "The layout is quite simple. Two sets of barracks, an administrative building, a dining facility, a gymnasium, and then firing ranges, obstacle courses, classrooms, exercise fields... The normal things you'd see at a military training base."

"Show me where the Hydra will be located," Stephenson said.

While Lawrence looked it up on the drawing, Paul asked, "What's the Hydra?"

"I guess I hadn't mentioned it," Stephenson replied.

"It'll go in over there on top of that rise," Lawrence said, pointing.

"Let's walk over, and I'll explain it," Stephenson told Paul, and headed toward the area. "We're quietly procuring the latest short-wave radio equipment from local enthusiasts, and we have an expert electronic broadcast theorist and engineer working on a technical advance. The idea is to set up a secure telecommunications relay station capable of sending and receiving messages from Great Britain and Western Europe as well as the United States and even down into South America. That's the capability we think it will have." He stopped and looked around. "The topography here lends to sending and receiving transmissions, and we can code messages safely."

"Seriously?" Paul said. "We've broken their codes. Why would we believe they haven't broken ours?"

Stephenson chuckled. "Remind me to explain that to you on the flight back to New York. Now regarding the short wave, our engineer, Benjamin deForest Bayly, is an electronics wizard. He says that theoretically we can do it. He's working on the technology. He expects it to be ready by next spring."

"And you think he can do it?"

Stephenson nodded patiently. "You don't know much about my business enterprises, Paul. They're far-flung and diversified. One of them participated in early concepts of television. The technology has been developing since late in the last century, but it's moving from mechanical to electronic imaging. It would be ready for commercialization but for this war. I'd like to see a unit in every house. The value of the technology is immense."

Listening with rapt if not challenged attention, Paul rubbed his chin. "I'm officially going to stop being amazed at anything," he said. "The idea of this relay station blew my mind, and now you're telling me leaps in television technology?"

"That's still down the road," Stephenson said, "but there's much more to come. There's an element I'll tell you about when we're on the plane."

A few hours later, as they flew back to New York, he told Paul, "There are some things that are top secret to the US and Great Britain, so I couldn't discuss them in front of Colonel Lawrence.

"When we made our bargain with President Roosevelt for support inside the Unites States, in addition to intelligence, part of what we offered was to give the US our full and complete radar technology, including our most advanced research. England is now able to put radar on some of its fighters to see and engage enemy aircraft at night. We're using it already against the *Luftwaffe* quite successfully. Our hope is that by pairing British research facilities with those of the US, we'll develop more advanced capabilities faster and sooner. Radar kept us in the fight over Britain."

Paul listened in amazement. "Technology and intelligence," he murmured. "That's our edge."

"It's not the whole package," Stephenson said. "Production capacity, levels of manpower, training, morale, communications—"

"You said you'd explain why we're confident the Germans can't break our codes."

"'Can't' might be too strong a term. We're confident that they haven't done it yet and doubt that they will, but they're still trying."

"How do we know they haven't yet?"

"Because the Germans are not very good at spy craft. We rounded up all the agents they sent to infiltrate Great Britain within weeks of their arrivals, but instead of arresting them, we turned them. They work for us now."

Seeing the astonishment on Paul's face, Stephenson remarked quietly, "I guess there is a lot to learn at this level."

45

March 24, 1941
Rockefeller Center, Manhattan, New York

"May I ask what your speech is intended to accomplish?" Paul asked.

"Good question," Donovan replied.

Stephenson listened to the exchange from behind his desk.

"Hitler is an emotional man," the general began. "He listens to his high command until someone crosses him on a level that he takes personally, and then he goes into tirades, and often fires the offender—or worse." He shifted in his seat and leaned forward. "Right now, we're in a bit of a lull strategically, but all the pieces are in place. Germany is poised to pounce in Greece. Yugoslavian partisans, led by their air force, are ready to break with the fascists, and we're about to enrage Hitler.

"That's the objective of my speech. The *führer* is still in a consultative mode with his generals. He'll be infuriated by what I say to the American people tomorrow, and he'll react emotionally. That will trigger German operations in Greece and limit his forces for Barbarossa. Then, he'll receive his surprise from Yugoslavia—and five months down the road, the Russian winter will hit him. I expect the *Wehrmacht* to be devastated by what happens there."

He stood. "Time for me to fly. If you'd like to see my speech, I've left a copy of it on Bill's desk." He grinned. "I'm wide open for critique." Shaking Paul's hand, he added, "I'll see you at the White House in the morning." Then he bade Stephenson farewell and departed.

Paul walked over, took the draft of Donovan's speech from Stephenson's desk, and read it, four short paragraphs. "I'm just struck by all the things that go on to fight this war that hardly anyone knows about," he told Stephenson. "I'm willing to bet that most Americans have never heard of General Donovan, and yet tomorrow he'll be elevated to national stature and address America about things we expect to affect the movement of armies across the globe. It's mind-boggling, but I wonder if history will record it or even take notice.

"What you and the general do is amazing. If anyone had told me about it, I wouldn't have believed it, and the only reason I do now is because I've been there in the meetings with Churchill. I traveled to Greece and saw the battlelines. I went to Yugoslavia and witnessed what happened there. And I still wonder if I've dreamt it.

"Here I am in New York City, living in a penthouse, and seeing things like—" He grasped at thoughts. "Like Camp X in Canada with its Hydra. It's all the stuff of spy and science fiction novels, except that I'm living it and seeing it. And I ask myself constantly, is this really going to win the war?"

The sides of Stephenson's mouth turned up and he regarded Paul with benevolence. "Have a seat, and let's talk through this. Maybe I can broaden your viewpoint." When they were both sitting, he continued, "We plucked you out of a traditional intelligence role in London and plopped you down here in America, and then took you to Canada, sent you to the Balkans—and as I recall, I even took you out on a local sortie with the FBI having to do with that sailor who was selling our convoys' courses and directions."

"How could I forget?" Paul said, feeling a mental tug from the moral struggles he had worked through over how he believed Stephenson had handled the matter.

"What you might not see clearly is the organization that supports us," Stephenson went on. "The sign on our door indicates that we're the British passport office, and we occupy two floors here in Rockefeller Center. That's a lot of people, but it's only the tip of the iceberg. We have at our disposal the assets of the formal sections of British intelligence, to include Bletchley and the newly forming SOE.

"Prime Minister Churchill asked me to take this job because I have large business interests in various parts of the world. I know intelligence, I know people, and I also employ my business assets when needed to further our cause. So, while it might seem that we have this small coterie that you readily see and includes Wild Bill because of his liaison role between us and the president, our undertakings often involve large numbers of people—most of whom you'll never meet or know how they're involved unless or until there's a reason."

Paul nodded and took a deep breath. "Operational security."

"Exactly. Does that add to your understanding?"

"It does, and the whole enterprise becomes even more amazing, but—" Paul hesitated.

"Spit it out," Stephenson said. "You've not been shy before."

Paul nodded. "I read the general's speech." He took a deep

breath. "I have to say, it was underwhelming, which causes me to ask, is that it? That's the speech to move armies?"

Stephenson laughed gently. "You'll get better at understanding subtleties. That's not anyone making that speech. That's a US Army general who reports directly to the president. His venue is national radio, and he'll speak to the American people after the president's introduction, so in effect, he'll speak for the president.

"Just two weeks ago, lend-lease was passed, and already American warships are under British command and control. And with Donovan's speech, the president will inform the *führer* that America is inching toward joining the fight while Hitler dithers over what to do in the Balkans and the Soviet Union.

"*Herr* Adolf will throw a fit, I promise you, and unleash his panzers into Greece, and when the coup is complete in Yugoslavia, he'll invade there too. He has no clue about the forces growing around him." He smiled up at Paul. "I can see on your face that you're uncertain how this will all play out. Obviously, I guarantee nothing, but I'm confident that within a few days, you'll start to see the results going the way we intend."

Paul grunted. "And if they do, Greeks and Yugoslavians will die in place of Soviets. That's a bitter pill." He caught Stephenson's steady gaze. "I get it. The pill is not as bitter as losing the war to a tyrant and having many more people slaughtered."

46

March 25, 1941
White House, Washington, DC

"The plan is working, Mr. President," Donovan said.

President Franklin Roosevelt peered through his spectacles across the breakfast table at Stephenson and Donovan in
his private dining room next to the Oval Office. Then he
glanced at Paul and gestured his way. "Good idea, bringing
him along. He works for you, eh, Little Bill?"

Although he addressed his query to Stephenson, Donovan
responded. "Captain Littlefield is solid, sir. I took him with me
through the Balkans." He added with a wry smile, "He's quirky
at times, but he can handle himself."

Roosevelt grunted. "Quirky is good. Look at where it got
my distant cousin, Ted. Anyway, I like Little Bill's idea of a
walking archive. Maybe you should get one." He turned to
Paul. "It's good that a young person is seeing how things
happen from the inside. After the war, when it's safe and
documents have been declassified, you should let the public

know of your experiences." His face suddenly turned solemn. "We don't want another war like this one."

He turned back to Donovan. "Go on with what you were saying about the plan."

"Yes, sir. Germany placed twelve panzer divisions on Bulgaria's southern border with Greece and warned Turkey not to interfere. With the British landing Force W on the east coast of Greece, and its drive across the country to support the war against Italy in Albania, Germany will invade soon. That will pin down *Wehrmacht* troops there.

"And we're only days away from a coup in Yugoslavia. What we say here today could prod it along, and I think this one will succeed. It'll create another ally for Great Britain, and that will surprise Hitler. He'll be forced to commit more troops to secure that flank. Mussolini's days must already be numbered, at least in the *führer's* mind. Benito is obviously no Julius Caesar."

Looking amused, Stephenson leaned back in his chair. "We're hearing through Bletchley that the chief of staff of the German supreme command, Field Marshal Keitel, is complaining of having to postpone Barbarossa by four weeks. He'll be frustrated further when he realizes that the invasion into Soviet territory will probably be delayed another two weeks." He chuckled. "And we were hoping for at least a day's delay."

The president laughed and then looked around for his aide. Spotting him, he called, "Where is this filming happening today?"

"In the Blue Room, sir."

Roosevelt nodded vigorously. "Good. Tell me again the rest of the preparations."

"Yes, sir. Your comments and the general's speech will be recorded on film and will go out immediately to all press outlets. In addition, it will be delivered to movie distributors to be released as newsreels for the beginning of each movie showing across the US and Britain, as we do regularly."

While he spoke, the president lit up a cigar and took a puff. "Good, good. Thank you," he told the aide, and turned back to Stephenson and Donovan. "These are my favorite," he declared, waving his cigar in the air. "I've got a box set aside for the prime minister. Be sure to pick it up on your way out."

Then he gestured toward his aide. "With that film's wide distribution, it ought to make its way to the *führer* and get his goat. He's the target audience."

"He's already riled up," Donovan observed. "This should be the finishing touch, Mr. President. I'm betting that we get our further postponement of Barbarossa."

Roosevelt gazed studiously at Donovan. "All right, Big Bill, let's get this done. You know the press is not fond of you lately. They won't like the elevation of your image that comes from my high praise and being seen on the stage with me."

Donovan laughed. "Are you kidding, sir? They love me. They just think I'm a clown."

The Blue Room, on the first floor of the White House, site of the only wedding of a president ever held there when Grover Cleveland married Frances Folsom in 1886, was oval-shaped and usually decorated in blues and whites. Customarily, it functioned as a room for receptions and receiving lines or occasional small dinners for state visitors or special guests of the White House.

A platform and podium had been erected at the end of the room near the windows with a ramp to accommodate the president's wheelchair. Most people knew of his affliction with polio, but the press treated news coverage of the three-term president such that the sight of him being pushed around did not dominate public reports.

Paul had entered the White House with some sense of wonder at its history and current position on the world stage, recalling Donovan's remarks about the British having burned it down. He watched as Roosevelt wheeled himself in, and then an aide pushed him into position behind the podium. Special shades, reflectors, and lights had been set up to cast the president and Donovan at their best.

Then, crew members took their positions, a director gave instructions, cameras whirred, and the president spoke. After introductory remarks, he said, "I sent my communications coordinator, General William Donovan, to the battlefront to review for me the state of the war and the attitudes and capabilities of Britain and her great people to weather this dark storm that settled on them. I wanted to know if they could turn it and emerge from it intact. He traveled the battlefronts, visited defensive positions, consulted with foreign leaders, and reported back to me. Concerning his odyssey, I am most happy to share remarks from my good friend, the Prime Minister of Great Britain." He held up a sheet of paper and read, 'Thank you for the magnificent work done by Donovan in the Balkans.'"

The president put the paper down and looked into the camera. "It was dangerous work, sensitive work, and work that was necessary if the United States is to proceed with wisdom during this time that the world is consumed in conflict. I asked him to share his perceptions with the American people, and so he will now report to you what he revealed to me. After he speaks, I'll deliver some remaining comments."

As the president was wheeled to a position behind the cameras where he could watch, Donovan took to the podium and waited for the director to signal him to speak. Paul and Stephenson watched from one side.

"I have been given an opportunity to study at first hand," the general began, "these great battles going on in the Atlantic, and in the Mediterranean, in Africa, in Greece, and in Albania. I have been able to form my conclusions on the basis of full information. These conclusions I will submit to my country for its use in furtherance of our national defense, an essential part of which is our policy of aid to Great Britain.

"We have no choice as to whether or not we will be attacked. That choice is Hitler's, and he has already made it, not for Europe alone, but for Africa, Asia, and the world. Our only choice is to decide whether or not we will resist it. And to choose in time, while resistance is still possible, while others are still able to stand with us.

"Let us keep this in mind—Germany is a formidable, a resourceful, and a ruthless foe. Do not underrate her. If we do —we deceive ourselves. Her victories have brought her new military and industrial strength. She got the jump at the start of the war and has kept it; but not yet has she made a full test. And until this test comes, it is better not to overrate her. But her greatest gains have been made through fear. Fear of the might of her war machine. So, she has played upon that fear, and her recent diplomatic victories are the product.

"But we must remember that there is a moral force in wars, that in the long run is stronger than any machine. And I say to you, my fellow citizens, all that Mr. Churchill has told you on the resolution and determination and valor and confidence of his people is true."

Paul listened, awestruck at Donovan's presence, and at the same words he had read the previous evening and discounted, which now in this setting seemed profound. He sensed for the first time that his own place in the great struggle might have significance. Only weeks ago in a royal palace, this same general had feigned public drunkenness as a means of advancing US national security interests; the results, some of which remained to be seen, were astoundingly successful.

The attack on their Humber along the coast road in Greece came to mind, when Paul had helped down from the overturned vehicle this same man who had just hurled a message that at once defied a tyrant and cast hope to a war-weary world. And he had struck terror in the heart of Prince Regent Paul so gently and smoothly.

As he descended from the podium, Donovan saw Paul eyeing him. "What? Did I mess up?" he whispered as they watched the president wheeled once more to the podium.

"No, sir," Paul replied, keeping his sense of wonder under tight control. "But may I say what a privilege it is to work with you."

Donovan grinned at him. "Don't go brown-nosin' me now that I'm a film star. You already chewed me out once." He tapped his head. "And I've got a long memory." He pointed toward the podium. "The president is ready to speak again."

"Thank you, General Donovan," Roosevelt said into his microphone while making eye contact with the general, "that was an excellent report." He turned to look into the camera. "As we can see, America, we face a dangerous situation, and we cannot much longer simply remain on the sidelines and hope. Our own security is imperiled. Therefore, I have also ordered that US Navy warships will protect British supply ships sailing into the European theater from Greenland, Newfoundland, and the West Indies, and of course along the American coasts. I further proclaim that the Red Sea and the Persian Gulf are no longer combat zones from which American ships can be excluded under our Neutrality Act. Having taken those decisions and issued those orders, let me emphasize that we seek war with no one. These new measures are defensive, but the nations of the world should take note that America will defend itself and its assets from any danger."

After the president had finished speaking and descended from the dais, he wheeled himself to Donovan and Paul accompanied by Stephenson. "That was a statesman's delivery," he remarked with enthusiasm to Donovan.

"I think America's enemies will take note of your strong action," the general replied, "and our friends will take heart."

Roosevelt turned to Stephenson. "And we have you to thank for suggesting that I take those actions. I had our legal beagles check out their lawfulness, and they assured me that under the Neutrality Act and given the circumstances, they are perfectly legal." He thrust an unlit cigar in his mouth and fumbled for his lighter. Then he grinned at Stephenson. "And what with all that's going on in Yugoslavia and Greece, the timing to announce our actions could not have been better." He lit his cigar and looked at Stephenson again with a querying expression. "What say you? How soon do you think *Herr* Adolf will see our film?"

"Why sir," Stephenson replied, the corners of his mouth turning up slightly, "I believe he'll be watching it by this time tomorrow."

47

March 27, 1941
Bletchley Park, England

"Sir, you asked me to expedite reports of significant events."

Commander Denniston removed his glasses as Claire proceeded into his office and took her seat. "Yes, Miss Little-field. What is it?"

"Major things are happening in Belgrade," she began. "Five days ago, as you must know, Hitler pointed out to Prince Regent Paul that Hungary, Bulgaria, and Romania had already aligned with his Axis powers under the Tripartite Pact, and he issued an ultimatum. Essentially, the regent was told to surrender his army, or Germany would invade. The regent set up conferences to meet Hitler's demands. Several high-level air force officers objected to capitulation. They've just staged a coup under the leadership of Yugoslav Air Force chief, General Dusan Simovic. They intend to declare that King Peter II has reached legal age and install him as the national leader today."

Denniston nodded. "That was done with British help. I'm

glad you're tracking. I'll get word up that the coup has taken place, although that might already have been reported through operational channels. Have you heard any reaction from Berlin?"

Claire arched her eyebrows. "We're hearing volumes. Hitler is throwing temper tantrums. He's also very upset about Britain's expedition into Greece on the east coast."

"As well he should, seeing his plans unravel. Anything from the Bulgarians?"

"The *Wehrmacht* is moving its 12th Army along the Greco-Bulgarian border in the Thrace region where it meets with Turkey's boundary. Hitler warned the Turks that he'll invade their country if it interferes with his plans in Greece."

Claire suddenly chuckled. "Stop me, sir, if I'm telling you things you already know."

"Of course, but too often what I get are reports with bare facts, and even analysis that doesn't pull the pieces together in a coherent picture. You're doing a great job. Are you seeing any signs that Hitler will invade Greece? Surely by now, he must've figured out that he'll only weaken his own forces allocated to go into the Soviet Union."

"He seems to be acting out of pure rage now. He takes what's going on in Yugoslavia as a personal affront, that he's being defied, but he hasn't yet seen British fingerprints on events there.

"Of course, he's already angry with us in the Greece-Bulgaria situation, but our part there is overt with our expeditionary force to reinforce the Greeks." She chuckled again. "On a personal note, sir, it's nice to imagine him raging because things are not going his way for a change."

Denniston laughed. "Yes, it is. All right, Miss Littlefield. Good report. I'll take your perspective higher." He rose from his seat and crossed the room to a radio. "Let's see if the BBC has picked up on the coup in Belgrade."

The radio squealed and squawked as it warmed up. Then music played, commercial announcements ran, and an anchorman reported the news. "To repeat an earlier story," he said, "Prince Regent Paul of Yugoslavia was removed from office today by air force officers staging a coup. BBC was informed that this action comes in the aftermath of an ultimatum delivered to the regent by Chancellor Adolf Hitler of Germany, demanding that the Yugoslavian army surrender to him or face invasion. Only two days ago, the now deposed Prince Regent Paul signed the Axis Pact's Tripartite Treaty. At the time, Alexander Cadogan, Britain's Permanent Under-Secretary of State for Foreign Affairs, stated, 'Yugoslavs seem to have sold their souls to the Devil.' Considering these new developments, Prime Minister Churchill issued a statement, as follows: 'Yugoslavia has found its soul.'"

Denniston clicked off the radio. "So, there you have it. Yugoslavia shifts into our sphere. That's enough to turn any Hun tyrant's face red. Thank you for coming, Miss Littlefield. Now the things to watch for are Hitler's military and political responses."

"I'll keep that in mind," Claire said as she headed through the door.

48

April 6, 1941
Rockefeller Center, Manhattan, New York

Bill Stephenson appeared in the doorway of his office across from Paul's desk and spoke urgently. "Come listen to this. It's the BBC. They're reporting live from Belgrade."

Paul bolted from his chair and hurried into Stephenson's office. The newsman had already begun his report:

"The bombing started early this morning, and the Nazis showed no mercy. Calling their action 'Operation Retribution,' their fighters strafed the streets, and their bombers dropped their deadly cargoes remorselessly. In a flash, centuries-old historic buildings were destroyed, including the royal palace. The National Library of Serbia is in flames, destroying hundreds of years of Serbian heritage. And when the raid was over, thousands lay dead in Belgrade's city center—mothers, fathers, children, toddlers, babies." The journalist's voice caught. "The bullets see no one. They strike indiscriminately, and now grandparents lie dead next to each other, never having seen the danger that killed them.

"This is a dark day for Belgrade, for Yugoslavia, that will be remembered long into the country's future. It will change the face of the city and the nature of the national culture that resulted because Yugoslavia dared to defy the man in Berlin. Time will tell how his gamble will be rewarded, but I know the Slavic people, and that population will not accept this savage slaughter of their families, friends, and neighbors without answering in full. Yugoslavia's defiance in the face of overwhelming military might well spread a glow across those countries the German war machine devoured. No longer will the Nazis be perceived as all-powerful and indestructible. Adolf Hitler has sown the wind. He will reap the whirlwind."

Stephenson clicked off the radio. Neither he nor Paul spoke at first, and then Stephenson said quietly, "The president has his Coventry."

49

May 11, 1941
Bletchley Park, England

Claire stared at the note she had just received from Commander Denniston. It read, "Ms. Littlefield, please meet me in Hut 8 immediately. Urgent."

She re-read it several times, and then, excusing herself from the team that handled analysis of decoded *Wehrmacht* and *Luftwaffe* messages in Hut 3, she hurried to meet with the commander. Barely four months had passed since she had joined the analysis group, and in the intervening weeks, she had seen little of him.

Hut 8, under the direction of a brilliant mathematician, Alan Turing, was where other cryptologists had spent months trying to break German naval codes, but the last Claire had heard, their best efforts had produced no breakthroughs. The group's consensus was that an additional security element had been added to the sending and receiving ends of the *Kriegsmarine's* Enigmas.

She entered the hut with some trepidation since Bletchley

employees adhered to operational security by not visiting areas in which they were not specifically authorized, and she had never been cleared for the naval part of the facility. Gripping the note firmly in her hand, she entered the hut, a nondescript, rectangular, single-story building with a tin roof among a row of such buildings built at one side of the Bletchley mansion. Inside, wide tables filled the length of the hut with young people, mostly women, seated around them and engrossed in marking up papers piled before them or keying at decoding machines that looked much like typewriters.

The scene was virtually the same as in Hut 6 where Claire had, prior to her promotion, decoded *Wehrmacht* and *Luftwaffe* radio traffic, the main difference being that the effort in Hut 6 had produced much actionable intelligence, often of high value, and was labeled as "Ultra." In Hut 8, although she observed the same level of diligence, what seemed to be missing was an air of confidence resulting from success. Yet as the door closed behind Claire and she looked across the studious heads, she noticed several women glancing at the far end of the room with expressions of anticipation, their bright eyes focused on a group of officials conferring there. Among them was Commander Denniston.

He spotted Claire and waved to her to join them. "We've had an intelligence coup," he said after making introductions. "What I'm getting ready to tell you was classified by the Admiralty as top secret. Only those in this room and of course our higher-ups know it.

"One of our ships, the *HMS Bulldog*, captured an enemy submarine two days ago, the *U110*. The German crew set scuttling charges that failed to detonate. So, the *Bulldog* sent over a boarding party, which brought back every document they could find. That was rather nervy considering that the explosives could have gone off at any time. But the Admiralty had sent out a letter instructing all ships to attempt to capture the encryption machine if the opportunity presented itself. And—"

His eyes went wide with excitement in his very gentle-manly British manner. "They succeeded. The crew of the *Bulldog* brought back an Enigma machine configured for Germany's navy. It's the missing link, so to speak, and now we have it." Denniston almost emerged from professional reserve into glee. "They would have brought the U-boat in as well, but high waves flooded the vessel and sank it, so they had to cut the towing cable."

Claire stared at him. "Are you saying that we can now decode and translate their navy's intercepted messages as easily as we can the *Wehrmacht's* and the *Luftwaffe's*? That's remarkable."

"I think that's the case, but the entire treasure trove is still on its way here. The ship will stop in Iceland. We've instructed them to photograph everything, and we're sending up a team to bring back the whole lot including the machine. Here's the thing—"

He interrupted himself and turned to the small group he had been conversing with. "You're all up to snuff," he told them. "Give me a few minutes to brief Miss Littlefield."

He took her elbow and guided her to a corner of the room. "Something is brewing in the North Sea. The Norwegian Resistance and the Swedes both sent reports of sightings of the *Bismarck* skirting their coasts, and communications in the area have grown in volume. If that battleship is on the move, it must be heading to Bergen in Norway for provisioning, and then it'll be setting out to the Atlantic."

"You think they'll try to run our blockade?"

"The *Bismarck* is useless to the Germans if it *doesn't* run it, and it's a terrible threat to our convoys if it does. But things get worse. We received word from the same sources that two battlecruisers, the *Scharnhorst* and the *Gneisenau*, had left the Baltic headed our way, and the heavy battlecruiser, *Prinz Eugen*, had already rounded Iceland."

He peered at Claire. "Are you taking this in? It's a lot."

Claire nodded. "I'm with you so far, sir. It's all so ominous."

"Agreed, but I'm told that this haul coming from *U110* contains not only an Enigma machine, but also the schedules for changing the settings disks, the courses and positions of current German ships at sea including their submarine wolf-packs, and diagrams showing how the *Kriegsmarine* sectioned off the Atlantic and assigned fleet and individual ship responsibilities. To have a prayer of keeping our supply lines open across the Atlantic, we must be able to track their ships. We've been able to do that to a degree from tracking where their radio transmissions originate, but we've not been able to know the content of those transmissions, which in any case are short and infrequent by design. The captured material should allow us to read their position reports to know exactly where they are and where they are going."

He caught himself. "Please excuse me. I'm prattling, but if we're right about *Bismarck's* movements and what we're getting from the *Bulldog*, the combined value is incalculable. We'll know where the *Bismarck* is as well as the position of every ship they put to sea and their planned movements, not to mention the German high command communications, just as we currently do with the *Wehrmacht* and *Luftwaffe*.

"If this comes about—the *Bulldog* haul—we'll be able to understand key communications as soon as they're received. Right now, we need access to key information as quickly as possible, particularly pertaining to the *Bismarck*.

"So, I'm asking you to come over to Hut 8 and go back to

decoding for a spell, until we've understood how this *Kriegs-marine* version of the Enigma machine works and have put our systems in place. I want you here with this team when that material comes in, to bring your combined decoding, linguistic, and analytical skills to bear to help expedite crucial messages forward. It's an incredible challenge. Are you up to it?"

Claire's face expressed both eagerness and concern. "I'm honored that you asked, sir, of course. But that's a huge responsibility. Are you sure I'm the one for this?"

"I'm sure, and I've already received Director Menzies' blessing."

Claire took a deep breath. "All right, if you're sure. When would I start?"

"Now. Your new co-workers will bring you up to speed on details, what's been done so far, and how they do it. You might recall that before we cracked the Enigma on the non-navy side, we were able to discern troop movements by the frequency, volume, and origin of messages. That's the level that the Hut 8 group is at now. Once we have in our hands the machine and the data that the *Bulldog* captured and understand how it works, we can 'let slip the hounds.' I'll want you to concentrate on messages coming to, from, or about the *Bismarck* and any of its significant support vessels. If you read or deduce anything along those lines, bring it to me immediately. Understood?"

"Yes, sir. Can someone put me in the big picture? I've focused on enemy ground and air forces in northern France and Berlin, but I know little about what's going on at sea, aside from what took place at Taranto. I know of the *Bismarck*, of course, but I don't understand why it strikes such terror. Isn't our *HMS Hood* equal to it?"

"Excellent question, Miss Littlefield, and one without easy

answers. The two ships are of equal length with similar weaponry, but their armaments are quite different. The *Hood* is a battlecruiser, much lighter, but might not be faster because it's much older. It's been our flagship since the last war, and it should have a greater range because of the difference in weight.

"The *Bismarck* is incredibly well protected with thick armor, and it's not agile, but it is fast. Perhaps faster than the *Hood*, but they've never done a footrace." He smiled wryly at his own humor. "The point is, the *Bismarck* can take the *Hood's* heavy shelling, but is the reverse true? We don't know the answer to that. Can the *Hood* maneuver quickly enough in the thick of battle to avoid being pounded by the *Bismarck's* huge guns? We don't know that answer either. So, if the *Bismarck* breaks out into the Atlantic, the battle that rages will resemble a chess match more than most, moving equivalently weighted pieces strategically to gain an advantage.

"We must win that battle, or Britain will suffer. The *Kriegsmarine* has been sinking our supply ships at an abysmal rate. We lost twenty-one merchant vessels in January and fifty-eight in February. That's against only twelve German U-boats destroyed in all last year. In that same time, we had fifteen million tons of cargo sunk, and thousands of sailors and merchant marines perished." He took a deep breath. "Mr. Churchill has said that the U-boat threat is the only thing about the war that he's ever really feared. In February, he came to believe that the nation could face starvation."

Claire put her hand to her mouth in astonishment. "I had no idea—"

Denniston grimaced. "Most people don't. Despite the Battle of Britain and the *blitz*, average Britons don't know how truly precarious our position is. Hitler figures that if he can't immediately invade, he can lay siege. And think about it, we're already rationing at one ounce of cheese and a minimal amount of meat per week, eight ounces of jam and margarine per month; and eggs, tomatoes, onions, and oranges have all but disappeared from store shelves."

Claire sighed. "I know. Is it possible that the *Kriegsmarine* is breaking our maritime codes? I mean, if they're having such success in finding and sinking our ships, that might explain how."

Denniston rubbed his chin. "It's a thought that's been raised elsewhere, but I don't think so. Hitler's got his U-boats out in wolfpacks. They spread across our shipping lanes watching for our convoys. When a submarine captain spots one, he shadows behind it on the surface and calls in the others in his pack. He takes command of the group, positions the other subs, and then they submerge and attack in strength from in front of our ships. We've tied up our battleships to protect convoys as a result, and the Germans have figured that out. They've learned that by avoiding our warships and attacking our merchant ships, they can starve us, as the *führer* intends.

"In the early days of the war, the *Kriegsmarine's* surface warships gave us the most problem. Now it's the submarines; but throw an impregnable *Bismarck* into the mix with its long-range heavy guns able to target multiple ships at a time and combine it with the ships I mentioned earlier as well as the wolfpacks, and they'll shut down our shipping. And here's the worst part—"

"The worst part, sir?" Claire interjected. "What you've just told me is quite bleak."

Denniston nodded solemnly. "You can see why capturing this naval Enigma and all the documents is so fortuitous. With them, we'll be able to steer our convoys around German positions. We must exploit that ability. They'll find an empty sea where they had expected to destroy another convoy."

"You were preparing to tell me the worst part."

"Ah, yes. Thanks for reminding me. The worst part." He leaned close to Claire. "They have a sister ship to the *Bismarck*, the *Tirpitz*, nearly set for service. It's undergoing sea trials now. The pair were bottlenecked in the Baltic to contain the Soviet navy should it attempt to break out of the Baltic, but their strategy might have changed, and the *Bismarck* might have slipped into the North Sea. That's bad enough, but if they get those two sister ships out into the Atlantic..." He rolled his eyes, leaving the sentence unfinished. "Our problem has been that we don't have enough vessels to defend against invasion as well as protect our commercial lanes. Just the *Bismarck* and the *Tirpitz* operating together would be a match for the whole of our Home Fleet."

His frustration was evident on his face. "All right then," he said, switching subjects. "I'll introduce you to Alan Turing and explain your role. He's a bit eccentric and can sometimes be difficult, but he's brilliant and completely absorbed in the mathematical and theoretical aspects of codebreaking. He'll be happy to have the benefit of your experience on his team."

Claire chuckled and lifted an eyebrow. "His reputation says otherwise. I hear he's rather a 'my way is best' sort of genius, but I'll put my best foot forward." She set a humorously determined expression on her face. "It's all for the cause, right?"

Denniston laughed. "You're a trooper, Miss Littlefield. We're fortunate to have you on our side." His demeanor became serious again. "Listen, you've proved your worth, and I've learned to pay attention to the instincts of good analysts. Last year, Harry Hinsley over in Hut 3 noticed a build-up of radio traffic around Norway. He tried to give warning to the extent of becoming a bother, but no one paid him any attention because he had long hair and was usually disheveled. Had we taken him seriously, we might have been better prepared for Germany's invasion of Norway and stopped Hitler right then and there. We could have avoided our humiliating evacuation from that country, and Neville Chamberlain might still be the prime minister. Ignoring Hinsley because he was disliked proved ruinous for Great Britain and Chamberlain's career."

He paused in thought. "And by the way, since I mentioned Hinsley, I should tell you that we previously ignored him a year ago when he warned that the *Scharnhorst* and the *Gneisenau* would sink our aircraft carrier, *HMS Glorious*. He was right." He shrugged. "Two points for this twenty-four-year-old upstart to zero for the combined upper echelon of British intelligence.

"We listen to him closely now, and he proposed a mission into the North Sea off of Iceland that was executed and now appears propitious to our success with this *Kriegsmarine* version of Enigma. You see, because Germany is farther east, they have a more difficult time in predicting weather, on which every mission counts for success. A while back, we captured a naval trawler with a naval Enigma, but by the time we boarded, the crew had tossed it overboard.

"That set Hinsley thinking that the *Kriegsmarine* must be keeping weather-monitoring trawlers off the coast of Iceland and that they must be sending their weather reports via coded messages. And of course, now we know that they were doing exactly that, and that these weather trawlers were manned by civilian crews.

"Hinsley suggested that if we were to execute a rapid raid against such a craft, the crew might, in their haste, throw the machine and codebooks overboard but forget to throw out the settings disks for the following months. He guessed that the disks might be held separately for safekeeping, probably in a safe, emphasizing that the mission should be conducted to look like an errant boarding, and the scuttling of the boat to look as though it had been done by the crew.

"It turns out Hinsley was right on all counts, and four days ago, we executed exactly that mission with precisely the result he predicted. We got the disks."

Denniston suddenly looked at Claire sharply. "You do understand that the settings in Enigma change periodically, and that is done by putting in new disks. On German naval vessels, that's once a month. If we have the machine and the settings, we can decode their messages."

"That gets to be more technical than I need, but I'm familiar with the concept."

"Hmm, yes. Well, I'm not sure if the lesson is that we should be more open to eccentricities or if eccentrics should try harder to be like the rest of us in how they present themselves. Seems like there ought to be some middle ground, but in any event, we must be diligent in digging out intelligence and communicating it. You've demonstrated your ability to do both. Let's put you to work."

"Thank you, sir. I hope not to disappoint anyone."

"Come along then. I'll introduce you."

"Wait, sir. There's one other thing I should bring to your attention."

Denniston's brows lifted, and he stared at Claire. "Bad news?"

"I'd say uncertain news. We don't have confirmation yet, but messages transmitted indicate that Hitler is shifting his bombing forces east in anticipation of his push into the Soviet Union. If correct, that should mean that nightly bombing of London and the rest of Great Britain is over."

The commander held Claire's steady gaze. "Could that be possible?"

"I think it might. Hitler is coming up against the grim reality that his resources are not limitless, and his priority for the moment seems to be shifting away from defeating us in our homeland."

Denniston raised his eyes heavenward as if sending a prayer. "Let's hope you're right, Miss Littlefield. That would be stupendous news."

50

May 15, 1941
London, England

Major Crockatt scrutinized Jeremy. "So, you're ready to come back to the fold?"

"I am, sir. The nightly bombings have stopped for the most part, the campaign to destroy the RAF ended eight months ago—"

"The air war goes on in other places."

"Yes, sir, but Hitler's immediate effort to destroy Britain seems to have been frustrated, at least for now, and I promised to return when the Battle of Britain was over. I think it's over."

"Well, Flight Lieutenant, you know the RAF was about to promote you."

"I know, sir. I'd still rather be where I can do the most good."

Crockatt chuckled. "Don't you mean that you'd rather be where you can get back to France?"

Jeremy blushed. "If you want me to confess that I'd welcome the chance to see Amélie, I'll gladly do it. However, that's not my guiding reason." He took a deep breath. "I feel indebted to Ferrand Boulier. I owe him my life."

Crockatt crossed his arms, shrugged, and arched his brow. "You went back and saved his. I'd say the balance is equal, and I'm sure he saw things the same way."

Jeremy nodded. "He didn't have to go out into that storm to rescue me, and doing it cost him his home, separation from his daughters, and finally, his life. I have to try to do for France what he can no longer do. The country is still important to winning the war, or we wouldn't have formed the SOE."

"Of course it's important, and we host the Free French under Charles De Gaulle right here in London. But this is a *world* war. Some people already call it the second world war, and we're fighting in Africa and Asia, on the ground and in the air."

Jeremy regarded the major with a puzzled look. "Are you saying that you don't want me to come back to MI-9?"

Crockatt smiled and shook his head. "Not at all. We'd welcome you back. But let's be sure you're using good judgment, limited though your choices might be."

"Sir, any choice I make will put me in danger. I doubt whether my skin will stop a bullet any better in North Africa or East Asia than it does in France."

"*Touché*, but you've got two personal interests across the Channel—Amélie in Marseille, and your brother in Colditz."

"I haven't let personal interests interfere before, and I've given no reason to believe I would start now."

"Granted, but you're asking to come back to MI-9. We have trained teams in France now. Their main objective is to help escaping prisoners evade capture. Quite a bit has developed since you left us nearly a year ago. When was that, last July?"

Feeling lightly reprimanded, Jeremy pursed his lips and nodded. "Late July."

"Then let me give you a sense of the lay of the land, to use a ground soldier's terminology. If you stay in the RAF, you'll soon be elevated to flight leader, and my guess is you'd have your pick of several assignments, most probably in North Africa or East Asia.

"You've already been in ground combat and on two covert missions, so I won't go over what that entails, but you were untrained for either role. We won't send you back to France without training, which at this point means three months."

Jeremy started to protest, but Crockatt held up his hand. "We have the luxury of more time at present. We didn't when we sent you out before."

"But sir, I've gained more experience."

"In flying, yes, and you're an ace and one of Cat's Eyes mates. We're all jolly proud of you. But the way that people's lives will rely on you is different. We know that you can do the job, but what you don't know could make a difference. We don't know what that is, and neither do you."

When he saw residual stubbornness in Jeremy's eyes, he added, "I'm sorry to put it to you this way, old boy, but that is our best offer, and I'm sure you'll find both SOE and MI-6 equally as insistent. I doubt that the RAF would release you to either of those sections anyway. They're not happy about letting you return to us, but that was the agreement I made with former Air Chief Marshal Dowding, and we put it in writing. As it was, I had to give him a jingle and get him to intervene with a call to his replacement to even consider your request to return."

Jeremy inhaled deeply, then exhaled. "Three months, eh?"

Leaning against his desk with his arms crossed, Crockatt affirmed with a slight nod.

"All right, then. When do I start?"

Crockatt smiled. "How about Monday, Captain. Today is

Thursday. Take a long weekend to see your sister and little Timmy. I'll have Vivian get word to you—"

"Sir, I was a lieutenant when I left here."

"You'll be a captain come Monday morning," Crockatt said, smiling. "The promotion is well deserved. Congratulations, and welcome back."

Jeremy beamed. "Thank you. It's good to be back."

Stony Stratford, England

Claire was delighted to see her little brother waiting for her when she descended from the bus that afternoon. "Jeremy, you're here. What a surprise." She glanced up at the skies. "This must be a side benefit of the *blitz* coming to an end."

"It is," Jeremy replied, laughing. "I have all weekend to spend with you and Timmy, and then I'm returning to the army."

Claire's eyes had started to widen with happiness, but just as suddenly, they clouded over. "Timmy will be ever so thrilled, but the last part of what you said doesn't sound good."

"No more night flying," Jeremy prodded, shaking his head close to her face. "I'll have my feet firmly planted on the ground." He looked down the street. "Let's stop in at The Bull. I'll buy you a drink and tell you all about it."

Claire's face clouded over even more. She cast a worried look down the street. "I haven't been back in there since—" She caught her breath. "Well, since we commemorated Shorty. I'm not sure I can—"

"Sure, you can," Jeremy assured her. He took both of her hands in his own. "We have friends there who cared about

Shorty and care about us. He wouldn't want to think that what happened to him would cast such a dark shadow that you forgo seeing them, and they wouldn't either." He tugged her arm. "Come on."

Reluctantly, Claire gave in. The Bull's manager greeted them at the door and guided them to their favorite table. "It's so good to see you," he said. Several patrons also greeted them as they made their way to their seats. They ordered drinks, and several minutes later, a waiter brought them.

Claire looked around at the familiar bar and piano, and the deeply polished wood-grained finishes with brass fittings. The sadness of her last visit to the pub held her momentarily, but she set the memory aside in favor of the first time Red had brought her there to meet Shorty and Andy, and then to celebrate Christmas. "We've had some good times in here," she murmured. Then she brightened up. "So, enlighten me on what you're up to. You've left the RAF?"

Jeremy nodded. "That will become official on Monday when I also become Captain Littlefield."

"Why Jeremy! I'm so proud of you. You survived the Battle of Britain and the *blitz*. And now you're a captain."

"Thank you, sister. I'm pleased to be alive and in one piece."

She cradled her face in her hands, supporting them with her elbows on the table. "I suppose I should be pleased for you, but the war's still on, just farther away. I imagine you'll be jumping into France at night again."

"The good news is that I'll be on the ground training here in Great Britain for three months. And I won't be jumping into France. Major Crockatt told me this morning of a new program that's in development using Lysander aircraft to land in France. It's supposed to be in operation by the time I complete training."

"So you'll be flying them?" Claire asked worriedly.

"No, no. But when I go, I'll be flown in one and climb down a ladder to the ground when it lands rather than jump out with a parachute. I'll return the same way."

Claire closed her eyes and held one hand to her forehead. "I guess that is some small comfort. Will you see Amélie?"

"I hope to, but Major Crockatt warned me to keep my focus on the mission."

"That's good advice," Claire said, pointing a playful finger in his face. "I love Amélie, and I don't want either of you to get killed. I'm curious about something, though. I've read about the Lysander. It's been around for several years. If the aircraft already exists, why does it take so long to put the program in place?"

Jeremy sighed and gave his sister a rueful look. "You're not going to want to hear this. The flights will go at night and land on unimproved fields. Informing the enemy of where we'll come in by putting in a lot of work on landing strips would never do. So, we have to identify the fields and train local partisans how to set up to receive the flights. And of course, not everyone in France is our friend, so anyone on the receiving party will have to be vetted. All of that takes time."

"I see. Then you don't know any detail about your first mission, not even when?"

"That is correct."

Claire breathed in deeply and closed her eyes. "Just please come home safely." When she reopened her eyes, she finished off her drink. "Enough sad talk. Timmy will be thrilled to see you."

51

May 25, 1941
Bletchley Park, England

An ache formed in the pit of Claire's stomach as she stared at the headlines of the *Sunday Dispatch*.

HMS HOOD SUNK

"Blown Up, Feared Few Survivors," Admiralty States

World's Largest Warship

Hurriedly, she read the article:

"The Admiralty announced last night that the battle cruiser *Hood*, the world's largest warship, blew up in a fight off the coast of Greenland when British forces met the Nazi battleship *Bismarck*. The *Bismarck* was damaged and British ships are carrying on the pursuit. It is feared there will be few survivors from *HMS Hood*. The battle cruiser received an unlucky hit in a magazine, which exploded. She was commanded by Captain R. Kerr, C.B.N., R.N., and was flying the flag of Vice Admiral L. E. Holland, C.B. The *Hood* had a normal complement of 1,341 officers and men. She was fitted with eight 15in. guns, twelve 5in. guns, and other armament. She also had four 21in. torpedo tubes above the waterline and one aircraft."

Claire skipped down to the description of the German ship:

"The *Bismarck*—a 35,000-ton battleship—was launched in Hitler's presence in 1939. It has an armament of eight 15in. guns, twelve 5.9in. guns. It carries four aircraft and had a top speed of 30 knots."

Claire hurried into Hut 8. Gloom cast a pall throughout its long interior, evidenced in the drooping shoulders and long stares of the decoders working at the tables. They continued their work, albeit with expressions varying between confusion, dismay, anger, and determination.

Denniston had entered the room from the other end and now conversed with Alan Turing. Then together, they turned to scan across the room.

"May I please have your attention," Turing called. "Commander Denniston has an announcement."

When everyone had turned to listen, Denniston stepped forward and cleared his throat. His face was taut; his voice shook. "I won't belabor the bad news regarding the *HMS Hood*," he said, "nor the impact of her loss on both our warfighting capability and public morale. To those of you with family and friends lost in the battle, my sincere condolences."

He looked at the floor as his jaw trembled. Then he took a deep breath and continued. "Two hours after the attack, Prime Minister Churchill sent out a command instructing every ship and aircraft within attack distance of the *Bismarck's* last known position to join in the search for her. In his own words"— Denniston drew a sheet of paper from his jacket and read from it—"'There is nothing more vital to the nation in this moment as the destruction of the *Bismarck*. I don't care how you do it. You must sink the *Bismarck*.'"

The commander paused and drew himself up, his eyes piercing as he scanned his audience. No one spoke. No one stirred.

"The prime minister's directive implies tasks for us in this room. We now have the *Kriegsmarine's* Enigma machine, and we have their disks with scheduled setting changes. Our task is clear. Whatever effort we've put into breaking German radio traffic to date, we will now double and triple it until the *Bismarck* is found and sent to the bottom of the North Atlantic."

When Denniston finished speaking, the room remained deadly quiet. He acknowledged his audience with a quick nod, then turned to leave the way he had come.

Claire hurried to follow him. "Sir, may I have a word with you?"

"Can we talk while we walk, or should this conversation be in my office?"

"It's probably best in your office."

They covered the distance through the halls quickly, and when they were seated, Claire began. "I think you're requesting more from Hut 8 than it can deliver at present."

The commander cast her a quizzical look and leaned forward. "Go on."

"It's a practical matter. We have one Enigma configured for *Kriegsmarine* messages. We'll have more soon, but that takes time, and only two weeks have gone by since we captured it. And there's another element."

"I'm listening."

"I've been watching the frequency of German naval radio transmissions and where they originate. They're not like the *Wehrmacht* or the *Luftwaffe*. Unlike those, the *Kriegsmarine's* are infrequent and short; and what we know of their origin and course is that being sea-based, they move—quickly.

"I've also been back to my old haunts at Hut 6 and discussed with the analysts in Hut 3. I think the naval Enigma will do wonders for us going forward, but expecting a lot out of it right now could lead to disappointment and missed opportunities."

"How so? I understand what you're saying about our new tool's limitations, but how will we miss opportunities."

"By looking for data from a place that can't give it. But intel is still available from where we've been receiving it all along, and that's Huts 3 and 6. It won't be perfect or as much as we'd like, but seeing cross-communications between the German services is not all that unusual, and of course, if they pertained to the *Kriegsmarine* and we read it, then it was most definitely sent in *Luftwaffe* and *Wehrmacht* codes. We might find something that could help track the *Bismarck* until we can pinpoint its location."

Denniston stared at Claire. Then he broke into a smile and leaned forward. "Miss Littlefield, I knew that bringing you over to Hut 8 was a good idea. Go to work. If you find anything, let me know immediately."

Claire swallowed hard when she left the commander's office as the implications of what she had just done descended on her. *I have him thinking I can produce something.*

She entered Hut 6, where she had begun work at Bletchley early the previous year. Most of her former coworkers still occupied their same seats, and she cast a glance wistfully to where she had sat during her days there. She had visited since joining the analysis team in Hut 3, as recently as this morning, but her status had just changed yet again. She had brought with her a note from Denniston that directed her previous supervisor to take instruction from Claire for the next few days and to give her project the highest priority.

The woman read the message, flashed her eyes at Claire, and announced the circumstances to the cryptologists. The atmosphere had already altered into one of urgency with the news of the *Hood*. Now it took a decided leap as the sense of what information was being sought settled onto the group. They went to work with set jaws.

Late that evening, Claire knocked on Denniston's door again. "I think we might have a start," she said on entering his office.

"How is that?"

"Hut 6 intercepted a very peculiar message from the *Luftwaffe* chief of staff this morning. It had been sent to one of his generals in Athens, Hans Jeshonnek. The chief implied that he had a son on board the *Bismarck* and wanted to know where it was going. Jeshonnek passed the message along to Admiral Lutjens aboard the *Bismarck*, who received the message and replied to it via the naval Enigma. The transmissions to and from Lutjens were in naval code. Hut 8 intercepted those messages between Jeshonnek and Lutjens but couldn't yet break them. But Jeshonnek converted them to *Luftwaffe* code and forwarded them back to the chief in Berlin.

"We had a little difficulty decoding the response at first because the German operator had made an error while keying in the—" Claire stopped talking, seeing that Denniston was gaping at her, and then continued, "But we figured out the mistake and the message translated clearly."

Denniston's face turned red, his eyes wide with excitement. "Are you saying that you've decoded a message containing the whereabouts of the *Bismarck*?"

"Yes, sir. We have the position and course set out clearly." She held out a piece of paper to him.

The commander leaped to his feet with such force that his chair fell backward. "Is that it?" He snatched it from her and stared at it. "Is this the message?"

Claire nodded. "That's it."

"Stay there," he said, and reached for the phone.

For the next twenty minutes Claire sat as Denniston made a series of calls while ignoring his overturned chair, and she heard him repeat her story several times. Finally, he hung up the phone, righted his seat, and sprawled into it, exhausted but obviously content. "Early tomorrow morning, our Coastal Command is sending up one of the American Catalina flying boats we have on loan to the area specified in this message to see if it can spot the *Bismarck*." His brow creased with incredulity. "It's being flown by a US Navy pilot, Ensign Leonard Smith. It's flying out of Londonderry." Then, he smiled at Claire. "Good work, Miss Littlefield."

Rockefeller Center, Manhattan, New York

Seeing the headlines that blared up at him from the newsstand, Paul was so shocked that he almost forgot his coffee.

1300 Dead As *Hood* Sinks In Battle
Death of a Titan

He grabbed his coffee and newspaper and began reading as he hurried to the elevator. He kept reading as it ascended.

"Britannia, self-proclaimed ruler of the waves, made one of its most somber announcements of the war yesterday. London acknowledged the German claim that the British battle cruiser *Hood* had been sunk...somewhere between Iceland and Greenland..."

Stephenson was already in his office with General Donovan when Paul arrived. The two sat in the area in front of the desk in deep discussion. Stephenson waved at Paul, summoning him to join them, and turned back to Donovan. "As I was saying," he told the general, "a Brit waking up and reading that the *Hood* had been sunk will be as traumatized as an American learning that the Statue of Liberty had been bombed and toppled. It looms that large in the British psyche. For twenty years, it has been the British Empire's flag-bearer around the globe, a symbol of her military might.

"She was sunk in two minutes." Stephenson leaned back in his seat and stared trancelike at the ceiling while all three men contemplated the event in silence. "The mightiest ship in the world was sunk in two minutes from nine miles away," he said at last, breaking the quiet. He shifted forward in his seat. "There was a lot of skill and luck in that shot. Reports filed by British officers on nearby ships say that the killing round struck just aft of the mid-deck. That's the only place it could have struck to have had such an effect."

"How's that?" Donovan inquired.

Stephenson sighed. "Originally, the *Hood* was lightly armored. Several years ago, as the *Bismarck* and the *Tirpitz* went into production, she was brought into drydock for re-fitting with heavier armor. But they only did the forward part of the ship. They intended to do the aft sections as well, but the *Hood* was so busy traipsing around the world to show the flag that the job never got done." He shook his head, failing at an attempt to hide disgust. "The ammunition magazines were immediately below where the killing round struck."

Silence descended again.

"What does that mean for our overall strategy?" Paul asked at last.

Stephenson stared at Paul absently and then shook himself out of his reverie. "It can't be allowed to change anything," he said after a moment. "We still must win the Atlantic, or Britain will starve." He took a deep breath. "Churchill is pulling out all the stops, and beyond soothing British sentiment, he really has no other choice. With the *Bismarck* loose in the Atlantic and the *Tirpitz* probably preparing to run the blockade..." He shook his head, leaving his obvious thought unspoken.

"Do we know the extent of damage to the *Bismarck*?" Donovan said.

Stephenson pursed his lips. "No, but it was streaming fuel oil as it left the battle site." He displayed rare disgust as he continued. "Our brand-new battleship, the *HMS Prince of Wales,* was also damaged in the encounter and couldn't follow. So, the *Bismarck* disappeared in the vastness of the Atlantic Ocean, waiting, I imagine, to be joined by its sister while the crew makes repairs."

Donovan stood, preparing to leave, and turned to Paul. "I had no idea about the stature of the *Hood* to your country-men," he said. "I'm sorry for its loss and that of your seamen."

Paul rose to his feet to acknowledge Donovan and escort him to the door. Stephenson also stood, shook hands with the general, and circled round to sit at his desk.

After Donovan had left, Paul returned to stand in front of Stephenson's desk. He held the newspaper in his hand. "Sir, if I may—"

Stephenson, who had begun perusing a document, looked up inquisitively. "Yes?"

"There's another article here that should interest you. It's short. I'll read it to you." He scanned down the paper's front page to the article with his finger. "The headline reads, 'US Months Ahead of Schedule,' and it goes on, '"The American industrial machine is performing marvels," says Lieutenant Commander R. Fletcher, M.P. Parliamentary Private Secretary to the First Lord of the Admiralty, at Ramsgate yesterday.

"'"The American steel industry,' he added, 'is producing at all but a fraction of capacity at one-hundred million tons, and in twelve months, military plan production has risen from four hundred and fifty to fourteen hundred a month and is still rising.'"

Paul finished the article and looked up to meet Stephenson's gaze.

"That's quite impressive," Stephenson said. "Thanks for showing it to me." He picked up the document he had begun reading and started studying it again.

Paul remained standing in front of the desk. "Sir—"

Stephenson looked up, puzzled. "Was there something else?"

"I was wondering," Paul began hesitantly, and then changed track. "You know it's been only two months since the president signed off on the Lend-Lease Act, and look how much America's already done."

"Agreed. I'd say that's quite a lot, and there's much more not reported in that article."

"That's exactly my point, sir. In view of how much the president's done and is doing, maybe we should re-think whether or not we need to continue with the other intelligence op." His voice turned mildly sarcastic. "The one to nudge American public opinion along."

Stephenson frowned, and for an instant, Paul thought he saw a flash of anger cross his face. "Captain Littlefield, your perceptions are valued, but when a decision is made, your job is to support it. That project you find so abhorrent is going

through. You don't have to like it, but you do have to do your
duty. Is that understood?"

Paul straightened to attention. "Doing my duty is never in
question, sir."

"Are you being asked to deceive the king, the prime minister, or any other British government official?"

"No, sir, but I don't see the sense of manipulating an ally. I
imagine that Mr. Roosevelt could be impeached for some of
his actions, not the least of which is allowing us to operate
here."

"And you might be right about that, but impeachment is
not conviction, and the US Constitution allows the president
very broad discretion and authority in taking action that only
he needs to approve to defend his country and its constitution.
I'm confident he would prevail in any impeachment effort.
Regardless, he's doing his job to protect his country and we
must do ours to protect Great Britain. The project goes
forward. Is that understood?"

"Yes, sir."

"Good. Then we'll forget that this conversation took
place." He started to direct his attention back to his document
but then looked up once more and smiled. "And let's hope the
Royal Navy finds the *Bismarck* and deals it a deathly blow."

52

May 27, 1941
North Atlantic Ocean

Pilot Officer John Moffat of the Royal Navy's Fleet Air Arm steadied himself in the ready room of the *HMS Ark Royal* as the aircraft carrier tossed in sixty-foot swells amidst peaks and troughs of the rough waters. "Ironic, isn't it?" he called to his navigator, Lieutenant John "Dusty" Miller, sitting across the table. "My father worked on this ship in the last war. He was an aeronautical engineer assigned under the first man who ever flew an airplane off a ship, Wing Commander Charles Samson." He laughed. "I wonder what the pair of them would think of our squadron today, firing at one of our own."

"Blimey, no one told us the *HMS Sheffield* was out there," Dusty objected. "Operations just pointed in the general direction and said, 'The *Bismarck* is out there. Find and sink her.'"

"Lucky for the *Sheffield* that we had those new magnetic detonators on the torpedoes," the gunner, A.J. Hayman, chimed in. He laughed. "Most of the fifteen planes in the squadron let their fish drop. Some must have hit, but not even one detonated."

Another pilot, Kenneth Pattison, lurched his way across the heaving floor and took a seat at the table with them. "And now they want us to do it again," he yelled above the sound of the moaning wind, the groaning ship, and the chatter of other pilots. "I just heard. Our 'Stringbags' are being fitted with the old torpedoes now."

Moffat gazed at him in disbelief. "Today? In this gale again. We're testing fate, I should say."

"Again," Pattison affirmed. "Since that Catalina spotted her yesterday morning, the entire fleet's been after her. I was just in the operations room, and a map there posted her run since our ships started closing in on her. She's heading southeast, probably to France for repairs at Brest—at least that's what the chaps in ops are thinking. She's leaving a stream of oil behind. She's too fast for our ships, so our job is to slow her down."

Moffat laughed. "If you want an airstrike done right, leave it to a Stringbag." He grinned. "Our Swordfish helped take out the French fleet in Algeria, sank the *FS Richelieu* at Dakar, destroyed half the Italian fleet at Taranto; and now they want us to go out in gale-force weather for a second run to take out the *Bismarck*?" He arched his brows. "It's all in a day's work. No other aircraft in existence could do it." He nudged Dusty. "But you know that our Stringbags are obsolete."

Dusty smiled back. "We'd better head on over for the briefing, such as it is."

"There's not going to be a briefing," Pattison said. "I just gave it to you. As soon as the kites are refitted with our old tubes, we fly out and try again to find the *Bismarck*."

Moffat's open-cockpit, three-seater biplane, officially known as a Fairey Swordfish, did not so much taxi along the aircraft carrier's deck as bounce over it until the ship fell away beneath him in a deep trough between mountainous waves. He had throttled up to maximum speed and set his trim to squeeze out all the lift he could; the tailwind whistling over the deck boosted him in front of a wall of ocean. He sat forward over his stick, pulled it back as far as he could, and with gritted teeth, willed the tiny aircraft to fly above the wave and into a gray sky with swirling black clouds over him. As the wind lifted his Swordfish, he could just see the tail of Kenneth Pattison's plane that had taken off ahead of him.

Behind him in the observer's seat, Dusty slapped Moffat's shoulder, and when the pilot turned, Dusty flashed Churchill's famous V-for-Victory sign. Wishing he felt as confident as he had sounded in the ready room before takeoff, Moffat faced the front and checked his instruments. With only a turbulent ocean below and rolling clouds above, he would need them.

Through high wind and violent clouds, he climbed to six thousand feet and finally broke into clearer skies. Circling wide before setting course, he was relieved to see that six Swordfish had already popped through the clouds, and within minutes, all fifteen fighters from the squadron had gathered.

His radio crackled, and he heard the squadron leader. "Red Flight, this is Red Leader. We'll take the northern route. Break. Blue One, this is Red Leader. Take your flight on the southern route parallel to us."

As each pilot responded, they formed their torpedo bombers in their respective flights. Moffat and his crew flew with Red Flight while Pattison formed up with Blue Flight. The Catalina had reported the *Bismarck* steaming southeast toward Brest, France, at thirty knots. Both flights headed in that general direction. The battle cruiser, *HMS Sheffield*, having suffered no damage from the friendly fire received earlier in the day, had used its high-speed capability to draw near but outside the firing range of the German behemoth. It shadowed the ship and broadcast its course and direction.

For two hours through the wind and rain, flying just above the clouds, the tiny biplanes plied through the gale. Then, midair explosions detonated all around them, alerting them that they had entered *Bismarck's* vicinity and been spotted.

Diving into the black, treacherous clouds with the rest of his flight spread to his left and right, Moffat glued his eyes to his altitude indicator, watching it spin around as he descended at a faster and faster rate. He broke clear of the clouds a hundred feet above sea level, and there, still several miles distant, sailed the *Bismarck*, in all her famed glory, fire spewing from her anti-aircraft guns.

Red Flight had emerged from the clouds aft of her port side, and as one, the pilots veered their rickety kites northward and then turned hard right to attack the ships broadside. They skimmed the tall waves at eighteen feet of altitude, the minimum required to release the torpedoes, and as they drew closer, the ship unleashed fire from its big five-inch guns, aiming them low to hit the ocean with explosive impact and spew plumes of water high in the air in hopes of snaring and bringing down the Swordfish.

By this time, realization had dawned on Moffat, and no doubt on the other pilots in the squadron, what must have been recognized with dismay by the German anti-aircraft gunners—their weapons could not shoot low enough to hit the planes flying so close to the surface of the water.

Keeping down as far as he dared, Moffat reduced his speed almost to a stall, a requirement to ensure that the torpedo positioned itself correctly when it splashed into the water. He flew in closer and closer until the ship was hardly more than a hundred yards away. Reaching down, he was about to release his torpedo when he felt Dusty's hand clamp down on his shoulder.

"Not yet," the navigator yelled into Moffat's ear. "I'll tell you when."

Turning in his seat, Moffat saw to his amazement that Dusty had climbed halfway out of the aircraft and was hanging on with the crooks of one elbow and knee while scanning the waves below. "We have to hit a trough," Dusty yelled. "If we hit a wave crest, the torpedo will go wild, and we'll miss."

Seconds passed. The *Bismarck* loomed larger and larger.

The boom, boom, boom of the big guns and the staccato of the anti-aircraft guns pounded in Moffat's ears to compete with his rapidly beating heart and the roar of wind. The pungent smell of exploding munitions spread all about, smothering the clean ocean air.

"Now!" Dusty called.

Moffat pulled the lanyard to release the tube.

The plane shuddered as it thrust higher in the air, the result of tossing off the weight of its cargo. Moffat remembered to stay over the torpedo to stabilize it with a thin wire as it hit the water and submerged.

Meanwhile, the *Bismarck's* guns continued to fire, and their rounds hissed overhead as they tried to fight off the aircraft swarming below the level of their decks on both sides of the ship. A stray thought struck Moffat. *This is not unlike the way Sir Francis Drake defeated the Spanish Armada.*

Yanking his mind back to the present, Moffat pulled his stick for a hard right turn, banked away from the vessel, and throttled up, gaining speed but staying below the elevation of the anti-aircraft guns.

"We have a trail," Dusty yelled from behind him. "We have a trail and—we've hit! I see a plume of water where we hit, a little forward of the stern."

Kenny Pattison emerged from the clouds at almost the same time as Moffat, to the *Bismarck's* starboard, opposite his fellow pilot.

His rickety torpedo plane hugged the waves as he sped over their crests, the salt spray reaching up to obscure his goggles, the *Bismarck's* rounds hissing past him to bury themselves in the churning Atlantic. He lined up, found a trough, and pulled the line to release the torpedo.

Nothing happened.

Pattison found himself and his crew with their heavy tube still slung beneath them and now having to climb rapidly amidship to avoid a collision. Higher and higher they flew while the anti-aircraft guns tracked them, and the *Bismarck's* rolling deck passed beneath them. Then they were clear of the ship and dived once again to skim the waves while the big guns generated mountainous plumes of water ahead of them and the anti-aircraft guns tried futilely to knock them from the sky.

"We have to make another round," Pattison called to his crew, thanking Fortune that he did not have to see their expressions.

He flew far out from the ship to make his turn, noting as he did so that his Swordfish was alone in the sky. His mates had dropped their tubes and headed back to the *Ark Royal.*

Pattison completed a wide turn and lined up to attack the *Bismarck* on the starboard side and began his run. At this distance, the ship appeared almost as a toy bobbing in the water, but as he drew closer and closer, it appeared larger and larger, with all its guns now trained on his Swordfish.

Keeping as close as possible to the prescribed eighteen feet above the tumultuous waves, through eruptions of water resulting from big-gun rounds, he closed the distance and slowed his plane to tube launch speed.

He pulled the lanyard.

The torpedo dropped away.

Pattison completed his launch maneuvers and then pulled a hard turn to the left, staying low. Daring to look back, he saw the torpedo's trail through the waves and then a plume of water as it hit near the stern. He remained only feet above the ocean's surface until he was well out of range of the anti-aircraft guns, and then climbed rapidly, setting his course back to the *Ark Royal*.

53

May 28, 1941
Bletchley Park, UK

Claire entered Commander Denniston's office with a message. "We received this a little while ago and just finished decoding it; and this time, it was our *Kriegsmarine* version of the Enigma that intercepted the message. It's from Admiral Lutjens aboard the *Bismarck* to Adolf Hitler. It's very short. If you like, I'll read it to you."

Denniston looked up and nodded grimly. "That should be interesting. Go ahead."

"It says, 'Ship unmanageable. We shall fight to the last shell. Long live Adolf Hitler.'" On finishing, Claire breathed out a sigh.

Denniston contemplated in silence a few moments. "That's consistent with what we know. We sent a squadron of Swordfish out to find and attack her with torpedoes. Three of them struck the *Bismarck*, two near the rudder. They must have damaged the steering because after their attack, the *Bismarck* only ran in circles." He smiled. "Good news is always welcome. I'm happy to say that all of our scrappy pilots in those rickety planes returned safely to their carrier."

He leaned forward. "Last night, our navy closed in and positioned around her for a final attack while our destroyers harassed her with torpedoes. Her guns were still very much a threat and she fought to the last. Two of our battleships, *Rodney* and *King George V*, moved in and pounded her. *Bismarck* returned fire with her broadside guns, but her projectiles fell short. Two more of our cruisers, the *Dorcetshire* and the *Norfolk*, joined the fight, and the *Rodney* moved in closer. Reports came in that *Bismarck's* turrets had been hit, and lower deck fires must have ignited. The final story is that the battleship has sunk under the waves. She is no more."

Denniston took a deep breath. "I have to say that I am in utter awe and admiration of the ship and crew."

Claire stood quietly listening until the commander had finished. The moment that they had anticipated to be celebratory seemed somber. "Were there any survivors?"

Denniston nodded. "Some. The *Rodney* stayed on station to pick them up, but then a German submarine threat caused it to move away. I think the figure is a hundred and eighteen saved. The survivors claim to have set charges to scuttle the ship. Maybe one day we'll know what was the final blow that brought her down."

"How many had been aboard the *Bismarck*?"

"Around thirty-four hundred."

Claire moved to one of the chairs and sat, her face drawn in sadness. "Such loss of life," she whispered. "So many young men."

Denniston said nothing, and they sat alone with their thoughts. Then Claire stood back up. "It's a relief that the

Bismarck is gone. Unfortunately, the war goes on and I must get back to work."

"Thank you, Miss Littlefield, and good job. You're a professional."

54

June 1, 1941
Marseille, France

"We can't wait," Fourcade told Henri. "The team coming from London won't be here for months. Since Jeannie left Dinard, we're not getting much intelligence out of northwestern France above Loire, particularly along the coast. We need a team up there now."

"Let me go up there and put some cells together. Phillippe can run things here in my absence. We're talking about a recruiting mission. I've done a good job in Marseille."

"You have," Fourcade replied. "But you know whoever you put in charge will have to relinquish authority to the new team leaders that London sends over. They're providing the funds."

"I'll make that clear. Will Jeremy be one of them?"

"According to our latest information, yes. British intelligence is insisting that everyone be fully trained before coming over, including—"

"He's young, but good. And experienced. I don't think

anyone I recruit will have a problem with him. Will they arrive by parachute?"

Fourcade shook her head. "By the time they come, SOE will have its special squadron operating to fly people in and out of enemy territory on the Lysander aircraft. The drop-off points will be scattered across the country, mostly along the south end of the Loire Valley. That's at the extreme of the Lysanders' range with enough fuel to get home, even with their extended fuel tanks. We'll take the passengers straight to safehouses in their areas of operations. You can scout them out while you're there. We'll need flat, open fields, wide enough for a small plane but not so wide that it can be seen for miles. The field will have to be unplowed and with no ditches. They'll be coming in at night."

Henri's eyes opened wide, and he whistled in amazement. "You're serious? How will they navigate?"

"By the light of the moon. And you'll need to train ground teams to guide them in with three pocket torches. The first of the guides will have to flash the Morse code for a single letter that will change for each landing. I'll give you all the particulars."

She cupped her hands along the edge of the table and pushed back. "Meanwhile, I have to go to Paris. I need to check on Jeannie and other people we have up there."

"Why don't I go with you? I can do some recruiting and then head west to prepare for the teams. We have time."

"Good idea. Take Amélie with you. We can teach her the landing procedures for the Lysander flights before we go, and she can help with training ground teams."

"Should we really take Amélie? Jeremy's flight might be one we'll prepare for."

Fourcade thought a moment without expression. "We can't expect to win this war by considering personal concerns too much. She's trained, and she's professional. So is Jeremy. She needs to be prepared for it if it happens and act appropriately. People at the landing sites should be thinking only of doing their jobs and being alert to anything around them that could sabotage the landing or cause it to be aborted." She smiled. "The two young lovers can see each other later in a safe place."

Henri nodded.

"Meanwhile," Fourcade went on, "there's another mission we need you to pull off ahead of coming to Paris. SOE is asking for information regarding the submarine pens near Bordeaux."

Henri grinned. "I know the place, and that should be easy. I'll get one of the officers drunk, steal his uniform, walk onto the base, get the intel, and walk off."

Fourcade shook her head in dismay. "Henri, after all the lectures you've given me on security, you suggest that? I don't want you killed."

He laughed. "To get that information, someone has to go in whether it's me or another person. To find and get close to a crewmember who'll take a bribe takes time. I can be on the base and back off within minutes, and I can be there and back within a matter of days."

"That's nearly four hundred miles each way. We shouldn't do so much circuitous travel. It's better if you take Amélie with you and go on from there to build the teams in the northwest. Just don't involve her in the submarine base mission. And keep in mind that Pétain has made clear that he's not happy with anti-German activities."

"So? We're not happy with him. You yourself had to talk Léon out of leading a coup against him in favor of more effective covert activity."

At mention of Léon, Fourcade turned crimson and averted her eyes. Henri noticed. "Ahh, you like him," he teased. "I thought I saw sparks fly when he was here. I think he likes you too."

"Nonsense. Let's stay on subject."

"Of course," Henri said, chuckling. "Anyway, Pétain hasn't yet started cracking down."

"But he will," Fourcade said. "All right, I'll give you the Bordeaux mission and you handle it within your section as you see fit, but I'm expecting you and Amélie to set up those teams for us in northwest France. Don't let me down."

"I won't, I assure you. I take as much precaution for my own security as I do for anyone else's. Now, going back to the Lysander flights, I'm curious about one aspect of them. How will we know that a flight is actually coming in? With weather changes and other potential conflicts, we can't possibly take for granted that a mission will go off as planned."

Fourcade chuckled. "You're right, but it's simpler than you might think. Be sure to listen to the BBC personal messages every night. We'll get information about the timeframe when flights are expected by other means, but final word that they're actually on their way will come over the BBC."

"How does that work?"

"Very easily. They've broadcast personal messages for years, like 'Happy birthday, Aunt Nancy.' The operation to bring Jeremy and his crew here is codenamed Caroline. Any message we hear that refers to Caroline *could* pertain to them. I say *could* because someone might request a genuine message for someone named Caroline.

"We listen for that operation name and a codeword specific to it. For instance, if the codeword is 'blue,' when we hear a message that has both the operation name and code-word in it—like, 'Caroline bought a blue dress today'—that tells us he's on his way."

Henri laughed in disbelief. "That's it?"

Fourcade smiled through pursed lips and nodded. "I told you. Simple."

"And all those other BBC personal messages?"

"They could be directed to other teams, or not. Some are real messages requested by ordinary citizens. Probably most of them are."

"That's ingenious," Henri concluded. "Now tell me what you need from the submarines."

55

June 8, 1941
Paris, France

"Who is it?" Fourcade asked cautiously, responding to a knock on the door to her apartment on Avenue Foch. She heard a series of raps that she recognized, swung the door open, and beamed in surprise at Phillippe Boutron. Her smile disappeared, replaced by concern, when she saw his face.

He hurried past her, and she closed the door. "What's wrong? You look so serious."

Phillippe raised a finger and motioned for her to follow him into the living room. When he reached the window, he peered down to the street and then whirled and paced across the room.

Watching him nervously, Fourcade sank into a seat. "Obviously, you have bad news. Let's have it."

"I do," he said. "And I'm angry too. What's happened should not have happened."

"Are we in immediate danger? Do we need to leave?"

Phillippe shook his head. "No. There's a little bright spot in all the news I have to tell, and that is that I was appointed to Pétain's intelligence staff. A former colleague who was kept on when most of the naval officers were released after the bombing of our fleet in Algeria recommended me. He's sympathetic to the Resistance and wants to help. I was recruiting him when he suggested I take this job.

"That's as good as the news gets. I accepted because I thought we could get useful information that way. It affords me the ability to move about freely, which is why I can say with confidence that we don't need to leave here in a hurry. But I still check."

"That's a relief, and I suppose I should congratulate you on your new job," Fourcade said, dumbfounded. "Will that detract from what you do for the Alliance?"

"We'll get to that. But first, I should tell you that Henri Schaerrer was captured by the Gestapo."

Fourcade gasped. "When? How? I met with him in Marseille just a week ago."

Of all her lieutenants, Henri ranked among her most favorite. Always friendly, even when pressed with concerns, he had been responsible for much of the rapid growth of her Resistance group by recruiting among his former naval colleagues.

"He was taken a few days ago. I don't have many details, except that when they arrested him, he had his pockets crammed full of classified information from the submarine pens near Bordeaux."

Fourcade listened as if in a trance. "I sent him on that mission personally."

"He should have taken more precautions," Phillippe said impatiently. "Apparently, he entered the base more than once and managed to get out some documents." He saw the anguish on Fourcade's face. "Look, I love Henri like a brother.

He brought me to you. He was always cautious about security for the rest of us, but he took too many personal risks."

"He did," Fourcade said mournfully. "I feel empty." A thought crossed her mind, and she brought her hand to her mouth. "What about Amélie? She went to the area with him. Was she taken too?"

"No. She made it to a safehouse, stayed there for two days, and then went back to Marseille. She's with Maurice now. He got a message to me with all I'm telling you."

Phillippe looked up at the ceiling, frowning. "There's more. Whether it's worse depends on perspective." He paused and took a deep breath. "Navarre and Léon went ahead with their plans to take over Algeria in preparation for a coup against Pétain. They were betrayed. Both were arrested along with others. I'm concerned that they could expose the operation in Marseille, and for that matter, here in Paris. The damage could even affect our friends in Dunkirk."

Fourcade sat transfixed, seeing visions of her carefully built Alliance network crumbling and people she loved being tortured and executed. At the mention of Léon, she had reacted spontaneously, but Phillippe appeared not to have noticed.

The faces of those who might suffer marched across Fourcade's mind, starting with Henri, Navarre, and Léon, already in custody; and continuing with Amélie, Chantal, Jeannie, Horton, Kenyon, Pierre, Maurice and his family, and others in and around Marseille. Then there were Nicolas, Jacques, Claude, Brigitte, and Théo in Dunkirk, and beyond them, myriad other names and faces who might be exposed under torture.

"What do you suggest we do?"

"First, you should leave Paris. Go to Pau near the southern border with Spain. When things die down, you can go back to

Marseille. It's usually safer there because most of the *gendarmeries* are sympathetic to the Resistance. They don't pay much attention to Pétain's directives regarding anti-German activities, but I'd wait to see if the organization there has been exposed.

"I can get word to Jeannie and the others here in Paris. Just tell me how to reach her. I'll instruct the leaders to lie low for a while until they hear from you."

Fourcade agreed and provided the names and contact information. Then she said, "Now, tell me how your job with Vichy intelligence affects what you can do for the Alliance."

Phillippe half-smiled. "It's ironic really. I went into the job intending to listen for useful intelligence, but I had to do something to look busy, so I wrote a report on how to reorganize the Vichy merchant marine. It was so well received that now my superiors want to appoint me to deputy military liaison at the Vichy embassy in Madrid." He scowled. "I don't want to do this, but I can't object without raising questions. I'll be limited in how much I can help the Resistance." He took a deep breath. "But there might be a positive coming out of it."

Fourcade looked at him quizzically. "What?"

"Spain is nominally a neutral country. It still maintains relations with Britain with all that means, including the use of a diplomatic pouch. I convinced my higher-ups to let me be the courier to carry the diplomatic mailbag between Spain and France. If you can get things to me in Pau, I can get them to Madrid and then to London. I take them under seal, so they won't be inspected when I cross the border."

Fourcade stared at him, dumbfounded. "You're joking."

Phillippe shook his head. "I'm not. I should even be able to get things through the opposite way too, but MI-6 and SOE are asking for so much information these days that we have to be careful about the volume of material. I'm sure the Gestapo has their tentacles down there and they don't necessarily trust Vichy-French officials."

"I guess it's worth a try," Fourcade said, "but you'd better be ready to hop over into Gibraltar and make your way to Britain, if need be, or get back to Marseille. I shall miss you."

"You haven't seen me that much lately anyway."

"But at least I knew that you were relatively safe. I'll worry more about you when you're in Madrid."

"We're always in danger, all of us, even if we do nothing," Phillippe said morosely. "Look at Henri, Navarre, and Léon."

"Yes, and I had a bit of a scare on the train coming to Paris. At the crossing point, I was selected by German officials for personal scrutiny. They took me to a room and ordered me to strip. If that wasn't humiliating enough, all of my clothes were inspected. They found nothing."

Phillippe's eyes widened in alarm. "Weren't you carrying MI-6 request-for-information questionnaires?"

Fourcade nodded and crossed the room to retrieve a wide-brimmed hat hanging on a rack. "I was wearing this," she said. Peeling back the lining under the brim, she showed him the incriminating papers. "That was a horrifying experience." The memory caused her face to tremble with emotion, and she fought it back. "I hope they don't torture our friends, but I expect they will. Navarre won't crack. I don't think Henri will either. I don't know Léon well enough to guess."

June 18, 1941
Marseille, France

When Fourcade climbed out of the small car that brought her to Maurice's farmhouse, Amélie and Chantal rushed to greet her, flinging their arms around her in an extended embrace. "I'm all right," she assured them while Maurice's three children looked on shyly.

"We were so scared for you," Chantal cried. "When we heard about Henri and the others…" Her voice trailed off.

"We're glad to see you," Amélie said firmly.

"And I'm glad to see you in one piece," Fourcade told Amélie. "I'll want to hear about what happened in Bordeaux."

Maurice stood behind the trio. He also gave Fourcade a welcome hug, and they all entered the house. "I think the villa is safe for your return, but wait a couple of days to double-check security. I've recruited some members of the police who watch out for us."

"And you can trust them?" Fourcade asked dubiously. "We think Navarre and Léon were done in by betrayal."

"We can never be completely sure about anyone," Maurice replied, "but I've known these men many years, and they love France and hate the Nazis. And don't forget that we have our own people watching out for us."

Fourcade stood on her toes to reach up and kiss his cheek. "I don't mean to make you think I doubt you, my big friend." She sighed. "We all have to trust someone."

Later, when they were settled in the living room and Maurice's children had been cleared from the house, Fourcade asked Amélie again what had happened to Henri.

"I don't know," Amélie replied. "He went on an operation that I wasn't informed about because I wasn't needed for it. I think he went into the submarine base at Bordeaux because when he was captured, he had on a navy uniform, and he was carrying classified papers. I know he had gone there several days earlier, and I'm sure he sent documents back from that venture.

"He might have been daring in the missions he took, but

he was careful with the information. I think he had just stolen more documents when the Gestapo got him.

"Anyway, another Resistance man watched out for him, and when Henri was arrested, that man ran to the safehouse and warned us to get out. I got well away, and wandered through crowded areas—markets, parks, busy streets—for hours before making my way to the next safehouse. I was always checking behind me, so I'm sure I wasn't followed."

"Do you have any idea how he was found out?"

"I can't decide if he was seen doing something suspicious or if he was betrayed. The man who watched out for him came to the second safehouse later. He said he had no chance to warn Henri. The Gestapo had been waiting a block outside the gate at the submarine base. Henri walked out with a group of other officers, and they came straight to him."

Fourcade contemplated the information. "Henri was the man who made us think about physical and operational security, and now he's gone." She turned to Maurice. "Did he teach you enough to take on the job?"

The big man sighed. "He taught me how critical it is and the measures he implemented. The job isn't one I want. Maybe you should ask Horton or Kenyon?"

"They don't have the reach into the French population. We need that. I'm sure they could both help, though."

"All right. I'll do it until someone better suited comes along."

Fourcade turned to Amélie. "Do you know the leaders northwest of Loire that Henri recruited?"

Amélie nodded. "I was there when he organized each cell and appointed a leader. If you want to go back up there, I can contact them and introduce you."

"That isn't what I have in mind. You were trained in

London. I want you to go back to the Bordeaux area to lead the section until the team from London arrives."

Amélie gasped, wide-eyed. "I can't. I've never led anything, and I was trained to be a courier, not a team leader."

"I had never led anything either before Navarre asked me to take over the Alliance in France. If we haven't learned the lesson about security with what's just happened, we never will. I'm at the center of the Alliance. I know too much. I can't expose myself to the cell leaders all over the country. Most of them only know me by my codename, Hérisson. The new ones Henri recruited already know you. We'll take steps to establish your authority."

"I'm not sure that will be enough for them to accept me."

"If they want to continue getting money, arms, equipment, and intelligence from the Alliance, they will. I wouldn't ask you to do it if I didn't have confidence in you. We need someone capable and trustworthy."

"I can go with her to help," Chantal chimed in, her eyes bright with anticipation.

"No," Fourcade said sharply. Seeing Chantal's crestfallen expression, she softened her tone. "Your sister will need a free mind. She can't be worrying about you."

A defiant look crossed Chantal's face. "I'll—"

"You'll what, Chantal?" Fourcade cut her off. "Run away and join another group? It's time to dispense with that threat. You've matured enough to recognize that if we're going to win this war, everyone has to perform where they are best."

She gestured toward Maurice. "He's told us what an incredible job you've done in reconnaissance around Marseille. That's likely to be important sooner than we can imagine. I want you here with him. Therefore, if you'll take the job, I'm appointing you as his special assistant for security, reconnaissance, and surveillance." She smiled. "It comes with pay."

Chantal sat speechless, staring at Fourcade, and then shifted her eyes to Amélie, Maurice, and back again to Fourcade. "I-I don't know what to say. I want to be with my sister, but I want to do the job where I can help the most."

Amélie had watched and listened to the exchange with anxious eyes. Now she stood and embraced Chantal. "Stay, little one," she whispered. "We'll always be together in spirit. You'll do a wonderful job for Maurice."

56

June 22, 1941
Bletchley Park, England

"They've done it, sir," Claire told Commander Denniston. "Germany started its invasion into the Soviet Union."

"I heard, through operational channels," Denniston replied. "Hitler had no choice at this point. He had posted nearly a third of his air and land forces along their common border, and he had depleted his fuel resources to the point that he needed Soviet oil to keep his army moving. What can you deduce from where the radio signals originate?"

"They're deploying, as expected, in three prongs: Army Group North is heading toward Leningrad with twenty-nine divisions, Army Group Center is aiming at Moscow with fifty divisions and two brigades, and Army Group South is marching toward Kiev with forty-six divisions."

The commander nodded. "The strange thing is that Stalin isn't responding. We've known that he didn't believe Hitler would break their non-aggression treaty despite our warnings, but he seems to be still operating under that illusion. Reports we're receiving through MI-6 tell us that he slept late and ordered no action at all once informed." He sighed. "What a strange world we live in."

Rockefeller Center, Manhattan, New York

"What do you make of Stalin's lack of response?" Paul asked Stephenson.

"I have no idea why, and it's costing him. His forces were caught flatfooted. The front is only hours old, and the Red Army is falling back. I believe the *Wehrmacht* has already advanced fifty miles in places." He chuckled. "Hitler sprung his surprise at the same time and on the same day of the year that Napoleon invaded Russia. He must not have read through history far enough to know how that ended up.

"Stalin's saving grace is that we can count on Adolf to make major strategic errors. Hitler's demonstrated that many times, but most dramatically by this Soviet invasion. As for how Joseph is reacting: I imagine he's in shock and probably humiliated by having ignored our warnings, but react he will. He'll mobilize or be de-throned, and he's in no mood to relinquish power. And then Hitler will learn viscerally of the industrial might Stalin orchestrated."

He took a deep breath. "The carnage will surmount any in history. The photos of devastation and atrocity coming in are quite stark, and this is just the beginning."

Oflag IV-C, Colditz, Germany

Lance re-read the letter in his hand. Purportedly from his sister, Claire, it made no sense, sharing memories of places they had never been and mentioning close friends he had never met. He realized with a sinking heart that no genuine news from home was contained in the missive. His duty was to turn it over to Chip, the British intelligence officer. He did so at morning roll call.

Then, while standing in formation waiting to be counted, he thought of his Polish friend and former fellow escapee, Miloš. The man had come to his room that morning shortly after dawn, and careful not to awaken the other prisoners in the room, he had poked lightly at Lance. When Lance opened his eyes, Miloš cautioned him to silence, and the two slipped out into the hall.

The Pole's excitement had been palpable. "Germany invaded the Soviet Union. Now, today. We heard it on our radio. The two devils will tear each other's limbs apart."

Lance had stared at the man, speechless, not so much because of the news but because he was still groggy from sleep. But as he began to comprehend what Miloš had said, bewilderment set in. "Are you sure? They're allies."

"Yes, I'm sure," came the animated reply, and Miloš continued with bright eyes in his broken English, which had improved since their escape attempts. "Your people will hear it when they wake up and listen to the BBC." He clapped Lance's shoulder and grinned. "I wanted you to be first to know it in the British. They like sleep."

Word of the purported invasion spread rapidly through whispered conversations among the prisoners, electrifying the atmosphere, generating much speculation about the veracity of the story. The Brits picked up the news from the BBC on their hidden radio, as Miloš had predicted, but the idea of Germany invading its ally seemed preposterous on its face.

Some reasoned that the Hun, being already engaged with Britain in England, North Africa, and the Baltics, would not only overextend its forces if it went after the Soviets, but would also lose the rear protection that the Soviets afforded. And if the report was true, could that be enough to bring the US into the war?

Many scoffed at the latter notion with disparaging comments. "Pshaw. The US is too self-absorbed to risk its neck."

"We can't have mama's boy getting roughed up in a real fight."

"Half of Americans support the Nazis."

"Why would they come to save Britain? They still remember the Revolution."

At mid-day, Chip sought Lance out while the latter played stoolball in the courtyard. Being one of the few competitive sports available to them as a pick-up game almost any time during daylight hours, the game was a favorite among the prisoners. Usually played on a grassy field, the game had been adapted to the constraints of the courtyard and its stone floor. As an ancient sport developed in Sussex and a possible ancestor to cricket, it required little equipment—a ball, a stool for a wicket, and anything that could be used for a bat.

Lance had been playing. When he saw Chip gesture to him, he called to another man on the sidelines to take his place, and, while wiping sweat from his brow, he joined the intelligence officer. "What's up?"

"We've decoded your letter. It arrived somewhat late, but it confirms what we heard on the BBC this morning about the invasion into Soviet territory."

Lance cast Chip a searching look. "That makes no sense. How could a letter mailed days or weeks ago confirm a report about an action that just took place today?"

Chip shrugged. "The decoded message simply said, 'Big news on June 22.' Granted, we're assuming that the big news is the invasion, but I'd be more surprised now if that isn't the case."

"I suppose you're right, but it would be nice to see another actual letter from home one of these days. Is that all you came to tell me?"

Chip shook his head. "No. The SBO would like to see you in his quarters."

"Uh-oh. That sounds serious. Any idea what it's about?"

Chip nodded grimly. "The *kommandant* received a report about your family on Sark. Guy will give you the specifics."

Lance sighed and dropped his head. "Ahh. If there's a way to make this war more miserable, leave it to the Nazis to figure it out."

Guy was apologetic. "You should know that you've been officially identified as a *prominente*. The *kommandant* informed me."

"How will that affect me now?"

"At present, it doesn't. The *kommandant* has no orders to transfer you, and I've convinced him that you're in no danger from us." He smirked. "As exalted as your lineage is, you're not related to the prime minister or the king."

"That's right, sir."

"Then for now, there's nothing to do but be aware of the situation and keep your background low-key. If it starts to become a concern, I'll let you know promptly."

"Thank you, sir."

Night fell, and silence settled. Then, a low, clear voice rang across the courtyard and echoed off the high inner walls of the dark castle and through the barracks within its cavernous interior. The singing was melodious, coming from the Polish section, and the tune was unmistakable, the "Song of the Volga Boatmen." "Yo ho heave, ho..."

Lance raised himself to rest on his elbows and cocked his ear. The singing continued, intermingled with loud guffaws and jeering catcalls.

Lance got out of bed and went to a window at the opposite end of the noncom room overlooking the courtyard. His room-mates grouped behind him to see what was happening. The single voice was joined by more, and then it was rapidly lost in a thunder of voices as prisoners all around the courtyard grouped around every window, thrusting and waving their arms between the bars and lustily singing the Volga song, echoing off the stone walls to mock the Germans and their invasion.

"You Nazis started too late," someone yelled. "The winters will eat you alive."

"You've never fought," another man called, "until you've fought a mad Russian."

"If Corporal Napoleon couldn't do it, the Austrian corporal certainly cannot."

In the courtyard, the sentries watched nervously, joined by reinforcements. These troops were new to the job, their unit having just relieved the previous one and being unaccustomed to occasional outbursts among the prison population. Then an officer strode to the center of the courtyard. He yelled something that Lance surmised to be a call for silence, but his voice was lost in the cacophony that mixed with hundreds more voices joining in to sing, full-throated, "Yo ho heave, ho..."

A beer bottle shattered on the ground with a loud popping noise, followed by another. The second one had been well-shaken, and it exploded with an even louder sound that sent the guards scurrying and then looking up and about for any more flying missiles. A loud whistle screeched across the courtyard—a prisoner doing a life-like imitation of a falling bomb from a Stuka. More prisoners generated the noises of roaring fighters and dive-bomber engines and explosions that sent the sentries looking wildly about and seeking shelter in a pandemonium against the incessant accompaniment of the low octave singing, "Yo ho heave, ho..."

After twenty minutes, the main portal opened wide, and three officers and several noncoms strode into the center of the courtyard. One apparently called for silence, but his voice was lost in the chaos. He turned to his party and began pointing in various directions and up at the windows. The group split up, with the other two officers moving adroitly to opposite ends of the courtyard, taking their sergeants and men with them.

Moments later, the sentries had been formed in two lines, with the front one kneeling while the back one remained standing. Both lines, on command, lifted their rifles to point at the crowded windows.

In a flash, the spaces were dark, the courtyard silent, as within the barracks, prisoners scurried to hide under beds and tables, in corners, outside their rooms in halls, and anywhere else they could find shelter. In the courtyard, clear commands rang out followed by the concussive sound of rifle fire, shattering glass, splintering wood, and the smack and ricochet of bullets against walls. When the firing stopped, all was quiet.

A special roll call was ordered. Lance stumbled into the cold air with his mates and formed up. A German noncom checked to see that no gaps occurred in the ranks. Then he counted the number of rows and columns, multiplied the two numbers, and reported the total. In other parts of the courtyard, the contingents from the other nationalities accomplished the same actions.

The *kommandant* appeared and took a position in front of the formations. Lance strained to hear, but the man did not address the rank and file. Instead, he summoned the senior officer of each national group and instructed them in tones too low to be heard across the distance. Then the *kommandant* left the courtyard.

Guy returned to the front of the British formation and addressed his contingent, his face grim. "As fun as tonight was, there could be penalties. What the *kommandant* told the senior officers was, and I quote, 'Throwing bottles at sentries is not gentlemanly behavior. In the future, you should not expect to be treated as gentlemen.'"

He raised an eyebrow. "I don't know what steps he intends or how far he'll take them, but I will tell you that he promised severe consequences if the bottle-throwing culprit doesn't own up." He rocked forward on his feet. "That's all I have. Go to bed."

At noon roll call, Lance once again stood in formation. Tension filled the air more than usual. The POWs generally remained quiet, and the guards were unusually alert. Otherwise, and surprisingly, the formation was conducted normally, with nothing untoward from either the prisoners or their captors.

After the formation was dismissed, Lance returned to his room where he found Miloš waiting for him. The Pole exhibited unusual and low morale. Lance studied his downcast demeanor. "How are things with your group after last night's riot."

Miloš shook his head slowly. "It's not fair. One of our lieutenants, Lieutenant Micky Surmanowics, confessed, but I'm sure he didn't do it."

Taken aback, Lance prodded, "Didn't he just come out of solitary?"

"He did." Miloš' eyes burned with ferocity. "He was there since the beginning of last November. That's eight months. He's one of the two who scaled down nearly four stories on a rope made from bedsheets."

"Why did he confess?"

"Because he's a good man and didn't want everyone else to suffer. He's going to be court-martialed next month. He's back in solitary now."

Lance grasped his friend's shoulder. "Miloš, we have to get out of here."

57

June 29, 1941
Oflag IV-C, Colditz, Germany

Stretched on a thin mattress with protruding steel springs that passed for a bed, Lance heard the jangling of keys before they were inserted into the lock, and then the clanging of tumblers as the lock turned and the door opened. Guy stepped inside the cell, a frown etched on his face.

Lance looked up at him, and then rose from his bunk and stood at attention. "I'm sorry, SBO. No excuse."

Guy heaved a sigh and sat in the single chair in the room at a small writing table across from the bunk. "Sit, sit. I won't stand on formality in here. I'm allowed by the Geneva Convention to visit you, to monitor your health and treatment." He looked around the cell dolefully. "This is a pretty dismal place."

"I've been in worse."

Guy nodded. "I will say that I'm a bit disappointed. I thought you understood the rules, and that there was a waiting list for escapes. You preempted everyone with your attempt, and your own reservation on the list was coming up." He scrutinized Lance, who had sat on the edge of the bed. "You know that some of our chaps confide in no one, and attempt escapes irrespective of rules and priorities. None have yet succeeded.

"I had thought you were above flouting our procedures. When prospective escapees go through our process, the escape committee provides money, food, clothing, maps, reconnaissance reports, forged papers, and whatever else is within our power to contribute. You went out with none of that.

"POWs who try on their own usually plan only for getting over the wall and not how they'll survive and get through the country, much less how they'll get across the border. Furthermore, they make things more difficult for those who follow the rules, sometimes interfering with others' plans by either making a simultaneous attempt or using an escape route that's discovered by the guards, closing it off for others."

Lance glanced at him with a worried look. "Did we do that, sir?"

Guy nodded reluctantly. "I'm afraid you did—not a scheduling conflict, but the method." He chuckled despite the seriousness. "Jumping on the back of a rubbish truck as it was heading out of the gate was ingenious, but now the guards inspect it every time. That route had been selected for an attempt by two others going together. Now they'll have to find another way, and they're likely to miss their dates. If that happens, their travel documents will have to be forged again." He waved his hand. "Etcetera."

Shamefaced, Lance returned Guy's steady gaze. He took a deep breath. "I truly am sorry, sir. I should have known better."

Guy studied Lance in silence and then said, "I'm going to

ask you a question, and then, depending on your response, I'll request a favor."

"I'll answer as best I can."

"Why did you go? It's as if you decided on the spur of the moment."

"I did, sir. I was put off by that bit about being classified as a *prominente* and felt I had to get out. The prospect of languishing in a cell like Romily's and then being used as a bargaining chip is not one I wish to encounter. I also saw how despondent Miloš became over Lieutenant Surmanowics' confession and court martial. By the way, is there any word on Miloš?"

Guy shook his head. "None yet. He might have made it home. Why were you re-captured right away, and he wasn't?"

"Hmph." Lance smirked. "He was smart enough to bring a bar of soap and a second set of clothing tightly wrapped. When we got off the truck, he went into an alley to find a faucet to wash off the smell, change clothes, and be on his merry way. I intended to steal some clothes. I found some hanging on a clothesline, but the *frau* saw me and came at me waving a broom and screaming. I took off at a run. Her neighbors heard the commotion and joined the chase. Then came the soldiers, and I was done in. Simple as that." He grinned. "I have to laugh, heartbreaking as my sob story is."

Guy laughed. "I admire your spirit." He sat quietly gathering his thoughts. Through a small, barred window, shouts and dull thumps drifted in from men playing stoolball in the courtyard with the occasional sharp order of a guard. Fortunately, the cell was dry and large enough to move about. "Are they feeding you well?"

Lance grinned. "They're feeding me. The term 'well' is relative. I'll survive."

"I'll press the *kommandant* to let me share some Red Cross

packages with you." His expression changed to one of concern. "I had not thought about how being listed as a *prominente* might affect your mentality. It's not a pleasant prospect."

"You had a request, sir?"

"Yes." Guy hesitated. "It was hard enough to ask before you revealed the worries of being a *prominente*. What you've just told me makes the request even more difficult."

"Ask away, sir. If it's within my power—"

"Don't finish that sentence until you've heard what I'm asking." Guy took a deep breath. "I'd like you to serve as assistant escape officer to Pat, and if he leaves, I'd like for you to take over for him. He's agreed to stay in place until late next year."

Dumbstruck, at first Lance could only stare. "Sir, you're asking me to volunteer not to escape?"

Guy's reluctance increased. "That's right. If you accept, you'll help prospective escapees with planning the details of their escapes, gathering materials, and coordinating whatever operational support they require. There is no reward for taking the job, and precious little that the honor will ever do for you. It's as purely selfless as you can get, but it's necessary."

Lance stared into nowhere for a time. Finally, he said, "That's a big request."

Guy nodded. "I know it is, and I appreciate that you haven't yet said no."

Lance stared at the floor for a time, unmoving. "It's not a job I'd look for, that's for certain. And I have to say that the *prominente* concern is on my mind. As I recall, you told me that *prominentes* could be held as bargaining chips, and failing that, they're likely to be executed." He laughed quietly. "So, if I commit to that, I could be signing my own death warrant."

"I understand, and that's not a light consideration. I'll tell you that we've implemented one of your early suggestions.

We've had a few prisoners fake escape attempts in which they remain here, hiding out in the attic and other places. They never wanted to try, but they were willing to help that way. As far as the guards were concerned, their escapes were successful, and since roll call is taken by the numbers present, they're not noticed when they substitute in for someone else. We call them floaters, and they attend roll call until the escape is discovered.

"So, if you'll take the job, I'll commit to this: if it looks like you'll be moved to a *prominente* cell, we'll pull you out immediately and have one of our floaters stand in for you. We'll plan and reserve an escape route for you not allowed to anyone else. And finally, if the occasion arises, we'll put you at the front of the list. Would that help?"

Lance looked askance at him. "It would certainly help in those circumstances, but it does nothing to change my current ones. I'm a prisoner of war, and every instinct in me screams for escape. I crave liberty more than I desire life. I want to breathe free air, and I want to go home."

Guy cleared his throat and scraped the chair on the floor as he rose and took a step toward the door. "I understand, Lance. I really do. No hard feelings. I had to ask."

Lance jumped up as well. "Wait, sir. I didn't say I wouldn't do it."

Startled, Guy turned back. "You will?"

Lance took a deep breath and closed his eyes momentarily. "Yes, sir. I will."

Still reacting with surprise, Guy said, "Do you mind if I ask why? You made your decision so quickly after such a profound defense of liberty."

"Because you asked."

Guy reached forward and gripped Lance's hand. "You have

my deep thanks, and I'm sure I speak for our whole British contingent."

Lance bobbed his head in response while staring vacantly as the full realization of what he had committed to descended on him. Then he gazed at Guy. "Just please see if you can get those Red Cross rations to me, would you, sir?"

58

September 6, 1941
London, England

"You're in demand, Captain," Major Crockatt told Jeremy. "The RAF would like to have you back, MI-6 tried pulling strings to bring you over there, and SOE wants another cooperative mission."

"It's nice to be popular," Jeremy joked. "We'll see if that's still the case when peace returns. What does SOE want?"

"As you would imagine, things are getting dicier in France. With the Germans bogging down in their advance on the Soviet Union while now being fully engaged in Yugoslavia and Greece, Hitler's grand plan for conquest is in disarray. That's good, but it means he'll lash out in unpredictable ways.

"In Vichy-France, General Pétain is under increasing pressure to crack down and put in place the same curbs as exist in occupied France—not that he objects. And he has an enthusiastic lieutenant in meeting those demands in the form of Vice President of the Council and Minister of Foreign Affairs, Admiral François Darlan.

"Darlan sees the future of France as the chief vassal state in a Germany that includes the European countries it's already conquered, so he sold the Germans a hundred and fifty trucks and tons of fuel for the war in North Africa. He even signed a tentative agreement for the Luftwaffe to use French airfields in Syria, resupply ports in Tunisia, and submarine barns in Dakar. Fortunately, some among the Vichy government wish to maintain an appearance of independence from Germany and managed to quash that second arrangement.

"But Darlan allows Germany's intelligence agencies, including the *Abwehr*, the SD, and the Gestapo to operate in Vichy France. That violates their armistice, but there it is. American diplomats report seeing German agents everywhere in Vichy—bars, restaurants, and even the opera.

"Darlan was furious to learn that the French Army's counterintelligence arm just broke up an *Abwehr* network operating in Marseille—"

Jeremy's attention was suddenly riveted on what the major said. "Marseille? Has Madame Fourcade been informed?"

"She has, and they're taking precautions. I know your personal concern. Amélie and Chantal are fine, at least according to our most recent information." He smiled. "For your benefit, Sergeant Horton included a snippet regarding their health and welfare in the last document drop that came to us via submarine."

"That's some small relief. So, Horton's doing well?"

"He is, I'm happy to say. He was a good choice for liaison. Fourcade likes him. Things are not as bad yet as in Northern France, but they will get that way soon if Pétain continues to allow German agents to operate so openly and in such numbers. Resistance members need to be careful in extending trust. Fortunately, the *gendarmes* there are not fond of Pétain,

Darlan, or the Nazis, so they basically ignore crackdown orders. I'm guessing they won't be allowed to do that forever."

Jeremy let out a deep breath and stared vacantly. "You can get so wrapped up in your own corner of the war that it's easy to forget what's going on elsewhere. It's funny, in a strange way. When I was flying, bringing down German fighters and bombers seemed like that was all there was to it. When the *Luftwaffe* stopped their *blitz* three months ago, the relief from not having to go up night after night was so great that—how do I say this without sounding totally naïve—a new day seemed to have dawned.

"Then while I was training, of course the war was always there, but in a faraway place. We didn't have much time to catch up or stay abreast of news. In my mind, the Nazis were in Northern France, and although they influenced Vichy, Amélie was far south in Marseille, safe and far removed from them. Now I find out that they're right on her doorstep."

Crockatt rose from the chair behind his desk and came around to lean against the front of it with his arms crossed, a grave expression on his face. "I should tell you that Amélie is active in the Resistance, but maybe you knew that."

"I did, but I didn't worry much because she was in Marseille."

"Her younger sister is as well."

Jeremy gasped and stared in disbelief. "She's too young. She should be staying safe and secure in some protected place."

"We're seeing quite a few young people in the Resistance, and there's no stopping them. They've been personally touched in one way or another. In Chantal's case, she's threatened to run away and join another organization if she's not allowed to participate. I hear that she's quite good at reconnaissance and as a courier."

Impatience overcame Jeremy, and he stood. "What do you want me to do?"

"I told you about the Boulier sisters because you should know to use all available resources, obviously within reason. Old people want to be in the fight too. As I recall, Ferrand's sister-in-law, Anna, was quite helpful in rescuing him, and she provided information that helped bring down Major Bergmann. He's dead."

Jeremy frowned in disgust but nodded. "That's a good thing."

"As I was about to say," Crockatt went on, "the SOE wants Fourcade to set up a new network in the northwest of France, closer to the coast, inside the occupied area. She's asked for you to be made available to be part of that."

"Of course. I'm surprised she hasn't sent Henri or Phillippe up to do that."

Crockatt grimaced. "Well, I have a bit of bad news in that regard. Henri was captured and we don't know where he's being held. And Phillippe is now doing duty ostensibly as a Vichy attaché in Madrid while funneling intelligence back and forth between British intelligence and Fourcade's group."

Jeremy folded his arms and dropped his jaw in astonishment.

"Fourcade's hands are tied if she wants SOE funding," Crockatt went on. If we're to provide money, we insist on having our teams there and being in charge. We've largely moved past doing only what is expedient, and SOE also insists on having a trained person to lead. You're trained, you're known to Fourcade and her network, and you're experienced. She wants you among anyone else we send, and we can send you on loan, but we won't agree to a permanent SOE reassignment. You won't be the only team leader going over this time. We're sending teams out as fast as we can."

Jeremy inhaled and rubbed the back of his neck. "That's tough. You're going to send me to France, but maybe somewhere that I can't see Amélie, knowing that she's doing dangerous things for the Resistance. When do I go?"

"Tonight. But there are some things to emphasize. Horton still does liaison for SOE and usually stays with Kenyon and the rest of the SOE group to blow things up. I have no complaints. He does a good job, and he belongs to SOE anyway." He peered into Jeremy's eyes. "But you belong to MI-9. I don't mind supporting their missions as long as ours get done."

"No worries about that. I'm intent on helping Lance if we can find a way."

"We're making headway on assisting POWs in general. We've developed escape maps that are printed on silk paper. They're thin, strong, and they don't make crinkling noises. We're in talks now with the makers of the Monopoly boardgame to put them inside the gameboards and ship them into POW camps via Red Cross parcels and family packages."

Jeremy gawked. "That's sensational. I'm awestruck."

"We're doing other things too. Our main task is to help prisoners escape, and then evade detection to come back to us."

"I'm fully on board with that."

Crockatt frowned. "I should comment on what you just said about Amélie and the dangers she faces, and your being elsewhere. I'd say, welcome to life in France.

"I might be speaking out of turn to mention this while I sit comfortably in this office, but that's the reality you're going into. For that matter, it's not that far removed from what our people experience in Great Britain, except that so far, we've been able to keep the Nazis off our doorsteps. But families are separated, loved ones killed, romances interrupted—"

Jeremy found himself speechless and staring into Crockatt's steady eyes. "You're right," he interjected. "I was thoughtless. Am I parachuting in?"

Crockatt shook his head. "The Lysander squadron is operational. They fly within seven nights on either side of a full moon. The rest of any month is too dark."

Jeremy sucked in his breath. "And that's better than jumping?"

"It is. We still drop equipment via parachutes, and I suppose we'll still do parachute drops when needed—we have the Halifax aircraft for that. But the Lysander pilots are dedicated to landing behind enemy lines. They've worked out their systems, and the ground crews in France are trained—the method works. We bring people back that way too." The major straightened up and went back to his seat. "You'll meet your courier and radio operator tonight before you take off. Do you have any more questions?"

"No. I should go get ready."

"Our procedures are a little different than when you went out last time. I won't be coming with you to the airfield. You'll be flying out of an unnamed location, but ahead of that you'll be driven to the house of Major Antony and Barbara Bertram in its vicinity. I won't tell you the name of the village, and we take measures, so you won't know it. That way if you're captured—"

Crockatt left the rest of the sentence unspoken. "Mrs. Bertram is quite instrumental in our operations as well as her husband, checking out everyone for anything that could incriminate you in enemy territory. They're a wonderful couple who see their mission as providing aid and comfort to our operatives as they leave and return to us. They give that personal touch that says to you on behalf of Britain, 'We care about you. Please come back to us safely.'"

For a split second, Crockatt's voice broke and his jaw tightened. He straightened and took a sharp breath. "Once we have mission go-ahead, a special station wagon will take your party to a secured area at the airfield. If the mission is scrubbed, you'll stay with the Bertrams until it's back on." He held out his palm. "That being the case, I'll say my goodbyes now."

Jeremy shook his hand. "Wish me luck."

The Bertrams occupied a charming stone cottage, and as Crockatt had said, the driver of the vehicle that transported the team took a circuitous route. Driving after dark in blackout conditions, Jeremy could not read the signs anyway.

Although his teammates, a man and a woman, were introduced to him prior to departure from a garage near Whitehall, no one spoke during the drive. For Jeremy, the tension was familiar and not as heightened as he had experienced flying into darkness night after night in the Beaufighters. However, he surmised that this was a first mission for the other two, and he imagined that they must be on edge, although both remained remarkably collected. They had greeted him professionally and he muttered that he would get to know them better when they reached their destination.

The truth was that Jeremy exercised the reserve he had built up against becoming too friendly with colleagues for having lost so many mates during the Battle of Britain and the *blitz*. His mind flitted to the last time he had parachuted into France at night. That had been a little over a year ago when he had been eager and met his teammates with enthusiasm. *What were their codenames? Brigitte and Théo, I think. I wonder if they're still alive.*

On arrival, he found the Bertrams to be as solicitous as

Crockatt had said. The major was a lean, rugged-looking, pipe-smoking man of medium height. Barbara was a bit shorter than he, slender, with light-colored, wavy hair.

They had already laid out a warm meal on the dining room table. Barbara fussed about seating them and ensuring everyone was comfortable.

A solemn quiet descended on the group as they began to eat. The major broke it by saying, "Conversation is difficult because you know where you're going, and we can't converse about details of each other's real private lives. So, I'll tell jokes, and if you would do me the favor, please pretend to laugh at them."

That brought about quiet chuckling, so he continued. "When we're done here, Barbara and I will check everything you're wearing and carrying with you for any labels or other hints that could show you came from England. We don't want to make things easy for the Hun."

Setting his reserve aside, Jeremy turned to the woman. "I've been rude while you're being brave." He extended his hand. "Call me Jeremy and we'll leave it at that. And your codename is?"

"Rowena," she replied, giving a nervous laugh. "I guess we're all tense. I'm the radio operator." She was dressed in a dark blue skirt with matching jacket. "My cover story is that I'm a schoolteacher. That's what I had intended for a career."

"And I go by Atlas," the man said, extending his hand. "I'm the courier." He was a burly man with a heavy beard and curly hair.

When neither was looking his way, Jeremy scrutinized them with a pang of misgivings. *They're so young. She can't be more than twenty, and he's not much older.*

"Do you mind?" Rowena interrupted his thoughts with a question for Barbara. "I'd like to get unpleasantries behind us, so I'll ask now." She hesitated as all eyes locked on her. "I have lethal pills—poison—in case I'm captured—"

"You'd like for me to sew them into a sleeve or something?" Barbara asked. When Rowena nodded, Barbara struggled to mask sadness. "Say no more. I've done it before. Of course I'll do yours." She looked at the others. "Anyone else?"

"I've got mine put away and easily accessible," Jeremy said.

"I do as well," Atlas echoed.

"Well then," the major broke in, "shall we get on and enjoy the meal."

Partway through the dinner, a telephone rang in the living room. Bertram went to answer it, and when he came back, he announced, "The mission's been scrubbed for tonight. Bad weather over the Channel extending beyond the French coast, and the prediction's not looking good for tomorrow."

An air of relief immediately lifted the atmosphere. Natural smiles appeared.

"What happens now?" Jeremy asked.

"You'll be our guests for as long as it takes to get good weather," Bertram said. "Your pilot, Captain Rymills, will be over soon. The pilots like to get to know their passengers whenever possible. The teams like that too; it sets them at ease. Rymills is very good for that. He flew night fighters before coming to the Lysanders."

"Captain Frank Rymills?" Jeremy inquired.

"Yes, do you know him?"

"I do," Jeremy said with pronounced enthusiasm, and laughed. "We called him 'Bunny.' We flew together. He's an excellent pilot."

59

September 7, 1941
RAF Martlesham Heath, Suffolk, England

Red sat at the back of the dispersal hut. "Disconsolate" was not the word he would use to describe his current mood, but he was unsettled. He would soon be the last of the original members in the 71 Eagle Squadron. His greatest friend in life, Andy Mamedoff, whom he had flown with all across California before defying US law to fly and fight with the RAF and picking up Shorty along the way, had just been slotted for a coveted flight commander's billet with the third unit composed of American-only pilots. It had just been formed, the 133 Eagle Squadron, at RAF Duxford near Cambridge.

Red missed Shorty and would miss Andy; they had been his buddies, his pals, his fellow fighter pilots. He set aside thoughts of Shorty. They depressed him. However, the thought of Andy Mamedoff brought a smile. The White Russian refugee would be the first American to be transferred to another American unit and the first to be promoted to leadership. Further, in only ten days, he would wed Penny Craven and be the first among the eagles to take a war bride. Red could not be happier for him.

He returned his thoughts to the present as more newer pilots entered the hut. Deep fatigue already showed on their faces, and they hardly spoke to one another. Gone was the camaraderie of earlier days when Red, Andy, Shorty, and Jeremy had trained together at RAF Hawarden in Wales. No more would they fly as they had at Middle Wallop, wingtip to wingtip, four fast friends out saving the world. The turns of battle had been hair-raising, but they had been thrilling too, and they had returned from missions flushed with the success of their exploits and ready to hit the taverns. *When was that? A year ago? A century?*

Then Jeremy had been downed in the last major daytime raid against Fighter Command. By the time he had healed and returned to 609 Squadron, Red, Andy, and Shorty had been transferred to 71 Eagle Squadron, an event they had looked forward to with anticipation. Then they found that they were loath to leave the place where they had launched on so many patrols, honed their combat skills, shot down German aircraft, and built enviable reputations. Only days after their new squadron was finally activated, Shorty had dived into that fateful cloud. *He must have hit the water at five hundred miles an hour, probably the result of vertigo.*

The four of them had survived Hitler's massive attacks against Fighter Command, and when those failed in bringing Great Britain to heel, the *führer* had sent the night raids with incendiaries and tons of explosive to pound the British population into submission. At last, seeming to accept that he could not dominate Great Britain and its stubborn prime minister in the immediate future, he had turned his attention north to the Soviet Union.

We survived all of that.

As more pilots trooped into the hut, they glanced at Red deferentially, almost reverently, the living legend among them who still flew and had taught or would teach them how to survive and win in aerial combat. Some of them puzzled over why Red himself had not been elevated to leadership, as Andy would be within days. His natural qualities in that regard were self-evident, even now when he kept a distance. When giving instruction, he was funny, patient, and caring, inspiring his new mates to be better. They *had* noticed that he tired easily, and when he returned from patrol, he immediately went to his room and crashed onto his bunk.

Red had heard some of the scuttle, none of it derogatory, all just wondering. He let it pass without comment. When asked, he would respond in his exaggerated Texas drawl, "Hey, I'm the old man in this outfit. I cain't keep up with you younger fellers."

Hmph. At twenty-four, I'm the old guy? Some of these pilots are a few years older than me.

He knew the truth. *My nemesis, lupus, is taking over.*

It was his secret; one he had shared with no one. Since learning that the disease had caused his collapse back at RAF Kirton Lindsey and that was why he woke up more fatigued and went to bed earlier and more exhausted than his buddies, he had continued to fight in the air with every ounce of energy. But his vitality waned on return to earth, and with it the gregarious, fun-loving disposition that had marked him and inspired his friends to follow him so readily. He had even distanced himself from Claire and Anne Haring, making no effort to contact the former during off hours, and neglecting to answer letters from the latter.

I hope I can make it to Andy's wedding. Overwhelming weariness could prevent him from making the overland trip to Epping where the wedding would be held, a distance of one-hundred-and-thirty miles roundtrip. He bore no envy for Andy for having gained leadership status while Red had not. He had known those opportunities were foreclosed when he heard the doctor's diagnosis.

The senior officers can see that I'm just not up to it. I'll be lucky if they let me fly much longer. He wondered if any of them had checked his health status with the doctor.

"Gentlemen, let me have your attention." The pilots gathered around Squadron Leader Stanley Meares. He was a good-looking fellow, Red could see that, with a narrow head, square jaw, light-colored hair, and intelligent eyes. "We're going up today," he said with a slight smile, "but it's no practice mission, and we won't be waiting on a clanging bell to scramble."

He waited for his words to settle in while the pilots exchanged puzzled glances. Standing with aching joints and drooping shoulders at the back of the group, Red pulled his head up and straightened his spine with a stirring of anticipated thrill.

"71 Eagle Squadron," Meares said dramatically, "today we go on the offensive. Today, we fly our first combat mission into France to destroy German targets."

Amidst whooping and hollering, Red smiled and looked around. "About damn time," he growled.

Two pilots close to him laughed and slapped his back. "You've been waiting a long time for this, haven't you, Red?" one said.

"Too long," he replied, ignoring the pain from the friendly clap.

Meares raised a hand for quiet. "This is a seek-and-destroy patrol," he said. "More of a probe to see what's out there. The weather's bad for flying but good for what we're going to do, which is fly in low under the clouds, shoot at anything that looks German, turn around when we get to the limit of our range, and scoot back."

"We're finally going to strike," someone called.

"Good day for it," another pilot said. "I like the weather for this."

"We'll surprise them. They're not looking to be attacked."

Once more, Meares quieted the squadron. "Now listen, we only have nine planes, and they've been 'rode hard and put up wet' a few times, as the saying goes, so no heroics and no unnecessary acrobatics. We get in, shoot what we find, and get out. If you come under fire, duck into some clouds and avoid contact. Understood?"

Five minutes later, nine Supermarine Spitfire IIAs rose into the sky. Red looked dully around his cockpit. Two weeks ago, they had been flying Hurricanes. He guessed this was a step up, but the squadron was already scheduled for the next version of the Spitfire by the end of the month, so he had refrained from looking for the fine differences between his previous fighter and this one. *If it flies, it's fast, can do a tight turn, and has plenty of firepower, I'm happy.*

They headed southeast toward northern France. Prior to reaching the coast, three of the Spitfires encountered mechanical malfunctions and returned to the airfield. Meares, Red, and four others pressed on.

Within minutes, they had streaked over the Channel, crossing into France between Dunkirk and the border with Belgium. *Wehrmacht* coastal gun crews had not spotted them in time to respond effectively, so they made a clean entry and sped inland.

They flew low, sometimes just above the trees, but the targets were sparse, with most of the military build-up concentrated along the coast. They strafed a few convoys, hit some obvious military bases, and looked for ammunition dumps.

Suddenly, when they were roughly seventy-five miles inland on a course toward Paris, their controller's voice came over the radio. "Red Leader, this is Control. A formation of bandits is shaping up behind you, between you and the coast, and headed your way. They're nearly on top of you."

"Roger," Meares replied. "We'll watch for them. The clouds are clearing. Visibility is a lot more than we expected."

"Understood. Look for them *now* at six o'clock. We count seventy-five of unknown type."

"Roger. Break. Red Flight, every man for himself."

Hearing the transmission, Red smiled. "Every man for himself?" he muttered. "What's that? I like 'tally-ho' better. And did Meares' voice just go up an octave?"

He banked hard right and began jinking across the fields. Dropping lower, barely skimming treetops, and dipping to fly between farm buildings, he started a wide turn to take him back toward the coast while searching for low clouds that offered concealment.

Then he saw the enemy formation, appearing at first as a swarm of bees that within seconds grew longer wings and stabilizers. Yellow flashes and smoke spouted from their guns as they descended.

He spotted a low cloud, but it was sufficiently high that he would expose himself by climbing to it. A quick glance around showed no better alternative, and the Germans, now diving, were rapidly closing the distance.

Red rotated the Spitfire to present less of a target and lifted his nose, throttling to maximum combat thrust. *Did the designers ever fix that carburetor problem?*

He leveled out at the base of the cloud and looked back over his shoulder. Most of the German fighters were still in a dive, but a few had peeled off, leveled out of their dives, turned, and started climbing toward him. Not far below, the earth turned and gyrated with every motion of his hand on the stick and his feet on the pedals.

He made out some details of the enemy aircraft. They were ME 110s, and several more pursued him, maneuvering to block his path to the Channel.

He continued toward the cloud at full power, changing direction every few seconds to avoid offering himself as an easy target. Even as he fled, quick thoughts of Shorty and Andy flashed through his mind. They knew how to maneuver with him to defeat the threat. The three of them had done it so many times over Kent and the waters south of there: calling to each other, warning of attacks from the rear, and handing off a bandit to whichever of them was best positioned to take it out. *Our new pilots are unseasoned. They don't know what to do.*

A plane appeared in his peripheral vision. On instinct he dove and turned. It flashed past him, spurting bullets and tracers that streaked by ahead of him. For a fleeting moment he caught a clear view of it and sucked in his breath.

The Messerschmitt's tail was covered from top to bottom with thin white stripes, each of them representing the kill of a British plane. There could be only two German fighter pilots with so many stripes: Major Adolf Galland and Lieutenant Joaquin Müncheberg.

Seconds later, another ME 110 streaked by with an even greater number of stripes. Red groaned. "Of all things, I've got to have two of Germany's greatest aces on me at the same time." He pushed the stick hard right, taking his Spitfire into as tight a turn as he could control, and sped into the cloud. *Maybe I can attack from there.*

60

September 8, 1941

"Won't this weather ever break?" Atlas said. "It's not as if I'm eager to get to my doom, but this sitting around—"

"You don't like our hospitality?" Major Bertram said, chuckling. "I'm joking, of course. The waiting can be the hardest part."

Bunny walked through the door in time to hear the conversation. He was a tall man and distinguished-looking, even for someone so young. His demeanor exuded humor and confidence, and he had light brown receding hair, and eyes that smiled even when serious. He and Jeremy had enjoyed re-acquainting during the hours of delay, with Bunny telling Jeremy, laughingly, "One of my mates says that piloting the Lysander is quite dodgy, like driving a London double-decker compared to the Spitfire or Beaufighter. I don't know why he would be so insulting. I rather like it."

Now, he stood in the middle of the living room floor. "There won't be any more waiting this round, not for another fifteen days. We've lost our window with the moon. You'll be

returned to London this afternoon and be back in two weeks."
He turned to Jeremy. "Major Crockatt sent a message for you
to call him."

Bertram gestured toward the phone, and Jeremy placed
the call. When he hung up, he had blanched, and he fought
back emotion.

Stony Stratford, England

The crunch of gravel on her driveway caused Claire to look
out her front window from her sofa where she played with
Timmy. She had arrived home from work at Bletchley Park a
few minutes earlier and expected no visitors, so she watched
with curiosity as a small government sedan drove into
sunlight from below twin rows of oaks and parked. The
driver's-side door opened, and Jeremy emerged.

"Jeremy's here," she told Timmy excitedly.

"Jermy?" the little boy squealed. "Jermy?"

Claire pointed and Timmy ran to look out the window.
Then she scooped him up and headed for the entrance.
When she opened it, Jeremy was already halfway up the front
path.

"Jermy!" Timmy called, and squirmed to be let down.

Claire laughed and lowered him to the ground. While the
little boy ran to greet Jeremy with a huge smile and wide-
spread arms, Claire advanced toward her brother. Then, the
look on his face brought her to a halt as her chest suddenly
tightened and her throat constricted.

Jeremy's face was long, his jaw taut, and his lips quivered.
He stooped to pick up Timmy, but not before Claire caught
sight of his eyes. They were horror-struck, and when Jeremy

raised Timmy, he brought the boy to his chest and held him close. His body shook.

"What?" Claire cried.

Jeremy did not answer. He only shook his head and swayed back and forth with Timmy.

Tears streamed down Claire's face. "No," she whispered, both hands engulfing her cheeks. "Who?"

Jeremy tried to speak. Claire ran and clung to him. "Who was it?" she whispered. "Not Red. Please tell me it's not Red."

Jeremy choked. "Red," he gasped.

Claire wept, her body shaking with grief. "Oh God, no," she moaned. "Please tell me it's not true."

Little Timmy, his eyes alternating between Jeremy and Claire, reached out and touched her face. "Don't cry, Gigi," he said in his tiny voice. "Everything will be all right. You'll see."

Claire encircled the child and Jeremy with her arms, and the three stood for several minutes on the garden path doing nothing but holding each other. The nanny had come to the door apparently intending to leave for the day, but seeing the drama before her, she came and started to take Timmy. He resisted, clinging to Jeremy.

"It's all right," he told her. "Thank you."

The nanny stood back observing for a moment, and then headed back inside. "I'll make some tea. You go on into the living room and I'll bring it to you."

Claire stepped back and wiped her eyes. Then Jeremy, still carrying the boy, walked up the path with her and entered the house.

"How did it happen?" Claire asked when they were seated on the sofa.

"The details are sketchy. Red's squadron was on its first offensive run into France. Clouds were low. They thought they could get in, do some damage, and get out." He told her as much as he knew. "They were caught deep inside France by seventy-five Messerschmitts. We lost two others, Hilard Fenlaw and Bill Nichols. Fenlaw was killed, but Nichols was wounded and captured. We've already received word on him.

"Another pilot, Bill Geiger, saw Red break away and go after one of the enemies, but then two top German aces, Galland and Müncheberg, came after him. His plane was shot up pretty bad, but he still attacked one of them."

Claire took a deep breath. "What do we know about Red for sure?"

Jeremy stood and rubbed his eyes. "He crash-landed. One of our chaps says he saw Red give a thumbs-up, but that's unconfirmed." He took a deep breath. "Red was known to the Germans because he was an original 'eagle' and an ace. Downing him would be a feather in anyone's cap. Contacts in France reported to Major Crockatt's office that German news announced that six of their pilots, including those two aces, claim to have shot him down."

"You don't think there's a chance he survived?"

Jeremy shook his head. "I suppose there's a slight chance, but we would have heard by now."

"How do you know that Fenlaw was killed?"

"He blew up in midair. No parachute."

Claire shuddered. "How did Andy take the news."

"I haven't seen him. I imagine quite hard, though I doubt he'll show it."

Fresh tears ran down Claire's face. "Andy's wedding is in one week. I'm not sure I can do it—go there." Her breath came in short gasps. "That celebration or memorial or whatever you call what we did for Shorty at The Bull was so painful. I don't know if I could do it again. And this isn't a memorial service, it's a wedding. Sadness is the last thing the couple needs, particularly in a war. Who knows how long we'll keep Andy?"

Her body shook. "How do I look happy when you and Andy are there without Red and Shorty? The four of you became such close friends. I grew to love them dearly."

Jeremy leaned over and held her. "I know," he said, "especially Red."

"Yes, especially Red," she sobbed. "I don't know if it would have gone further. I never got the chance to find out." She wiped her eyes and took a deep breath. "I can't keep doing this."

She felt Timmy nudging her knee, and when she glanced down at him, he looked at her with large, solemn eyes. "I love you, Gigi."

"Oh, I love you too," she said, reaching down and lifting him into her arms.

Jeremy regarded the two of them. "That's the second time he's called you Gigi."

"Well, he must call me something, and I'm not his mum or his aunt. What happens if bona fide family shows up and claims him? I don't want to confuse him."

Jeremy tousled Timmy's hair. "I know I'm being selfish, but I pray that doesn't happen. I want to see him grow up."

"And we will, one way or another. You'll see."

Jeremy chuckled involuntarily. "He's sounding like you already. Did you hear him outside on the path? He used your 'you'll see' phrase." He looked into Claire's face. "Let me know about the wedding. Under the circumstances—"

"Of course I'll go," Claire sniffed. "How could I do otherwise?"

61

September 15, 1941
Epping, England

The trip from Stony Stratford had not taken long. Jeremy had driven up the night before from RAF Middle Wallop, spent the night, and escorted Claire and Timmy to Epping, a town that Winston Churchill had served while a member of parliament, situated seventeen miles northeast of London in the county of Essex. The crowd was not large, mainly because of wartime restrictions and rationing.

The intelligence officer for 71 Squadron, Robbie Robinson, hosted the wedding and reception, having arranged for the ceremony at a local church and a luncheon afterward at a nearby inn. He met the Littlefields and Timmy at the door and led them to their seats.

Perhaps because time had passed since learning of Red's passing, Claire found the prospect of attending the affair not as difficult as she had thought it would be. She expected sad moments, but she looked forward to seeing Andy and meeting his bride.

The ceremony, held in a centuries-old chapel, was short. One of Andy's squadron mates, Vic Bono, a pilot officer neither Jeremy nor Claire had met before, stood as best man. He comported himself well, but Claire found that she once more fought tears on seeing Vic standing where Red should have been. Unfortunately, most of the squadron were on readiness and could not attend the festivities, so most of the guests came from among Penny's family and friends.

Seeing the couple together, Claire was amazed at the similarities between their faces. Same cheek structures, same shape of lips, eyes, and noses, and even the same height, although with her hat, Penny appeared slightly taller. She was pretty and vivaciously feminine; he was decidedly masculine. Together, Claire thought they made a cute and happy couple.

At the luncheon, Timmy fidgeted through the routine of toasts and speeches. Claire and Jeremy took turns bouncing him on their knees and otherwise amusing him. She noticed that Penny, while beaming as a bride would, carried an air of uncertainty and sadness which she seemed to share with Andy through exchanged glances that carried an endearing sense of intimacy. Seated at a table facing their guests, they reached for each other and held hands. For his part, Andy listened to the toasts and speeches; and then suddenly, he stood.

As if seized by premonition, Claire gulped and turned to search Jeremy's face for an indication of what might take place. His eyes were on Andy.

"I'd like to say something," Andy began, and a hush fell over the crowd as if everyone might have anticipated his intention. He held a glass of wine in his hand. "A week and a day ago," he said, "I lost the best friend I've ever had, Pilot Officer Red Tobin." His eyes turned red and his voice broke. He struggled to continue. "You know our story, so I won't tell it again."

Taking a deep breath, he went on. "I want to say—"

He took another deep breath as his lips quivered. "I want to say that he should be here." He shook his head. "No. I mean to say that Red, you are here." He placed his right hand over the left side of his chest and looked skyward. "In my heart, where you will always be."

He gazed across the crowd. "And so, I propose a toast to you, Red. Those who knew you well, loved you. You fooled the FBI. You fought the British bureaucracy and made them take us. Without you, I wouldn't be here."

Fighting tears and sniffles, the guests lifted their glasses and drank to Red.

Struggling to control her emotions, Claire grabbed Jeremy's arm with both hands and squeezed it, biting her lower lip. Finding it a losing battle, she buried her face in a kerchief and turned. Jeremy leaned over her protectively while Timmy rested his head on her knee.

Moments later, a woman above them said, "I'm so sorry. May I help?"

Jeremy looked up. Penny stood there. "I've heard so much about you, Claire. You meant a lot to our lost eagles, and you still do, to Andy—"

Just then, a deep, throaty roar rode the air, grew in volume, and descended on the guests. Recognizing the sound, Jeremy looked skyward. Two Hurricanes, flying barely above the rooftop, zoomed over the gardens. As they cleared the reception area, they waggled their wings, lifted their noses, and climbed almost vertically in the sky. They reached their zenith and rounded their loops with their cockpits down. Then, as they screamed toward earth, they rotated upright, flew low over the reception once more, and departed, executing barrel rolls.

While the Hurricanes performed their antics, the guests

cheered in amazement at the maneuvers. Spirits rose. Timmy watched the performance in wonder, at first fearful, and then jumping up and down and pointing with delight.

"Would you like to come with me?" Penny asked Claire. "I'd love to spend some time getting to know you and introducing you to my family and friends. Bring Timmy along. They'll love him."

Claire looked at Jeremy uncertainly.

"Go on," he said. "You'll feel better. Andy's coming this way. We can catch up."

"I'm glad you came," Andy said. "Claire too." He and Jeremy had retired to a quiet place on the grounds. The other guests had given them space to visit. Most were pleased to shower attention on Timmy, the little boy most of them had heard of for being saved from the shipwreck.

Jeremy looked into the sky. "That was a terrific display those Hurricanes put on. Were they your mates from the 71st?"

Andy nodded with a slight smile. "The two who flew over the inn were Bill Geiger and Ed Bateman. That was Bono's idea. They couldn't be here because it's too far by car when they're on readiness—which they are now—but it's only a few minutes by air, and if they're scrambled, their controller would divert them to where they needed to be.

"I saw four more buzz the village. They'll probably pay hell for that. Today is market day in Epping, and flying that low, I'm sure they scattered pigs, chickens, sheep, not to mention scaring the townspeople. The mayor's a good man, though, and so are the villagers. They'll forgive rambunctious young pilots who risk their lives daily for them and want to celebrate a mate's wedding."

"I heard you were shot down and wounded last month. How well are you mending?"

Andy grinned. "What you heard was probably exaggerated —and happened at Middle Wallop over a year ago before you joined us."

Taken aback, Jeremy chuckled. "One of your mates just told me about it a few minutes ago. You never mentioned it."

"It wasn't much of a deal. My only injuries were a wounded ego and a bruised back."

"I heard that your Spitfire took twenty-nine hits from 20 mm cannon and machine gun fire—eight through the prop, twenty through the fuselage, and one through the armor plating—a total loss."

"Yep, I'm surprised they let me fly again," Andy joked. "I had to get better at evasive maneuvers."

Jeremy chuckled. "Well, I'm glad you're well and safe. And congratulations! Penny is beautiful and sweet. Her gesture to Claire just now was kind and will be remembered. And well done on your promotion to command too."

Andy smiled. "I'm a lucky man, Jeremy. When my parents escaped Stalin, they never saw the Battle of Britain or the *blitz* in my future. I came through, and now I'm married to an heiress." He chuckled. "That boggles my mind. I think what she saw in me must be how alike we look. Anyway, who knows what will happen next?" He sighed and tossed his head. "Tell me what you're doing now. The last time we saw each other, you were in night fighters. Since Hitler isn't bombing us every night lately, what are you flying?"

"Nothing now," Jeremy lamented. "My agreement with Major Crockatt was that I'd come back to MI-9 when the air war over Britain had come to an end. He got that in writing from Air Chief Marshal Dowding. The raids have pretty much wound down, so I'm out of the skies and back to ground-pounding."

"Ah, I pity you. Does that mean you're back to covert work in France? Will you get to see Amélie?"

"Right now, I seem to be on perpetual waiting on account of weather, but yes, that's the plan. Going back to MI-9 was my choice, to do covert work in France. I hope to see Amélie, but I don't want to put her in greater jeopardy. It's been nearly a year since I've seen her. By now, she probably doesn't remember me, and you know what surrounds women in France—French men."

Andy grunted. "Those French men have as much on their plates these days as we do, and no one who saw you and Amélie together would believe she's forgotten you." He glanced around. "Look, here's a piece of friendly advice from a buddy—or mate, as you would say. If I've learned nothing else in this war, it's that none of us knows how much time we have. If you love that girl and if you get another chance, you'd better grab her and don't let go.

"Hell, *make* the chance if you have to. You're tenacious enough. She might look small and harmless, but those of us who know how she's handled all the crap in France know that she's one rare, tough cookie, worth fighting for to keep in your life." He paused. "Not to mention that she's beautiful." He clapped Jeremy's shoulder. "Anyway, that's my advice."

Jeremy smiled. "We think alike." He glanced into the sky, contemplating. "You know, of the seven 'eagles' on the roster of The Few, only you, Donahue, and a chap named Haviland are left."

Andy clapped him on the shoulder. "I try not to think about that too much."

"Sorry. My point is that you all sacrificed a great deal to

fight for Great Britain, and you're still here. We'll never forget what you've done, I promise you. Our nation is grateful."

Andy nodded acknowledgment. "When Red and I first talked about crossing the pond, we intended to join the Finns against the Soviet Union. Shorty had the same idea, but we left Canada too late. The Finns were beaten. So then, we were going to fight for France. We watched that defeat up close and had to skedaddle across the Channel to the white cliffs. This whole escapade started as a lark for us, an adventure. We knew we *could* be killed. None of us thought we *would* be, but —" He shrugged and remained silent a moment. "We learned about courage and endurance from you, your family, and your country. We stayed because it's the right fight. You reminded me of what my parents went through, escaping Stalin to get to freedom." He chuckled. "Basically, the same struggle the United States went through to get our liberty."

Jeremy laughed. "That's a bit of a strained analogy. Regardless, it seems the colonies have made a go of it on their own after all."

"And on that note, let's rejoin the party, shall we?"

"Yes, but just one more question. When do you take command of your flight at 133 Eagle Squadron?"

"In three days."

September 22, 1941
The Downs Near Petworth, UK

"I'm not optimistic about the weather," Bunny told Jeremy. The team had been driven back to the Bertrams' house that morning. "I give us no chance of getting out today and little tomorrow. We're getting too late in the year. The cross-

Channel weather is terrible, and we're not like the bombers and fighters—we can't fly above it. We have to go in low, sometimes only fifty feet above the ground, and of course, always at night."

He glanced somberly at Jeremy. "I heard about your friend, Red Tobin. I'm sorry."

"It happens," Jeremy said, keeping his emotion buried. "So now we sit."

"As we've done for much of the war, around the dispersal huts," Bunny responded. "This isn't much different." He looked around at the well-appointed warmth of the Bertrams' living room. "Except that it's more comfortable here."

"That it is," Jeremy said, picking up a magazine and sinking into one of the overstuffed chairs while looking out the window at the rolling countryside. "That it is."

62

October 8, 1941
RAF Sealand, Wales, UK

Andy lowered the landing gear on his Hurricane, tail number Z3781. He flared, settled onto the runway, and taxied to a refueling station, waved in by ground crew. The six fighters from his 133 Eagle Squadron's Blue Flight followed him. Nearby the kites belonging to Red Flight and the four spare aircraft followed suit at another station. The trip from RAF Fowlmere had been uneventful.

Several days prior, the pilots of the entire squadron had grumbled while being briefed regarding their next posting to RAF Eglington in Northern Ireland. Squadron Leader George Brown had raised a hand for quiet. "Fighter Command decided that we need more flight training," he told them.

"It's called the island of never-ending rain," someone had called out. "How will we train when the weather is always meant for ducks?"

"I understand, gentlemen, but ours is not to pick and choose—"

"Ours is but to do and die—in foul weather. Pun intended."

The room had erupted in scornful laughter.

Once more, Brown called for quiet. "Let's be serious a moment, shall we? You're all good pilots, but you're not yet accomplished *combat* pilots. On your first day at Fowlmere, you watched the class before yours celebrate their graduation with a station fly-past. No one needs reminding of the catastrophe when one of the instructors flew into and sawed off the tail of another instructor, who was a hero of the Battle of Britain. And only twelve days ago, two of your squadron mates, Walt Soares and Charlie Barrell, collided on final approach. You all attended their funerals.

"So, don't tell me that you're ready for battle without more practice. I understand that you came over from America to fight, but we must give you the utmost chance of surviving the battles unscathed, and part of that is through training."

Then the disgruntled mood in the room changed to ringing cheers when Brown announced, "And by the way, while at Eglinton, you'll be trading your Hurricane MK IIBs for Supermarine Spitfire IIAs."

In the interim to their departure, the grumbling did not entirely cease. However, by the time the day had come and pre-checks had been completed, the squadron had accepted their lot. They had lifted into the air this morning with only the normal back-and-forth joshing, characteristic of military everywhere.

They had landed for fuel at Sealand an hour after takeoff, and each pilot had his fighter serviced. While they waited, Andy and Brown stood together studying the sky over the sea, visible beyond the runway toward Ireland.

"Those clouds don't look good," Andy said.

"Agreed. The next stop is Andreas Airfield on the Isle of

Man. That's a little shorter than the distance we just flew. Unless a storm blows up, we should be all right."

"I hope. The last leg is a little farther than the first one."

"Let's brief the men. If we get into sticky weather, they'll have to make individual judgment calls about turning back to Sealand or continuing on to Andreas."

———

Apprehension seized Andy as he led his flight back into the skies heading out over the Irish Sea. The sky had grown darker, and winds buffeted his Hurricane. Scanning the fighters under his charge, he saw them being tossed about just as he was.

"Blue Flight," he called, "increase your interval. Pay attention to your instruments. This will be a rough ride."

As he listened for each pilot to acknowledge, his mind went to Penny. "Pretty Penny," he had started calling her.

"That's so *gauche*," she had responded, but she liked it.

He could hardly believe his luck when they first met, and she had showed him particular attention. Before then, whenever he, Red, and Shorty went out together, Red had always been the one the girls sought out—well, before Red had suddenly quieted down and become withdrawn. That had puzzled Andy. *What happened to him?*

Andy was known for being audacious in his own right, but until the time that Red had collapsed, he could never seem to escape the tall pilot's shadow. *Did his collapse have something to do with the way he withdrew from everyone?*

In any event, lively, friendly, partyer Penny had shown no interest in anyone else from the moment they met, and he was thrilled to be with her. She had been upset at the news that the 133rd would transfer to Northern Ireland. "That's so far away," she had cried. "I won't get to see you."

"I'll be back somewhere in England in three months," he had assured her, "and I'll spend every moment with you that I'm not flying."

Early this morning, before leaving their house, she had wept. "I can't be left alone."

He tried to comfort her. "Darling, you have lots of friends to keep you company."

She had shaken her head miserably. "I have lots of people who like to be around me because I have lots of money." She had kissed him and held him passionately. "You didn't know I was rich when we met, and I didn't bring it up."

"I learned that tidbit from Claire last Christmas. I was in shock."

"I remember." She laughed through her tears. "I thought you were going to break up with me because you thought you couldn't measure up." She threw her arms around Andy's neck and whispered, "I wouldn't have anyone else. I love you."

A sense of misgiving overtook Andy. *The last thing Penny told me was, I love you. Did I respond?*

For a fleeting moment, knowing the answer to that question overrode everything else. Then a strong gust thrust Andy high. The clouds had grown darker and thicker. He checked his instruments, in particular his lateral pitch. *Step on the ball.*

A stout headwind burned up his fuel. Darkness closed around him. Peering through it, he saw none of his flight-mates.

His radio crackled. "Blue Leader, this is Blue Five. I'm feeling the onset of vertigo. Heading back."

"Blue Leader, this is Blue Six. Ditto."

"Roger. Be safe. I'll see you both at destination when you get there."

Some minutes later, Andy's radio crackled again, with traffic from Red Flight.

"Red Leader, this is Red Three. I'm off course, but I'm across the water. Weather is lighter. I see an airfield. I'm going to set down and wait this out."

"This is Red Two. I see Red Three. I'll follow him down."

"Red Two and Three, this is Red Leader. Roger."

Meanwhile, the turbulence around Andy had turned vicious, with sheets of rain pounding against his windshield and threatening to deafen him. He glued his eyes to his instruments. "Blue Two, Three, and Four, status?" he called.

"This is Blue Two. I've seen no break."

"This is Blue Three. Same."

"This is Blue Four. Same."

Andy closed his eyes momentarily and shook his head. Those were his youngest and most inexperienced fighters. "This is Blue Leader. If you see a break in the clouds, take it. No heroics. Get on the ground as quickly and safely as you can."

Thankfully, they acknowledged his transmission.

A faint call came through from another Red Flight fighter. "This is Red Five. I've spotted an airfield. I'll ride out the storm there."

"This is Red Leader, Roger."

———

A farmer in Maughold on the Isle of Man heard a low rumble above the roar of wind and pounding rain. He had heard the sound before and figured that fighters must be flying nearby.

This time, however, the tenor of the engines was different, louder. He walked out onto his front porch and cupped his ear toward them. Then he saw them fly across a field to his front, four of them, coming fast and too low.

He sucked in his breath in horror.

They plowed into a low-rise hill across the field from his house. A thunderous explosion shot flames high into the sky followed by rapid, irregular popping as ammunition burned off in a machine gun staccato.

The farmer raced into the darkness and rain, and he soon sensed other people, men and women, young and old, running to the burning aircraft. But when they came near, blazing heat and random bullets held them back.

Nothing could be done for the pilots who were doubtless already dead. When the ammunition had stopped burning off, the farmer continued pressing as close as the heat allowed until he could read the only one of the tail numbers that was not scorched off: Z3781.

63

October 9, 1941
London, England

"You didn't waste any time getting here," Major Crockatt told Jeremy. "It's still early morning."

"We've reached the end of our window again," Jeremy replied. They sat across the desk from one another in the major's office. "This waiting is a killer. We were supposed to be in France more than a month ago."

"You and all the other teams that should have flown out, not to mention the equipment that is sorely needed there. Let's hope for a break in the next moon cycle. Will you be staying with your sister?"

Jeremy affirmed. "That's where I'm headed this afternoon. At least I'll get to spend some time with her and Timmy."

"Check in by phone once in a while over the next couple of weeks, but otherwise relax and enjoy yourself. You've earned it."

"Hmph. It's hard to relax when people you love are in harm's way."

Crockatt smiled wryly. "I understand, but give it a try."

"Listen, on the way up here, I heard on the news that some chaps from the 133rd had been lost in a storm. Could I prevail on Vivian to call over to Fighter Command and check the names? Andy Mamedoff is a flight commander in that squadron."

"Certainly." He pushed a button on his desk, and moments later, the secretary appeared in his doorway. Crockatt explained the request, and Vivian left, closing the door behind her.

"What do you hear from your parents on Sark?" Crockatt asked.

Jeremy sighed. "Nothing good. They know their letters will be censored, so they don't tell us much of substance, and they wouldn't want to worry us with their suffering anyway. The good news is that they're still writing, which means they're still alive."

"That's a sorry situation, the Channel Isles. To have left British territory undefended is unimaginable."

"Agreed, but I've come to accept that the prime minister had no choice. I'm not surprised that my parents chose to stay. I probably could have predicted that, but I still might wring their necks the next time I see them for having done so, whenever that is."

Vivian hurried in, an anxious look on her face. She glanced furtively at Jeremy and then handed the major a note.

He read it quickly, grimaced, and looked up at Jeremy. "I'm afraid we've received a bit of bad news." He handed the note to Jeremy.

Stony Stratford, England

Reading on her sofa in the living room, Claire heard gravel crunching on her driveway. As on the day when Jeremy came to tell her of Red's passing, she was not expecting visitors. She jerked her head up and stared out the window with apprehension.

A small government sedan broke from beneath the oaks into waning sunlight. She inhaled sharply, brought a hand up in front of her mouth, started to rise, and called to the nanny. "Would you please take Timmy to play in the back garden? Someone is here to see me."

The nanny hurried in, glanced out the window, and shook her head sadly without a word. Then she picked up Timmy. He protested, but she promised him a sugar biscuit, and that mollified the child.

Tears had already formed in Claire's eyes when she opened the door. Jeremy had exited the car and was halfway up the garden path. The look on his face confirmed her fears.

"Andy?" she gasped, and as Jeremy nodded, she turned pale. He hurried to her and wrapped his arms around her.

"Oh my God," Claire said suddenly. "What about Penny? That poor girl. She's not been married even a month. She'll be all alone. I must go to her."

"I brought her here. I hope you don't mind. She's in the car."

"She's here?" Claire wiped her eyes and stared at the car. "Of course I don't mind." She hurried to the sedan and opened the passenger side door. Inside, Penny sat with her face in her hands. When she removed them and peered up, she looked exhausted and confused.

Claire leaned in and hugged her. "I'm so sorry," she whispered. "I have no words for my anguish, which can't approach your own."

Both women shook as grief overtook them. Jeremy joined

them, standing just behind Claire, and when they had calmed down, he helped bring Penny into the house.

―――――――

"I got the news at Major Crockatt's office this morning," Jeremy told Claire when Penny had fallen into fitful sleep in the guest bedroom. "I'd heard that the 133rd had been scattered with some planes and pilots lost, so I asked him to inquire to find out who."

He took a deep breath. "I couldn't believe when I learned that Andy had gone down. He was such a good and experienced pilot. He'd told me that Penny felt alone despite her wealth, and she had said she hoped you and she could become friends. She loved meeting you at the wedding.

"I drove up there as soon as I heard. I arrived at their cottage just after she had been informed of the tragedy by the sergeant major. He and the rest of the ground crew were due to start their convoy to Eglington today, and he was the senior man present. Penny was in no shape to be left alone."

"I'm glad you brought her," Claire said. "This is a horrible thing to face, especially alone." She sank into it. "How long, little brother? How much longer must good people endure these ravages of dictators." She buried her face in her hands.

Jeremy went to the bar and pulled out two tumblers. "Care for a drink?"

"I could use one. Thanks."

He poured them, brought one to Claire, and sat next to her. "I wish I had an answer. I imagine there will always be one somewhere in the world. This one in Germany is particularly nasty."

"The one in Moscow isn't any better. He just doesn't threaten us at the moment."

Jeremy agreed and gestured toward the room where Penny slept. "You're going to keep her here?"

"She's welcome to stay as long as she wants."

"Good. Did I mention that I'll be staying too?"

Claire's face brightened with a smile. "That's wonderful. Are you on leave?"

"Of sorts. I'll have to check in from time to time."

A frown furrowed Claire's brow. "You're being a bit cryptic. What's my little brother up to these days?"

Jeremy smiled. "What will you be doing at your job tomorrow?"

She frowned with a hint of somber mock petulance. "Ask me no questions, and I'll tell you no lies?"

"Exactly," Jeremy said grimly. "But I will tell you that when I report back in, you might not hear from me for a while."

As soon as he said the words, Claire's shoulders drooped, but her face became resolute. She set her jaw, straightened her back, and gazed at Jeremy. "I'm getting beyond tears. That doesn't mean I love you less. From now on, I'll save my emotions for the day when we can celebrate the end of this nightmare, and we won't have to grieve for yet another loved one dying too young."

Jeremy nodded solemnly and glanced toward the bedroom where Penny slept. "Do you have any ideas about how to help her?"

"I do. She's bright and well educated, and after she's had time to mourn, she'll need to get busy doing something to keep her mind occupied. I'm on good terms with my superiors. I'll talk to them about hiring her—that is, if she wants to. She has the qualifications they look for."

64

October 23, 1941
The Downs Near Petworth, England

Bunny strode into the Bertrams' living room. "The weather's looking good," he announced. "We might take a few bumps along the way, but I think we have a good chance of flying out tonight."

Jeremy and his team had arrived there the night before. They looked up anxiously and then at each other, and the atmosphere suddenly took on a subdued quality. Each face tightened from relaxed to professionally neutral with hooded eyes.

Bunny took in the transformation. "I'm sorry. This is a case where good news is bad news, isn't it?" He took a deep breath and blew it out.

"We volunteered," Rowena said, taking to her feet. "Thank you. I'll get ready."

Barbara Bertram entered the room from the kitchen, and from the expressions on her guests' faces, she read what was taking place. "Oh dear," she sniffed. "Antony will be so upset that he's not here to see you off." Then she hugged all three members of the team. "Take care of them," she admonished Bunny as tears formed in her eyes.

"I'll do my best, mum." He turned to the group. "We'll have snacks on the plane, but I'd avoid drinking much liquid from here until we reach your destination. We have no facilities on board, and it's a long flight."

Near dusk, they rode in a special station wagon with darkened windows, taking a winding route. When they emerged from the vehicle, they found themselves behind a high, solid gate blocking their views except along the length of the runway, but some ethereal quality in the air made Jeremy believe that he knew where they were: RAF Tangmere, where he had flown so many missions prior to transferring to Middle Wallop to be with Red, Andy, and Shorty.

He scrutinized the landscape he *could* see in the waning light beyond the end of the runway, certain that he recognized the shape of rolling hills in the distance. Then, he glanced wistfully in what he estimated to be the direction of the churchyard of St. Mary's and St. Blaise in Boxgrove, where he and his mates had buried his great friend, mentor, and Olympic gold medalist, another American eagle who had flown for Great Britain and given his life for her, Billy Fiske.

A Lysander sat on the apron. It gave an aura of strength and versatility with its monstrous Mercury engine and tri-bladed propeller jutting pugnaciously skyward, huge cowlings over its front landing gear, and double-struts supporting wings of a wide and peculiar shape. Strapped to the underside of its short fuselage was a torpedo-like tank that provided added fuel for extended range.

Bunny was already there. He guided the group to the steel ladder welded to the fuselage behind the wing and forward of the stabilizer. "This is it," he said grimly. "Just a reminder: when we land, get out quickly and follow your guide away from the aircraft. I won't be on the ground more than three minutes." He reached forward and shook the hand of each team member, telling them, "Thank you for what you do."

Then he helped them climb the ladder into the cramped rear compartment. Moments later, the ignition cranked, the propeller turned, the engine roared to life, and the aircraft taxied to the runway before lifting into the night sky.

Flying low by the light of a slender, waxing moon, Rymills guided his tiny, lone aircraft across the turbulent waves of the English Channel, crossing into France between Luc-sur-Mer and Ouistreham along the Normandy coast. Heading south, he entered the Loire Valley and followed it.

His only navigational instruments were a map and a compass, although he had flown the route enough times that the valley itself and some landmarks had become familiar sufficiently that he amusingly stated a belief that God had put them there at creation to aid Lysander pilots flying at night. Nevertheless, the rumble of the gigantic engine along with the cramped cockpit and low light made navigating difficult, and if he happened to drop his map from his knee, searching for it by torchlight became a challenge he preferred to avoid.

Tonight, he would be delivering his passengers to a field near Montrichard in the Cher Valley of Torraine Province. He imagined that the area must be beautiful with rivers and streams; intermittent forests; and wide, open fields on gently rolling hills; but having seen it only at night, he could not know for sure. The Resistance group there had been thoughtful enough to have planted potatoes at one end of the landing field and wildflowers at the opposite end so that spotting it and gauging its length from the air at night by the light of moon and stars had been made less difficult.

On a previous landing there, grateful Resistance members had given him a bottle of wine. Later, back at Tangmere, he had studied the label and determined that the wine had been produced in that province, and on further study, he had learned that Torraine hosted many vineyards.

Bunny knew the ground team to be competent. On hearing the Lysander, one member with a pocket torch flashed a single letter of the alphabet in Morse code at the approach end of the field. Receiving a return signal from Bunny, the second person would flash another torch. When the aircraft had touched down, a third member stationed off the field halfway down its length flashed a third signal, letting Bunny know where along the field he should stop.

Squashed together in the small compartment behind the cockpit, Jeremy, Rowena, and Atlas felt every vibration, jarring turn, bank of the aircraft, and bump of the entire flight. They sat in the dark, mentally and emotionally stretched, hearing the rush of wind over the skin of the aircraft and its moans and screeches from metal rubbing metal when they encountered turbulence. As they neared the time that they knew instinctively that their flight must soon be over, their hearts beat faster, their hands became clammy, and adrenaline revived them to alertness.

Since the Lysander had flown so low to the ground, their descent had occurred almost undetected. Their first clue was a sudden upward swing of the nose as the plane flared, and then a thud with a lurch as its front landing gear hit the ground.

Then, after the rear wheel settled and a very short taxi, the aircraft came to a halt.

Almost before the engine cut to an idling hum, someone outside climbed the ladder and pulled the compartment open. "*Vite, vite!*" a figureless voice urged, and the three passengers scrambled down.

As soon as they were on the ground and clear of the ladder, they heard new passengers scrambling up. Within three minutes, Bunny flew his aircraft back into the moonlit sky, leaving the three arrivals with their unknown hosts.

65

October 24, 1941
Montrichard, France

Jeremy eyed the young man sitting across a long table from him. They were in a dimly lit, underground wine cellar. Several of the Resistance group's members, men and women, were grouped around them, some sitting at the table, some standing. They wore tired, neutral expressions. None were hostile, but none were openly friendly, although some repressed smiles while glancing furtively at their comrades.

The reception team had been efficient, whisking their charges away from the field in small trucks and vans. The drive had not been long, but it had been bumpy, and when the vehicles finally came to a stop, Jeremy, Rowena, and Atlas had found themselves in front of a barn stuffed with stale and decaying hay. From there, they had followed their guides through the barnyard into a stone courtyard to another non-descript building, and then down some dark stairs into their present location.

The young man eyed them coolly. "Welcome to France,"

he said, but his voice lacked warmth. "I am Jean Monmousseaux. My codename is Faucon. If you are tired, we can speak in the morning, but I think the sooner the better." He looked across the group. "Which one of you is Labrador?"

Jeremy raised his hand. "That would be me."

Faucon regarded him appraisingly. "I hear your French is very good—that you can pass for a Frenchman."

"I do my best," Jeremy replied. He studied Faucon. He was roughly Jeremy's age, mid-twenties, and he seemed generally friendly. But on this night, at least, he projected an edge that added to Jeremy's unease, and probably to Atlas' and Rowena's as well.

Faucon had a wide, square face with strong features and a slightly receding hairline with nevertheless full, thick hair that lent him a rugged, distinguished look. He was fairly tall and muscular, and he carried himself with a confident, no-nonsense demeanor.

"If there is something urgent to discuss, by all means, you and I can do so now," Jeremy replied evenly. "It's been a long day, though, and if you wouldn't mind, I'd like to release my colleagues to get some sleep."

"I'd prefer to stay," Rowena interjected quickly.

"As would I," Atlas added. "I'm not feeling that we are wanted here, and if there's an issue about that, I'd prefer we find out about it now."

Faucon alternated his eyes between the three of them. "I think that's better, although I have no problem discussing with only the team leader." He locked his eyes on Jeremy. "If that's what you prefer."

"Faucon," Jeremy said with a touch of sternness in his tone. "Is that what you wish to be called?"

Faucon nodded. "I prefer that you get used to using my codename. The chance for slip-ups is reduced."

"Then why did you tell us your real name?"

Faucon gave a smile under narrowed eyes. "Because if you will be here for any time at all, you will know who I am. My name is known in these regions."

Jeremy nodded. "Fair enough." He glanced at the people assembled around them. "Your group was very effective tonight. They've been trained well. We appreciate their reception."

Faucon acknowledged with a slight bow of his head.

Jeremy locked eyes with him. "If there's an issue, let's hear it. Like my colleague, Atlas, I'm not feeling any warmth."

Faucon half-snickered. "Atlas? Seriously?"

Atlas shrugged. "I didn't pick my codename. If you don't like it, we can change it."

Faucon waved aside the matter and focused again on Jeremy. "I think you should know some of our history here, since the Germans occupied the north of France." His tone took on an angry quality. "Our province, Touraine, is famous for growing wine." He glanced at Jeremy as if expecting a reaction. "Wine might seem like a fanciful indulgence for the rich, but it is our livelihood."

Around him, the gathered Resistance members nodded and voiced their agreement. Faucon continued, his voice sounding hollow. "The Germans laid waste to it," he hissed. "They try to ship our wine to Germany at prices they set that impoverish us, and they take our foodstuffs too, our produce. In the sixteen months since they invaded, they've turned our fertile valley into a wasteland, and our people face starvation."

"We hope to help drive them out," Jeremy said. "What's the problem? I can't sort through it if I don't know what it is."

Faucon took a deep breath, looking thoughtful. "I appreciate that you risked your lives to come here." He paused and stared directly into Jeremy's eyes. "I've been led to understand that I should take orders from you."

Jeremy leaned back in surprise. "That's a strong way of putting it. I think I'd describe my relationship with you as a cooperative one. The nub of the matter is that if England is to supply arms, equipment, and money—literally money dropped in bundles by the thousands of francs—then it should have some say in how those resources are distributed and used. I am the conduit."

Faucon nodded. "I know that, but I should inform you of some things." He leaned forward. "I served in Charles de Gaulle's tank regiment. I fought the Germans in pitched battle. I joined one of the earliest Resistance groups, called Combat, and I organized the local group. I know what I'm doing."

"No argument there," Jeremy said, "and you are to be lauded. That should make things easier for us."

"Let's get to the heart of the issue." Faucon took on a challenging tone once more. "Several weeks ago, maybe two months, a man came here—a former French naval officer, but I think he was Swiss."

Jeremy looked up sharply.

"He brought with him a young lady," Faucon continued. "She was very nice and capable, and they brought promises of British resources, and sure enough, some arrived by parachute, including money. We are duly grateful. And I will say that he was effective in recruiting new members and joining groups together."

Jeremy listened now with rapt attention.

"And then he did something very stupid," Faucon continued. "He came here with a mission to go to Bordeaux to obtain intelligence about the submarine pens. But instead of assigning someone to do it, he went himself." He shook his head. "Granted, not anyone could go in and out of the base like he did, and the requested intelligence was of sufficient technical difficulty that a naval officer should have done it." He thrust a finger in the air and growled. "He should not have been both the leader and the operative on the ground."

His next words struck Jeremy like a thunderclap. "He was captured."

"How? Where?"

"Coming out of the gate, by the Gestapo. And for that to have happened, someone betrayed him." A fresh round of anger crossed Faucon's face. "He was here preaching operational security and training on tactical measures and procedures with other members of his group that he brought, including two British soldiers. They taught ground tactics and demolitions, and that was great."

"Two Brits?" Jeremy interrupted in surprise. "Do you know their names?"

Faucon shook his head. "They were only here for two weeks, and then returned to wherever they came from. We only used codenames."

That had to be Horton and Kenyon. "Sorry to interrupt. Go on."

"We appreciate the help, but in the final analysis, this Swiss naval officer, by his stupidity, exposed our organization, and when it was all over, we were reduced to the same level we had been before his arrival. That was particularly harmful because this was the central group that was uniting the others before he came. That's why he sought us out."

Faucon's voice took on a plaintive tone. "Some of our people were captured. One woman, a girl really, not even out of her teens, was beaten senseless and her right breast was cut off. She died without giving up any information. Others did, though, and a few escaped or were never captured."

He looked up grimly. "We caught the traitor. He won't

betray anyone again. And I will admit that we used this naval officer's methods to increase our security."

Jeremy listened in stunned silence, and for a time, no one spoke, but his heart and mind raced. "You mentioned a woman who came with him. What was her role?"

"She had been trained in London to be a courier as well as a radio operator, when need be, but we never received a radio."

"We brought one with us," Jeremy said, and indicating Rowena, he added, "and an operator. And the radio is smaller and more powerful than its predecessor model."

"That's good," Faucon said, bestowing an appreciative look on Rowena.

"What happened to the woman?" Jeremy asked, containing his anxiety.

"She managed to get to a second safehouse. And to give credit where credit is due, we had it set up at the Swiss man's insistence. She waited a few days and then managed to get back here." He exhaled. "I think she was supposed to occupy your position until you arrived, but she was in no way qualified for that. I heard about some things that happened to her. She lost her home in Dunkirk, her father was killed, and I heard she saved her sister from rape. She's brave, and London trained her well for her job, but leading is a completely different skill. She'll get there, but she's not there yet."

Jeremy searched the anxious and determined faces surrounding him, suddenly hoping to see Amélie among them. "Where is she now?"

"I sent her back to wherever she came from." Faucon chuckled. "I think it was Marseille. The Swiss officer let some things drop. If he ever escapes or is turned loose, he could learn a few things about operational security." He sighed. "The woman is a nice person, but she had no role here. She had no communication to her leader, she brought no experience in tactical operations or organization, and no ability to acquire resources. We all liked her." With his last statement, he peered around the room for agreement, and his comrades nodded and made sounds of assent. "But she was a fish out of water." He grunted. "The fact remains that someone somewhere decided that she was more qualified than me or anyone in this area to lead an organization that came together and was effective without their help. We see the value of a united effort, but there won't be one if all decisions are made at a level so high, we can't even see it."

"Good point." Jeremy turned to Atlas and Rowena. "Any questions or comments?"

When they both declined, he asked Faucon, "So, what do you suggest?"

Faucon spread his arms apart, gripped the sides of the table, and leaned back. "I'm glad you asked that question in that way." He took a deep breath. "I think you should stay here for a week or two. Maybe three or four. Get out and meet the groups that the Swiss man had strung together. Listen to their concerns, their setups, what they've done to date. Assess their various abilities. We want British aid, but we don't want to trade one form of dictatorship for another, with or without the money you bring."

He suddenly scowled and pointed a finger at Jeremy as a thought crossed his mind. "You'll need to be careful. The Germans have taken many of our young men as prisoners of war, and there's talk of taking more for forced labor in their 'fatherland.'" He said the word derisively. "We'll be your guides and provide security."

He dropped his hands and leaned forward over the table. "When you've done all of that, go back to Marseille or wherever it is that your higher headquarters is located. Tell them what you've observed.

"De Gaulle wants to build a Free French Army to fight alongside Britain when an invasion becomes possible. We want to help to bring that about." He held out his hand. "If you can agree to that, then I'll say again, welcome to France."

Jeremy studied Faucon. Around them, no one moved or spoke. He turned to his mates. They returned his gaze without expression. Then he looked at the anxious faces hovering over them. At last, he reached across the table and gripped Faucon's hand in both of his own. *"Vive la France."*

66

October 27, 1941
Rockefeller Center, Manhattan, New York

"So, tonight is the big night," Paul said morosely as he entered Stephenson's office and took a seat in front of his desk.

"Oh, cheer up. We're going to win this war and preserve Western civilization. Surely that must count for something."

"You know my reservations."

Stephenson looked up impatiently. "With that supercilious attitude, we'd be sure to lose the war. Think of what that would mean to England, to your family and friends, and to your parents on Sark Island. You've mentioned more than once that they must be just above famine rations by now. How will you feel about your righteousness when they starve because actions we could have taken were below our moral code?"

Stephenson became noticeably angry as he spoke, warming to his arguments. "Hitler is putting people on cattle cars and shipping them to their deaths. Should we allow him to continue because we have weak stomachs for hard choices?

Ten days ago, the Nazis fired on the *USS Kearny* in waters off of Iceland, the second US navy ship in less than a month, and the US is still neutral. Do we let that go unpunished? Or should we wait for the next one or the one after that?"

He stood and came around his desk, standing in front of Paul with legs spread apart and hands on hips. "You cling to this notion that if we stay absolutely spotless morally, somehow we'll bring evil to its knees. Well, when is evil so great that all measures should be taken against it? When should we take them in this conflict? After the first mentally deficient child was euthanized for the good of society; after the second? How about the third? Is the millionth sufficient?"

Paul listened, captured by Stephenson's passion.

"Hitler has already crossed the threshold of evil that obligates us to act," Little Bill continued. "And don't forget that God himself sent the flood to stamp out evil and only discriminated with respect to Noah and his family. Then there was the Angel of Death and the blights and plagues in Egypt. Today, we'd call the latter two biological warfare, but they seem to have been morally acceptable weapons at the time to address the wickedness of that day.

"He's executed homosexuals for being homosexual. He's killed Poles for being Polish, Czechs for being Czechs; the Jewish death count grows, and God only knows what the toll is now. He still fights Britain in Africa, terrorizes in the Balkans, and four months ago he turned on his ally, the Soviet Union.

"Stop equating our deceptions with the evil of the Third Reich. I frankly find it offensive. We are not raiding Jewish homes and throwing their families into the streets and terrorizing and killing them. On the contrary, we sacrifice our young men by the hundreds of thousands in bloody conflict to stop his wickedness. We are not promoting a single race as being superior to all others. And we have no global dictatorial aims."

Stephenson caught himself and stepped down his anger. "We *are* attempting to stop a man who is the incarnation of all that evil and do it before he develops the atomic means to enslave the world. You've been around enough to know that we are not talking science fiction. He's close to the ability to do exactly that, and only Great Britain stands in his way.

"We fed Hitler lies. We aggravated the fight in Greece to tie up his resources in the Balkans. We agitated in Yugoslavia to cause the coup there precisely to delay Hitler's invasion of the Soviet Union and make him defend Romania's oil fields. We hoped to cost him at least a day, and we got six weeks. His troops are already struggling in the mud trying to get to Moscow, and freezing weather has not even begun to set in there."

"Winter is now our weapon, and we'll defeat Hitler because of the deceptive actions we took. In so doing, we'll ally with Russia and deny Hitler Soviet industrial power, military armaments, and the Red Army. Now, our task is to involve the United States. We still cannot win the war without America."

He stopped for breath and continued with a stern tone and narrowed eyes looking directly into Paul's. "It's time for you to decide to grow up, join in the responsibility for our decisions and actions, or move aside. Great Britain is a tiny island country fighting for survival. It has no time for halfway measures or moral handwringing. And it has no need to apologize."

When he had finished speaking, Stephenson stood staring at Paul, and then, as if realizing he might have carried the vehemence of his argument past his intention, he closed his eyes briefly, rubbed his forehead, and returned to his seat.

Paul had sat in shock during the onslaught, and when it

was over, he stood slowly. Approaching Stepheson's desk, he said, "Sir, may I speak."

Stephenson gazed up at him with an almost sheepish look and remnants of defiance. "Of course," he said brusquely. "I've never stopped you. If you're going to stay, please turn on the radio. The president's Navy Day address is about to begin."

"I want to say, sir, that working with you is an honor of a lifetime, one I will always cherish."

"But—"

"No buts. I'm thickheaded, but I see your points. They might be difficult to accept, but I do accept them, and no one can argue that my country is in a death struggle. I won't bring up the matter again." With that, Paul walked over and turned on the radio.

"I'm glad to see you coming to your senses," Stephenson said gruffly, and bestowed the only broad smile Paul had ever seen on him, albeit with still a slight frown.

"Do you suppose the president will address what happened to the *Kearny*?" Paul asked, returning to his seat while the radio warmed up.

"His time is wasted if he doesn't," Stephenson replied. "A Nazi submarine fired on and damaged a US warship. Germany had been given fair warning that British ships sailed under US protection. It's the first time that Americans might sense that the war can come to their shores very quickly irrespective of anything we do. The Atlantic and Pacific don't provide the same protections they once did."

By the time Paul returned to his seat, President Roosevelt had finished his opening remarks and was into the body of his speech.

"Many American-owned merchant ships have been sunk on the high seas. One American destroyer was attacked on September 4. Another destroyer was attacked and hit on

October 17. Eleven brave and loyal men of our Navy were killed by the Nazis.

"We have wished to avoid shooting. But the shooting has started. And history has recorded who fired the first shot. In the long run, however, all that will matter is who fired the last shot.

"America has been attacked. The *USS Kearny* is not just a Navy ship. She belongs to every man, woman, and child in this nation. Illinois, Alabama, California, North Carolina, Ohio, Louisiana, Texas, Pennsylvania, Georgia, Arkansas, New York, Virginia—those are the home states of the honored dead and wounded of the *Kearny*. Hitler's torpedo was directed at every American, whether he lives on our seacoasts or in the innermost part of the nation, far from the seas and far from the guns and tanks of the marching hordes of would-be conquerors of the world.

"The purpose of Hitler's attack was to frighten the American people off the high seas—to force us to make a trembling retreat. This is not the first time he has misjudged the American spirit. That spirit is now aroused."

Stephenson stirred behind the desk, looking up from a sheet of paper he had been glancing at while the president spoke. He held it up for Paul to see. "This is an advance copy of his speech. He's doing a good job—hitting all the points. Our contribution is about to come up."

Despite his comments to Stephenson before the speech began, Paul's stomach tightened as he listened with strained attention while the president continued. He brushed his hands over his trousers to wipe away gathering moisture.

The president pressed on.

"I have in my possession a secret map made in Germany by Hitler's government—by the planners of the new world order. It is a map of South America and a part of Central

America, as Hitler proposes to reorganize it. Today in this area there are fourteen separate countries. The geographical experts of Berlin, however, have ruthlessly obliterated all existing boundary lines and have divided South America into five vassal states, bringing the whole continent under their domination. And they have also so arranged it that the territory of one of these new puppet states includes the Republic of Panama and our great lifeline—the Panama Canal.

"That is his plan. It will never go into effect.

"This map makes clear the Nazi design not only against South America but against the United States itself.

"Your government has in its possession another document made in Germany by Hitler's government. It is a detailed plan, which, for obvious reasons, the Nazis did not wish and do not wish to publicize just yet, but which they are ready to impose a little later on a dominated world—if Hitler wins. It is a plan to abolish all existing religion—Protestant, Catholic, Mohammedan, Hindu, Buddhist, and Jewish alike. The property of all churches will be seized by the Reich and its puppets. The cross and all other symbols of religion are to be forbidden. The clergy are to be forever silenced under penalty of the concentration camps, where even now so many fearless men are being tortured because they have placed God above Hitler.

"In the place of the churches of our civilization, there is to be set up an international Nazi church—a church which will be served by orators sent out by the Nazi government. In the place of the Bible, the words of *Mein Kampf* will be imposed and enforced as Holy Writ. And in place of the cross of Christ will be put two symbols—the swastika and the naked sword.

"A god of blood and iron will take the place of the God of love and mercy. Let us well ponder that statement which I have made tonight.

"These grim truths which I have told you of the present and future plans of Hitlerism will, of course, be hotly denied tonight and tomorrow in the controlled press and radio of the Axis Powers. And some Americans—not many—will continue to insist that Hitler's plans need not worry us and that we should not concern ourselves with anything that goes on beyond rifle shot of our own shores."

Stephenson slapped the desk and stood. "It's done," he said. "The president made the case. I believe now that America will be with us." He came around and stood by the front of the desk, holding his chin in one hand while listening to the broadcast.

Then he turned a curious eye on Paul. "When it comes to national security, do you think it more acceptable to deceive a friend into spreading a lie, or for that friend to do so knowingly?"

Paul stared, bewildered by the question. "Sir, are you saying that Roosevelt—"

"I'm making no statement. I'm merely posing a question, and you may consider it rhetorical." He turned to listen once more and consulted the advance copy of the speech. "He's finishing up now. Let's listen."

"It has not been easy for us Americans to adjust ourselves to the shocking realities of a world in which the principles of common humanity and common decency are being mowed down by the firing squads of the Gestapo. We have enjoyed many of God's blessings. We have lived in a broad and abundant land, and by our industry and productivity we have made it flourish.

"There are those who say that our great good fortune has betrayed us; that we are now no match for the regimented masses who have been trained in the Spartan ways of ruthless brutality. They say that we have grown fat, and flabby, and lazy, and that we are doomed.

"But those who say that know nothing of America or of American life.

"They do not know that this land is great because it is a land of endless challenge. Our country was first populated, and it has been steadily developed, by men and women in whom there burned the spirit of adventure and restlessness and individual independence which will not tolerate oppression.

"Ours has been a story of vigorous challenges which have been accepted and overcome, challenges of uncharted seas, of wild forests and desert plains, of raging floods and withering drought, of foreign tyrants and domestic strife, of staggering problems, social, economic, and physical; and we have come out of them the most powerful Nation, and the freest, in all of history.

"Today in the face of this newest and greatest challenge of them all, we Americans have cleared our decks and taken our battle stations. We stand ready in the defense of our Nation and the faith of our fathers to do what God has given us the power to see as our full duty."

Stephenson walked over to the console and clicked off the radio. "It will happen. I make no prediction about when, but in due course, America will fight alongside us. Of that, I am sure." He gave Paul an appraising glance. "Are you still with us?"

Paul stood. "I am, sir. I have my misgivings. I can't help that—"

"No one's asked you to give them up. You're a man of integrity, Paul. If we had more like you, we might not be in this war. And your courage is tested." He chuckled. "God knows your mouth works." Becoming serious once more, he added,

"It's enough for us that you'll do your duty, give us your best counsel, and obey lawful commands."

"I have two questions, sir, if you'll indulge me. How did the map and the story of its origin get to the president?"

"I gave it to Donovan," Stephenson replied with no evidence of remorse. "I told him that our operatives had taken it from a German agent in Argentina."

Paul grimaced. "I understand," he said reluctantly.

"What's your second question?"

"How will we know if it had any effect?"

Stephenson conferred one of his enigmatic smiles. "We should never get our hopes too high, but don't forget that this operation has two parts, and the objective is to get Hitler to declare war on the United States. That second part must still play out. A young army captain from the White House will visit Senator Wheeler's office very soon."

"To deliver the victory plan, an exercise in fiction, written for Hitler's benefit."

"Precisely." Stephenson looked at his watch. "And now, we should be off to Camp X to see how progress there is coming. I want to know if our Hydra network is going to work. That will be an unparalleled communications capability."

67

November 15, 1941
Marseille, France

Madame Fourcade approached Maurice's vegetable warehouse cautiously. Of late, she had begun receiving people
there because with her frequent and extended absences, her
sudden appearances at the villa accompanied by many visitors
coming and going at different times might attract attention.
Maurice had brought the matter to her, making a point that
Chantal had raised the issue with the suggestion that the
warehouse might be a better place to meet Resistance
members since frequent guests throughout the day would be
considered normal. She had recently turned sixteen and had
twisted back and forth, unable to hide a smile of pride as
Maurice discussed the matter with Fourcade.

On this morning, Fourcade had arrived minutes before the
warehouse's scheduled opening and became immediately
wary on seeing a tall man wearing an overcoat and fedora
lounging in front of the door. She proceeded, intending to
pass on by if her suspicions were not allayed. However, as she

drew near, her heart missed a beat as her subconscious mind recognized before her conscious mind did a vaguely familiar figure; and then it leaped when the man turned, and she recognized the face. Major Léon Faye.

Taking a breath and failing at subduing a smile, Fourcade slowed her pace to a measured step. "You took your time revisiting us," she called as she drew near.

Léon lifted his face to see better below his hat and smiled, a charming, broad expression that lit up his handsome face. He stepped forward and kissed her on both cheeks. "I know. It's very bad of me," he said playfully. "You see, I've been on a grand tour of Italy, North Africa, and the French chateaux."

Taking a furtive look about and seeing nothing concerning, Fourcade unlocked the door and invited him inside. "I'll show you around."

Once in the warehouse office, Léon turned immediately serious. "Navarre instructed me to offer you safe passage to Algeria. The word we've received is that your network was compromised and is non-existent. He's worried that you'll be captured." He paused and added, "I worry too."

With a sudden welling in her chest, Fourcade glanced at him sharply. She took a breath to calm her beating heart. "I think you'll find the stories of our demise to be slightly exaggerated," she said, remembering Mark Twain. "As it happens, my former chief of staff, a man by the name of Gavarni, turned out to be a mercenary. He had great ideas of how we could convert the Alliance to work for Vichy and make us both rich. I had to let him go, with prejudice—"

Léon took a deep breath. "I won't ask what that means."

Fourcade chuckled. "He wasn't harmed, but we took steps to cut him off and we keep tabs on him. So, I'm now looking for a new chief of staff if you're open to the job."

Léon laughed, but seeing that Fourcade was not joking, he stopped short. "You're serious?"

"If you have time," Fourcade replied, "you should stay here for the day and see for yourself whether Alliance is alive or I should seek shelter in Algeria; and then make up your mind. The offer will still be open."

Disconcerted, Léon pursed his lips and nodded. "All right. You're on."

"I should tell you," Fourcade continued, "the British were unsure of how to handle the Alliance leadership when Navarre left for Algeria. For a time, I kept the situation from them for being unsure of how they would react to a woman running the show, but we soon overcame their reticence with our effectiveness. They need our network."

A knock on the door interrupted their conversation, and Chantal entered. Smiling shyly at Léon, she greeted them. "Two men are waiting to see you," she told Fourcade. "Ernest Siegrist and Georges Guillot."

"Bring them in," Fourcade said, and as Chantal went to escort the men, she explained to Léon, "They were policemen in Paris who joined an anti-Nazi intelligence group. The Gestapo demolished it, but these two officers escaped and want to stay active in the Resistance. London confirmed their story for us, and now they are here."

When her business with the two former policemen was concluded, a woman entered the office. Fourcade introduced her to Léon. "This is Denise Centore, a professional historian. I've hired her to be my assistant."

She turned to Denise. "You look concerned."

Denise, short and stocky, nodded. She held out a piece of brown wrapping paper with writing on it. "This invisible ink that MI-6 sent out through diplomatic pouch becomes visible under heat. They've been sending messages on packages that end up sometimes in hot places. This one reports German anti-aircraft positions in Boulogne. If the Germans see others like this, Phillippe's operation in Madrid will end, and he'll probably be arrested."

"Inform London immediately," Fourcade said sharply. As Denise departed, Fourcade explained Phillippe's activities in Madrid.

"That's quite remarkable," he said.

Fourcade nodded. "Yes, and the British have developed silk paper that doesn't rustle. It takes an element of risk away for couriers who carry written messages."

Chantal came in again, escorting a courier with several transcribed radio messages, including a high-priority one. "These were received by our radio operator, Émile Andoly," Fourcade told Léon. "We have radios here, in Paris, Pau, the Loire Valley, and Dunkirk for now. More will come with SOE and MI-9 teams as our network and others expand."

Fourcade thanked the courier and dismissed her. "I should tell you, Léon," she said, rising and putting an arm around Chantal's shoulders, "that this young lady has become increasingly important around here. In addition to being one of our most trusted couriers, she's also done some of the most amazing reconnaissance work for us, finding and sketching all kinds of military targets in the Marseille area. If the shooting war ever reaches here, the enemy will be surprised at how prepared we are, in part due to her work."

Chantal blushed and retreated through the door.

"Her sister, Amélie, has been in northwest France, in the Loire Valley. She was with Henri there to develop new groups until a team leader from London arrived to take her place." She smiled gently. "That's a sweet-sour love story I'll have to tell you about one day."

"Where is she now?"

"Here, in Marseille. She's one of our best operatives, but I think I put her in over her head in Loire. I put her in a leadership position, and she wasn't ready yet."

While she spoke, she opened the priority message. She read it quickly and, grim-faced, handed it to Léon. It was from an Alliance agent who had managed to open several German crates at the Marseille port. The labels showed them to be the property of the German armistice commission. However, they contained rifles, ammunition, and other military items, and were en route to the *Wehrmacht's* Afrika Corps.

Léon whistled in amazement. "These even show the sailing dates and the ships that will carry them."

Fourcade nodded. "We'll send that to London with a request that the ships be bombed once they put to sea. I expect that they will be."

As the morning wound on, more people with more intelligence came by to see Fourcade until, at last, Léon said, "Your point's made. Alliance is alive and well." He stood and inhaled expansively. "I could use some lunch. Care to join me? We could go to one of the black-market bars."

Fourcade shook her head. "I'll be recognized there. I can't take the risk."

"Then come to my hotel room," he replied with his best innocent smile. "You'll feast on *foie gras* and a bottle of Monbazillac."

There, they continued the conversation.

"Where have you been and what have you been doing all this time?" Fourcade asked. "We tried to keep track of you, but after Navarre escaped from prison in North Africa, that became impossible. He's hiding out in Pau now."

"I wasn't as fortunate as he was," Léon said wryly. "I was in prison the whole time, although I moved from one to another a couple of times. Who knows why? Bureaucratic decisions rarely make sense. Anyway, I was rotting away." He chuckled. "I didn't come out too worse for wear."

"I'd say not," Fourcade said, regarding him coyly behind a glass of wine. "You look like you kept yourself in good physical shape."

"Ah, you noticed. I had you in mind when I did my daily workouts."

Fourcade gulped, the air seemed suddenly warm, and to avoid wading into deep waters, she changed the subject. "Do you know the British have a new air service? It started operations a couple of months ago, and they fly people and equipment in and out, landing in open fields. They fly at night by the light of the moon, and our people guide them to the landing strips by flashlight. In fact, one of the team leaders I mentioned earlier, Jeremy Littlefield, the one on the other side of the love story I mentioned—he came over that way."

Léon shook his head in disbelief. "So many people doing so many things." He took a deep breath and let it out. "What is your greatest concern now?"

Fourcade thought deeply. "Navarre wasn't entirely wrong: our network was infiltrated and nearly destroyed. We've rebuilt much of it, but we have sectors still needing repair, and we need to open new ones. The British will support us with resources, but we need qualified people to recruit, train, plan, and lead."

"I can be part of that," Léon said without hesitation, "and I can bring some air force officers with me—senior people who know how to organize and execute."

Fourcade's breath caught, and she brought her hands to her face. "Would you do that?" A shadow of doubt crossed her face. "Would they accept my leadership? I'm not prepared to relinquish it. I built the Alliance organization in France, and then re-built it, established relations with the Brits, and secured their aid. The people involved know and trust me. If you'll be my chief of staff, I see you and me sharing responsibilities and tasks, but ultimately, my decisions are final. Can your colleagues live with that? I'm a woman."

Léon laughed. "I *had* noticed. And I don't know why men of principle and discipline wouldn't accept your leadership. You've proven yourself. I'm prepared to."

Hardly believing her ears, Fourcade said, "Then you'll be my chief of staff?" She held her breath.

Léon stood and regarded her with a solemn but slightly amused expression. "If you'll have me."

Thrilled, Fourcade jumped up from her seat and threw her arms around him. He embraced her, and then kissed her lips.

The air had turned bitterly cold, and snow fell as Fourcade walked with Léon back to the warehouse. Nevertheless, she felt a glow that had been absent from her life for many years. She ascribed it to her growing affection for Léon and her success in winning him to actively support her beloved Alliance.

Chantal waited for them at the front door, and Fourcade noticed that she was not smiling. "Is something wrong?"

Chantal gestured toward the office. "Maurice is waiting for you in there with Gabriel Rivière."

"This sounds serious," Fourcade told Léon as they made their way through the warehouse. "Gabriel is a local operative and highly reliable. Whatever news he has, we'll have to believe it."

Inside the office, Maurice rose from the chair behind the desk. His big eyes stared at Fourcade sadly as she entered, and his jaw hung open, slack. He gestured toward Gabriel, a man sitting in front of him of similar size and build enough that the two men could be brothers.

Gabriel also stood and faced Fourcade. He held his hands in front of him, fidgeting with a hat.

Sudden trepidation seized Fourcade. "What is it?" she said. "Just tell me."

"Madame, I'm so sorry to be the one to bring this news," Gabriel said. "We heard it a short while ago." He took a breath, and his voice broke as he said, "Henri was executed two days ago." Then a ferocious growl entered his voice. "He will be avenged." He stopped talking as Maurice came around the desk.

Fourcade reeled, holding back sobs as Maurice wrapped his arms around her. "I sent him on that mission," she cried. "It's my fault he's dead. He was my friend. I loved him dearly."

Léon stood respectfully aside while Maurice and Gabriel tried to console her. Chantal entered the room and stood close to her, at a loss for what to do.

"He'll be avenged," Gabriel repeated. "I promise you."

Fourcade shook her head and fought for composure. "That would harm the Resistance," she said through anguished moans. "Henri would not want that. We must carry on."

68

November 26, 1941
Rockefeller Center, Manhattan, New York

Stephenson called Paul into his office. "The second part of our planned deception that you had objected to is about to trigger. As you know, Senator Burton Wheeler has made himself a particularly useful tool. His rants against the administration have been so loud, frequent, and vociferous that his reactions to anything are predictable. We'll make use of that.

"A US Marine lieutenant colonel is coming here this morning, but he won't be in uniform. He'll appear familiar to you, but I assure you that the two of you have never met. Depending on the message he brings, I'll send a wire to London. It will set several things rolling. I'll show it to you before I send it.

"Meanwhile, regarding Senator Wheeler. He spread rumors that the map the president referenced in his speech on Navy Day was a forgery, and he even stated on the senate floor that 'perhaps it originated in New York, in the minds of gentlemen closely associated to the British government.'" He harrumphed. "Maybe Wheeler can get the family of Gottfried Sanstede to believe that rubbish."

"Who, sir?"

"The late Mr. Sanstede. He was a German military attaché in Argentina. He copied the original map that his ambassador had held. I don't know why he did it or what he intended to do with it, but the fact is that it was taken from his courier by British agents in South America organizing anti-Nazi resistance movements in case Hitler attempts military operations there.

"Unfortunately for Sanstede, after the president's Navy Day speech, the Gestapo traced the leak to him and executed him. So much for Mr. Wheeler's theory.

"Still, the senator will be useful. Remember that the objective is to get Germany to declare war on the US, not the other way around."

A knock on the door interrupted their conversation, and a secretary escorted in the man Stephenson had been expecting. Then she left, closing the door behind her.

When Paul first saw the man's face, he recognized that Stephenson had been correct, the officer did look familiar, but at first Paul could not discern why that was the case. Then the officer extended his hand and introduced himself. "Lieutenant-colonel James Roosevelt," he said, and when Paul almost gaped, he added, "I get that a lot, and yes, I am the president's son, and yes, I'm going bald."

"He's an excellent conduit," Stephenson said, chuckling while offering a seat. "People expect to see him at the White House, and they don't follow him." He turned to James. "So, what's the word?"

James' face turned grim as he sat down. "My father says that negotiations with the Japanese are leading nowhere."

"I didn't expect that they would be positive," Stephenson

said in an equally foreboding tone. "I'll inform the prime minister."

***

November 27, 1941
London, England

Prime Minister Churchill read Stephenson's telegram three times to be sure he had understood it correctly, although the message was quite simple. It said, "JAPANESE NEGOTIA- TIONS OFF. SERVICES EXPECT ACTION WITHIN TWO WEEKS."

69

Washington, DC

A US Army captain in full uniform hurried up the stairs of the senate office building carrying a briefcase. He stopped at the information desk and then followed directions to the office of Senator Burton K. Wheeler of Montana, where he presented himself and requested to speak with the senator on a national security matter of utmost urgency. When asked for his name, he stated that he preferred to remain anonymous. At that point, the intern screening him noticed that the captain had removed his nametag from his jacket.

"If I can't speak with him, at least allow me to put what I have into the hands of his chief of staff or someone with a clearance high enough to know its contents. It's marked top secret." He leaned over and spoke quietly in conspiratorial tones. "I'm not supposed to have taken this out of the facility where I work." He jutted his chin toward the White House. "I'm doing this out of concern for the American people. I don't want to see us go to war."

Now fully attentive, the intern pushed a button, and soon a

tall, thin man appeared with round spectacles and scarcely any vestige of personality or hair. The intern conferred with him in whispers, the two glancing furtively at the captain at intermittent intervals. Then the thin man approached him.

"May I see what you've brought?"

"Certainly, sir, if you'll take me to a secure facility. Are you cleared for classified material?"

"I assure you that I am, Captain. I'm the senator's chief of staff. Would his office be suitable? He's not here now and you've already broken classified material-handling protocol. You can show it to me there or I can call security. Either way, if what you have in that briefcase is truly top secret, you're not leaving this office with it."

The captain glanced around, apparently suddenly nervous. "I guess that'll have to do."

In the office festooned with colors and symbols of national pride, the captain looked around in wonder at the trappings of power. "I came to the right place," he said, and smiled. "Senator Wheeler is famous for his dedication to keeping America safe from foreign wars."

"May I see what you brought," the chief of staff said. "I don't have a lot of time."

"Oh, yes, sir." The captain sat on a fine, multicolored divan and pulled from his valise a box much like those used to store typing paper. "Here it is, sir," he said, lifting the lid so that the cover page of a document was visible.

The staffer peered at it, his eyes widening in surprise. As the captain handed the box to him, he took it with an air of not wanting to touch it. The cover was stamped TOP SECRET, and the title read, "Victory Program," and under it, the thesis, "Germany First."

"This is the plan the president intends to implement to win the war," the captain said. "That means, obviously, that he plans to go to war." He looked at his watch. "Look, I really have to go. I'll be missed if I'm out of my office much longer."

The chief of staff crossed the room and set the box in the middle of the desk. "I'll see that the senator gets it," he said.

November 29, 1941
Rockefeller Center, Manhattan, New York

"Have you seen the report in the *Chicago Tribune*," Paul asked when Stephenson entered his office.

Stephenson's lips turned up slightly. "Read it to me," he said. "Just the first sentence past the headline."

Paul read the brief passage. "'A confidential report prepared by the joint Army and Navy command by direction of President Roosevelt...is a blueprint for total war.'"

"Wheeler couldn't keep a national secret if his mother's life depended on it," Stephenson said scornfully. "Certainly, he's proven that he places his own judgment above those of the president and the national intelligence apparatus. I would say that within five days, a copy of that document will be in Hitler's hands."

"If I may be so bold, sir, essentially what you believe is that the United States will be at war with Germany very soon."

"Yes, I believe that. And further, I believe Japan will attack within the same timeframe. The Americans think so too. They just don't know where the attack will take place, and we don't either. We've had sightings of the Imperial Navy off Indochina, so a weak consensus is that Japan will attack easy prey among Britain's Far East colonies. I'll tell you honestly, I wish I had greater insight on that side of the planet. The Japanese are a wily bunch and very capable. They might yet surprise us."

December 3, 1941
Bletchley Park, England

Claire hurried through the halls to Commander Denniston's office. She knocked, but then entered without waiting to be summoned. "I'm sorry, sir. I thought you should see this immediately."

Denniston looked up from a document, surprised. "Tell me the gist."

Claire took a breath. "This is coming straight from the German high command in Berlin. Hitler's intelligence people have somehow got their hands on a three-hundred-and-fifty-page top-secret document that they claim was prepared at the direction of the US president. It's titled "Victory Program," and it purports to be Roosevelt's plan for all-out war, with the main tenet being to defeat Germany first. The *führer* has seen it and is livid. He's told his inner circle that he intends to declare war on the United States, and they are trying to talk him out of it."

As she spoke, the commander leaned forward in his chair, his eyes narrowing and his hands gripping the edge of his desk. "Thank you," he said tersely. "I'll run it up. Be sure to keep mum about it."

"Yes, sir, although I think I'll finish for the day and head home now, if I may. I need a stiff drink."

"Don't drink alone," Denniston admonished Claire as she headed for the door. "And come in sober. Things are likely to get active over the next few days."

"Of course, sir. I have that new girl, Penny Mamedoff in Hut 6, staying with me. We'll commiserate and watch out for each other. And I have Timmy to look after, so I can't get too blown away."

"Right. Any word from your brothers?"

"Only Lance, sir. Still stashed away at Colditz." Her voice caught. "But he seems healthy. I have no idea where the other two are, and nothing encouraging from my parents."

"Keep a stiff upper lip. You'll meet again. I'm sure of it."

"Of course."

December 6, 1941
Rockefeller Center, Manhattan, New York

"We're on the verge," Stephenson told Paul. "I can feel it."

He handed across two sheets of paper. "This went to the president from London at three o'clock this morning, London time. That would be nine o'clock in DC. Read it."

Paul took them with an ominous sense. The first was a cover sheet, marked, *Triple Priority—Most Urgent—Personal and Secret to the President.*

The second sheet carried the message. It read, "British Admiralty reports that at 0300 hours London time this morning two Japanese groups seen off Cambodia Point sailing westward toward Malaya and Thailand...First group, twenty-five transports, six cruisers, ten destroyers. Second group, ten transports, two cruisers, ten destroyers..."

Paul looked up anxiously. "Where are they going, sir?"

"I wish I knew, Paul. I really wish I knew."

Washington, DC

Lieutenant Commander Alwin Kramer, USN, stared at the message received at 0128 hours. He was the Japanese-language expert on duty at the Navy Department. Stunned at the message received from Bainbridge Island at the US Navy's intercept station in the Puget Sound, he read and re-read it several times in both Japanese and English to be sure the translation was correct. Then he grabbed his jacket and ran for the door.

"Sir, where're you going?" his senior NCO called after him.

"To the State Department. They need to see this."

"That's eight blocks away, sir. It's freezing outside. We don't have a duty vehicle."

Kramer halted, breathing hard. "I'll run it, Sergeant Major. We're about to be at war in the Pacific." He jammed the paper in the NCO's face. "Read this."

The man did. The message read, "Tokyo instructs its ambassador at the embassy in Washington, DC to inform the United States that negotiations are to cease an hour after midday, local."

70

December 7, 1941
Rockefeller Center, Manhattan, New York

Sitting at his desk, Paul heard a loud exclamation, and seconds later, Stephenson appeared in the doorway, looking unsettled. "Come in here," he said urgently. "You need to hear this."

Paul bounded out of his chair and hurried into the office where Little Bill already stood by the console that held his radio, turning the dial. The receiver squawked and emitted other electronic noises before settling on the announcer's clear voice.

"This just in," the newsman said. "The Japanese attack on Hawaii's Pearl Harbor continues. Within an hour and five minutes, the battleship *Arizona* was completely destroyed and four others severely damaged."

Paul glanced sharply at Stephenson as the newsman continued, "Eyewitnesses say they see black smoke rising out of the naval base, and they hear the buzz of Japanese aircraft flying overhead, recognized by the red 'rising sun' insignias on the wings. They've heard multiple explosions that still continue."

The man's voice faded a moment, and then he was back, his tone filled with emotion. "We're starting to get word of the death toll, and it is significant. Hangars are on fire with men trapped inside. Fighters are being shot up on the runway as they taxi for takeoff."

He broke off momentarily and then went on. "We'll continue with up-to-the-minute reports as more information comes in, but ladies and gentlemen, this is a cataclysmic event. As stated at the outset of this report, the United States is under attack by the Japanese at Pearl Harbor. They staged a surprise raid at dawn that still continues, and it can mean only one thing. America is at war."

Stephenson turned the radio off with a click. Walking back to his desk, he sat in his chair and leaned back. "We're in it now," he muttered.

Paul stared at him. Mental and emotional numbness crept through his being. "Did we know this was coming?"

"Excuse me?"

Paul stood listlessly, confused images of the past months flitting into his mind and just as quickly darting out as he struggled to formulate a rational thought. "We did everything we knew how to get the US in the war against Germany," he heard himself say. Instinctively, he knew he was heading into muddy waters, but he could not seem to stop himself. "Was there another Stephenson-type person in Los Angeles or San Francisco working behind the scenes to develop what just happened?"

Stephenson sat up and peered at Paul. "Not that I know of. Are you joking?" By the look on his face, he might have been on the verge of severe anger. "I don't like what you're implying."

"Why not? If it was acceptable to maneuver the United States into the war in Europe and Africa, why not in the Far East? And who would have done that?"

"If it was done, I had no knowledge of it," Stephenson said, severity creeping into his voice. "You're challenging above your level, Captain. Please note that nothing we have done has killed Americans or destroyed their facilities, so I don't quite see the parallel you suggest. Japan needed no provocation to invade Manchuria and its other conquests. Obviously, it sees the US as a major obstacle to its ambitions, and from what I've heard of the attack so far, it closely resembles what Britain did to the Italians at Taranto. Britain's aim in our raid was to preempt the Italian navy from dominating the Mediterranean. I'd say that the Japanese had a similar objective in the Pacific and used similar means to achieve it, but their objective isn't defensive. It's conquest. Time will tell how successful they were."

He stood and leaned over the desk on tightly curled fists. "And if you're done with pontificating, you might want to climb down from that high horse. We knew the war was coming, but not like this. The president is convening a meeting of his top advisers at three o'clock this afternoon. I'm sure Donovan will be there. I was speaking with him on the phone as the news started coming in. He says Mr. Roosevelt is angry but clearly composed and keeping his cool. He's working on his address to the American people with Grace Tully, his private secretary, right now. We've got work to do to learn what the US response will be and what Britain's should be."

Paul listened with a sinking feeling, chagrinned that he

had spoken impulsively from emotion without analysis. "I'm sorry, sir. That was wrong of me. What do you expect the president's response to be?"

"Roosevelt will ask Congress to declare war—against Japan—and they will. I'll call the prime minister and relay Donovan's comments so he gets the picture as near as we can give him from the horse's mouth. With any luck, he'll speak to the president, but that's far from assured. Mr. Roosevelt is rather busy."

"How can I help?"

The ends of Stephenson's lips lifted slightly. "Good recovery. Your heart's in the right place, Paul, even if your brain takes a wayward stroll once in a while." Then he looked down at some notes on his desk. "Call down to our embassy. Get a directory of the Japanese delegation. Write up a background synopsis of the ambassador and his chief advisors. Also, we should know soon which Japanese commanders and ships were involved in the attack. Get me as much information as you can on the principals. If you have any trouble getting cooperation, use my name, but be judicious about it. That should keep you busy for a while. We'll talk more when we know more. Meanwhile, keep an ear open for a call from Donovan. If I'm busy, interrupt me."

Bletchley Park, England

Claire was in Hut 8 when the news reached there. Immediately, someone wheeled a cart into the decoding room with a radio tuned to BBC, and together everyone present listened to the continuing reports. She watched the faces of her colleagues, noting the mixed dread and elation. Dread at the obvious escalation of the war, and elation that at long last, the United States would fight alongside Great Britain. For a moment, time seemed to have stood still, and when it started again, a new, more uncertain, and frightening age seemed to have emerged.

71

December 8, 1941
Sark Island, English Channel Isles

"Are you sure this is a safe hiding place?" Stephen said, glancing about the storage room dubiously.

"It's as safe as any," Marian replied. She stood in front of a high stack of trunks, boxes, and suitcases left in her care by residents of the island who, for one reason or another, had left without knowing when they would return. "The soldiers have looked in here several times, but they never do more than a cursory search."

She started moving items aside. "I keep the radio in a trunk all the way at the back and on the bottom, and if someone comes to the door, our poodles sound the alarm, and then I can make great fanfare of moving through the house trying to quiet them while the radio is being put away. It's worked so far."

"Yes, but after today, I expect the penalties for keeping and listening to the radio will become far more stringent. In other places, the Nazis have put people to death for exactly that."

Marian frowned with a sardonic expression. "So much for being ambassadors of goodwill. Mr. Roosevelt is bound to speak soon, and I want to hear what he has to say. The prime minister should be speaking too."

"But news of the Japanese attack is only rumor. Who told you about it?"

"One of the fishermen. He heard it from one of the guards on his boat. The German was taunting him about it, but our man only understood a little of what was said—just 'attack,' 'Japan,' and 'America.'"

"That's a little flimsy."

"Agreed, but the rumor is making the rounds. By now, I suspect most of our islanders have heard it, and if it's true, I'm sure others heard it by different means."

Stephen heaved a sigh. "Well, double-checking to make sure we've covered all the risks never hurts. I'll instruct the servant to keep watch while we're listening."

As they talked, Marian worked through the pile of luggage until she reached the trunk with the radio. "Another rumor is that Mr. Roosevelt would address the American nation today. If we've missed the broadcast, I'm sure it will be repeated."

While Stephen went to instruct the servant, she opened the trunk, pulled the radio out, and plugged it in. By the time Stephen returned, it had warmed up and she had tuned it to the BBC. They listened to a few minutes of music and commercial messages, and then a newscaster spoke.

"For those just learning of the Japanese attack on Pearl Harbor, we'll be providing details throughout the day."

Marian and Stephen exchanged grim glances. "I guess the rumor's true," he said.

"At present," the newscaster continued, "we await the president of the United States, who is expected to address Congress in a few minutes. Those familiar with the content of his speech say that he dictated and edited his speech himself and that it is short. He preferred it over a seventeen-page draft submitted by the Pentagon—"

The newsman was cut short by blaring music after which he said, "The president is at the rostrum. Let's listen."

Then, Roosevelt spoke, his voice strong and resolute.

"Mr. Vice President, Mr. Speaker, Members of the Senate, and of the House of Representatives: Yesterday, December 7, 1941—a date which will live in infamy—the United States of America was suddenly and deliberately attacked by naval and air forces of the Empire of Japan.

"The United States was at peace with that nation and, at the solicitation of Japan, was still in conversation with its government and its emperor looking toward the maintenance of peace in the Pacific. Indeed, one hour after Japanese air squadrons had commenced bombing in the American island of Oahu, the Japanese ambassador to the United States and his colleague delivered to our Secretary of State a formal reply to a recent American message. And while this reply stated that it seemed useless to continue the existing diplomatic negotiations, it contained no threat or hint of war or of armed attack."

The president then proceeded through a short review of the planning that must have gone into the attack and the deception Japan used to mollify the US while it proceeded to execute its war campaign, and he detailed the damage done to America's navy and the death toll exacted. He pointed out that the offensive had included almost simultaneous attacks extending over a wide area of the Pacific, including Malaya, Hong Kong, Guam, the Philippine Islands, Wake Island, and Midway Island.

He spoke in grave terms of the American people's understanding of what the calamity implied about their very lives; and he stated that he had directed the Army and Navy to take all measures to defend the safety of the nation, saying, "... always will our whole nation remember the character of the onslaught against us."

The president paused momentarily, and then made his final comments.

"No matter how long it may take us to overcome this premeditated invasion, the American people in their righteous might will win through to absolute victory.

I believe that I interpret the will of the Congress and of the people when I assert that we will not only defend ourselves to the uttermost but will make it very certain that this form of treachery shall never again endanger us.

"Hostilities exist. There is no blinking at the fact that our people, our territory, and our interests are in grave danger.

"With confidence in our armed forces, with the unbounding determination of our people, we will gain the inevitable triumph—so help us God.

"I ask that the Congress declare that since the unprovoked and dastardly attack by Japan on Sunday, December 7, 1941, a state of war has existed between the United States and the Japanese empire."

Thunderous applause erupted over the radio, but the news anchor cut in, silencing it. "Those were the remarks by President Roosevelt calling on Congress to declare war on Japan. In a few minutes, Mr. Churchill will broadcast his statement on the attack, which we will also bring to you."

Marian turned to face Stephen. "The whole world is at war now," she said, a fearful tone creeping into her voice despite her best effort to quell it.

Stephen grasped her hand and kissed it. "Japan is allied with Germany. A declaration of war on the Third Reich must soon follow. What that probably means to us is that demands on our resources will increase, imported supplies will be fewer, and the German authorities will be more oppressive."

Marian bowed her head, shaking it with eyes closed. "And I urged our people to stay on the island. I hope they can forgive me." She looked up suddenly, gazing at Stephen with despairing eyes. "How do you think this will affect Lance?"

Stephen did not reply. He moved close to her and embraced her. They sat without moving until they heard their poodles barking. The servant hurried in to reassure them that there had been no cause for alarm. A neighbor had stopped by to find out if the household had heard the news.

Oflag IV-C, Colditz, Germany

In the highest, most secret niche of Colditz Castle, a small group gathered. Among them were the operators of the hand-fashioned radio assembled by brilliant and creative engineers using bits of wire and parts smuggled into the camp in family parcels, bribed from willing guards or civilian workers and vendors, or stolen from German equipment.

With the operators were the leaders of the British contin-gent, including Guy, Pat, Chip, and Lance. Around them were the "reporters," British POWs who each morning gathered to receive the day's news from the BBC, and then made rounds to the various barracks rooms to disseminate it to the rest of the British POW population. Similar procedures were practiced by each nationality.

On this morning, the British POWs eyed each other somberly as President Roosevelt finished speaking and they waited to hear from Prime Minister Churchill. Then, amid whining electronic noises, the statesman's voice resounded.

"As soon as I heard last night that Japan had attacked the United States, my first feeling was that Parliament should be immediately summoned. We are fighting for the maintenance of a parliamentary system, and it is indispensable to our system of Government that Parliament should play its full part in all the important acts of the state and on all the great occasions in the conduct of the war. The great number of members who attended in spite of the shortness of the notice shows the zeal and strictness with which the members of both Houses attend to their duties.

"You will remember that a month ago, with the full approval of the nation and of the Empire, I pledged the word of Great Britain that should the United States become involved in a war with Japan, a British declaration would follow within the hour. I therefore spoke to President Roosevelt on the Atlantic telephone last night with a view to arranging the timing of our respective declarations. The President told me that he would this morning send a message to Congress, which of course as you all know is the instrument, the constitutional instrument, by which alone a United States declaration of war can be made.

"And I assured him that we would follow immediately. However, it soon appeared that British territory in Malaya had also been the object of a Japanese attack, and later on it was announced from Tokyo that the Japanese High Command—not the Imperial Japanese Government—but the Japanese High Command had declared that a state of war existed with Great Britain and the United States."

The prime minister's speech was longer than Roosevelt's had been, but the gathering listened with rapt attention as Churchill summarized the history of relations with Japan and the patience with which the United States had attempted to resolve their differences. Then he entered into his final remarks.

"We have at least four-fifths of the population of the globe upon our side. We are responsible for their safety—we are responsible for their future. And as I told the House of Commons this afternoon, in the past we had a light which flickered, in the present we have a light which flames, and in the future, there will be a light which will shine calm and resplendent over all the land and all the sea."

The speech ended, and the group began dispersing amidst concerned discussion. As Pat and Lance made their way back down into the main areas of the castle, Pat asked Lance what he thought of the situation.

"I dunno," Lance replied. "I'm still trying to absorb what just happened. Japan and Germany are formal allies, so I suppose Hitler will declare war on the United States, in which case America will join the war in Europe on our side. I can see where that might make our guards a little fidgety. Things might become more difficult for us until we and the Germans see how things play out for them on the ground. Control of the Suez Canal just became much more crucial, which probably means that fighting in North Africa will become more intense. And of course, there was that map that Roosevelt referenced a couple of months back about Hitler's plans for South America. With this new twist, that's got to make the Panama Canal a critical piece of geography too.

"How all of that will affect us here is hard to say. We're removed from the hard fighting by a considerable distance, but as resources are spread thin, we're likely to feel it."

When Lance had finished speaking, Pat glanced at him in surprise. "That was quite a soliloquy, Sergeant, and an impressive analysis. You must have been paying more attention in school than you let on."

Lance grinned back at him. "No, sir, plenty of my mates can attest that the opposite was the case. Here there's nothing to do but learn, and any tidbit that gets us closer to being out of here lodges in this thick skull." He tapped his temple. "Facts and figures take their time to get inside my head, but once there, they stay. Then they bounce around until I can make use of them."

Pat laughed. "It's good to have you around, Lance Little-field. Here we are, the two of us, aching to get out more than most and with the skills that increase our probabilities, and we're acquiescing to SBO's pitiful plea for us to stay."

"Yes, sir. Some would call us daft, but there it is."

EPILOGUE

December 11, 1941
Afrika Corps Headquarters, near Tobruk, Libya, North
Africa

"It's so good to see you here and healthy," Field Marshal Erwin
Rommel greeted *Oberst* Meier warmly. "How's the leg?"

"Probably as good as it's going to get, but at least I can
fully exercise now." He glanced around the operations tent
where they stood. "And I'm released for combat duty. It is my
honor and privilege to serve with you again, *Herr* Field
Marshal."

"Let's take a walk in the desert where we can talk,"
Rommel said. "Have you heard this morning's news?" he asked
as they moved outside the tent and past myriad panzers, troop
carriers, antennas, and other war materiel.

"The driver informed me on the way in from the airfield.
Germany and Italy declared war on the United States?"

"Yes." Rommel glanced around before continuing. "That
was a mistake. There is no combination of nations that can
match America's industrial might, and they proved during the

last war that they can mobilize quickly." He stared out over the desert toward British forces.

"Did you know that Prime Minister Churchill sent his entire tank force down here to North Africa on the same day that the French government vacated Paris?"

"I hadn't put that together, sir."

"Churchill plays to win," Rommel said. "His seasoned veterans were trapped at Dunkirk, and he evacuated them. But they had barely arrived in England when he was already sending a tank force to Egypt. The logistics and timing alone would tell you that the troops he sent to Africa were newly recruited, poorly trained, and unseasoned, and in fact, that's what we found. Our forces rolled over them.

"But that's no longer the case. The British soldiers here now are veterans. They've fought us for eighteen months, they were reinforced by the regular army that was rescued from Dunkirk, and their replacements are better trained. Here at Tobruk, they've taken everything we've thrown at them since last year, and now their 8th Army has come to relieve them."

Rommel exhaled. "That American lend-lease program brought the British better equipment and supplies with remarkable speed, and the re-supply is more frequent. And soon, they'll be joined by American soldiers." He paused and swung around with a slight smile. "Do I sound like a pessimist?"

"You sound like a combat leader taking stock of the lay of the land, *mein Herr*, without which victory is impossible."

Rommel sighed. "Almost the entire high command advised Hitler against this declaration, but he was livid about a report our agents in the US intercepted called the Victory Program."

"I've heard of it, and generally know its content."

"Since Germany has already pulled the trigger, I expect

that Roosevelt will ask Congress very soon to declare war on us, probably today. A runner will bring me a transcript if that happens. And when it happens, the scales will be weighed against us. We can only hope that the Japanese will wear America down in the Far East sufficiently for us to do the same in the west. Then, maybe we have a chance to win."

"I fear, sir, that this man from Austria could bring about the destruction of our fatherland."

Rommel swung around sharply in front of Meier. "I fear the same, but we will speak no more about it today." He chuckled. "There is one bright spot in our favor."

Meier listened expectantly.

"The Americans have an overly ambitious military attaché in their Cairo embassy, a Brevet Colonel Fellers. He's a West Point graduate, no less, and he likes to go into the British combat lines, attend their staff meetings, gather information, and send long, detailed reports to his bosses in the United States, encrypting it with what the Americans call their Black Code. Undoubtedly, they think it's unbreakable.

"What Fellers doesn't know is that last month, Italy's military intelligence sent two of their paramilitary police and two embassy employees into the American embassy at night—a burglary. They came away with the Black Code and all the documentation needed to use it. They quickly photographed it and returned the materials, so the Americans didn't know they had it.

"The Italians suddenly knew the enemy dispositions from these Feller reports as soon as they were sent. They kindly shared them with us but would not provide the actual code material. What they don't know is that, within the past weeks, we've broken the Black Code too. Now, we can read the reports as fast as the Italians do, or for that matter, as fast as the Americans can. That's how, for the past week, I've known each morning the positions of British forces from the night before." Rommel laughed. "It's a tremendous advantage to exploit until the Americans figure out that we've got their code or until they routinely change it. We also have some of the British codes, which has been a big help."

"It's funny you should mention that," Meier interjected. "When I was at Dinard, I sometimes had this strange sense that Great Britain knew what was going on inside our headquarters. We'd move troops, ships, stores, and they'd bomb them. I sometimes wondered if they had broken our codes, but when I went to study our Enigma, I could see that was impossible."

"I heard about some of what took place there. What about that girl—"

"Jeannie Rousseau."

"Yes. I heard there was some concern that she might be a spy."

"If you had known her, sir, you would have seen that to be preposterous. She was a very able linguist and translator and helped us willingly—and charmingly, I might add—in matters dealing with the public in Dinard. But no one ever saw her taking notes or listening where she shouldn't have. She never acted nervously or was seen to be in places where she shouldn't be. I concluded that Major Bergmann, the SS officer who reported her to the Gestapo, had it in for her in the same way he did the Boulier family in Dunkirk." He related what had happened to the major. "In all honesty, I was glad to see him go. Like most people in the SS and the Gestapo, he had no morals, and his loyalty was to his ambition and not to our country."

"I remember him," Rommel mused. "As I recall, he tried to drive a wedge between you and the *führer*."

"And you, sir. If he had succeeded with me, he would have been after you. He did not like regular military officers."

"Well, thankfully, he's no longer a problem." Rommel glanced at a soldier tromping through the desert sand toward them. "Here comes the news we were expecting."

The soldier saluted both officers and handed a wrinkled piece of paper to the field marshal. He took and read it. "Cry havoc and let slip the dogs of war," he muttered, handing the crumpled message to Meier.

"Sir?"

"We are at war with the United States."

Marseille, France

Madame Fourcade turned off the radio and looked about at the group sitting around the terrace table. From off in the distance, she heard the whisper of the sea.

"It's done," she said. "The US is formally at war with Germany."

Looking somber, Léon weighed in. "This should be good for us, and I hope it is, but unintended consequences always play in. I see a long war ahead."

Amélie had sat quietly listening. When Fourcade looked her way for comment, at first, Amélie merely shook her head, but then she said, "We hoped for America to come into the war. We even expected it. The surprise was the Japanese attack. We're in for a long fight, but we have a much better chance now of winning." A wistful look crossed her face. "Personal plans will be delayed for a long, long time."

Fourcade reached across and squeezed her hand. "Better days are ahead. We'll have some dark ones in between, but sunny days will return. I believe that." She glanced around at the others. "Anyone else?"

Horton started to speak, but then he looked across the table and saw Chantal watching him with starry eyes. He blushed and refrained from saying anything.

Sitting next to him, Maurice caught the exchange and nudged Horton with a slight smile. Then he returned Fourcade's glance and shook his head. "It's all been said. I'm glad America will fight with us."

"Kenyon? Pierre?" Fourcade asked. They both shook their heads.

"In that case, tonight we both mourn America's tragedy and celebrate the new alliance. This is the beginning. We're turning the storm." With the sun setting behind her, she stood and smiled. "So, let's bring out refreshments, relax, and enjoy each other's company." As an afterthought, she added, "While we can."

As everyone trooped to the house to help bring out the food, Fourcade pulled Amélie aside and together they strolled into the garden. "Do we have any word from Jeannie?"

"Yes. The Gestapo is giving her no problems in Paris. She's taken a job with a company that supplies materials to the *Wehrmacht*. That positions her well to penetrate German senior command there. She's going to take it slow."

Fourcade exhaled. "I wish her the very best. I'd like you to remain as her primary contact for our purposes." She beamed with pride. "What the two of you accomplished—"

"With Phillipe, Chantal—"

"Yes, yes, of course, and those in the Loire Valley, and your family and friends at Dunkirk too. I don't mean to slight anyone. Have you heard from them?"

"I have. Things are relatively quiet in Dunkirk now. Jacques took over leadership of the Boulier network and is teaching my cousin, Nicolas, to keep things together while he goes to England for training. You know Jacques is Jewish?"

"I did know that. I shudder to think what will happen to him if he's ever captured."

"Let's pray he never is. He's a wonderful man."

"I am so proud of your sister, Chantal, but at the same time, I ache for her. This is no way for a girl to grow up. You know she thinks she likes Sergeant Horton in a romantic way."

Amélie smiled. "I think it's obvious to everyone, including him. He sees her as a little girl, but they're only three and a half years apart. By the time this war is over, he might view her differently, and they're both too young anyway."

"You're right, of course, and yet he's a combat veteran and she—" Fourcade stopped herself.

"...pushed a man over a cliff." Amélie finished the sentence and sighed. "The war, the war, the war. It overshadows everything."

Seeing Amélie's lips quiver, Fourcade grasped her arm. "You want to know about Jeremy, and I wish I had something good to tell you. I don't. But I also have nothing bad to report. As the British say, keep a stiff upper lip."

Silhouetted against a blue sky with the Mediterranean shimmering beyond Marseille, Amélie nodded. "I will."

Up on the terrace, an indistinct commotion started, with loud shouting. Together, the two women turned anxiously, but their vantage was too low to see what was transpiring. Cautiously, they approached, and when they could view over the lip of the steps, they saw the entire group gathered at the center of the terrace, celebrating.

Exchanging questioning glances, they mounted the stairs and hurried across. As they did, the gathering parted, and a disheveled man with tired features emerged, smiling broadly.

Amélie stared in disbelief. Tears of joy streamed down her

face as she ran to throw her arms around Jeremy. They held each other and kissed, ignoring those around who watched, smiling and laughing; and when they parted, Jeremy looked across at Fourcade's beaming face.

"I have many things to report," he told her. "Later." Then he returned his full attention to Amélie.

THE GIANT AWAKENS
Book #4 in the After Dunkirk series

The world is at war.

Japan has just attacked Pearl Harbor. In London, Prime Minister Churchill disappears. In Washington, President Roosevelt faces an alliance with conflicting objectives. In the Soviet Union, dictator Joseph Stalin watches a Nazi onslaught maul his country.

From their isolated perch on Sark Island, feudal rulers Dame Marian Littlefield and her husband oppose their German occupiers in the only way left to them—through a battle of wits. They wonder about the location and well-being of their offspring, Paul, Claire, Lance, and Jeremy.

Meanwhile, Paul engages in intelligence operations in Manhattan and Washington, DC. Claire works with Americans decoding enemy messages. Lance conspires to escape with other POWs at Oflag IV-C within the walls of Colditz Castle. Jeremy leaves his heart with Amélie in France to join the British commandos for the greatest raid in history.

And in Moscow, the Russian winter has just set in.

Get your copy today at AuthorLeeJackson.com

JOIN THE READER LIST

Never miss a new release! Sign up to receive exclusive updates from author Lee Jackson.

**Join today at
AuthorLeeJackson.com**

YOU MIGHT ALSO ENJOY...

The After Dunkirk Series

After Dunkirk

Eagles Over Britain

Turning the Storm

The Giant Awakens

The Reluctant Assassin Series

The Reluctant Assassin

Rasputin's Legacy

Vortex: Berlin

Fahrenheit Kuwait

Target: New York

Never miss a new release! Sign up to receive exclusive updates from author Lee Jackson.

AuthorLeeJackson.com/Newsletter

AUTHOR'S NOTE

An anecdote is worthwhile hearing when it tells of unusual or remarkable events. Without at least one of those elements, there is no story to tell. A point can be reached at which a tale reaches beyond our ability to suspend disbelief, at which point, our own tolerance for the absurd kicks in. I mention this because a few readers have mentioned that stories I've written about seem to go past that point of believability. The truth is, sadly, that most of what I write happened to someone. I might change the names, the dates, or some of the details in order for the book to flow, but beyond entertainment, a chief objective of mine is to honor those who fought for us by writing about their incalculable courage by representing their deeds as closely as possible to the way they occurred. For example, Jeannie Rousseau did live and work as a translator in the German army headquarters in Dinard, France. She spoke five languages fluently, as represented, and graduated from the prestigious institution indicated. That said, no direct evidence is available that she had any bearing on informing the British about German plans. However, she did possess the remarkable memory as described, she was arrested by the

Gestapo, and she was released under pressure from the German headquarters, and then ordered to vacate Dinard and stay away from the French Atlantic coast. The later remarkable contributions stemming from her photographic memory in Paris is a matter of record which will be covered later in this series, as well as the dear price she paid for performing what she considered to be her duty.

As a further example, the pilots of the Swordfish "Stringbags" in their engagements against the Italian navy at Taranto and later against the *Bismarck* is almost exactly as history recorded them, minus the initial dialogue, but including the gunner who held on to the side of the aircraft to ensure that his pilot dropped the torpedo at the best possible moment. That was no Hollywood addition to heroics for the sake of drama. But setting that aside, just that those pilots took off for a second time in gale-force conditions to hunt down and engage the *Bismarck* boggles my mind. If I were to add any action, it would only diminish what they did.

Even the shenanigans inside Colditz are based on real accounts. My intent is to bring you as much of a panoply of historical events that shaped the war and our lives, and of course, as a primary objective, to provide quality entertainment.

ACKNOWLEDGMENTS

There are too many people to thank without inadvertently leaving someone out, and most know who you are and my deep gratitude. However, two I must mention, one whose name must remain anonymous; and the other is BG (Ret.) Lance Betros for their concentrated feedback and advice. Their encouragement along with that of family and friends kept me working when I might have otherwise whiled away hours accomplishing nothing.

ABOUT THE AUTHOR

Lee Jackson is the internationally bestselling and award-winning author of The Reluctant Assassin series and the After Dunkirk series. He graduated from West Point and is a former Infantry Officer of the US Army. He deployed to Iraq and Afghanistan, splitting 38 months between them as a senior intelligence supervisor for the Department of the Army. His novels are enjoyed by readers around the world. Lee lives and works with his wife in Texas.

LeeJackson@AuthorLeeJackson.com

Made in United States
Orlando, FL
18 December 2021

12142107R00340